MONKEY WARRIORS . . . FULL OF SURPRISES . . .

For one instant man and kzin stood twenty paces apart, unmoving. Goon leaped for the nearest weapon, the beam rifle Puss had dropped, and saw Locklear release the short arrow. It missed by a full armspan and now, his bloodlust rekindled and with no fear of such a marksman, Goon dropped the rifle and pulled Yellowbelly's stiletto from his own arm. He turned toward Locklear, who was unaccountably running *toward* him instead of fleeing as a monkey should flee a leopard, and threw his head back in a battle scream.

Locklear's second arrow, fired from a distance of five paces, pierced the roof of Goon's mouth, its stainless steel barb severing nerve bundles at the brain stem. Goon fell like a jointed tree, knees buckling first, arms hanging, and the ground's impact drove the arrow tip out the back of his head, slippery with gore. Goon's head lay two paces from Locklear's feet. He neither breathed nor twitched.

Locklear hurried to the side of poor, courageous, ill-starred Puss and saw her gazing calmly at him. "One for you, one for me, Puss. Only two more to go."

"I wish—I could live to celebrate that," she said, more softly than he had ever heard her speak.

"You're too tough to let a little burn," he began.

"They shot tiny things, too," she said, a finger migrating to a bluish perforation at the side of her rib cage. "Coughing blood. Hard to breathe," she managed.

He knew then that she was dying.

Baen Books by Jerry Pournelle & S.M. Stirling
The Prince

The "War World" series
Blood Feuds
Blood Vengeance

Baen Books by Jerry Pournelle
Janissaries
Birth of Fire

Baen Books by S.M. Stirling
The Draka series:
The Domination
Drakon
Drakas! (anthology)

with James Doohan:
The Flight Engineer series:
The Rising
The Privateer
The Independent Command

with David Drake:
The Forge
The Chosen
The Reformer

The City Who Fought (with Anne McCaffrey)
The Ship Avenged

Snowbrother

THE HOUSES OF THE KZINTI

JERRY POURNELLE
S.M. STIRLING
DEAN ING

THE HOUSES OF THE KZINTI

A Baen Books Original Omnibus

Baen Publishing Enterprises
P.O. Box 1403
Riverdale, NY 10471
www.baen.com

ISBN: 0-7434-3577-X

Cover art by Larry Elmore

First printing, December 2002

Library of Congress Cataloging-in-Publication Data

Pournelle, Jerry, 1933-
The houses of the Kzinti / by Jerry Pournelle, S.M. Stirling & Dean Ing.
p. cm.
"A Baen Books original omnibus"—T.p. verso.
Contents: Cathouse / by Dean Ing — The children's hour / by Jerry Pournelle & S.M. Stirling.
ISBN 0-7434-3577-X
1. Human-alien encounters—Fiction. 2. Life on other planets—Fiction. 3. Science fiction, American. I. Ing, Dean. II. Stirling, S.M. III. Ing, Dean. Cathouse. IV. Pournelle, Jerry, 1933– Children's hour. V. Title.

PS3566.O815 H67 2002
813'.54—dc21

2002028324

Distributed by Simon & Schuster
1230 Avenue of the Americas
New York, NY 10020

Produced by Windhaven Press, Auburn, NH
Printed in the United States of America

10 9 8 7 6 5 4 3 2 1

Contents

THE HOUSES OF THE KZINTI

Cathouse

by Dean Ing

Sampling war's minor ironies: Locklear knew so little about the *Weasel* or wartime alarms, he thought the klaxon was hooting for planetfall. That is why, when the *Weasel* winked into normal space near that lurking kzin warship, little Locklear would soon be her only survivor. The second irony was that, while the Interworld Commission's last bulletin had announced sporadic new outbursts of kzin hostility, Locklear was the only civilian on the *Weasel* who had never thought of himself as a warrior and did not intend to become one.

Moments after the *Weasel*'s intercom announced completion of their jump, Locklear was steadying himself next to his berth, waiting for the ship's gravity-polarizer to kick in and swallowing hard because, like ancient French wines, he traveled poorly. He watched with envy as Herrera, the hairless, whipcord-muscled Belter in the other bunk, swung out with one foot planted on the deck and the other against the wall. "Like a cat," Locklear said admiringly.

"That's no compliment anymore, flatlander," Herrera said. "It looks like the goddam tabbies want a fourth war. You'd think they'd learn," he added with a grim headshake.

Locklear sighed. As a student of animal psychology in general, he'd known a few kzinti well enough to admire the way they learned. He also knew Herrera was on his way to enlist if, as seemed likely, the kzinti were spoiling for another war. And in that case, Locklear's career was about to be turned upside down. Instead of a scholarly life puzzling out the meanings of Grog forepaw gestures and kzin ear-twitches, he would probably be conscripted into some warren full of psych warfare pundits, for the duration. These days, an ethologist had to be part historian, too—Locklear remembered more than he liked about the three previous man-kzin wars.

And Herrera was ready to fight the kzinti already, and Locklear had called *him* a cat. Locklear opened his mouth to apologize but the klaxon drowned him out. Herrera slammed the door open, vaulted into the passageway reaching for handholds.

"What's the matter," Locklear shouted. "Where are you—?"

Herrera's answer, half-lost between the door-slam and the klaxon, sounded like "atta nation" to Locklear, who did not even know the drill for a deadheading passenger during battle stations. Locklear was still waiting for a familiar tug of gravity when that door sighed, the hermetic seal swelling as always during a battle alert, and he had time to wonder why Herrera was in such a hurry before the *Weasel* took her fatal hit amidships.

An energy beam does not always sound like a thunderclap from inside the stricken vessel. This one sent a faint crackling down the length of the *Weasel*'s hull, like the rustle of pre-space parchment crushed in a man's hand. Sequestered alone in a two-man cabin near the ship's aft galley, Locklear saw his bunk leap toward him, the inertia of his own body wrenching his grip from his handhold near the door. He did not have time to consider the implications of a blow powerful enough to send a twelve-hundred-ton Privateer-class patrol ship tumbling like a pinwheel, nor the fact that the blow itself was the reaction from most of the *Weasel*'s air, exhausting to space in explosive decompression. And because his cabin had no external viewport, he could not see the scatter of human bodies into the void. The last thing he saw was the underside of his bunk, and the metal brace that caught him above the left cheekbone. Then he knew only a mild curiosity: wondering why he heard something like the steady sound of a thin whistle underwater, and why that yellow flash in his head was followed by an infrared darkness crammed with pain.

It was the pain that brought him awake; that, and the sound of loud static. No, more like the zaps of an arc welder in the hands of a novice—or like a catfight. And then he turned a blurred mental page and *knew* it, the way a Rorschach blot suddenly becomes a face half-forgotten but always feared. So it did not surprise him, when he opened his eyes, to see two huge kzinti standing over him.

To a man like Herrera they would merely have been massive. To Locklear, a man of less than average height, they were enormous; nearly half again his height. The broadest kzin, with the notched right ear and the black horizontal furmark like a frown over his eyes, opened his mouth in what, to humans, might be a smile. But kzinti smiles showed dagger teeth and always meant immediate threat. This one was saying something that sounded like, "Clash-rowll whuff, rurr fitz."

Locklear needed a few seconds to translate it, and by that time the second kzin was saying it in Interworld: "Grraf-Commander says, 'Speak when you are spoken to.' For myself I would prefer that you remained silent. I have eaten no monkey-meat for too long."

While Locklear composed a reply, the big one—the Grraf-Commander, evidently—spoke again to his fellow. Something about whether the monkey knew his posture was deliberately obscene. Locklear, lying on his back on a padded table as big as a Belter's honeymoon bed, realized his arms and legs were flung wide. "I am not very fluent in the Hero's tongue," he said in passable Kzin, struggling to a sitting position as he spoke.

As he did, some of that pain localized at his right collarbone. Locklear moved very slowly thereafter. Then, recognizing the dot-and-comma-rich labels that graced much of the equipment in that room, he decided not to ask where he was. He could be nowhere but an emergency surgical room for kzin warriors. That meant he was on a kzin ship.

A faint slitting of the smaller kzin's eyes might have meant determination, a grasping for patience, or—if Locklear recalled the texts, and if they were right, a small "if" followed by a very large one—a pause for relatively cold calculation. The smaller kzin said, in his own tongue, "If the monkey speaks the Hero's tongue, it is probably as a spy."

"My presence here was not my idea," Locklear pointed out, surprised to find his memory of the language returning so quickly. "I boarded the *Weasel* on command to leave a dangerous region, not to enter one. Ask the ship's quartermaster, or check her records."

The commander spat and sizzled again: "The crew are all carrion. As you will soon be, unless you tell us why, of all the monkeys on that ship, you were the only one so specially protected."

Locklear moaned. This huge kzin's partial name and his scars implied the kind of warrior whose valor and honor forbade lies to a captive. All dead but himself? Locklear shrugged before he thought, and the shrug sent a stab of agony across his upper chest. "Sonofabitch," he gasped in agony. The navigator kzin translated. The larger one grinned, the kind of grin that might fasten on his throat.

Locklear said in Kzin, very fast, "Not you! I was cursing the pain."

"A telepath could verify your meanings very quickly," said the smaller kzin.

"An excellent idea," said Locklear. "He will verify that I am no spy, and not a combatant, but only an ethologist from Earth. A kzin acquaintance once told me it was important to know your forms of address. I do not wish to give offense."

"Call me Tzak-Navigator," said the smaller kzin abruptly, and grasped Locklear by the shoulder, talons sinking into the human flesh. Locklear moaned again, gritting his teeth. "You would attack? Good," the navigator went on, mistaking the grimace, maintaining his grip, the formidable kzin body trembling with intent.

"I cannot speak well with such pain," Locklear managed to grunt. "Not as well-protected as you think."

"We found you well-protected and sealed alone in that ship," said the commander, motioning for the navigator to slacken his hold. "I warn you, we must rendezvous the *Raptor* with another Ripping-Fang class cruiser to pick up a full crew before we hit the Eridani worlds. I have no time to waste on such a scrawny monkey as you, which we have caught nearer our home worlds than to your own."

Locklear grasped his right elbow as support for that aching collarbone. "I was surveying life-forms on purely academic study—in peacetime, so far as I knew," he said. "The old patrol craft I leased didn't have a weapon on it."

"You lie," the navigator hissed. "We saw them."

"The *Weasel* was not my ship, Tzak-Navigator. Its commander brought me back under protest; said the Interworld Commission wanted noncombatants out of harm's way—and here I am in its cloaca."

"Then it was already well-known on that ship that we are at war. I feel better about killing it," said the commander. "Now, as to the ludicrous cargo it was carrying: what is your title and importance?"

"I am scholar Carroll Locklear. I was probably the least

important man on the *Weasel*—except to myself. Since I have nothing to hide, bring a telepath."

"Now it gives orders," snarled the navigator.

"Please," Locklear said quickly.

"Better," the commander said.

"It knows," the navigator muttered. "That is why it issues such a challenge."

"Perhaps," the commander rumbled. To Locklear he said, "A skeleton crew of four rarely includes a telepath. That statement will either satisfy your challenge, or I can satisfy it in more—conventional ways." That grin again, feral, willing.

"I meant no challenge, Grraf-Commander. I only want to satisfy you of who I am, and who I'm not."

"We know *what* you are," said the navigator. "You are our prisoner, an important one, fleeing the Patriarchy rim in hopes that the monkeyship could get you to safety." He reached again for Locklear's shoulder.

"That is pure torture," Locklear said, wincing, and saw the navigator stiffen as the furry orange arm dropped. If only he had recalled the kzinti disdain for torture earlier! "I am told you are an honorable race. May I be treated properly as a captive?"

"By all means," the commander said, almost in a purr. "We eat captives."

Locklear, slyly: "Even important ones?"

"If it pleases me," the commander replied. "More likely you could turn your coat in the service of the Patriarchy. I say you could; I would not suggest such an obscenity. But that is probably the one chance your sort has for personal survival."

"My sort?"

The commander looked Locklear up and down, at the slender body, lightly muscled with only the deep chest to suggest stamina. "One of the most vulnerable specimens of monkeydom I have ever seen," he said.

That was the moment when Locklear decided he was at war. "Vulnerable, and important, and captive. Eat me," he said, wondering if that final phrase was as insulting in Kzin as it was in Interworld. Evidently not . . .

"Gunner! Apprentice Engineer," the commander called suddenly, and Locklear heard two responses through the ship's intercom. "Lock this monkey in a wiper's quarters." He turned to his navigator. "Perhaps Fleet Commander Skrull-Rrit will want this one alive. We shall know in an eight-squared of duty watches." With that, the huge kzin commander strode out.

—∿— —∿— —∿—

After his second sleep, Locklear found himself roughly hustled forward in the low-polarity ship's gravity of the *Raptor* by the nameless Apprentice Engineer. This smallest of the crew had been a kitten not long before and, at two-meter height, was still filling out. The transverse mustard-tinted band across his abdominal fur identified Apprentice Engineer down the full length of the hull passageway.

Locklear, his right arm in a sling of bandages, tried to remember all the mental notes he had made since being tossed into that cell. He kept his eyes downcast to avoid a challenging look—and because he did not want his cold fury to show. These orange-furred monstrosities had killed a ship and crew with every semblance of pride in the act. They treated a civilian captive at best like playground bullies treat an urchin, and at worst like food. It was all very well to study animal behavior as a detached ethologist. It was something else when the toughest warriors in the galaxy attached you to their food chain.

He slouched because that was as far from a military posture as a man could get—and Locklear's personal war could hardly be declared if he valued his own pelt. He would try to learn where hand weapons were kept, but would try to seem stupid. He would . . . he found the last vow impossible to keep with the Grraf-Commander's first question.

Wheeling in his command chair on the *Raptor*'s bridge, the commander faced the captive. "If you piloted your own monkeyship, then you have some menial skills." It was not a question; more like an accusation. "Can you learn to read meters if it will lengthen your pathetic life?"

Ah, there *was* a question! Locklear was on the point of lying, but it took a worried kzin to sing a worried song. If they needed him to read meters, he might learn much in a short time. Besides, they'd know bloody well if he lied on this matter. "I can try," he said. "What's the problem?"

"Tell him," spat Grraf-Commander, spinning about again to the holo screen.

Tzak-Navigator made a gesture of agreement, standing beside Locklear and gazing toward the vast humped shoulders of the fourth kzin. This nameless one was of truly gigantic size. He turned, growling, and Locklear noted the nose scar that seemed very appropriate for a flash-tempered gunner. Tzak-Navigator met his gaze and paused, with the characteristic tremor of a kzin who prided himself on physical control. "Ship's Gunner, you are relieved. Adequately done."

With the final phrase, Ship's Gunner relaxed his ear umbrellas and stalked off with a barely creditable salute. Tzak-Navigator pointed to the vacated seat, and Locklear took it. "He has got us lost," muttered the navigator.

"But you were the navigator," Locklear said.

"Watch your tongue!"

"I'm just trying to understand crew duties. I asked what the problem was, and Grraf-Commander said to tell me."

The tremor became more obvious, but Tzak-Navigator knew when he was boxed. "With a four-kzin crew, our titles and our duties tend to vary. When I accept duties of executive officer and communications officer as well, another member may prove his mettle at some simple tasks of astrogation."

"I would think Apprentice Engineer might be good at reading meters," Locklear said carefully.

"He has enough of them to read in the engine room. Besides, Ship's Gunner has superior time in grade; to pass him over would have been a deadly insult."

"Um. And I don't count?"

"Exactly. As a captive, you are a nonperson—even if you have skills that a gunner might lack."

"You said it was adequately done," Locklear pointed out.

"For a gunner," spat the navigator, and Locklear smiled. A kzin, too proud to lie, could still speak with mental reservations to an underling. The navigator went on: "We drew first blood with our chance sortie to the galactic West, but Ship's Gunner must verify gravitational blips as we pass in hyperdrive."

Locklear listened, and asked, and learned. What he learned initially was fast mental translation of octal numbers to decimal. What he learned eventually was that, counting on the gunner to verify likely blips of known star masses, Grraf-Commander had finally realized that they were monumentally lost, light-years from their intended rendezvous on the rim of known space. *And that rendezvous is on the way to the Eridani worlds,* Locklear thought. He said, as if to himself but in Kzin, "Out Eridani way, I hear they're always on guard for you guys. You really expect to get out of this alive?"

"No," said the navigator easily. "Your life may be extended a little, but you will die with heroes. Soon."

"Sounds like a suicide run," Locklear said.

"We are volunteers," the navigator said with lofty arrogance, making no attempt to argue the point, and then continued his instructions.

Presently, studying the screen, Locklear said, "That gunner has us forty parsecs from anyplace. Jump into normal space long enough for an astrogation fix and you've got it."

"Do not abuse my patience, monkey. Our last Fleet Command message on hyperwave forbade us to make unnecessary jumps."

After a moment, Locklear grinned. "And your commander doesn't want to have to tell Fleet Command you're lost."

"What was that thing you did with your face?"

"Uh,—just stretching the muscles," Locklear lied, and pointed at one of the meters. "There; um, that was a field strength of, oh hell, three eights and four, right?"

Tzak-Navigator did not have to tremble because his four-fingered hand was in motion as a blur, punching buttons. "Yes. I have a star mass and," the small screen stuttered its chicken-droppings in Kzinti, "here are the known candidates."

Locklear nodded. In this little-known region, some star masses, especially the larger ones, would have been recorded. With several fixes in hyperdrive, he could make a strong guess at their direction with respect to the galactic core. But by the time he had his second group of candidate stars, Locklear also had a scheme.

Locklear asked for his wristcomp, to help him translate octal numbers—his chief motive was less direct—and got it after Apprentice Engineer satisfied himself that it was no energy weapon. The engineer, a suspicious churl quick with his hands and clearly on the make for status, displayed disappointment at his own findings by throwing the instrument in Locklear's face. Locklear decided that the kzin lowest on the scrotum pole was most anxious to advance by any means available. And that, he decided, just might be common in all sentient behavior.

Two hours later by his wristcomp, when Locklear tried to speak to the commander without prior permission, the navigator backhanded him for his trouble and then explained the proper channels. "I will decide whether your message is worth Grraf-Commander's notice," he snarled.

Trying to stop his nosebleed, Locklear told him.

"A transparent ruse," the navigator accused, "to save your own hairless pelt."

"It would have that effect," Locklear agreed. "Maybe. But it would also let you locate your position."

The navigator looked him up and down. "Which will aid us in our mission against your own kind. You truly disgust me."

In answer, Locklear only shrugged. Tzak-Navigator wheeled and crossed to the commander's vicinity, stiff and proper, and spoke rapidly for a few moments. Presently, Grraf-Commander motioned for Locklear to approach.

Locklear decided that a military posture might help this time, and tried to hold his body straight despite his pains. The commander eyed him silently, then said, "You offer me a motive to justify jumping into normal space?"

"Yes, Grraf-Commander: to deposit an important captive in a lifeboat around some stellar body."

"And why in the name of the Patriarchy would I want to?"

"Because it is almost within the reach of plausibility that the occupants of this ship might not survive this mission," Locklear said with irony that went unnoticed. "But en route to your final glory, you can inform Fleet Command where you have placed a vitally important captive, to be retrieved later."

"You admit your status at last."

"I have a certain status," Locklear admitted. *It's damned low, and that's certain enough.* "And while you were doing that in normal space, a navigator might just happen to determine exactly where you are."

"You do not deceive me in your motive. If I did not locate that spot," Tzak-Navigator said, "no Patriarchy ship could find you—and you would soon run out of food and air."

"And you would miss the Eridani mission," Locklear reminded him, "because we aren't getting any blips and you may be getting farther from your rendezvous with every breath."

"At the least, you are a traitor to monkeydom," the navigator said. "No kzin worthy of the name would assist an enemy mission."

Locklear favored him with a level gaze. "You've decided to waste all nine lives for glory. Count on me for help."

"Monkeys are clever where their pelts are concerned," rumbled the commander. "I do not intend to miss rendezvous, and this monkey must be placed in a safe cage. Have the crew provision a lifeboat but disable its drive, Tzak-Navigator. When we locate a stellar mass, I want all in readiness for the jump."

The navigator saluted and moved off the bridge. Locklear received permission to return to his console, moving slowly, trying to watch the commander's furry digits in preparation for a jump that might be required at any time. Locklear punched several notes into the wristcomp's memory; you could never tell when a scholar's notes might come in handy.

Locklear was chewing on kzin rations, reconstituted meat which met human teeth like a leather brick and tasted of last week's oysters, when the long-range meter began to register. It was not much of a blip but it got stronger fast, the vernier meter registering by the time Locklear called out. He watched the commander, alone while the rest of the crew were arranging that lifeboat, and used his wristcomp a few more times before Grraf-Commander's announcement.

Tzak-Navigator, eyeing his console moments after the jump and still light-minutes from that small stellar mass, was at first too intent on his astrogation to notice that there was no nearby solar blaze. But Locklear noticed, and felt a surge of panic.

"You will not perish in solar radiation, at least," said Grraf-Commander in evident pleasure. "You have found yourself a black dwarf, monkey!"

Locklear punched a query. He found no candidate stars to match this phenomenon. "Permission to speak, Tzak-Navigator?"

The navigator punched in a final instruction and, while his screen flickered, turned to the local viewscreen. "Wait until you have something worth saying," he ordered, and paused, staring at what that screen told him. Then, as if arguing with his screen, he complained, "But known space is not old enough for a completely burnt-out star."

"Nevertheless," the commander replied, waving toward the screens, "if not a black dwarf, a very, very brown one. Thank that lucky star, Tzak-Navigator; it might have been a neutron star."

"And a planet," the navigator exclaimed. "Impossible! Before its final collapse, this star would have converted any nearby planet into a gas shell. But there it lies!" He pointed to a luminous dot on the screen.

"That might make it easy to find again," Locklear said with something akin to faint hope. He knew, watching the navigator's split concentration between screens, that the kzin would soon know the *Raptor*'s position. No chance beyond this brown dwarf now, an unheard-of anomaly, to escape this suicide ship.

The navigator ignored him. "Permission for proximal orbit," he requested.

"Denied," the commander said. "You know better than that. Close orbit around a dwarf could rip us asunder with angular acceleration. That dwarf may be only the size of a single dreadnought, but its mass is enormous enough to bend distant starlight."

While Locklear considered what little he knew of collapsed star matter, a cupful of which would exceed the mass of the greatest warship in known space, the navigator consulted his astrogation screen again. "I have our position," he said at last. "We were on the way to the galactic rim, thanks to that untrained—well, at least he is a fine gunner. Grraf-Commander, I meant to ask permission for orbit around the planet. We can discard this offal in the lifeboat there."

"Granted," said the commander. Locklear took more notes as the two kzinti piloted their ship nearer. If lifeboats were piloted with the same systems as cruisers, and if he could study the ways in which that lifeboat drive could be energized, he might yet take a hand in his fate.

The maneuvers took so much time that Locklear feared the kzin would drop the whole idea, but, "Let it be recorded that I keep my bargains, even with monkeys," the commander grouched as the planet began to grow in the viewport.

"Tiny suns, orbiting the planet? Stranger and stranger," the navigator mused. "Grraf-Commander, this is—not natural."

"Exactly so. It is artificial," said the commander. Brightening, he added, "Perhaps a special project, though I do not know how we could move a full-sized planet into orbit around a dwarf. Tzak-Navigator, see if this tallies with anything the Patriarchy may have on file." No sound passed between them when the navigator looked up from his screen, but their shared glance did not improve the commander's mood. "No? Well, backup records in triplicate," he snapped. "Survey sensors to full gain."

Locklear took more notes, his heart pounding anew with every added strangeness of this singular discovery. The planet orbited several light-minutes from the dead star, with numerous satellites in synchronous orbits, blazing like tiny suns—or rather, like spotlights in imitation of tiny suns, for the radiation from those satellites blazed only downward, toward the planet's surface. Those satellites, according to the navigator, seemed to be moving a bit in complex patterns, not all of them in the same ways—and one of them dimmed even as they watched.

The commander brought the ship nearer, and now Tzak-Navigator gasped with a fresh astonishment. "Grraf-Commander, this planet is dotted with force-cylinder generators. Not complete shells, but open to space at orbital height. And the beam-spread of each satellite's light flux coincides with the edge of each force cylinder. No, not all of them; several of those circular areas are not bathed in any light at all. Fallow areas?"

"Or unfinished areas," the commander grunted. "Perhaps we have discovered a project in the making."

Locklear saw blazes of blue, white, red, and yellow impinging in vast circular patterns on the planet's surface. *Almost as if someone had placed small models of Sirius, Sol, Fomalhaut, and other suns out here,* he thought. He said nothing. If he orbited this bizarre mystery long enough, he might probe its secrets. If he orbited it too long, he would damned well die of starvation.

Then, "Homeworld," blurted the astonished navigator, as the ship continued its close pass around this planet that was at least half the mass of Earth.

Locklear saw it too, a circular region that seemed to be hundreds of kilometers in diameter, rich in colors that reminded him of a kzin's fur. The green expanse of a big lake, too, as well as dark masses that might have been mountain crags. And then he noticed that one of the nearby circular patterns seemed achingly familiar in its colors, and before he thought, he said it in Interworld:

"Earth!"

The commander leaped to a mind-numbing conclusion the moment before Locklear did. "This can only be a galactic prison—or a zoo," he said in a choked voice. "The planet was evidently moved here, after the brown dwarf was discovered. There seems to be no atmosphere outside the force walls, and the planetary surface between those circular regions is almost as cold as interstellar deeps, according to the sensors. If it is a prison, each compound is well-isolated from the others. Nothing could live in the interstices."

Locklear knew that the commander had overlooked something that could live there very comfortably, but held his tongue awhile. Then, "Permission to speak," he said.

"Granted," said the commander. "What do you know of this—this thing?"

"Only this: whether it is a zoo or a prison, one of those compounds seems very Earthlike. If you left me there, I might find air and food to last me indefinitely."

"And other monkeys to help in Patriarch-knows-what," the navigator put in quickly. "No one is answering my all-band queries, and we do not know who runs this prison. The Patriarchy has no prison on record that is even faintly like this."

"If they are keeping heroes in a kzinti compound," grated the commander, "this could be a planet-sized trap."

Tzak-Navigator: "But whose?"

Grraf-Commander, with arrogant satisfaction: "It will not matter whose it is, if they set a vermin-sized trap and catch an armed lifeboat. There is no shell over these circular walls, and if there were, I would try to blast through it. Re-enable the lifeboat's drive. Tzak-Navigator, as Executive Officer you will remain on alert in the *Raptor.* For the rest of us: sound planetfall!"

Caught between fright and amazement, Locklear could only hang on and wait, painfully buffeted during reentry because the kzin-sized seat harness would not retract to fit his human frame. The lifeboat, the size of a flatlander's racing yacht, descended in a broad spiral, keeping well inside those invisible force-walls that might have damaged the craft on contact. At last the commander set his ship on a search pattern that spiraled inward while maintaining perhaps a kilometer's height above the yellow grassy plains, the kzin-colored steaming jungle, the placid lake, the dark mountain peaks of this tiny, synthesized piece of the kzin homeworld.

Presently, the craft settled near a promontory overlooking that lake and partially protected by the rise of a stone escarpment—the landfall of a good military mind, Locklear admitted to himself. "Apprentice-Engineer: report on environmental conditions," the commander ordered. Turning to Locklear, he added, "If this is a zoo, the zookeepers have not yet learned to capture heroes—nor any of our food animals, according to our survey. Since your metabolism is so near ours, I think this is where we shall deposit you for safekeeping."

"But without prey, Grraf-Commander, he will soon starve," said Apprentice Engineer.

The heavy look of the commander seemed full of ironic amusement. "No, he will not. Humans eat monkeyfood, remember? This specimen is a *kshat.*"

Locklear colored but tried to ignore the insult. Any creature willing to eat vegetation was, to the kzinti, *kshat,* an herbivore capable of eating offal. And capable of little else. "You might leave me some rations anyway," he grumbled. "I'm in no condition to be climbing trees for food."

"But you soon may be, and a single monkey in this place could hide very well from a search party."

Apprentice-Engineer, performing his extra duties proudly, waved a digit toward the screen. "Grraf-Commander, the gravity constant is exactly home normal. The temperature, too; solar flux, the same; atmosphere and microorganisms as well. I suspect that the builders of this zoo planet have buried gravity polarizers with the force cylinder generators."

"No doubt those other compounds are equally equipped to surrogate certain worlds," the commander said. "I think, whoever they are—or were—the builders work very, very slowly."

Locklear, entertaining his own scenario, suspected the builders worked very slowly, all right—and in ways, with motives, beyond the understanding of man or kzin. But why tell his suspicions to Scarface? Locklear had by now given his own private labels to these infuriating kzinti, after noting the commander's face-mark, the navigator's tremors of intent, the gunner's brutal stupidity and the engineer's abdominal patch: to Locklear, they had become Scarface, Brick-shitter, Goon, and Yellowbelly. Those labels gave him an emotional lift, but he knew better than to use them aloud.

Scarface made his intent clear to everyone, glancing at Locklear from time to time, as he gave his orders. Water and rations for eight duty watches were to be offloaded. Because every kzin craft has special equipment to pacify those kzinti who displayed criminal behavior, especially the Kdaptists with their treasonous leanings toward humankind, Scarface had prepared a *zzrou* for their human captive. The *zzrou* could be charged with a powerful soporific drug, or—as the commander said in this case—a poison. Affixed to a host and tuned to a transmitter, the *zzrou* could be set to inject its material into the host at regular intervals—or to meter it out whenever the host moved too far from that transmitter.

Scarface held the implant device, no larger than a biscuit with vicious prongs, in his hand, facing the captive. "If you try to extract this, it will kill you instantly. If you somehow found the transmitter and smashed it—again you would die instantly. Whenever you stray two steps too far from it, you will suffer. I shall set it so that you can move about far enough to feed yourself, but not far enough to make finding you a difficulty."

Locklear chewed his lip for a moment, thinking. "Is the poison cumulative?"

"Yes. And if you do not know that honor forbids me to lie, you will soon find out to your sorrow." He turned and handed a small device to Yellowbelly. "Take this transmitter and place it where no monkey might stumble across it. Do not wander more than eight-cubed paces from here in the process—and take a sidearm and a transceiver with you. I am not absolutely certain the place is uninhabited. Captive! Bare your back."

Locklear, dry-mouthed, removed his jacket and shirt. He watched Yellowbelly bound back down the short passageway and, soon afterward, heard the sigh of an air lock. He turned casually, trying to catch sight of him as Goon was peering through the viewport, and then he felt a paralyzing agony as Scarface impacted the prongs of the *zzrou* into his back just below the left shoulder blade.

His first sensation was a chill, and his second was a painful reminder of those *zzrou* prongs sunk into the muscles of his back. Locklear eased to a sitting position and looked around him. Except for depressions in the yellowish grass, and a terrifyingly small pile of provisions piled atop his shirt and jacket, he could see no evidence that a kzin lifeboat had ever landed here. "For all you know, they'll never come back," he told himself aloud, shivering as he donned his garments. Talking to himself was an old habit born of solitary researches, and made him feel less alone.

But now that he thought on it, he couldn't decide which he dreaded most, their return or permanent solitude. "So let's take stock," he said, squatting next to the provisions. A kzin's rations would last three times as long for him, but the numbers were depressing: within three flatlander weeks he'd either find water and food, or he would starve—if he did not freeze first.

If this was really a compound designed for kzin, it would be chilly for Locklear—and it was. The water would be drinkable, and no doubt he could eat kzin game animals if he found any that did not eat him first. He had already decided to head for the edge of that lake, which lay shining at a distance that was hard to judge, when he realized that local animals might destroy what food he had.

Wincing with the effort, he removed his light jacket again. They had taken his small utility knife but Yellowbelly had not checked his grooming tool very well. He deployed its shaving blade instead of the nail pincers and used it to slit away the jacket's epaulets, then cut carefully at the triple-folds of cloth, grateful for his accidental choice of a woven fabric. He found that when trying to break a thread, he would cut his hand before the thread parted. Good; a single thread would support all of those rations but the water bulbs.

His wristcomp told him the kzin had been gone an hour, and the position of that ersatz 61 Ursa Majoris hanging in the sky said he should have several more hours of light, unless the builders of this zoo had fudged on their timing. "Numbers," he said. "You need better numbers." He couldn't eat a number, but knowing the right ones might feed his belly.

In the landing pad depressions lay several stones, some crushed by the cruel weight of the kzin lifeboat. He pocketed a few fragments, two with sharp edges, tied a third stone to a twenty-meter length of thread and tossed it clumsily over a branch of a vine-choked tree. But when he tried to pull those rations up to suspend them out of harm's way, that thread sawed the pulpy branch in two. Sighing, he began collecting and stripping vines. Favoring his right shoulder, ignoring the pain of the *zzrou* as he used his left arm, he finally managed to suspend the plastic-encased bricks of leathery meat five meters above the grass. It was easier to cache the water, running slender vines through the carrying handles and suspending the water in two bundles. He kept one brick and one water bulb, which contained perhaps two gallons of the precious stuff.

And then he made his first crucial discovery, when a trickle of moisture issued from the severed end of a vine. It felt cool, and it didn't sting his hands, and taking the inevitable plunge he licked at a droplet, and then sucked at the end of that vine. Good clean water, faintly sweet; but with what subtle poisons? He decided to wait a day before trying it again, but he was smiling a ferocious little smile.

Somewhere within an eight-cubed of kzin paces lay the transmitter for that damned thing stuck into his back. No telling exactly how far he could stray from it. "Damned right there's some telling," he announced to the breeze. "Numbers, numbers," he muttered. And straight lines. If that misbegotten son of a hairball was telling the truth—and a kzin always did—then Locklear would know within a step or so when he'd gone too far. The safe distance from that transmitter would probably be the same in all directions, a hemisphere of space to roam in. Would it let him get as far as the lake?

He found out after sighting toward the nearest edge of the lake and setting out for it, slashing at the trunks of jungle trees with a sharp stone to blaze a straight-line trail. Not exactly straight, but nearly so. He listened hard at every step, moving steadily downhill, wondering what might have a menu with his name on it.

That careful pace saved him a great deal of pain, but not enough of it to suit him. Once, studying the heat-sensors that guided a captive rattlesnake to its prey back on Earth, Locklear had been bitten on the hand. It was like that now behind and below his left shoulder, a sudden burning ache that kept aching as he fell forward, writhing, hurting his right collarbone again. Locklear scrambled backward five paces or so and the sting was suddenly, shockingly, absent. That part wasn't like a rattler bite, for sure. He cursed, but knew he had to do it: moved forward again, very slowly, until he felt the lancing bite of the *zzrou.* He moved back a pace and the sting was gone. "But it's cumulative," he said aloud. "Can't do this for a hobby."

He felled a small tree at that point, sawing it with a thread tied to stones until the pulpy trunk fell, held at an angle by vines. Its sap was milky. It stung his finger. Damned if he would let it sting his tongue. He couldn't wash the stuff off in lake water because the lake was perhaps a klick beyond his limit. He wondered if Yellowbelly had thought about that when he hid the transmitter.

Locklear had intended to pace off the distance he had moved from his food cache, but kzin gravity seemed to drag at his heels and he knew that he needed numbers more exact than the paces of a tiring man. He unwound all of the thread on the ball, then sat down and opened his grooming tool. Whatever forgotten genius had stamped a five-centimeter rule along the length of the pincer lever, Locklear owed him. He measured twenty of those lengths and then tied a knot. He then used that first one-meter length to judge his second knot; used it again for the third; and with fingers that stung from tiny cuts, tied two knots at the five-meter point. He tied three knots at the ten-meter point, then continued until he had fifteen meters of surveying line, ignoring the last meter or so.

He needed another half-hour to measure the distance, as straight as he could make it, back to the food cache: 437 meters. He punched the datum into his wristcomp and rested, drinking too much from that water bulb, noting that the sunlight was making longer shadows now. The sundown direction was "West" by definition. And after sundown, what? Nocturnal predators? He was already exhausted, cold, and in need of shelter. Locklear managed to pile palmlike fronds as his bed in a narrow cleft of the promontory, made the best weapon he could by tying fist-sized stones two meters apart with a thread, grasped one stone and whirled the other experimentally. It made a satisfying whirr—and for all he knew, it might even be marginally useful.

The sunblaze fooled him, dying slowly while it was still halfway to his horizon. He punched the time into his wristcomp, and realized that the builders of this zoo might be limited in the degree to which they could surrogate a planetary surface, when other vast circular cages were adjacent to this one. It was too much to ask that any zoo cage be, for its specimens, the best of all possible worlds.

Locklear slept badly, but he slept. During the times when he lay awake, he felt the silence like a hermetic seal around him, broken only by the rasp and slither of distant tree fronds in vagrant breezes. Kzin-normal microorganisms, the navigator had said; maybe, but Locklear had seen no sign of animal life. Almost, he would have preferred stealthy footfalls or screams of nocturnal prowlers.

The next morning he noted on his wristcomp when the ersatz kzinti sun began to blaze—not on the horizon, but seeming to kindle when halfway to its zenith—rigged a better sling for his right arm, then sat scratching in the dirt for a time. The night had lasted thirteen hours and forty-eight minutes. If succeeding nights were longer, he was in for a tooth-chattering winter. But first: FIND THAT DAMNED TRANSMITTER.

Because it was small enough to fit in a pocket. And then, ah then, he would not be held like a lapdog on a leash. He pounded some kzin meat to soften it and took his first sightings while swilling from a water bulb.

The extension of that measured line, this time in the

opposite direction, went more quickly except when he had to clamber on rocky inclines or cut one of those pulpy trees down to keep his sightings near-perfect. He had no spirit level, but estimated the inclines as well as he could, as he had done before, and used the wristcomp's trigonometric functions to adjust the numbers he took from his surveying thread. That damned kzin engineer was the kind who would be half-running to do his master's bidding, and an eight-cubed of his paces might be anywhere from six hundred meters to a kilometer. Or the hidden transmitter might be almost underfoot at the cache; but no more than a klick at most. Locklear was pondering that when the *zzrou* zapped him again.

He stiffened, yelped, and whirled back several paces, then advanced very slowly until he felt its first half-hearted bite, and moved back, punching in the datum, working backward using the same system to make doubly sure of his numbers. At the cache, he found his two new numbers varied by five meters and split the difference. His southwest limit had been 437 meters away, his northeast limit 529; which meant the total length of that line was 966 meters. It probably wasn't the full diameter of his circle, but those points lay on its circumference. He halved the number: 483. That number, minus the 437, was 46 meters. He measured off forty-six meters toward the northeast and piled pulpy branches in a pyramid higher than his head. This point, by God, *was* one point on the full diameter of that circle perpendicular to his first line! Next he had to survey a line at a right angle to the line he'd already surveyed, a line passing through that pyramid of branches.

It took him all morning and then some, lengthening his thread to be more certain of that crucial right angle before he set off into the jungle, and he measured almost seven hundred meters before that bloody damned *zzrou* bit him again, this time not so painfully because by that time he was moving very slowly. He returned to the pyramid of branches and struck off in the opposite direction, just to be sure of the numbers he scratched in the dirt using the wristcomp. He was filled with joy when the *zzrou* faithfully poisoned him a bit over 300 meters away, within ten meters of his expectation.

Those first three limit points had been enough to rough out the circle; the fourth was confirmation. Locklear knew that he had passed the transmitter on that long northwest leg; calculated quickly, because he knew the exact length of that diameter, that it was a bit over two hundred meters from his pyramid; and measured off the distance after lunch.

"Just like that fur-licking bastard," he said, looking around him at the tangle of orange, green and yellow jungle growth. "Probably shit on it before he buried it."

Locklear spent a fruitless hour clearing punky shrubs and man-high ferns from the soft turf before he saw it, and of course it was not where he had been looking at all. "It" was not a telltale mound of dirt, nor a kzin footprint. It was a group of three globes of milky sap, no larger than water droplets, just about knee-high on the biggest palm in the clearing. And just about the right pattern for a kzin's toe-claws.

He moved around the trunk, as thick as his body, staring up the tree, now picking out other sets of milky puncture marks spaced up the trunk. More kzin clawmarks. Softly, feeling the gooseflesh move down his arms, he called, "Ollee-ollee-all's-in-free," just for the hell of it. And then he cut the damned tree down, carefully, letting the breeze do part of the work so that the tree sagged, buckled, and came down at a leisurely pace.

The transmitter, which looked rather like a wristcomp without a bracelet, lay in a hole scooped out by Yellowbelly's claws in the tender young top of the tree. It was sticky with sap, and Locklear hoped it had stung the kzin as it was stinging his own fingers. He wiped it off with vine leaves, rinsed it with dribbles of water from severed vines, wiped it off again, and then returned to his food cache.

"Yep, the shoulder hurts, and the damned gravity doesn't help but," he said, and yelled it at the sky, "Now I'm loose, you rat-tailed sons of bitches!"

He spent another night at the first cache, now with little concern about things that went boomp in the ersatz night. The sunblaze dimmed thirteen hours and forty-eight minutes after it began, and Locklear guessed that the days and nights of this synthetic arena never changed. "It'd be tough to develop a cosmology here," he said aloud, shivering because his right shoulder simply would not let him generate a fire by friction. "Maybe that was deliberate." If he wanted to study the behavior of intelligent species without risking their learning too much, and had not the faintest kind of ethics about it, Locklear decided he might imagine just such a vast enclosure for the kzinti. Only they were already a spacefaring race, and so was humankind, and he could have *sworn* the adjacent area on this impossible zoo planet was a ringer for one of the wild areas back on Earth. He cudgeled his memory until he recalled the lozenge shape of that lake seen from orbit, and the earthlike area.

"Right—about—there," he said, nodding to the southwest, across the lake. "If I don't starve first."

He knew that any kzinti searching for him could simply home in on the transmitter. Or maybe not so simply, if the signal was balked by stone or dirt. A cave with a kink in it could complicate their search nicely. He could test the idea—at the risk of absorbing one zap too many from that infuriating *zzrou* clinging to his back.

"Well, second things second," he said. He'd attended to the first things first. He slept poorly again, but the collarbone seemed to be mending.

Locklear admitted an instant's panic the next morning (he had counted down to the moment when the ersatz sun began to shine, missing it by a few seconds) as he moved beyond his old limit toward the lake. But the *zzrou* might have been a hockey puck for its inertness. The lake had small regular wavelets—*easy enough to generate if you have a timer on your gravity polarizer,* he mused to the builders—and a narrow beach that alternated between sand and pebbles. No prints of any kind, not even birds or molluscs. If this huge arena did not have extremes of weather, a single footprint on that sand might last a geologic era.

The food cache was within a stone's throw of the kzin landing, good enough reason to find a better place. Locklear found one, where a stream trickled to the lake (pumps, or rainfall? Time enough to find out), after cutting its passage down through basalt that was half-hidden by foliage. Locklear found a hollow beneath a low waterfall and, in three trips, portaged all his meagre stores to that hideyhole with its stone shelf. The water tasted good, and again he tested the trickle from slashed vines because he did not intend to stay tied to that lakeside forever.

The channel cut through basalt by water told him that the stream had once been a torrent and might be again. The channel also hinted that the stream had been cutting its patient way for tens of centuries, perhaps far longer. "Zoo has been here a long time," he said, startled at the tinny echo behind the murmur of water, realizing that he had begun to think of this planet as "Zoo." It might be untenanted, like that sad remnant of a capitalist's dream that still drew tourists to San Simeon on the coast of Earth's California. Cages for exotic fauna, but the animals long since gone. *Or never introduced?* One more puzzle to be shelved until more pieces could be studied.

During his fourth day on Zoo, Locklear realized that the water was almost certainly safe, and that he must begin testing the tubers, spiny nuts, and poisonous-looking fruit that he had been eyeing with mistrust. Might as well test the stuff while circumnavigating the lake, he decided, vowing to try one new plant a day. Nothing had nibbled at anything beyond moss-like growths on some soft-surfaced fruit. He guessed that the growths meant that the fruit was overripe, and judged ripeness that way. He did not need much time deciding about plants that stank horribly, or that stung his hands. On the seventh day on Zoo, while using a brown plant juice to draw a map on plastic food wrap (a pathetic left-handed effort), he began to feel distinct localized pains in his stomach. He put a finger down his throat, bringing up bits of kzin rations and pieces of the nutmeats he had swallowed after trying to chew them during breakfast. They had gone into his mouth like soft rubber capsules, and down his throat the same way.

But they had grown tiny hair-roots in his belly, and while he watched the nasty stuff he had splashed on stone, those roots continued to grow, waving blindly. He applied himself to the task again and finally coughed up another. How many had he swallowed? Three, or four? He thought four, but saw only three, and only after smashing a dozen more of the nutshells was he satisfied that each shell held three, and only three, of the loathsome things. Not animals, perhaps, but they would eat you nonetheless. Maybe he should've named the place "Herbarium." The hell with it:

"Zoo" it remained.

On the ninth day, carrying the meat in his jacket, he began to use his right arm sparingly. That was the day he realized that he had rounded the broad curve of the lake and, if his brief memory of it from orbit was accurate, the placid lake was perhaps three times as long as it was wide. He found it possible to run, one of his few athletic specialties, and despite the wear of kzin gravity he put fourteen thousand running paces behind him before exhaustion made him gather high grasses for a bed.

At a meter and a half per step, he had covered twenty-one klicks, give or take a bit, that day. Not bad in this gravity, he decided, even if the collarbone was aching again. On his abominable map, that placed him about midway down the long side of the lake. The following morning he turned west, following another stream through an open grassy plain, jogging, resting, jogging. He gathered tubers floating downstream and ate one, fearing that it would surely be deadly because it tasted like a wild strawberry.

He followed the stream for three more days, living mostly on those delicious tubers and water, nesting warmly in thick sheaves of grass. On the next day he spied a dark mass of basalt rising to the northwest, captured two litres of water in an empty plastic bag, and risked all. It was well that he did for, late in the following day with heaving chest, he saw clouds sweeping in from the north, dragging a gray downpour as a bride drags her train. That stream far below and klicks distant was soon a broad river which would have swept him to the lake. But now he stood on a rocky escarpment, seeing the glisten of water from those crags in the distance, and knew that he would not die of thirst in the highlands. He also suspected, judging from the shredded-cotton roiling of cloud beyond those crags, that he was very near the walls of his cage.

Even for a runner, the two-kilometer rise of those crags was daunting in high gravity. Locklear aimed for a saddleback only a thousand meters high where sheets of rain had fallen not long before, hiking beside a swollen stream until he found its source. It wasn't much as glaciers went, but he found green depths of ice filling the saddleback, shouldering up against a force wall that beggared anything he had ever seen up close.

The wall was transparent, apparent to the eye only by its effects and by the eldritch blackness just beyond it. The thing was horrendously cold, seeming to cut straight across hills and crags with an inner border of ice to define this kzin compound. Locklear knew it only seemed straight because the curvature was so gradual. When he tossed a stone at it, the stone slowed abruptly and soundlessly as if encountering a meters-deep cushion, then slid downward and back to clatter onto the minuscule glacier. Uphill and down, for as far as he could see, ice rimmed the inside of the force wall. He moved nearer, staring through that invisible sponge, and saw another line of ice a klick distant. Between those ice rims lay bare basalt, as uncompromisingly primitive as the surface of an asteroid. Most of that raw surface was so dark as to seem featureless, but reflections from ice lenses on each side dappled the dark basalt here and there. The dapples of light were crystal clear, without the usual fuzziness of objects a thousand meters away, and Locklear realized he was staring into a vacuum.

"So visitors to Zoo can wander comfortably around with gravity polarizer platforms between the cages," he said aloud, angrily because he could see the towering masses of conifers in the next compound. It was an Earth compound, all right—but he could see no evidence of animals across that distance, and that made him fiercely glad for some reason. He ached to cross those impenetrable barriers, and his vision of lofty conifers blurred with his tears.

His feet were freezing, now, and no vegetation grew as near as the frost that lined the ice rim. "You're good, but you're not perfect," he said to the builders. "You can't keep the heat in these compounds from leaking away at the rims." Hence frozen moisture and the lack of vegetation along the rim, and higher rainfall where clouds skirted that cold force wall.

Scanning the vast panoramic arc of that ice rim, Locklear noted that his prison compound had a gentle bowl shape, though some hills and crags surged up in the lowlands. *Maybe using the natural contours of old craters? Or maybe you made those craters.* It was an engineering project that held tremendous secrets for humankind, and it had been there for one hell of a long time. Widely spaced across that enormous bowl were spots of dramatic color, perhaps flowers. *But they won't scatter much without animal vectors to help the wind disperse seeds and such. Dammit, this place wasn't finished!*

He retraced his steps downward. There was no point in making a camp in this inclement place, and with every sudden whistle of breeze now he was starting to look up, scanning for the kzin ship he knew might come at any time. He needed to find a cave, or to make one, and that would require construction tools.

Late in the afternoon, while tying grass bundles at the edge of a low rolling plain, Locklear found wood of the kind he'd hardly dared to hope for. He simply had not expected it to grow horizontally. With a thin bark that simulated its surroundings, it lay mostly below the surface with shallow roots at intervals like bamboo. Kzinti probably would've known to seek it from the first, damn their hairy hides. The stuff—he dubbed it shamboo—grew parallel to the ground and arrow-straight, and its foliage popped up at regular intervals too. Some of its hard, hollow segments stored water, and some specimens grew thick as his thighs and ten meters long, tapering to wicked growth spines on each end. Locklear had been walking over potential hiking staffs, construction shoring, and rafts for a week without noticing. He pulled up one the size of a javelin and clipped it smooth.

His grooming tool would do precision work, but Locklear abraded blisters on his palms fashioning an axehead from a chertlike stone common in seams where basalt crags soared from the prairie. He spent two days learning how to socket a handaxe in a shamboo handle, living mostly on tuberberries and grain from grassheads, and elevated his respect for the first tool-using creatures in the process.

By now, Locklear's right arm felt almost as good as new, and the process of rediscovering primitive technology became a compelling pastime. He was so intent on ways to weave split shamboo filaments into cordage for a firebow, while trudging just below the basalt heights, that he almost missed the most important moment of his life.

He stepped from savannah grass onto a gritty surface that looked like other dry washes, continued for three paces, stepped up onto grassy turf again, then stopped. He recalled walking across sand-sprinkled tiles as a youth, and something in that old memory made him look back. The dry wash held wave-like patterns of grit, pebbles, and sand, but here and there were bare patches.

And those bare patches were as black and as smooth as machine-polished obsidian.

Locklear crammed the half-braided cord into a pocket and began to follow that dry wash up a gentle slope, toward the cleft ahead, and toward his destiny.

His heart pounding with hope and fear, Locklear stood five meters inside the perfect arc of obsidian that formed the entrance to that cave. No runoff had ever spilled grit across the smooth broad floor inside, and he felt an irrational concern that his footsteps were defiling something perfectly pristine, clean and cold as an ice cavern. But a far, *far* more rational concern was the portal before him, its facing made of the same material as the floor, the opening itself four meters wide and just as high. A faint flickering luminescence, as of gossamer film stretched across the portal, gave barely enough light to see. Locklear saw his reflection in it, and wanted to laugh aloud at this ragged, skinny, barrel-chested apparition with the stubble of beard wearing stained flight togs. And the apparition reminded him that he might not be alone.

He felt silly, but after clearing his throat twice he managed to call out: "Anybody home?"

Echoes; several of them, more than this little entrance space could possibly generate. He poked his sturdy shamboo hiking staff into the gossamer film and jumped when stronger light flickered in the distance. "Maybe you just eat animal tissue," he said, with a wavering chuckle. "Well—" He took his grooming pincers and cut away the dried curl of skin around a broken blister on his palm, clipped away sizeable crescents of fingernails, tossed them at the film.

Nothing but the tiny clicks of cuticles on obsidian, inside; *that's* how quiet it was. He held the pointed end of the staff like a lance in his right hand, extended the handaxe ahead in his left. He *was* right-handed, after all, so he'd rather lose the left one . . .

No sensation on his flesh, but a sudden flood of light as he moved through the portal, and Locklear dashed backward to the mouth of the cave. "Take it easy, fool," he chided himself. "What did you see?"

A long smooth passageway; walls without signs or features; light seeming to leap from obsidian walls, not too strong but damned disconcerting. He took several deep breaths and went in again, standing his ground this time when light flooded the artificial cave. His first thought, seeing the passageway's apparent end in another film-spanned portal two hundred meters distant, was, *Does it go all the way from Kzersatz to Newduvai?* He couldn't recall when he'd begun to think of this kzin compound as Kzersatz and the adjoining, Earthlike, compound as Newduvai.

Footfalls echoing down side corridors, Locklear hurried to the opposite portal, but frost glistened on its facing and his staff would not penetrate more than a half-meter through the luminous film. He could see his exhalations fogging the film. The resistance beyond it felt spongy but increasingly hard, probably an extension of that damned force wall. If his sense of direction was right, he should be just about beneath the rim of Kzersatz. No doubt someone or something knew how to penetrate that wall, because the portal was there. But Locklear knew enough about force walls and screens to despair of getting through it without better understanding. Besides, if he did get through he might punch a hole into vacuum. If his suspicions about the builders of Zoo were correct, that's exactly what lay beyond the portal.

Sighing, he turned back, counting nine secondary passages that yawned darkly on each side, choosing the first one to his right. Light flooded it instantly. Locklear gasped.

Row upon row of cubical, transparent containers stretched down the corridor for fifty meters, some of them tiny, some the size of a small room. And in each container floated a specimen of animal life, rotating slowly, evidently above its own gravity polarizer field. Locklear had seen a few of the creatures; had seen pictures of a few more; all, every last one that he could identify, native to the kzin homeworld. He knew that many museums maintained ranks of pickled specimens, and told himself he should not feel such a surge of anger about this one. *Well, you're an ethologist, you twit,* he told himself silently. *You're just pissed off because you can't study behaviors of dead animals.* Yet, even taking that into consideration, he felt a kind of righteous wrath toward builders who played at godhood without playing it perfectly. It was a responsibility he would never have chosen. He did not yet realize that he was surrounded with similar choices.

He stood before a floating *vatach,* in life a fast-moving burrower the size of an earless hare, reputedly tasty but too mild-mannered for kzinti sport. No symbols on any container, but obvious differences among the score of *vatach* in those containers.

How many sexes? He couldn't recall. "But I bet you guys would," he said aloud. He passed on, shuddering at the critters with fangs and leathery wings, marveling at the stump-legged creatures the height of a horse and the mass of a rhino, all in positions that were probably fetal though some were obviously adult.

Retracing his steps to the *vatach* again, Locklear leaned a hand casually against the smooth metal base of one container. He heard nothing, but when he withdrew his hand the entire front face of the glasslike container levered up, the *vatach* settling gently to a cage floor that slid forward toward Locklear like an offering.

The *vatach* moved.

Locklear leaped back so fast he nearly fell, then darted forward again and shoved hard on the cage floor. Back it went, down came the transparent panel, up went the *vatach,* inert, into its permanent rotating waltz.

"Stasis fields! By God, they're alive," he said. The animals hadn't been pickled at all, only stored until someone was ready to stock Kzersatz. *Vatach* were edible herbivores—but if he released them without natural enemies, how long before they overran the whole damned compound? And did he really want to release their natural enemies, even if he could identify them?

"Sorry, fellas. Maybe I can find you an island," he told the little creatures, and moved on with an alertness that made him forget the time. He did not consider time because the glow of illumination did not dim when the sun of Kzersatz did, and only the growl of his empty belly sent him back to the cave entrance where he had left his jacket with his remaining food and water. Even then he chewed tuberberries from sheer necessity, his hands trembling as he looked out at the blackness of the Kzersatz night. Because he had passed down each of those eighteen side passages, and knew what they held, and knew that he had some godplaying of his own to ponder.

He said to the night and to himself, "Like for instance, whether to take one of those goddamned kzinti out of stasis."

His wristcomp held a hundred megabytes, much of it concerning zoology and ethology. Some native kzin animals were marginally intelligent, but he found nothing whatever in memory storage that might help him communicate abstract ideas with them. "Except the tabbies themselves, eighty-one by actual count," he mused aloud the next morning, sitting in sunlight outside. "Damned if I do. Damned if I don't. Damn if I know which is the damnedest," he admitted. But the issue was never very much in doubt; if a kzin ship did return, they'd find the cave sooner or later because they were the best hunters in known space. He'd make it expensive in flying fur, maybe—but there seemed to be no rear entrance. Well, he didn't have to go it alone; Kdaptist kzinti made wondrous allies. Maybe he could convert one, or win his loyalty by setting him free.

If the kzin ship didn't return, he was stuck with a neolithic future or with playing God to populate Kzersatz, unless—"Aw shitshitshit," he said at last, getting up, striding into the cave. "I'll just wake the smallest one and hope he's reasonable."

But the smallest ones weren't male; the females, with their four small but prominent nipples and the bushier fur on their tails, were the runts of that exhibit. In their way they were almost beautiful, with longer hindquarters and shorter torsos than the great bulky males, all eighty-one of the species rotating nude in fetal curls before him. He studied his wristcomp and his own memory, uncomfortably aware that female kzin were, at best, morons. Bred for bearing kits, and for catering to their warrior males, female kzinti were little more than ferociously protected pets in their own culture.

"Maybe that's what I need anyhow," he muttered, and finally chose the female that bulked smallest of them all. When he pressed that baseplate, he did it with grim forebodings.

She settled to the cage bottom and slid out, and Locklear stood well away, axe in one hand, lance in the other, trying to look as if he had no intention of using either. His Adam's apple bobbed as the female began to uncoil from her fetal position.

Her eyes snapped open so fast, Locklear thought they should have clicked audibly. She made motions like someone waving cobwebs aside, mewing in a way that he found pathetic, and then she fully noticed the little man standing near, and she screamed and leaped. That leap carried her to the top of a nearby container, *away* from him, cowering, eyes wide, ear umbrellas folded flat.

He remembered not to grin as he asked, "Is this my thanks for bringing you back?"

She blinked. "You (something, something) a devil, then?"

He denied it, pointing to the scores of other kzin around her, admitting he had found them this way.

If curiosity killed cats, this one would have died then and there. She remained crouched and wary, her eyes flickering around as she formed more questions. Her speech was barely understandable. She used a form of verbal negation utterly new to him, and some familiar words were longer the way she pronounced them. The general linguistic rule was that abstract ideas first enter a lexicon as several words, later shortened by the impatient.

Probably her longer words were primitive forms; God only knew how long she had been in stasis! He told her who he was, but that did not reduce her wary hostility much. She had never heard of men. Nor of any intelligent race other than kzinti. Nor, for that matter, of spaceflight. But she was remarkably quick to absorb new ideas, and from Locklear's demeanor she realized all too soon that *he,* in fact, was scared spitless of *her.* That was the point when she came down off that container like a leopard from a limb, snatched his handaxe while he hesitated, and poked him in the gut with its haft.

It appeared, after all, that Locklear had revived a very, *very* old-fashioned female.

"You (something or other) captive," she sizzled, unsheathing a set of shining claws from her fingers as if to remind him of their potency. She turned a bit away from him then, looking sideways at him. "Do you have sex?"

His Adam's apple bobbed again before he intuited her meaning. Her first move was to gain control, her second to establish sex roles. A bright female; yeah, that's about what an ethologist should expect . . . "Humans have two sexes just as kzinti do," he said, "and I am male, and I won't submit as your captive. You people eat captives. You're not all that much bigger than I am, and this lance is sharp. I'm your benefactor. Ask yourself why I didn't spear you for lunch before you awoke."

"If you could eat me, I could eat you," she said. "Why do you cut words short?"

Bewildering changes of pace but always practical, he thought. Oh yes, an exceedingly bright female. "I speak modern Kzinti," he explained. "One day we may learn how many thousands of years you have been asleep." He enjoyed the almost human widening of her yellow eyes, and went on doggedly. "Since I have honorably waked you from what might have been a permanent sleep, I ask this: what does your honor suggest?"

"That I (something) clothes," she said. "And owe you a favor, if nakedness is what you want."

"It's cold for me, too." He'd left his food outside but was wearing the jacket, and took it off. "I'll trade this for the axe."

She took it, studying it with distaste, and eventually tied its sleeves like an apron to hide her mammaries. It could not have warmed her much. His question was half disbelief: "That's it? Now you're clothed?"

"As (something) of the (something) always do," she said. "Do you have a special name?"

He told her, and she managed "Rockear." Her own name, she said, was (something fiendishly tough for humans to manage), and he smiled. "I'll call you 'Miss Kitty.' "

"If it pleases you," she said, and something in the way that phrase rolled out gave him pause.

He leaned the shamboo lance aside and tucked the axe into his belt. "We must try to understand each other better," he said. "We are not on your homeworld, but I think it is a very close approximation. A kind of incomplete zoo. Why don't we swap stories outside where it's warm?"

She agreed, still wary but no longer hostile, with a glance of something like satisfaction toward the massive kzin male rotating in the next container. And then they strolled outside into the wilderness of Kzersatz which, for some reason, forced thin mewling *miaows* from her. It had never occurred to Locklear that a kzin could weep.

As near as Locklear could understand, Miss Kitty's emotions were partly relief that she had lived to see her yellow fields and jungles again, and partly grief when she contemplated the loneliness she now faced. *I don't count,* he thought. *But if I expect to get her help, I'd best see that I do count.*

Everybody thinks his own dialect is superior, Locklear decided. Miss Kitty fumed at his brief forms of Kzinti, and he winced at her ancient elaborations, as they walked to the nearest stream. She had a temper, too, teaching him genteel curses as her bare feet encountered thorns. She seemed fascinated by this account of the kzin expansion, and that of humans, and others as well through the galaxy. She even accepted his description of the planet Zoo though she did not seem to understand it.

She accepted his story so readily, in fact, that he hit on an intuition. "Has it occurred to you that I might be lying?"

"Your talk is offensive," she flared. "My benefactor a criminal? No. Is it common among your kind?"

"More than among yours," he admitted, "but I have no reason to lie to you. Sorry," he added, seeing her react again. *Kzinti don't flare up at that word today; maybe all cusswords have to be replaced as they weaken from overuse.* Then he told her how man and kzin got along between wars, and ended by admitting it looked as if another war was brewing, which was why he had been abandoned here.

She looked around her. "Is Zoo your doing, or ours?"

"Neither. I think it must have been done by a race we know very little about: Outsiders, we call them. No one knows how many years they have traveled space, but very, very long. They live without air, without much heat. Just beyond the wall that surrounds Kzersatz, I have seen airless corridors with the cold darkness of space and dapples of light. They would be quite comfortable there."

"I do not think I like them."

Then he laughed, and had to explain how the display of his teeth was the opposite of anger.

"Those teeth could not support much anger," she replied, her small pink ear umbrellas winking down and up. He learned that this was her version of a smile.

Finally, when they had taken their fill of water, they returned as Miss Kitty told her tale. She had been trained as a palace *prret;* a servant and casual concubine of the mighty during the reign of *Rrawlrit* Eight and Three. Locklear said that the "Rritt" suffix meant high position among modern kzinti, and she made a sound very like a human sniff. *Rrawlritt* was the arrogant son of an arrogant son, and so on. He liked his females, lots of them, especially young ones. "I was (something) than most," she said, her four-digited hand slicing the air at her ear height.

"Petite, small?"

"Yes. Also smart. Also famous for my appearance," she added without the slightest show of modesty. She glanced at him as though judging which haunch might be tastiest. "Are you famous for yours?"

"Uh—not that I know of."

"But not unattractive?"

He slid a hand across his face, feeling its stubble. "I am considered petite, and by some as, uh, attractive." *Two or three are "Some." Not much, but some . . .*

"With a suit of fur you would be (something)," she said, with that ear-waggle, and he quickly asked about palace life because he damned well did not want to know what that final word of hers had meant. It made him nervous as hell. Yeah, but what *did* it mean? Mud-ugly? Handsome? Tasty? *Listen to the lady, idiot, and quit suspecting what you're suspecting.*

She had been raised in a culture in which females occasionally ran a regency, and in which males fought duels over the argument as to whether females were their intellectual equals. Most thought not. Miss Kitty thought so, and proved it, rising to palace prominence with her backside, as she put it.

"You mean you were no better than you should be," he commented.

"What does that mean?"

"I haven't the foggiest idea, just an old phrase." She was still waiting, and her aspect was not benign. "Uh, it means nobody could expect you to do any better."

She nodded slowly, delighting him as she adopted one of the human gestures he'd been using. "I did too well to suit the males jealous of my power, Rockear. They convinced the regent that I was conspiring with other palace *prrets* to gain equality for our sex."

"And were you?"

She arched her back with pride. "Yes. Does that offend you?"

"No. Would you care if it did?"

"It would make things difficult, Rockear. You must understand that I loathe, admire, hate, desire kzintosh—male kzin. I fought for equality because it was common knowledge that some were planning to breed *kzinrret,* females, to be no better than pets."

"I hate to tell you this, Miss Kitty, but they've done it."

"Already?"

"I don't know how long it took, but—" He paused, and then told her the worst. Long before man and kzin first met, their females had been bred into brainless docility. Even if Miss Kitty found modern sisters, they would be of no help to her.

She fought the urge to weep again, strangling her miaows with soft snarls of rage.

Locklear turned away, aware that she did not want to seem vulnerable, and consulted his wristcomp's encyclopedia. The earliest kzin history made reference to the downfall of a *Rrawlrit* the fifty-seventh—Seven Eights and One, and he gasped at what that told him. "Don't feel too bad, Miss Kitty," he said at last. "That was at least forty thousand years ago; do you understand eight to the fifth power?"

"It is very, very many," she said in a choked voice.

"It's been more years than that since you were brought here. How did you get here, anyhow?"

"They executed several of us. My last memory was of grappling with the lord high executioner, carrying him over the precipice into the sacred lagoon with me. I could not swim with those heavy chains around my ankles, but I remember trying. I hope he drowned," she said, eyes slitted. "Sex with him had always been my most hated chore."

A small flag began to wave in Locklear's head; he furled it for further reference. "So you were trying to swim. Then?"

"Then suddenly I was lying naked with a very strange creature staring at me," she said with that ear-wink, and a sharp talon pointed almost playfully at him. "Do not think ill of me because I reacted in fright."

He shook his head, and had to explain what *that* meant, and it became a short course in subtle nuances for each of them. Miss Kitty, it seemed, proved an old dictum about downtrodden groups: they became highly expert at reading body language, and at developing secret signals among themselves. It was not Locklear's fault that he was constantly, and completely unaware, sending messages that she misread.

But already, she was adapting to his gestures as he had to her language. "Of all the kzinti I could have taken from stasis, I got you," he chuckled finally, and because her glance was quizzical, he told a gallant half-lie; "I went for the prettiest, and got the smartest."

"And the hungriest," she said. "Perhaps I should hunt something for us."

He reminded her that there was nothing to hunt. "You can help me choose animals to release here. Meanwhile, you can have this," he added, offering her the kzinti rations.

The sun faded on schedule, and he dined on tuberberries while she devoured an entire brick of meat. She amazed him by popping a few tuberberries for dessert. When he asked her about it, she replied that certainly kzinti ate vegetables in her time; why should they not?

"Males want only meat," he shrugged.

"They would," she snarled. "In my day, some select warriors did the same. They claimed it made them ferocious and that eaters of vegetation were mere *kshauvat,* dumb herbivores; we *prret* claimed their diet just made them hopelessly aggressive."

"The word's been shortened to *kshat* now," he mused. "It's a favorite cussword of theirs. At least you don't have to start eating the animals in stasis to stay alive. That's the good news; the bad news is that the warriors who left me here may return at any time. What will you do then?"

"That depends on how accurate your words have been," she said cagily.

"And if I'm telling the plain truth?"

Her ears smiled for her: "Take up my war where I left it," she said.

Locklear felt his control slipping when Miss Kitty refused to wait before releasing most of the *vatach*. They were nocturnal with easily-spotted burrows, she insisted, and yes, they bred fast—but she pointed to specimens of a winged critter in stasis and said they would control the *vatach* very nicely if the need arose. By now he realized that this kzin female wasn't above trying to vamp him; and when that failed, a show of fang and talon would succeed.

He showed her how to open the cages only after she threatened him, and watched as she grasped waking *vatach* by their legs, quickly releasing them to the darkness outside. No need to release the (something) yet, she said; Locklear called the winged beasts "batowls." "I hope you know what you're doing," he grumbled. "I'd stop you if I could do it without a fight."

"You would wait forever," she retorted. "I know the animals of my world better than you do, and soon we may need a lot of them for food."

"Not so many; there's just the two of us."

The cat-eyes regarded him shrewdly. "Not for long," she said, and dropped her bombshell. "I recognized a friend of mine in one of those cages."

Locklear felt an icy needle down his spine. "A male?"

"Certainly not. Five of us were executed for the same offense, and at least one of them is here with us. Perhaps those Outsiders of yours collected us all as we sank in that stinking water."

"Not *my* Outsiders," he objected. "Listen, for all we know they're monitoring us, so be careful how you fiddle with their setup here."

She marched him to the kzin cages and purred her pleasure on recognizing two females, both *prret* like herself, both imposingly large for Locklear's taste. She placed a furry hand on one cage, enjoying the moment. "I could release you now, my sister in struggle," she said softly. "But I think I shall wait. Yes, I think it is best," she said to Locklear, turning away. "These two have been here a long time, and they will keep until—"

"Until you have everything under your control?"

"True," she said. "But you need not fear, Rockear. You are

an ally, and you know too many things we must know. And besides," she added, rubbing against him sensuously, "you are (something)."

There was that same word again, *t'rralap* or some such, and now he was sure, with sinking heart, that it meant "cute." He didn't feel cute; he was beginning to feel like a Pomeranian on a short leash.

More by touch than anything else, they gathered bundles of grass for a bower at the cave entrance, and Miss Kitty showed no reluctance in falling asleep next to him, curled becomingly into a buzzing ball of fur. But when he moved away, she moved too, until they were touching again. He knew beyond doubt that if he moved too far in the direction of his lance and axe, she would be fully awake and suspicious as hell.

And she'd call my bluff, and I don't want to kill her, he thought, settling his head against her furry shoulder. *Even if I could, which is doubtful. I'm no longer master of all I survey. In fact, now I have a mistress of sorts, and I'm not too sure what kind of mistress she has in mind. They used to have a word for what I'm thinking. Maybe Miss Kitty doesn't care who or what she diddles; hell, she was a palace courtesan, doing it with males she hated. She thinks I'm t'rralap. Yeah, that's me, Locklear, Miss Kitty's trollop; and what the hell can I do about it? I wish there were some way I could get her back in that stasis cage* . . . And then he fell asleep.

To Locklear's intense relief, Miss Kitty seemed uninterested in the remaining cages on the following morning. They foraged for breakfast and he hid his astonishment as she taught him a dozen tricks in an hour. The root bulb of one spiny shrub tasted like an apple; the seed pods of some weeds were delicious; and she produced a tiny blaze by rapidly pounding an innocent-looking nutmeat between two stones. It occurred to him that nuts contained great amounts of energy. A pile of these firenuts, he reflected, might be turned into a weapon . . .

Feeding hunks of dry brush to the fire, she announced that those root bulbs baked nicely in coals. "If we can find clay, I can fire a few pottery dishes and cups, Rockear. It was part of my training, and I intend to have everything in domestic order before we wake those two."

"And what if a kzin ship returns and spots that smoke?"

That was a risk they must take, she said. Some woods

burned more cleanly than others. He argued that they should at least build their fires far from the cave, and while they were at it, the cave entrance might be better disguised. She agreed, impressed with his strategy, and then went down on all-fours to inspect the dirt near a dry wash. As he admired her lithe movements, she shook her head in an almost human gesture. "No good for clay."

"It's not important."

"It is vitally important!" Now she wheeled upright, impressive and fearsome. "Rockear, if any kzintosh return here, we must be ready. For that, we must have the help of others—the two *prret*. And believe me, they will be helpful only if they see us as their (something)."

She explained that the word meant, roughly, "paired household leaders." The basic requirements of a household, to a kzin female, included sleeping bowers—easily come by—and enough pottery for that household. A male kzin needed one more thing, she said, her eyes slitting: a *wtsai*.

"You mean one of those knives they all wear?"

"Yes. And you must have one in your belt." From the waggle of her ears, he decided she was amused by her next statement: "It is a—badge, of sorts. The edge is usually sharp but I cannot allow that, and the tip must be dull. I will show you why later."

"Dammit, these things could take weeks!"

"Not if we find the clay, and if you can make a *wtsai* somehow. Trust me, Rockear; these are the basics. Other kzinrret will not obey us otherwise. They must see from the first that we are proper providers, proper leaders with the pottery of a settled tribe, not the wooden implements of wanderers. And they must take it for granted that you and I," she added, "are (something)." With that, she rubbed lightly against him.

He caught himself moving aside and swallowed hard. "Miss Kitty, I don't want to offend you, but, uh, humans and kzinti do not mate."

"Why do they not?"

"Uhm. Well, they never have."

Her eyes slitted, yet with a flicker of her ears: "But they could?"

"Some might. Not me."

"Then they might be able to," she said as if to herself. "I thought I felt something familiar when we were sleeping."

She studied his face carefully. "Why does your skin change color?"

"Because, goddammit, I'm upset!" He mastered his breathing after a moment and continued, speaking as if to a small child, "I don't know about kzinti, but a man can *not,* uh, mate unless he is, uh—"

"Unless he is intent on the idea?"

"Right!"

"Then we will simply have to pretend that we do mate, Rockear. Otherwise, those two kzinrret will spend most of their time trying to become your mate and will be useless for work."

"Of all the . . ." he began, and then dropped his chin and began to laugh helplessly. Human tribal customs had been just as complicated, once, and she was probably the only functioning expert in known space on the customs of ancient kzinrret. "We'll pretend, then, up to a point. Try and make that point, ah, not too pointed."

"Like your *wtsai,"* she retorted. "I will try not to make your face change color."

"Please," he said fervently, and suggested that he might find the material for a *wtsai* inside the cave while she sought a deposit of clay. She bounded away on all-fours with the lope of a hunting leopard, his jacket a somehow poignant touch as it flapped against her lean belly.

When he looked back from the cave entrance, she was a tiny dot two kilometers distant, coursing along a shallow creekbed. "Maybe you won't lie, and I've got no other ally," he said to the swift saffron dot. "But you're not above misdirection with your own kind. I'll remember that."

Locklear cursed as he failed to locate any kind of tool chest or lab implements in those inner corridors. But he blessed his grooming tool when the tip of its pincer handle fitted screwheads in the cage that had held Miss Kitty prisoner for so long. He puzzled for minutes before he learned to turn screwheads a quarter-turn, release pressure to let the screwheads emerge, then another quarter-turn, and so on, nine times each. He felt quickening excitement as the cage cover detached, felt it stronger when he disassembled the base and realized its metal sheeting was probably one of a myriad stainless steel alloys. The diamond coating on his nail file proved the sheet was no indestructible substance. It was thin enough to flex, even to be dented by a whack against an adjoining cage. It might take awhile, but he would soon have his *wtsai* blade.

And two other devices now lay before him, ludicrously far advanced beyond an ornamental knife. The gravity polarizer's main bulk was a doughnut of ceramic and metal. Its switch, and that of the stasis field, both were energized by the sliding cage floor he had disassembled. The switches worked just as well with fingertip pressure. They boasted separate energy sources which Locklear dared not assault; anything that worked for forty thousand years without harming the creatures near it would be more sophisticated than any fumble-fingered mechanic.

Using the glasslike cage as a test load, he learned which of the two switches flung the load into the air. The other, then, had to operate the stasis field—and both devices had simple internal levers for adjustments. When he learned how to stop the cage from spinning, and then how to make it hover only a hand's breadth above the device or to force it against the ceiling until it creaked, he was ecstatic. Then he energized the stasis switch with a chill of gooseflesh. Any prying paws into those devices would not pry for long, unless someone knew about that inconspicuous switch. Locklear could see no interconnects between the stasis generator and the polarizer, but both were detachable. If he could get that polarizer outside—Locklear strode out of the cave laughing. It would be the damnedest vehicle ever, but its technologies would be wholly appropriate. He hid the device in nearby grass; the less his ally knew about such things, the more freedom he would have to pursue them.

Miss Kitty returned in late afternoon with a sopping mass of clay wrapped in greenish-yellow palm leaves. The clay was poor quality, she said, but it would have to serve—and why was he battering that piece of metal with his stone axe?

If she knew a better way to cut off a *wtsai*-sized strip of steel than bending it back and forth, he replied, he'd love to hear it. Bickering like an old married couple, they sat near the cave mouth until dark and pursued their separate Stone-Age tasks. Locklear, whose hand calluses were still forming, had to admit that she had been wonderfully trained for domestic chores; under those quick four-digited hands of hers, rolled coils of clay soon became shallow bowls with thin sides, so nearly perfect they might have been turned on a potter's wheel. By now he was calling her "Kit," and she seemed genuinely pleased when he praised her work. Ah, she said, but wait until the pieces were sun-dried to leather hardness; then she would make the bowls lovely with talon-etched decoration. He objected that decoration took time. She replied curtly that kzinrret did not live for utility alone.

He helped pull flat fibers from the stalks of palm leaves, which she began to weave into a mat. "For bedding," he asked? "Certainly not," she said imperiously; "for the clothing which modesty required of kzinrret." He pursued it: "Would they really care all that much with only a human to see them?" "A human *male,*" she reminded him; if she considered him worthy of mating, the others would see him as a male first, and a non-kzin second. He was half-amused but more than a little uneasy as they bedded down, she curled slightly facing away, he crowded close at her insistence, "—For companionship," as she put it.

Their last exchange that night implied a difference between the rigorously truthful male kzin and their females. "Kit, you can't tell the others we're mated unless we are."

"I can ignore their questions and let them draw their own conclusions," she said sleepily.

"Aren't you blurring that fine line between half-truths and, uh, non-truths?"

"I do not intend to discuss it further," she said, and soon was purring in sleep with the faint growl of a predator.

He needed two more days, and a repair of the handaxe, before he got that jagged slice of steel pounded and, with abrasive stones, ground into something resembling a blade. Meanwhile, Kit built her open-fired kiln of stones in a ravine some distance from the cave, ranging widely with that leopard lope of hers to gather firewood. Locklear was glad of her absence; it gave him time to finish a laminated shamboo handle for his blade, bound with thread, and to collect the thickest poles of shamboo he could find. The blade was sharp enough to trim the poles quickly, and tough enough to hold an edge.

He was tying crosspieces with plaited fiber to bind thick shamboo poles into a slender raft when, on the third day of those labors, he felt a presence behind him. Whirling, he brandished his blade. "Oh," he said, and lowered the *wtsai.* "Sorry, Kit. I keep worrying about the return of those kzintosh."

She was not amused. "Give it to me," she said, thrusting her hand out.

"The hell I will. I need this thing."

"I can see that it is too sharp."

"I need it sharp."

"I am sure you do. I need it dull." Her gesture for the blade was more than impatient.

Half straightening into a crouch, he brought the blade up again, eyes narrowed. "Well, by God, I've had about all your whims I can take. You want it? Come and get it."

She made a sound that was deeper than a purr, putting his hackles up, and went to all-fours, her furry tailtip flicking as she began to pace around him. She was a lovely sight. She scared Locklear silly. "When I take it, I will hurt you," she warned.

"If you take it," he said, turning to face her, moving the *wtsai* in what he hoped was an unpredictable pattern. *Dammit, I can't back down now. A puncture wound might be fatal to her, so I've got to slash lightly.* Or maybe he wouldn't have to, when she saw he meant business.

But he did have to. She screamed and leaped toward his left, her own left hand sweeping out at his arm. He skipped aside and then felt her tail lash against his shins like a curled rope. He stumbled and whirled as she was twisting to repeat the charge, and by sheer chance his blade nicked her tail as she whisked it away from his vicinity.

She stood erect, holding her tail in her hands, eyes wide and accusing. "You—you insulted my tail," she snarled.

"Damn tootin'," he said between his teeth.

With arms folded, she turned her back on him, her tail curled protectively at her backside. "You have no respect," she said, and because it seemed she was going to leave, he dropped the blade and stood up, and realized too late just how much peripheral vision a kzin boasted. She spun and was on him in an instant, her hands gripping his wrists, and hurled them both to the grass, bringing those terrible ripping foot talons up to his stomach. They lay that way for perhaps three seconds. "Drop the *wtsai,*" she growled, her mouth near his throat. Locklear had not been sure until now whether a very small female kzin had more muscular strength than he. The answer was not just awfully encouraging.

He could feel sharp needles piercing the skin at his stomach, kneading, releasing, piercing; a reminder that with one move she could disembowel him. The blade whispered into the grass. She bit him lightly at the juncture of his neck and shoulder, and then faced him with their noses almost touching. "A love bite," she said, and released his wrists, pushing away with her feet.

He rolled, hugging his stomach, fighting for breath, grateful that she had not used those fearsome talons with her push. She found the blade, stood over him, and now no sign of her anger remained. *Right; she's in complete control,* he thought.

"Nicely made, Rockear. I shall return it to you when it is presentable," she said.

"Get the hell away from me," he husked softly.

She did, with a bound, moving toward a distant wisp of smoke that skirled faintly across the sky. If a kzin ship returned now, they would follow that wisp immediately.

Locklear trotted without hesitation to the cave, cursing, wiping trickles of blood from his stomach and neck, wiping a tear of rage from his cheek. There were other ways to prove to this damned tabby that he could be trusted with a knife. One, at least, if he didn't get himself wasted in the process.

She returned quite late, with half of a cooked *vatach* and tuberberries as a peace offering, to find him weaving a huge triangular mat. It was a sail, he explained, for a boat. She had taken the little animal on impulse, she said, partly because it was a male, and ate her half on the spot for old times' sake. He'd told her his distaste for raw meat and evidently she never forgot anything.

He sulked awhile, complaining at the lack of salt, brightening a bit when she produced the *wtsai* from his jacket which she still wore. "You've ruined it," he said, seeing the colors along the dull blade as he held it. "Heated it up, didn't you?"

"And ground its edge off on the stones of my hot kiln," she agreed. "Would you like to try its point?" She placed a hand on her flank, where a man's kidney would be, moving nearer.

"Not much of a point now," he said. It was rounded like a formal dinner knife at its tip.

"Try it here," she said, and guided his hand so that the blunt knifetip pointed against her flank. He hesitated. "Don't you want to?"

He dug it in, knowing it wouldn't hurt her much, and heard her soft miaow. Then she suggested the other side, and he did, feeling a suspicious unease. That, she said, was the way a *wtsai* was best used.

He frowned. "You mean, as a symbol of control?"

"More or less," she replied, her ears flicking, and then asked how he expected to float a boat down a dry wash, and he told her because he needed her help with it. "A skyboat? Some trick of man, or kzin?"

"Of man," he shrugged. It was, so far as he knew, uniquely his trick—and it might not work at all. He could not be sure about his other trick either, until he tried it. Either one might get him killed.

When they curled up to sleep again, she turned her head and whispered, "Would you like to bite my neck?"

"I'd like to bite it off."

"Just do not break the skin. I did not mean to make yours bleed, Rockear. Men are tender creatures."

Feeling like an ass, he forced his nose into the fur at the curve of her shoulder and bit hard. Her miaow was familiar. And somehow he was sure that it was not exactly a cry of pain. She thrust her rump nearer, sighed, and went to sleep.

After an eternity of minutes, he shifted position, putting his knees in her back, flinging one of his hands to the edge of their grassy bower. She moved slightly. He felt in the grass for a familiar object; found it. Then he pulled his legs away and pressed with his fingers. She started to turn, then drew herself into a ball as he scrambled further aside, legs tingling.

He had not been certain the stasis field would operate properly when its flat field grid was positioned beneath sheaves of grass, but obviously it was working. Indeed, his lower legs were numb for several minutes, lying in the edge of the field as they were when he threw that switch. He stamped the pins and needles from his feet, barely able to see her inert form in the faint luminosity of the cave portal. Once, while fumbling for the *wtsai,* he stumbled near her and dropped to his knees.

He trembled for half a minute before rising. "Fall over her now and you could lie here for all eternity," he said aloud. Then he fetched the heavy coil of fiber he'd woven, with those super-strength threads braided into it. He had no way of lighting the place enough to make sure of his work, so he lay down on the sail mat inside the cave. One thing was sure: she'd be right there the next morning.

He awoke disoriented at first, then darted to the cave mouth. She lay inert as a carven image. The Outsiders probably had good reason to rotate their specimens, so he couldn't leave her there for the days—or weeks!—that temptation suggested. He decided that a day wouldn't hurt, and hurriedly set about finishing his airboat. The polarizer was lashed to the underside of his raft, with a slot through the shamboo so that he could reach down and adjust the switch and levers. The crosspieces, beneath, held the polarizer off the turf.

Finally, with a mixture of fear and excitement, he sat down in the middle of the raft-bottomed craft and snugged fiber straps across his lap. He reached down with his left hand, making sure the levers were pulled back, and flipped the switch. Nothing. Yet. When he had moved the second lever halfway, the raft began to rise very slowly. He vented a whoop—and suddenly the whole rig was tipping before he could snap the switch. The raft hit on one side and crashed flat like a barn door with a tooth-loosening impact.

Okay, the damn thing was tippy. He'd need a keel—a heavy rock on a short rope. Or a little rock on a long rope! He erected two short lengths of shamboo upright with a crosspiece like goalposts, over the seat of his raft, enlarging the hole under his thighs. Good; now he'd have a better view straight down, too. He used the cord he'd intended to bind Kit, tying it to a twenty-kilo stone, then feeding the cord through the hole and wrapping most of its fifteen-meter length around and around that thick crosspiece. Then he sighed, looked at the westering sun, and tried again.

The raft was still a bit tippy, but by paying the cordage out slowly he found himself ten meters up. By shifting his weight, he could make the little platform slant in any direction, yet he could move only in the direction the breeze took him. By adjusting the controls he rose until the heavy stone swung lazily, free of the ground, and then he was drifting with the breeze. He reduced power and hauled in on his keel weight until the raft settled, and then worked out the needed improvements. Higher skids off the ground, so he could work beneath the raft; a better method for winding that weight up and down; and a sturdy shamboo mast for his single sail—better still, a two-piece mast bound in a narrow A-frame to those goalposts. It didn't need to be high; a short catboat sail for tacking was all he could handle anyhow. And come to think of it, a pair of shamboo poles pivoted off the sides with small weights at their free ends just might make automatic keels.

He worked on that until a half-hour before dark, then carried his keel cordage inside the cave. First he made a slip noose, then flipped it toward her hands, which were folded close to her chin. He finally got the noose looped properly, pulled it tight, then moved around her at a safe distance, tugging the cord so that it passed under her neck and, with sharp tugs, down to her back. Then another pass. Then up to her neck, then around her flexed legs. He managed a pair of half-hitches before he ran short of cordage, then fetched his shamboo lance. With the lance against her throat, he snapped off the stasis field with his toe.

She began her purring rumble immediately. He pressed lightly with the lance, and then she waked, and needed a moment to realize that she was bound. Her ears flattened. Her grin was nothing even faintly like enjoyment. "You drugged me, you little *vatach.*"

"No. Worse than that. Watch," he said, and with his free hand he pointed at her face, staring hard. He toed the switch again and watched her curl into an inert ball. The half-hitches came loosed with a tug, and with some difficulty he managed to pull the cordage away until only the loop around her hand remained. He toed the switch again; watched her come awake, and pointed dramatically at her as she faced him. "I loosened your bonds," he said. "I can always tie you up again. Or put you back in stasis," he added with a tight smile, hoping this paltry piece of flummery would be taken as magic.

"May I rise?"

"Depends. Do you see that I can defeat you instantly, anytime I like?" She moved her hands, snarling at the loop, starting to bite it asunder. "Stop that! Answer my question," he said again, stern and unyielding, the finger pointing, his toe ready on the switch.

"It seems that you can," she said grudgingly.

"I could have killed you as you slept. Or brought one of the other *prret* out of stasis and made her my consort. Any number of things, Kit." Her nod was slow, and almost human. "Do you swear to obey me hereafter, and not to attack me again?"

She hated it, but she said it: "Yes. I—misjudged you, Rockear. If all men can do what you did, no wonder you win wars."

He saw that this little charade might get him in a mess later. "It is a special trick of mine; probably won't work for male kzin. In any case, I have your word. If you forget it, I will make you sorry. We need each other, Kit; just like I need a sharp edge on my knife." He lowered his arm then, offering her his hand. "Here, come outside and help me. It's nearly dark again."

She was astonished to find, from the sun's position, that she had "slept" almost a full day. But there was no doubting he had spent many hours on that airboat of his. She helped him for a few moments, then remembered that her kiln would now be cool, the bowls and water jug waiting in its primitive chimney. "May I retrieve my pottery, Rockear?"

He smiled at her obedient tone. "If I say no?"

"I do it tomorrow."

"Go ahead, Kit. It'll be dark soon." He watched her bounding away through high grass, then hurried into the cave. He had to put that stasis gadget back where he'd got it or, sure as hell, she'd figure it out and one fine day *he* would wake up hogtied. Or worse.

Locklear's praise of the pottery was not forced; Kit had a gift for handcrafts, and they ate from decorated bowls that night. He sensed her new deference when she asked, "Have you chosen a site for the manor?"

"Not until I've explored further. We'll want a hidden site we can defend and retreat from, with reliable sources of water, firewood, food—not like this cave. And I'll need your help in that decision, Kit."

"It must be done before we wake the others," she said, adding as if to echo his own warnings, "And soon, if we are to be ready for the kzintosh."

"Don't nag," he replied. He blew on blistered palms and lay full-length on their grassy bower. "We have to get that airboat working right away," he said, and patted the grass beside him. She curled up in her usual way. After a few moments he placed a hand on her shoulder.

"Thank you, Rockear," she murmured, and fell asleep. He lay awake for another hour, gnawing the ribs of two sciences. The engineering of the airboat would be largely trial and error. So would the ethology of a relationship between a man and a kzin female, with all those nuances he was beginning to sense. How, for example, did a kzin make love? Not that he intended to—*unless,* a vagrant thought nudged him, *I'm doing some of it already . . .*

Two more days and a near-disastrous capsizing later, Locklear found the right combination of ballast and sail. He found that Kit could sprint for short distances faster than he could urge the airboat, but over long distances he had a clear edge. Alone, tacking higher, he found stronger winds that bore him far across the sky of Kzersatz, and once he found himself drifting in cross-currents high above that frost line that curved visibly, now, tracing the edge of the force cylinder that was their cage.

He returned after a two-hour absence to find Kit weaving more mats, more cordage, for furnishings. She approached the airboat warily, mistrusting its magical properties but relieved to see him. "You'll be using this thing yourself, pretty soon, Kit," he confided. "Can you make us some decent ink and paper?"

In a day, yes, she said, if she found a scroll-leaf palm, to soak, pound, and dry its fronds. Ink was no problem. Then hop aboard, he said, and they'd go cruising for the palm. *That* was a problem; she was plainly terrified of flight in any form. Kzinti were fearless, he reminded her. Females were not, she said, adding that the sight of him dwindling in the sky to a scudding dot had "drawn up her tail"—a fear reaction, he learned.

He ordered her, at last, to mount the raft, sitting in tandem behind him. She found the position somehow obscene, but she did it. Evidently it was highly acceptable for a male to crowd close behind a female, but not the reverse. Then Locklear recalled how cats mated, and he understood. "Nobody will see us, Kit. Hang on to these cords and pull only when I tell you." With that, he levitated the airboat a meter, and stayed low for a time—until he felt the flexure of her foot talons relax at his thighs.

In another hour they were quartering the sky above the jungles and savannahs of Kzersatz, Kit enjoying the ride too much to retain her fears. They landed in a clearing near the unexplored end of the lake, Kit scrambling up a thick palm to return with young rolled fronds. "The sap stings when fresh," she said, indicating a familiar white substance. "But when dried and reheated it makes excellent glue." She also gathered fruit like purple leather melons, with flesh that smelled faintly of seafood, and stowed them for dinner.

The return trip was longer. He taught her how to tack upwind and later, watching her soak fronds that night inside the cave, exulted because soon they would have maps of this curious country. In only one particular was he evasive.

"Rockear, what is that thing I felt on your back under your clothing," she asked.

"It's, uh, just a thing your warriors do to captives. I have to keep it there," he said, and quickly changed the subject.

In another few days, they had crude air maps and several candidate sites for the manor. Locklear agreed to Kit's choice as they hovered above it, a gentle slope beneath a cliff overhang where a kzinrret could sun herself half the day. Fast-growing hardwoods nearby would provide timber and firewood, and the stream burbling in the throat of the ravine was the same stream where he had found that first waterfall down near the lake, and had conjectured on the age of Kzersatz. She rubbed her cheek against his neck when he accepted her decision.

He steered toward the hardwood grove, feeling a faint dampness on his neck. "What does that mean?"

"Why—marking you, of course. It is a display of affection." He pursued it. The ritual transferred a pheromone from her furry cheeks to his flesh. He could not smell it, but she maintained that any kzin would recognize her marker until the scent evaporated in a few hours.

It was like a lipstick mark, he decided—"Or a hickey with your initials," he told her, and then had to explain himself. She admitted he had not guessed far off the mark. "But hold on, Kit. Could a kzin warrior track me by my scent?"

"Certainly. How else does one follow a spoor?"

He thought about that awhile. "If we come to the manor and leave it always by air, would that make it harder to find?"

Of course, she said. Trackers needed a scent trail; that's why she intended them to walk in the nearby stream, even if splashing in water was unpleasant. "But if they are determined to find you, Rockear, they will."

He sighed, letting the airboat settle near a stand of pole-straight trees, and as he hacked with the dulled *wtsai,* told her of the new weaponry: projectiles, beamers, energy fields, bombs. "When they do find us, we've got to trap them somehow; get their weapons. Could you kill your own kind?"

"They executed me," she reminded him and added after a moment, "Kzinrret weapons might be best. Leave it to me." She did not elaborate. Well, women's weapons had their uses.

He slung several logs under the airboat and left Kit stone-sharpening the long blade as he slowly tacked his way back to their ravine. Releasing the hitches was the work of a moment, thick poles thudding onto yellow-green grass, and soon he was back with Kit. By the time the sun faded, the *wtsai* was biting like a handaxe and Kit had prepared them a thick grassy pallet between the cliff face and their big foundation logs. It was the coldest night Locklear had spent on Kzersatz, but Kit's fur made it endurable.

Days later, she ate the last of the kzin rations as he chewed a fishnut and sketched in the dirt with a stick. "We'll run the shamboo plumbing out here from the kitchen," he said, "and dig our escape tunnel out from our sleep room parallel with the cliff. We'll need help, Kit. It's time."

She vented a long purring sigh. "I know. Things will be different, Rockear. Not as simple as our life has been."

He laughed at that, reminding her of the complications they had already faced, and then they resumed notching logs, raising the walls beyond window height. Their own work packed the earthen floors, but the roofing would require more hands than their own. That night, Kit kindled their first fire in the central room's hearth, and they fell asleep while she tutored him on the ways of ancient kzin females.

Leaning against the airboat alone near the cave, Locklear felt new misgivings. Kit had argued that his presence at the awakenings would be a Bad Idea. Let them grow used to him slowly, she'd said. Stand tall, give orders gently, and above all don't smile until they understand his show of teeth. *No fear of that,* he thought, shifting nervously a half-hour after Kit disappeared inside. *I don't feel like smiling.*

He heard a shuffling just out of sight; realized he was being viewed covertly; threw out his chest and flexed his pectorals. Not much by kzin standards, but he'd developed a lot of sinew during the past weeks. He felt silly as hell, and those other kzinrret had not made him any promises. The *wtsai* felt good at his belt.

Then Kit was striding into the open, with an expression of strained patience. Standing beside him, she muttered, "Mark me." Then, seeing his frown: "Your cheek against my neck, Rockear. *Quickly.*"

He did so. She bowed before him, offering the tip of her tail in both hands, and he stroked it when she told him to. Then he saw a lithe movement of orange at the cave and raised both hands in a universal weaponless gesture as the second kzinrret emerged, watching him closely. She was much larger than Kit, with transverse stripes of darker orange and a banded tail. Close on her heels came a third, more reluctantly but staying close behind as if for protection, with facial markings that reminded Locklear of an ocelot and very dark fur at hands and feet. They were admirable creatures, but their ear umbrellas lay flat and they were not yet his friends.

Kit moved to the first, urging her forward to Locklear. After a few tentative sniffs the big kzinrret said, in that curious ancient dialect, "I am (something truly unpronounceable), prret in service of Rockear." She bent toward him, her stance defensive, and he marked her as Kit had said he must, then stroked her tabby-banded tail. She moved away and the third kzinrret approached, and Locklear's eyes widened as he performed the greeting ritual. She was either potbellied, or carrying a litter!

Both of their names being beyond him, he dubbed the larger one Puss; the pregnant one, Boots. They accepted their new names as proof that they were members of a very different kind of household than any they had known. Both wore aprons of woven mat, Kit's deft work, and she offered them water from bowls.

As they stood eyeing one another speculatively, Kit surprised them all. "It is time to release the animals," she said. "My lord Rockear-the-magician, we are excellent herders, and from your flying boat you can observe our work. The larger beasts might also distract the kzintosh, and we will soon need meat. Is it not so?"

She *knew* be couldn't afford an argument now—and besides, she was right. He had no desire to try herding some of those big critters outside anyhow, and kzinti had been doing it from time immemorial. *Damned clever tactic, Kit; Puss and Boots will get a chance to work off their nerves, and so will I.* He swept a permissive arm outward and sat down in the airboat as the three kzin females moved into the cave.

The next two hours were a crash course in zoology for Locklear, safe at fifty-meter height as he watched herds, coveys, throngs and volleys of creatures as they crawled, flapped, hopped and galumphed off across the yellow prairie. A batowl found a perch atop his mast, trading foolish blinks with him until it whispered away after another of its kind. One huge ruminant with the bulk of a rhino and murderous spikes on its thick tail sat down to watch him, raising its bull's muzzle to issue a call like a wolf. An answering howl sent it lumbering off again, and Locklear wondered whether they were to be butchered, ridden, or simply avoided. He liked the last option best.

When at last Kit came loping out with shrill screams of false fury at the heels of a collie-sized, furry tyrannosaur, the operation was complete. He'd half-expected to see a troop of more kzinti bounding outside, but Kit was as good as her word. None of them recognized any of the other stasized kzinti, and all seemed content to let the strangers stay as they were.

The airboat did not have room for them all, but by now Kit could operate the polarizer levers. She sat ahead of Locklear for decorum's sake, making a show of her pairing with him, and let Puss and Boots follow beneath as the airboat slid ahead of a good breeze toward their tacky, unfinished little manor. "They will be nicely exhausted," she said to him, "by the time we reach home."

Home. My God, it may be my home for the rest of my life, he thought, watching the muscular Puss bound along behind them with Boots in arrears. *Three kzin courtesans for company; a sure 'nough cathouse! Is that much better than having those effing warriors return? And if they don't, is there any way I could get across to my own turf, to Newduvai?* The gravity polarizer could get him to orbit, but he would need propulsion, and a woven sail wasn't exactly de rigueur for travel in vacuum, and how the hell could he build an airtight cockpit anyhow? Too many questions, too few answers, and two more kzin females who might be more hindrance than help, hurtling along in the yellowsward behind him. One of them pregnant.

And kzin litters were almost all twins, one male. Like it or not, he was doomed to deal with at least one kzintosh. The notion of killing the tiny male forced itself forward. He quashed the idea instantly, and hoped it would stay quashed. *Yeah, and one of these days it'll weigh three times as much as I do, and two of these randy females will be vying for mating privileges.* The return of the kzin ship, he decided, might be the least of his troubles.

That being so, the least of his troubles could kill him.

Puss and Boots proved far more help than hindrance. Locklear admitted it to Kit one night, lying in their small room off the "great hall," itself no larger than five meters by ten and already pungent with cooking smokes. "Those two hardly talk to me, but they thatch a roof like crazy. How well can they tunnel?"

This amused her. "Every pregnant kzinrret is an expert at tunneling, as you will soon see. Except that you will not see. When birthing time nears, a mother digs her secret birthing place. The father sometimes helps, but oftener not."

"Too lazy?"

She regarded him with eyes that reflected a dim flicker from the fire dying in the next room's hearth, and sent a shiver through him. "Too likely to eat the newborn male," she said simply.

"Good God. Not among modern kzinti, I hope."

"Perhaps. Females become good workers; males become aggressive hunters likely to challenge for household mastery. Which would *you* value more?"

"My choice is a matter of record," he joked, adding that they were certainly shaping the manor up fast. That, she said, was because they knew their places and their leaders. Soon they would be butchering and curing meat, making (something) from the milk of ruminants, cheese perhaps, and making ready for the kittens. Some of the released animals seemed already domesticated. A few *vatach,* she said, might be trapped and released nearby for convenience.

He asked if the others would really fight the returning kzin warriors, and she insisted that they would, especially Puss. "She was a highly valued *prret,* but she hates males," Kit warned. "In some ways I think she wishes to be one."

"Then why did she ask if I'd like to scratch her flanks with my *wtsai,*" he asked.

"I will claw her eyes out if you do," she growled. "She is only negotiating for status. Keep your blade in your belt," she said angrily, with a metaphor he could not miss.

That blade reminded him (as he idly scratched her flanks with its dull tip to calm her) that the cave was now a treasury of materials. He must study the planting of the fast-growing vines which, according to Kit, would soon hide the roof thatching; those vines could also hide the cave entrance. He could scavenge enough steel for lances, more of the polarizers to build a whopping big airsloop, maybe even— He sat up, startling her. "Meat storage!"

Kit did not understand. He wasn't sure he wanted her to. He would need wire for remote switches, which might be recovered from polarizer toroids if he had the nerve to try it.

"I may have a way to keep meat fresh, Kit, but you must help me see that no one else touches my magics. They could be dangerous." She said he was the boss, and he almost believed it.

Once the females began their escape tunnel, Locklear rigged a larger sail and completed his mapping chores, amassing several scrolls which seemed gibberish to the others. And each day he spent two hours at the cave. When vines died, he planted others to hide the entrance. He learned that polarizers and stasis units came in three sizes, and brought trapped *vatach* back in large cages he had separated from their gravity and stasis devices. Those clear cage tops made admirable windows, and the cage metal was then reworked by firelight in the main hall.

Despite Kit's surly glances, he bade Puss sit beside him to learn metalwork, while Boots patiently wove mats and formed trays of clay to his specifications for papermaking. One day he might begin a journal. Meanwhile he needed awls, screwdrivers, pliers—and a longbow with arrows. He was all thumbs while shaping them.

Boots became more shy as her pregnancy advanced. Locklear's new social problem became the casual nuances from Puss that, by now, he knew were sexual. She rarely spoke unless spoken to, but one day while resting in the sun with the big kzinrret he noticed her tailtip flicking near his leg. He had noticed previously that a moving rope or vine seemed to mesmerize a kzin; they probably thought it fascinated him as well.

"Puss, I—uh—sleep only with Kit. Sorry, but that's the way of it."

"Pfaugh. I am more skilled at *ch'rowl* than she, and I could make you a pillow of her fur if I liked." Her gaze was calm, challenging; to a male kzin, probably very sexy.

"We must all work together, Puss. As head of the household, I forbid you to make trouble."

"My Lord," she said with a small nod, but her ear-flick was amused. "In that case, am I permitted to help in the birthing?"

"Of course," he said, touched. "Where is Boots, anyway?"

"Preparing her birthing chamber. It cannot be long now," Puss added, setting off down the ravine.

Locklear found Kit dragging a mat of dirt from the tunnel and asked her about the problems of birthing. The hardest part, she said, was the bower—and when males were near, the hiding. He asked why Puss would be needed at the birthing.

"Ah," said Kit. "It is symbolic, Rockear. You have agreed to let her play the mate role. It is not unheard-of, and the newborn male will be safe."

"You mean, symbolic like our pairing?"

"Not quite that symbolic," she replied with sarcasm as they distributed stone and earth outside. "Prret are flexible."

Then he asked her what *ch'rowl* meant.

Kit vented a tiny miaow of pleasure, then realized suddenly that he did not know what he had said. Furiously: "She used that word to you? I will break her tail!"

"I forbid it," he said. "She was angry because I told her I slept only with you." Pleased with this, Kit subsided as they moved into the tunnel again. Some kzin words, he learned, were triggers. At least one seemed to be blatantly lascivious. He was deflected from this line of thought only when Kit, digging upward now, broke through to the surface.

They replanted shrubs at the exit before dark, and lounged before the hearthfire afterward. At last Locklear yawned; checked his wristcomp. "They are very late," he said.

"Kittens are born at night," she replied, unworried.

"But—I assumed she'd tell us when it was time."

"She has not said eight-cubed of words to you. Why should she confide that to a male?"

He shrugged at the fire. Perhaps they would always treat him like a kzintosh. He wondered for the hundredth time whether, when push came to shove, they would fight with him or against him.

In his mapping sorties, Locklear had skirted near enough to the force walls to see that Kzersatz was adjacent to four other compounds. One, of course, was the tantalizing Newduvai. Another was hidden in swirling mists; he dubbed it Limbo. The others held no charm for him; he named them Who Needs It, and No Thanks. He wondered what collections of life forms roamed those mysterious lands, or slept there in stasis. The planet might have scores of such zoo compounds.

Meanwhile, he unwound a hundred meters of wire from a polarizer, and stole switches from others. One of his jury-rigs, outside the cave, was a catapult using a polarizer on a sturdy frame. He could stand fifty meters away and, with his remote switch, lob a heavy stone several hundred meters. Perhaps a series of the gravity polarizers would make a kind of mass driver—a true space drive! There was yet hope, he thought, of someday visiting Newduvai.

And then he transported some materials to the manor where he installed a stasis device to keep meat fresh indefinitely; and late that same day, Puss returned. Even Kit, ignoring their rivalry, welcomed the big kzinrret.

"They are all well," Puss reported smugly, paternally. To Locklear's delighted question she replied in severe tones, "You cannot see them until their eyes open, Rockear."

"It is tradition," Kit injected. "The mother will suckle them until then, and will hunt as she must."

"I am the hunter," Puss said. "When we build our own manor, will your household help?"

Kit looked quickly toward Locklear, who realized the implications. *By God, they're really pairing off for another household,* he thought. After a moment he said, "Yes, but you must locate it nearby." He saw Kit relax and decided he'd made the right decision. To celebrate the new developments, Puss shooed Locklear and Kit outside to catch the late sun while she made them an early supper. They sat on their rough-hewn bench above the ravine to eat, Puss claiming she could return to the birthing bower in full darkness, and Locklear allowed himself to bask in a sense of well-being. It was not until Puss had headed back down the ravine with food for Boots, that Locklear realized she had stolen several small items from his storage shelves.

He could accept the loss of tools and a knife; Puss had, after all, helped him make them. What caused his cold sweat was the fact that the tiny *zzrou* transmitter was missing. The *zzrou* prongs in his shoulder began to itch as he thought about it. Puss could not possibly know the importance of the transmitter to him; maybe she thought it was some magical tool—and maybe she would destroy it while studying it. "Kit," he said, trying to keep the tremor from his voice, "I've got a problem and I need your help."

She seemed incensed, but not very surprised, to learn the function of the device that clung to his back. One thing was certain, he insisted: the birthing bower could not be more than a klick away. Because if Puss took the transmitter farther than that, he would die in agony. Could Kit lead him to the bower in darkness?

"I might find it, Rockear, but your presence there would

provoke violence," she said. "I must go alone." She caressed his flank gently, then set off slowly down the ravine on all-fours, her nose close to the turf until she disappeared in darkness.

Locklear stood for a time at the manor entrance, wondering what this night would bring, and then saw a long scrawl of light as it slowed to a stop and winked out, many miles above the plains of Kzersatz. Now he knew what the morning would bring, and knew that he had not one deadly problem, but two. He began to check his pathetic little armory by the glow of his memocomp, because that was better than giving way entirely to despair.

When he awoke, it was to the warmth of Kit's fur nestled against his backside. *There was a time when she called this obscene,* he thought with a smile—and then he remembered everything, and lit the display of his memocomp. Two hours until dawn. How long until death, he wondered, and woke her.

She did not have the *zzrou* transmitter. "Puss heard my calls," she said, "and warned me away. She will return this morning to barter tools for things she wants."

"I'll tell you who else will return," he began. "No, don't rebuild the fire, Kit. I saw what looked like a ship stationing itself many miles away overhead, while you were gone. Smoke will only give us away. It might possibly be a Manship, but—expect the worst. You haven't told me how you plan to fight."

His hopes fell as she stammered out her ideas, and he countered each one, reflecting that she was no planner. They would hide and ambush the searchers—but he reminded her of their projectile and beam weapons. Very well, they would claim absolute homestead rights accepted by all ancient Kzinti clans—but modern Kzinti, he insisted, had probably forgotten those ancient immunities.

"You may as well invite them in for breakfast," he grumbled. "Back on earth, women's weapons included poison. I thought you had some kzinrret weapons."

"Poisons would take time, Rockear. It takes little time, and not much talent, to set warriors fighting to the death over a female. Surely they would still respond with foolish bravado?"

"I don't know; they've never seen a smart kzinrret. And

ship's officers are very disciplined. I don't think they'd get into a free-for-all. Maybe lure them in here and hit 'em while they sleep . . ."

"As you did to me?"

"Uh no, I—yes!" He was suddenly galvanized by the idea, tantalized by the treasures he had left in the cave. "Kit, the machine I set up to preserve food is exactly the same as the one I placed under you, to make you sleep when I hit a foot switch." He saw her flash of anger at his earlier duplicity. "An ancient sage once said anything that's advanced enough beyond your understanding is indistinguishable from magic, Kit. But magic can turn on you. Could you get a warrior to sit or lie down by himself?"

"If I cannot, I am no *prret,*" she purred. "Certainly I can *leave* one lying by himself. Or two. Or . . ."

"Okay, don't get graphic on me," he snapped. "We've got only one stasis unit here. If only I could get more—but I can't leave in the airboat without that damned little transmitter! Kit, you'll have to go and get Puss now. I'll promise her anything within reason."

"She will know we are at a disadvantage. Her demands will be outrageous."

"We're *all* at a disadvantage! Tell her about the kzin warship that's hanging over us."

"Hanging magically over us," she corrected him. "It is true enough for me."

Then she was gone, loping away in darkness, leaving him to fumble his way to the meat storage unit he had so recently installed. The memocomp's faint light helped a little, and he was too busy to notice the passage of time until, with its usual sudden blaze, the sunlet of Kzersatz began to shine.

He was hiding the wires from Puss's bed to the foot switch near the little room's single doorway when he heard a distant roll of thunder. No, not thunder: it grew to a crackling howl in the sky, and from the nearest window he saw what he most feared to see. The kzin lifeboat left a thin contrail in its pass, circling just inside the force cylinder of Kzersatz, and its wingtips slid out as it slowed. No doubt of the newcomer now, and it disappeared in the direction of that first landing, so long ago. If only he'd thought to booby-trap that landing zone with stasis units! Well, he might've, given time.

He finished his work in fevered haste, knowing that time was now his enemy, and so were the kzinti in that ship, and so, for all practical purposes, was the traitor Puss. *And Kit? How easy it will be for her to switch sides! Those females will make out like bandits wherever they are, and I may learn Kit's decision when these goddamned prongs take a lethal bite in my back. Could be any time now.* And then he heard movements in the high grass nearby, and leaped for his longbow.

Kit flashed to the doorway, breathless. "She is coming, Rockear. Have you set your sleeptrap?"

He showed her the rig. "Toe it once for sleep, again for waking, again for sleep," he said. "Whatever you do, don't get near enough to touch the sleeper, or stand over him, or you'll be in the same fix. I've set it for maximum power."

"Why did you put it here, instead of our own bed?"

He coughed and shrugged. "Uh,—I don't know. Just seemed like—well, hell, it's *our* bed, Kit! I, um, didn't like the idea of your using it, ah, the way you'll have to use it."

"You are an endearing beast," she said, pinching him lightly at the neck, "to bind me with tenderness."

They both whirled at Puss's voice from the main doorway: "Bind who with tenderness?"

"I will explain," said Kit, her face bland. "If you brought those trade goods, display them on your bed."

"I think not," said Puss, striding into the room she'd shared with Boots. "But I will show them to you." With that, she sat on her bed and reached into her apron pocket, drawing out a *wtsai* for inspection.

An instant later she was unconscious. Kit, with Locklear kibitzing, used a grass broom to whisk the knife safely away. "I should use it on her throat," she snarled, but she let Locklear take the weapon.

"She came of her own accord," he said, "and she's a fighter. We need her, Kit. Hit the switch again."

A moment later, Puss was blinking, leaping up, then suddenly backing away in fear. "Treachery," she spat.

In reply, Locklear tossed the knife onto her bed despite Kit's frown. "Just a display, Puss. You need the knife, and I'm your ally. But I've got to have that little gadget that looks like my wristcomp." He held out his hand.

"I left it at the birthing bower. I knew it was important," she said with a surly glance as she retrieved the knife. "For its return, I demand our total release from this household, I demand your help to build a manor as large as this, wherever

I like. I demand teaching in your magical arts." She trembled, but stood defiant; a dangerous combination.

"Done, done, and done," he said. "You want equality, and I'm willing. But we may all be equally dead if that kzin ship finds us. We need a leader. Do you have a good plan?"

Puss swallowed hard. "Yes. Hunt at night, hide until they leave."

Sighing, Locklear told her that was no plan at all. He wasted long minutes arguing his case: Puss to steal near the landing site and report on the intruders; the return of his *zzrou* transmitter so he could try sneaking back to the cave; Kit to remain at the manor preparing food for a siege—and to defend the manor through what he termed guile, if necessary.

Puss refused. "My place," she insisted, "is defending the birthing bower."

"And you will not have a male as a leader," Kit said. "Is that not the way of it?"

"Exactly," Puss growled.

"I have agreed to your demands, Puss," Locklear reminded her. "But it won't happen if the kzin warriors get me. We've proved we won't abuse you. At least give me back that transmitter. Please," he added gently.

Too late, he saw Puss's disdain for pleading. "So that is the source of your magic," she said, her ears lifting in a kzinrret smile. "I shall discover its secrets, Rockear."

"He will die if you damage it," Kit said quickly, "or take it far from him. You have done a stupid thing; without this manbeast who knows our enemy well, we will be slaves again. To males," she added.

Puss sidled along the wall, now holding the knife at ready, menacing Kit until a single bound put her through the doorway into the big room. Pausing at the outer doorway she stuck the *wtsai* into her apron. "I will consider what you say," she growled.

"Wait," Locklear said in his most commanding tone, the only one that Puss seemed to value. "The kzintosh will be searching for me. They have magics that let them see great distances even at night, and a big metal airboat that flies with the sound of thunder."

"I heard thunder this morning," Puss admitted.

"You heard their airboat. If they see you, they will probably capture you. You and Boots must be very careful, Puss."

"And do not hesitate to tempt males into (something) if you can," Kit put in.

"Now you would teach me my business," Puss spat at Kit, and set off down the ravine.

Locklear moved to the outer doorway, watching the sky, listening hard. Presently he asked, "Do you think we can lay siege to the birthing bower to get that transmitter back?"

"Boots is a suckling mother, which saps her strength," Kit replied matter-of-factly. "So Puss would fight like a crazed warrior. The truth is, she is stronger than both of us."

With a morose shake of his head, Locklear began to fashion more arrows while Kit sharpened his *wtsai* into a dagger, arguing tactics, drawing rough conclusions. They must build no fires at the manor, and hope that the searchers spread out for single, arrogant sorties. The lifeboat would hold eight warriors, and others might be waiting in orbit. Live captives might be better for negotiations than dead heroes—"But even as captives, the bastards would eat every scrap of meat in sight," Locklear admitted.

Kit argued persuasively that any warrior worth his *wtsai* would be more likely to negotiate with a potent enemy. "We must give them casualties," she insisted, "to gain their respect. Can these modern males be that different from those I knew?"

Probably not, he admitted. And knowing the modern breed, he knew they would be infuriated by his escape, dishonored by his shrewdness. He could expect no quarter when at last they did locate him. "And they won't go until they do," he said. On that, they agreed; some things never changed.

Locklear, dog-tired after hanging thatch over the gleaming windows, heard the lifeboat pass twice before dark but fell asleep as the sun faded.

Much later, Kit was shaking him. "Come to the door," she urged. "She refuses to come in."

He stumbled outside, found the bench by rote, and spoke to the darkness. "Puss? You have nothing to fear from us. Had a change of heart?"

Not far distant: "I hunted those slopes where you said the males left you, Rockear."

It was an obvious way to avoid saying she had reconnoitered as he'd asked, and he maintained the ruse. "Did you have good hunting?"

"Fair. A huge metal thing came and went and came again.

I found four warriors, in strange costume and barbaric speech like yours, with strange weapons. They are making a camp there, and spoke with surprise of seeing animals to hunt." She spoke slowly, pausing often. He asked her to describe the males. She had no trouble with that, having lain in her natural camouflage in the jungle's verge within thirty paces of the ship until dark. *Must've taken her hours to get here in the dark over rough country,* he thought. *This is one tough bimbo.*

He waited, his hackles rising, until she finished. "You're sure the leader had that band across his face?" She was. She'd heard him addressed as "Grraf-Commander." One with a light-banded belly was called "Apprentice Something." And the other two tallied, as well. "I can't believe it," he said to the darkness. "The same foursome that left me here! If they're all down here, they're deadly serious. Damn their good luck."

"Better than you think," said Puss. "You told me they had magic weapons. Now I believe it."

Kit, leaning near, whispered into Locklear's ear. "If she were injured, she would refuse to show her weakness to us."

He tried again. "Puss, how do you know of their weapons?"

With dry amusement and courage, the disembodied voice said, "The usual way: the huge sentry used one. Tiny sunbeams that struck as I reached thick cover. They truly can see in full darkness."

"So they've seen you," he said, dismayed.

"From their shouts, I think they were not sure what they saw. But I will kill them for this, sentry or no sentry."

Her voice was more distant now. Locklear raised his voice slightly: "Puss, can we help you?"

"I have been burned before," was the reply.

Kit, moving into the darkness quietly: "You are certain there are only four?"

"Positive," was the faint reply, and then they heard only the night wind.

Presently Kit said, "It would take both of us, and when wounded she will certainly fight to the death. But we might overpower her now, if we can find the bower."

"No. She did more than she promised. And now she knows she can kill me by smashing the transmitter. Let's get some sleep, Kit," he said. Then, when he had nestled behind her, he added with a chuckle, "I begin to see why the kzinti decided to breed females as mere pets. Sheer self-defense."

"I would break your tail for that, if you had one," she replied in mock ferocity. Then he laid his hand on her flank, heard her soft miaow, and then they slept.

Locklear had patrolled nearly as far as he dared down the ravine at midmorning, armed with his *wtsai,* longbow, and an arrow-filled quiver rubbing against the *zzrou* when he heard the first scream. He knew that Kit, with her short lance, had gone in the opposite direction on her patrol, but the repeated kzin screams sent gooseflesh up his spine. Perhaps the tabbies had surrounded Boots, or Puss. He nocked an arrow, half climbing to the lip of the ravine, and peered over low brush. He stifled the exclamation in his throat.

They'd found Puss, all right—or she'd found them. She stood on all-fours on a level spot below, her tail erect, its tip curled over, watching two hated familiar figures in a tableau that must have been as old as kzin history. Almost naked for this primitive duel, ebony talons out and their musky scent heavy on the breeze, they bulked stupefyingly huge and ferocious. The massive gunner, Goon, and engineer Yellowbelly circled each other with drawn stilettoes. What boggled Locklear was that their modern weapons lay ignored in neat groups. Were they going through some ritual?

They were like hell, he decided. From time to time, Puss would utter a single word, accompanied by a tremor and a tail-twitch; and each time, Yellowbelly and Goon would stiffen, then scream at each other in frustration.

The word she repeated was *ch'rowl.* No telling how long they'd been there, but Goon's right forearm dripped blood, and Yellowbelly's thigh was a sodden red mess. Swaying drunkenly, Puss edged nearer to the weapons. As Yellowbelly screamed and leaped, Goon screamed and parried; bearing his smaller opponent to the turf. What followed then was fast enough to be virtually a blur in a roil of Kzersatz dust as two huge tigerlike bodies thrashed and rolled, knives flashing, talons ripping, fangs sinking into flesh.

Locklear scrambled downward through the grass, his progress unheard in the earsplitting caterwauls nearby. He saw Puss reach a beam rifle, grasp it, swing it experimentally by the barrel. That's when he forgot all caution and shouted, "No, Puss! Put the stock to your shoulder and pull the trigger!"

He might as well have told her to bazzfazz the shimstock; and in any case, poor valiant Puss collapsed while trying to figure the rifle out. He saw the long ugly trough in her side then, caked with dried blood. A wonder she was conscious, with such a wound. Then he saw something more fearful still, the quieter thrashing as Goon found the throat of Yellowbelly, whose stiletto handle protruded from Goon's upper arm.

Ducking below the brush, Locklear moved to one side, nearer to Puss, whose breathing was as labored as that of the males. Or rather, of one male, as Goon stood erect and uttered a victory roar that must have carried to Newduvai. Yellowbelly's torn throat pumped the last of his blood onto alien dust.

"I claim my right," Goon screamed, and added a Word that Locklear was beginning to loathe. Only then did the huge gunner notice that Puss was in no condition to present him with what he had just killed to get. He nudged her roughly, and did not see Locklear approach with one arrow nocked and another held between his teeth.

But his ear umbrellas pivoted as a twig snapped under Locklear's foot, and Goon spun furiously, the big legs flexed, and for one instant man and kzin stood twenty paces apart, unmoving. Goon leaped for the nearest weapon, the beam rifle Puss had dropped, and saw Locklear release the short arrow. It missed by a full armspan and now, his bloodlust rekindled and with no fear of such a marksman, Goon dropped the rifle and pulled Yellowbelly's stiletto from his own arm. He turned toward Locklear, who was unaccountably running *toward* him instead of fleeing as a monkey should flee a leopard, and threw his head back in a battle scream.

Locklear's second arrow, fired from a distance of five paces, pierced the roof of Goon's mouth, its stainless steel barb severing nerve bundles at the brain stem. Goon fell like a jointed tree, knees buckling first, arms hanging, and the ground's impact drove the arrow tip out the back of his head, slippery with gore. Goon's head lay two paces from Locklear's feet. He neither breathed nor twitched.

Locklear hurried to the side of poor, courageous, ill-starred Puss and saw her gazing calmly at him. "One for you, one for me, Puss. Only two more to go."

"I wish—I could live to celebrate that," she said, more softly than he had ever heard her speak.

"You're too tough to let a little burn," he began.

"They shot tiny things, too," she said, a finger migrating to a bluish perforation at the side of her rib cage. "Coughing blood. Hard to breathe," she managed.

He knew then that she was dying. A spray of slugs, roughly

aimed at night from a perimeter-control smoothbore, had done to Puss what a beam rifle could not. Her lungs filling slowly with blood, she had still managed to report her patrol and then return to guard the birthing bower. He asked through the lump in his throat, "Is Boots all right?"

"They followed my spoor. When I—came out, twitching my best *prret* routine—they did not look into the bower."

"Smart, Puss."

She grasped his wrist, hard. "Swear to protect it—with your life." Now she was coughing blood, fighting to breathe.

"Done," he said. "Where is it, Puss?"

But her eyes were already glazing. Locklear stood up slowly and strode to the beam rifle, hefting it, thinking idly that these weapons were too heavy for him to carry in one trip. And then he saw Puss again, and quit thinking, and lifted the rifle over his head with both hands in a manscream of fury, and of vengeance unappeased.

The battle scene was in sight of the lake, fully in the open within fifty paces of the creek, and he found it impossible to lift Puss. Locklear cut bundles of grass and spread them to hide the bodies, trembling in delayed reaction, and carried three armloads of weapons to a hiding place far up the ravine just under its lip. He left the dead kzinti without stripping them; perhaps a mistake, but he had no time now to puzzle out tightband comm sets or medkits. Later, if there was a later . . .

He cursed his watery joints, knowing he could not carry a kzin beam rifle with its heavy accumulator up to the manor. He moved more cautiously now, remembering those kzin screams, wondering how far they'd carried on the breeze, which was toward the lake. He read the safety legends on Goon's sidearm, found he could handle the massive piece with both hands, and stuck it and its twin from Yellowbelly's arsenal into his belt, leaving his bow and quiver with the other weapons.

He had stumbled within sight of the manor, planning how he could unmast the airboat and adjust its buoyancy so that it could be towed by a man afoot to retrieve those weapons, when a crackling hum sent a blast of hot air across his cheeks. Face down, crawling for the lip of the ravine, he heard a shout from near the manor.

"Grraf-Commander, the monkey approaches!" The reply,

deep-voiced and muffled, seemed to come from inside the manor. So they'd known where the manor was. Heat or motion sensors, perhaps, during a pass in the lifeboat—not that it mattered now. A classic pincers from down and up the ravine, but one of those pincers now lay under shields of grass. They could not know that he was still tethered invisibly to that *zzrou* transmitter. But where was Kit?

Another hail from Brickshitter, whose tremors of impatience with a beam rifle had become Locklear's ally: "The others do not answer my calls, but I shall drive the monkey down to them."

Well, maybe he'd intended merely to wing his quarry, or follow him.

You do that, Locklear thought to himself in cold rage as he scurried back in the ravine toward his weapons cache; *you just do that, Brickshitter.* He had covered two hundred meters when another crackle announced the pencil-thin beam, brighter than the sun, that struck a ridge of stone above him.

White-hot bees stung his face, back and arms; tiny smoke trails followed fragments of superheated stone into the ravine as Locklear tumbled to the creek, splashing out again, stumbling on slick stones. He turned, intending to fire a sidearm, but saw no target and realized that firing from him would tell volumes to that big sonofabitchkitty behind and above him. Well, they wouldn't have returned unless they wanted him alive, so Brickshitter was just playing with him, driving him as a man drives cattle with a prod. Beam weapons were limited in rate of fire and accumulator charge; maybe Brickshitter would empty this one with his trembling.

Then, horrifyingly near, above the ravine lip, the familiar voice: "I offer you honor, monkey."

Whatthehell: the navigator knew where his quarry was anyhow. Mopping a runnel of blood from his face, Locklear called upward as he continued his scramble. "What, a prisoner exchange?" He did not want to be more explicit than that.

"We already have the beauteous kzinrret," was the reply that chilled Locklear to his marrows. "Is that who you would have sacrificed for your worthless hide?"

That tears it; no hope now, Locklear thought. "Maybe I'll give myself up if you'll let her go," he called. *Would I? Probably not. Dear God, please don't give me that choice because I know there would be no honor in mine . . .*

"We have you caged, monkey," in tones of scorn. "But

Grraf-Commander warned that you may have some primitive hunting weapon, so we accord you some little honor. It occurs to me that you would retain more honor if captured by an officer than by a pair of rankings."

Locklear was now only a hundred meters from the precious cache. *He's too close; he'll see the weapons cache when I get near it and that'll be all she wrote. I've got to make the bastard careless and use what I've got.* He thought carefully how to translate a nickname into Kzin and began to ease up the far side of the ravine. "Not if the officer has no honor, you trembling shitter of bricks," he shouted, slipping the safety from a sidearm.

Instantly a scream of raw rage and astonishment from above at this unbelievably mortal insult, followed by the head and shoulders of an infuriated navigator. Locklear aimed fast, squeezed the firing stud, and saw a series of dirt clods spit from the verge of the ravine. The damned thing shot low!

But Brickshitter had popped from sight as though propelled by levers, and now Locklear was climbing, stuffing the sidearm into his belt again to keep both hands free for the ravine, and when he vaulted over the lip into low brush, he could hear Brickshitter babbling into his comm unit.

He wanted to hear the exchange more than he wanted to move. He heard: ". . . has two kzin handguns—of course I saw them, and heard them; had I been slower he would have an officer's ears on his belt now!—Nossir, no reply from the others. How else would he have hero's weapons? What do you think?—I think so, too."

Locklear began to move out again, below brush-tops, as the furious Brickshitter was promising a mansack to his commander as a trophy. *And they won't get that while I live,* he vowed to himself. In fact, with his promise, Brickshitter was admitting they no longer wanted him alive. He did not hear the next hum, but saw brush spatter ahead of him, some of it bursting into flame, and then he was firing at the exposed Brickshitter who now stood with brave stance, seven and a half feet tall and weaving from side to side, firing once a second, as fast as the beam rifle's accumulator would permit.

Locklear stood and delivered, moving back and forth. At his second burst, the weapon's receiver locked open. He ducked below, discarded the thing, and drew its twin, estimating he had emptied the first one with thirty rounds. When next he lifted his head, he saw that Brickshitter had outpaced him across the ravine and was firing at the brush again. Even as the stuff ahead of him was kindling, Locklear noticed that the brush behind him flamed higher than a man, now a wildfire moving in the same direction as he, though the steady breeze swept it away from the ravine. His only path now was along the ravine lip, or in it.

He guessed that this weapon would shoot low as well, and opened up at a distance of sixty paces. Good guess; Brickshitter turned toward him and at the same instant was slapped by an invisible fist that flung the heavy rifle from his grasp. Locklear dodged to the lip of the ravine to spot the weapons, saw them twenty paces away, and dropped the sidearm so that he could hang onto brush as he vaulted over, now in full view of Brickshitter.

Whose stuttering fire with his good arm reminded Locklear, nearly too late, that Brickshitter had other weapons beside that beam rifle. Spurts of dirt flew into Locklear's eyes as he flung himself back to safety. He crawled back for the sidearm, watching the navigator fumble for his rifle, and opened up again just as Brickshitter dropped from sight. More wasted ammo.

Behind him, the fire was raging downslope toward their mutual dead. Across the ravine, Brickshitter's enraged voice: "Small caliber flesh wound in the right shoulder but I have started brush fires to flush him. I can see beam rifles, close-combat weapons and other things almost below him in the ravine.—Yessir, he is almost out of ammunition and wants that cache.—Yessir, a few more bolts. An easy shot."

Locklear had once seen an expedition bundle burn with a beam rifle in it. He began to run hard, skirting still-smouldering brush and grass, and had already passed the inert bodies of their unprotesting dead when the ground bucked beneath him. He fell to one knee, seeing a cloud of debris fan above the ravine, echoes of the explosion shouldering each other down the slopes, and he knew that Brickshitter's left-armed aim had been as good as necessary. Good enough, maybe, to get himself killed in that cloud of turf and stone and metal fragments, yes, and good wooden arrows that had made a warrior of Locklear. Yet any sensible warrior knows how to retreat.

The ravine widened now, the creek dropping in a series of lower falls, and Locklear knew that further headlong flight would send him far into the open, so far that the *zzrou* would kill him if Brickshitter didn't. And Brickshitter could track his spoor—but not in water. Locklear raced to the creek, heedless of the misstep that could smash a knee or ankle, and began to negotiate the little falls.

The last one faced the lake. He turned, recognizing that he had cached his pathetic store of provisions behind that waterfall soon after his arrival. It was flanked by thick fronds and ferns, and Locklear ducked into the hideyhole behind that sheet of water streaming wet, gasping for breath.

A soft inquiry from somewhere behind him. He whirled in sudden recognition. *It's REALLY a small world,* he thought idiotically. "Boots?" No answer. Well, of course not, to his voice, but he could see the dim outline of a deep horizontal tunnel, turning left inside its entrance, with dry grasses lining the floor. "Boots, don't be afraid of me. Did you know the kzin males have returned?"

Guarded, grudging it: "Yes. They have wounded my mate."

"Worse, Boots. But she killed one," *—it was her doing as surely as if her fangs had torn out Yellowbelly's throat—*"and I killed another. She told me to—to retrieve the things she took from me." It seemed his heart must burst with this cowardly lie. He was cold, exhausted, and on the run, and with the transmitter he could escape to win another day, and, and— And he wanted to slash his wrists with his *wtsai.*

"I will bring them. Do not come nearer," said the soft voice, made deeper by echoes. He squatted under the overhang, the plash of water now dwindling, and he realized that the blast up the ravine had made a momentary check-dam. He distinctly heard the mewing of tiny kzin twins as Boots removed the security of her warm, soft fur. A moment later, he saw her head and arms. Both hands, even the one bearing a screwdriver and the transmitter, had their claws fully extended and her ears lay so flat on her skull that they might have been caps of skin. Still, she shoved the articles forward.

Pocketing the transmitter with a thrill of undeserved success, he bade her keep the other items. He showed her the sidearm. "Boots, one of these killed Puss. Do you see that it could kill you just as easily?"

The growl in her throat was an illustrated manual of counterthreat.

"But I began as your protector. I would never harm you or your kittens. Do you see that now?"

"My head sees it. My heart says to fight you. Go."

He nodded, turned away, and eased himself into the deep pool that was now fed by a mere trickle of water. Ahead was the lake, smoke floating toward it, and he knew that he could run safely in the shallows hidden by smoke without leaving prints. And fight another day. And, he realized, staring back at the once-talkative little falls, leave Boots with her kittens where the cautious Brickshitter would almost certainly find them because now the mouth of her birthing bower was clearly visible.

No, I'm damned if you will!

"So check into it, Brickshitter," he muttered softly, backing deep into the cool cover of yellow ferns. "I've still got a few rounds here, if you're still alive."

He was alive, all right. Locklear knew it in his guts when a stone trickled its way down near the pool. He knew it for certain when he felt soft footfalls, the almost silent track of a big hunting cat, vibrate the damp grassy embankment against his back. He eased forward in water that was no deeper than his armpits, still hidden, but when the towering kzin warrior sprang to the verge of the water he made no sound at all. He carried only his sidearm and knife, and Locklear fired at a distance of only ten paces, actually a trifling space.

But a tremendous trifle, for Brickshitter was well-trained and did not pause after his leap before hopping aside in a squat. He was looking straight at Locklear and the horizontal spray of slugs ceased before it reached him. Brickshitter's arm was a blur. Foliage shredded where Locklear had hidden as the little man dropped below the surface, feeling two hot slugs trickle down his back after their velocity was spent underwater.

Locklear could not see clearly, but propelled himself forward as he broke the surface in a desperate attempt to reach the other side. He knew his sidearm was empty. He did not know that his opponent's was, until the kzin navigator threw the weapon at him, screamed, and leaped.

Locklear pulled himself to the bank with fronds as the big kzin strode toward him in water up to his belly. Too late to run, and Brickshitter had a look of cool confidence about him. *I like him better when he's not so cool.* "Come on, you *kshat,* you *vatach*'s ass," he chanted, backing toward the only place where he might have safety at his back—the stone shelf before Boots's bower, where great height was a disadvantage. "Come on, you fur-licking, brickshitting hairball, do it!" Leaping and screaming, screaming and leaping; "you stupid no-name," he finished, wondering if the last was an insult.

Evidently it was. With a howling scream of savagery, the big kzin tried to leap clear of the water, falling headlong as Locklear reached the stone shelf. Dagger now in hand, Brickshitter floundered to the bank spitting, emitting a string of words that doubled Locklear's command of kzinti curses. Then, almost as if reading Locklear's mind, the navigator paused a few paces away and held up his knife. And his voice, though quivering, was exceedingly mild. "Do you know what I am going to do with this, monkey?"

To break through this facade, Locklear made it offhanded. "Cut your *ch'rowl*ing throat by accident, most likely," he said.

The effect was startling. Stiffening, then baring his fangs in a howl of frustration, the warrior sprang for the shelf, seeing in midleap that Locklear was waiting for exactly that with his *wtsai* thrust forward, its tip made needle-sharp by the same female who had once dulled it. But a kzin warrior's training went deep. Pivoting as he landed, rolling to one side, the navigator avoided Locklear's thrust, his long tail lashing to catch the little man's legs.

Locklear had seen that one before. His blade cut deeply into the kzin's tail and Brickshitter vented a yelp, whirling to spring. He feinted as if to hurl the knife and Locklear threw both arms before his face, seeing too late the beginning of the kzin's squatting leap in close quarters, like a swordsman's balestra. Locklear slammed his back painfully against the side of the cave, his own blade slashing blindly, and felt a horrendous fiery trail of pain down the length of his knife arm before the graceful kzin moved out of range. He switched hands with the *wtsai*.

"I am going to carve off your maleness while you watch, monkey," said Brickshitter, seeing the blood begin to course from the open gash on Locklear's arm.

"One word before you do," Locklear said, and pulled out all the stops. "*Ch'rowl* your grandmother. *Ch'rowl* your patriarch, and *ch'rowl* yourself."

With each repetition, Brickshitter seemed to coil into himself a bit farther, his eyes not slitted but saucer-round, and with his last phrase Locklear saw something from the edge of his vision that the big kzin saw clearly. Ropelike, temptingly bushy, it was the flick of Boots's tail at the mouth of her bower.

Like most feline hunters from the creche onward, the kzin

warrior reacted to this stimulus with rapt fascination, at least for an instant, already goaded to insane heights of frustration by the sexual triggerword. His eyes rolled upward for a flicker of time, and in that flicker Locklear acted. His headlong rush carried him in a full body slam against the navigator's injured shoulder, the *wtsai* going in just below the rib cage, torn from Locklear's grasp as his opponent flipped backward in agony to the water. Locklear cartwheeled into the pool, weaponless, choosing to swim because it was the fastest way out of reach.

He flailed up the embankment searching wildly for a loose stone, then tossed a glance over his shoulder. The navigator lay on his side, half out of the water, blood pumping from his belly, and in his good arm he held Locklear's *wtsai* by its handle. As if his arm were the only part of him still alive, he flipped the knife, caught it by the tip, forced himself erect.

Locklear did the first thing he could remember from dealing with vicious animals: reached down, grasped a handful of thin air, and mimicked hurling a stone. It did not deter the navigator's convulsive move in the slightest, the *wtsai* a silvery whirr before it thunked into a tree one pace from Locklear's breast. The kzin's motion carried him forward into the water, face down. He did not entirely submerge, but slid forward inert, arms at his sides. Locklear wrestled his blade from the tree and waited, his chest heaving. The navigator did not move again.

Locklear held the knife aloft, eyes shut, for long moments, tears of exultation and vengeance coursing down his cheeks, mixing with dirty water from his hair and clean blood from his cheek. His eyes snapped open at the voice.

"May I name my son after you, Rockear?" Boots, just inside the overhang, held two tiny spotted kittens protectively where they could suckle. It was, he felt, meant to be an honor merely for him to see them.

"I would be honored, Boots. But the modern kzin custom is to make sons earn their names, I think."

"What do I care what they do? We are starting over here."

Locklear stuffed the blade into his belt, wiping wet stuff from his face again. "Not unless I can put away that scarfaced commander. He's got Kit at the manor—unless she has him. I'm going to try and bias the results," he said grimly, and scanned the heights above the ravine.

To his back, Boots said, "It is not traditional, but—if you come for us, we would return to the manor's protection."

He turned, glancing up the ravine. "An honor. But right now, you'd better come out and wait for the waterfall to resume. When it does, it might flood your bower for a few minutes." He waved, and she waved back. When next he glanced downslope, from the upper lip of the ravine, he could see the brushfire dwindling at the jungle's edge, and water just beginning to carve its way through a jumble of debris in the throat of the ravine, and a small lithe orange-yellow figure holding two tiny spotted dots, patiently waiting in the sunlight for everything he said to come true.

"Lady," he said softly to the waiting Boots, "I sure hope you picked a winner."

He could have disappeared into the wilds of Kzersatz for months but Scarface, with vast advantages, might call for more searchers. Besides, running would be reactive, the act of mindless prey. Locklear opted to be proactive—a hunter's mindset. Recalling the violence of that exploding rifle, he almost ignored the area because nothing useful could remain in the crater. But curiosity made him pause, squinting down from the heights, and excellent vision gave him an edge when he saw the dull gleam of Brickshitter's beam rifle across the ravine. It was probably fully discharged, else the navigator would not have abandoned it. But Scarface wouldn't know that.

Locklear doubled back and retrieved the heavy weapon, chuckling at the sharp stones that lay atop the turf. Brickshitter must have expended a few curses as those stones rained down. The faint orange light near the scope was next to a legend in Kzinti that translated as "insufficient charge." He thought about that a moment, then smeared his own blood over the light until its gleam was hidden. Shouldering the rifle, he set off again, circling high above the ravine so that he could come in from its upper end. Somehow the weapon seemed lighter now, or perhaps it was just his second wind. Locklear did not pause to reflect that his decision for immediate action brought optimism, and that optimism is another word for accumulated energy.

The sun was at his back when he stretched prone behind low cover and paused for breath. The zoom scope of the rifle showed that someone had ripped the thatches from the manor's window bulges, no doubt to give Scarface a better view. *Works both ways, hotshot,* he mused; but though he could see through the windows, he saw nothing move. Presently he began to crawl forward and down, holding the heavy rifle in the crooks of his arms, abrading his elbows as he went from brush to outcrop to declivity. His shadow stretched before him. Good; the sun would be in a watcher's eyes and he was dry-mouthed with awareness that Scarface must carry his own arsenal.

The vines they had planted already hid the shaft of their escape tunnel but Locklear paused for long moments at its mouth, listening, waiting until his breath was quiet and regular. What if Scarface were waiting in the tunnel? He ducked into the rifle sling, put his *wtsai* in his teeth, and eased down feet-first using remembered hand and footholds, his heart hammering his ribs. Then he scuffed earth with his knee and knew that his entry would no longer be a surprise if Scarface was waiting. He dropped the final two meters to soft dirt, squatting, hopping aside as he'd seen Brickshitter do.

Nothing but darkness. He waited for his panting to subside and then moved forward with great caution. It took him five minutes to stalk twenty meters of curving tunnel, feeling his way until he saw faint light filtering from above. By then, he could hear the fitz-rowr of kzin voices. He eased himself up to the opening and peered through long slits of shamboo matting that Boots had woven to cover the rough walls.

" . . . Am learning, milady, that even the most potent Word loses its strength when used too often," a male voice was saying. Scarface, in tones Locklear had never expected to hear. "As soon as this operation is complete, rest assured I shall be the most gallant of suitors."

Locklear's view showed only their legs as modern warrior and ancient courtesan faced each other, seated on benches at the rough-hewn dining table. Kit, with a sulk in her voice, said, "I begin to wonder if your truthfulness extends to my attractions, milord."

Scarface, fervently: "The truth is that you are a warrior's wildest fantasies in fur. I cannot say how often I have wished for a mate I could actually talk to! Yet I am first Grraf-Commander, and second a kzintosh. Excuse me," he added, stood up, and strode to the main doorway, now in full view of Locklear. His belt held ceremonial *wtsai,* a sidearm and God knew what else in those pockets. His beam rifle lay propped beside the doorway. Taking a brick-sized device from his broad belt, he muttered, "I wonder if this rude hut is interfering with our signals."

A click and then, in gruff tones of frustrated command, he

said, "Hunt leader to all units: report! If you cannot report, use a signal bomb from your beltpacs, dammit! If you cannot do that, return to the hut at triple time or I will hang your hides from a pennant pole."

Locklear grinned as Scarface moved back to the table with an almost human sigh. *Too bad I didn't know about those signal bombs. Warm this place up a little. Maybe I should* go *back for those beltpacs.* But he abandoned the notion as Scarface resumed his courtship.

"I have hinted, and you have evaded, milady. I must ask you now, bluntly: will you return with me when this operation is over?"

"I shall do as the commander wishes," she said demurely, and Locklear grinned again. She hadn't said "Grraf-Commander"; and even if Locklear didn't survive, *she* might very well wind up in command. Oh sure, she'd do whatever the commander liked.

"Another point on which you have been evasive," Scarface went on; "your assessment of the monkey, and what relationship he had to either of you." Locklear did not miss this nuance; Scarface knew of two kzinrret, presumably an initial report from one of the pair who'd found Puss. He did not know of Boots, then.

"The manbeast ruled us with strange magic forces, milord. He made us fearful at times. At any time he might be anywhere. Even now." *Enough of that crap,* Locklear thought at her, even though he felt she was only trying to put the wind up Scarface's backside. *Fat chance! Lull the bastard, put him to sleep.*

Scarface went to the heart of his question. "Did he act honorably toward you both?"

After a long pause: "I suppose he did, as a manbeast saw honor. He did not *ch'rowl* me, if that is—"

"Milady! You will rob the Word of its meaning, or drive me mad."

"I have an idea. Let me dance for you while you lie at your ease. I will avoid the term and drive you only a little crazy."

"For the eighth-squared time, I do not need to lie down. I need to complete this hunt; duty first, pleasure after. I—what?"

Locklear's nose had brushed the matting. The noise was faint, but Scarface was on his feet and at the doorway, rifle in hand, in two seconds. Locklear's nose itched, and he pinched his nostrils painfully. It seemed that the damned tabby was never completely off-guard, made edgy as a *wtsai* by his failure to contact his crew. Locklear felt a sneeze coming, sank down on his heels, rubbed furiously at his nose. When he stood up again, Scarface stood a pace outside, demanding a response with his comm set while Kit stood at the doorway. Locklear scratched carefully at the mat, willing Kit alone to hear it. No such luck.

Scarface began to pace back and forth outside, and Locklear scratched louder. Kit's ear-umbrellas flicked, lifted. Another scratch. She turned, and saw him move the matting. Her mouth opened slightly. *She's going to warn him,* Locklear thought wildly.

"Perhaps we could stroll down the ravine, milord," she said easily, taking a few steps outside.

Locklear saw the big kzin commander pass the doorway once, twice, muttering furiously about indecision. He caught the words, " . . . Return to the lifeboat with you now if I have not heard from them very soon," and knew that he could never regain an advantage if that happened. He paced his advance past the matting to coincide with Scarface's movements, easing the beam rifle into plain sight on the floor, now with his head and shoulders out above the dusty floor, now his waist, now his—his—his sneeze came without warning.

Scarface leaped for the entrance, snatching his sidearm as he came into view, and Locklear gave himself up then even though he was aiming the heavy beam rifle from a prone position, an empty threat. But a bushy tail flashed between the warrior's ankles, and his next bound sent him skidding forward on his face, the sidearm still in his hand but pointed away from Locklear.

And the muzzle of Locklear's beam rifle poked so near the commander's nose that he could only focus on it cross-eyed. Locklear said it almost pleasantly: "Could even a monkey miss such a target?"

"Perhaps," Scarface said, and swallowed hard. "But I think that rifle is exhausted."

"The one your nervous brickshitting navigator used? It probably was," said Locklear, brazening it out, adding the necessary lie with, "I broiled him with this one, which doesn't have that cute little light glowing, does it? Now then: skate that little shooter of yours across the floor. Your crew is all bugbait, Scarface, and the only thing between you and kitty heaven is my good humor."

Much louder than need be, unless he was counting on Kit's help: "Have you no end of insults? Have you no sense of honor? Let us settle this as equals." Kit stood at the doorway now.

"The sidearm, Grraf-Commander. Or meet your ancestors. Your crew tried to kill me—and monkey see, monkey do."

The sidearm clattered across the rough floor mat. Locklear chose to avoid further insult; the last thing he needed was a loss of self-control from the big kzin. "Hands behind your back. Kit, get the strongest cord we have and bind him; the feet, then the hands. And stay to one side. If I have to pull this trigger, you don't want to get splattered."

Minutes later, holding the sidearm and sitting at the table, Locklear studied the prisoner who sat, legs before him, back against the doorway, and explained the facts of Kzersatz life while Kit cleaned his wounds. She murmured that his cheek scar would someday be *t'rralap* as he explained the options. "So you see, you have nothing to lose by giving your honorable parole, because I trust your honor. You have everything to lose by refusing, because you'll wind up as barbecue."

"Men do not eat captives," Scarface said. "You speak of honor and yet you lie."

"Oh, I wouldn't eat you. But *they* would. There are two kzinrret here who, if you'll recall, hate everything you stand for."

Scarface looked glumly at Kit. "Can this be true?"

She replied, "Can it be true that modern kzinrret have been bred into cattle?"

"Both can be true," he conceded. "But monk—men are devious, false, conniving little brutes. How can a kzinrret of your intelligence approve of them?"

"Rockear has defeated your entire force—with a little help," she said. "I am content to pledge my honor to a male of his resourcefulness, especially when he does not abuse his leadership. I only wish he were of our race," she added wistfully.

Scarface: "My parole would depend on your absolute truthfulness, Rockear."

A pause from Locklear, and a nod. "You've got it as of now, but no backing out if you get some surprises later."

"One question, then, before I give my word: *are all my crew truly casualties?*"

"Deader than this beam rifle," Locklear said, grinning, holding its muzzle upward, squeezing its trigger.

Later, after pledging his parole, Scarface observed reasonably that there was a world of difference between an insufficient charge and *no* charge. The roof thatching burned slowly at first; slowly enough that they managed to remove everything worth keeping. But at last the whole place burned merrily enough. To Locklear's surprise, it was Scarface who mentioned safe removal of the *zzrou,* and pulled it loose easily after a few deft manipulations of the transmitter.

Kit seemed amused as they ate al fresco, a hundred meters from the embers of their manor. "It is a tradition in the ancient culture that a major change of household leadership requires burning of the old manor," she explained with a smile of her ears.

Locklear, still uneasy with the big kzin warrior so near and now without his bonds, surreptitiously felt the sidearm in his belt and asked, "Am I not still the leader?"

"Yes," she said. "But what kind of leader would deny happiness to his followers?" Her lowered glance toward Scarface could hardly be misunderstood.

The ear umbrellas of the big male turned a deeper hue. "I do not wish to dishonor another warrior, Locklear, but—if I am to remain your captive here as you say, um, such females may be impossibly overstimulating."

"Not to me," Locklear said. "No offense, Kit; I'm half in love with you myself. In fact, I think the best thing for my own sanity would be to seek, uh, females of my own kind."

"You intended to take us back to the manworlds, I take it," said Scarface with some smugness.

"After a bit more research here, yes. The hell with wars anyhow. There's a lot about this planet you don't know about yet. Fascinating!"

"You will never get back in a lifeboat," said Scarface, "and the cruiser is now only a memory."

"You didn't!"

"I assuredly did, Locklear. My first act when you released my bonds was to send the self-destruct signal."

Locklear put his head between his hands. "Why didn't we hear the lifeboat go up?"

"Because I did not think to set it for destruct. It is not exactly a major asset."

"For me it damned well is," Locklear growled, then went on. "Look here: I won't release Kit from any pair-bonding to me unless you promise not to sabotage me in any way. And I further promise not to try turning you over to some military bunch, because I'm the, uh, mayor of this frigging planet and I can declare peace on it if I want to. Honor bound, honest injun, whatever the hell that means, and all the rigamarole that goes with it. Goddammit, I could have blown your head off."

"But you did not know that."

"With the sidearm, then! Don't *ch'r*—don't fiddle me around. Put your honor on the line, mister, and put your big paw against mine if you mean it."

After a long look at Kit, the big kzin commander reached out a hand, palm vertical, and Locklear met it with his own. "You are not the man we left here," said the vanquished kzin, eyeing Locklear without malice. "Brown and tough as dried meat—and older, I would say."

"Getting hunted by armed kzinti tends to age a feller," Locklear chuckled. "I'm glad we found peace with honor."

"Was any commander," the commander asked no one in particular, "ever faced with so many conflicts of honor?"

"You'll resolve them," Locklear predicted. "Think about it: I'm about to make you the head captive of a brand new region that has two newborn babes in it, two intelligent kzinrret at least, and over an eight-squared other kzinti who have been in stasis for longer than you can believe. Wake 'em, or don't, it's up to you, just don't interfere with me because I expect to be here part of the time, and somewhere else at other times. Kit, show him how to use the airboat. If you two can't figure out how to use the stuff in this Outsider zoo, I miss my—"

"Outsiders?" Scarface did not seem to like the sound of that.

"That's just my guess," Locklear shrugged. "Maybe they have hidden sensors that tell 'em what happens on the planet Zoo. Maybe they don't care. What I care about, is exploring the other compounds on Zoo, one especially. I may not find any of my kind on Newduvai, and if I do they might have foreheads a half-inch high, but it bears looking into. For that I need the lifeboat. Any reason why it wouldn't take me to another compound on Zoo?"

"No reason." After a moment of rumination, Scarface put on his best negotiation face again. "If I teach you to be an expert pilot, would you let me disable the hyperwave comm set?"

Locklear thought hard for a similar time. "Yes, if you swear to leave its local functions intact. Look, fella, we may want to talk to one another with it."

"Agreed, then," said the kzin commander. That night, Locklear slept poorly. He lay awake for a time, wondering if Newduvai had its own specimen cave, and whether he could find it if one existed. The fact was that Kzersatz simply lacked the kind of company he had in mind. *Not even the right kind of cathouse,* he groused silently. He was not enormously heartened by the prospect of wooing a Neanderthal nymphet, either. Well, that was what field research was for. *Please, God, at least a few Cro-Magnons! Patience, Locklear, and earplugs,* because he could not find sleep for long.

It was not merely that he was alone, for the embers near his pallet kept him as toasty as kzinrret fur. No, it was the infernal yowling of those cats somewhere below in the ravine.

Briar Patch

by Dean Ing

If Locklear had been thinking straight, he never would have stayed in the god business. But when a man has been thrust into the Fourth Man-Kzin War, won peace with honor from the tigerlike kzinti on a synthetic zoo planet, and released long-stored specimens so that his vast prison compound resembles the kzin homeworld, it's hard for that man to keep his sense of mortality.

It's hard, that is, until someone decides to kill him. His first mistake was lust, impure and simple. A week after he paroled Scarface, the one surviving kzin warrior, Locklear admitted his problem during supper. "All that caterwauling in the ravine," he said, refilling his bowl from the hearth stewpot, "is driving me nuts. Good thing you haven't let the rest of those kzinti out of stasis; the racket would be unbelievable!"

Scarface wiped his muzzle with a brawny forearm and handed his own bowl to Kit, his new mate. The darkness of the huge Kzersatz region was tempered only by coals, but Locklear saw those coals flicker in Scarface's cat eyes. "A condition of my surrender was that you release Kit to me," the big kzin growled. "And besides: do humans mate so quietly?"

Because they were speaking Kzin, the word Scarface had used was actually "ch'rowl"—itself a sexual goad. Kit, who was refilling the bowl, let slip a tiny mew of surprise and pleasure. "Please, milord," she said, offering the bowl to Scarface. "Poor Rockear is already overstimulated. Is it not so?" Her huge eyes flicked to Locklear, whom she had grown to know quite well after Locklear waked her from age-long sleep.

"Dead right," Locklear agreed with a morose glance. "Not by the word; by the goddamn deed!"

"She is mine," Scarface grinned; a kzin grin, the kind with big fangs and no amusement.

"Calm down. I may have been an animal psychologist, but I only have letches for human females," Locklear gloomed toward his kzin companions. "And every night when I hear you two flattening the grass out there," he nodded past the half-built walls of the hut, "I get, uh, . . ." He did not know how to translate "horny" into Kzin.

"You get the urge to travel," Scarface finished, making it not quite a suggestion. The massive kzin stared into darkness as if peering across the force walls surrounding Kzersatz. Those towering invisible walls separated the air, and lifeforms, of Kzersatz from other synthetic compounds of this incredible planet, Zoo. "I can see the treetops in the next compound as easily as you, Locklear. But I see no monkeys in them."

Before his defeat, Scarface had been "Graf-Commander." The same strict kzin honor that bound him to his surrender, forbade him to curse his captor as a monkey. But he could still sharpen the barb of his wit. Kit, with real affection for Locklear, did not approve. "Be nice," she hissed to her mate.

"Forget it," Locklear told her, stabbing with his Kzin *wtsai* blade for a hunk of meat in his stew. "Kit, he's stuck with his military code, and it won't let him insist that his captor get the hell out of here. But he's right. I still don't know if that next compound I call Newduvai is really Earth-like." He smiled at Scarface, remembering not to show his teeth, and added, "Or whether it has my kind of monkey."

"And we must not try to find out until your war wounds have completely healed," Kit replied.

The eyes of man and kzin warrior met. "Whoa," Locklear said quickly, sparing Scarface the trouble. "*We* won't be scouting over there; I will, but you won't. I'm an ethologist," he went on, holding up a hand to bar Kit's interruption. "If Newduvai is as completely stocked as Kzersatz, somebody—maybe the Outsiders, maybe not, but damn certain a long time ago—*some*body intended all these compounds to be kept separate. Now, I won't say I haven't played god here a little . . ."

"And intend to play it over there a lot," said Kit, who had never yet surrendered to anyone.

"Hear me out, I'm not going to start mixing species from Kzersatz and Newduvai any more than I already have, and that's final." He pried experimentally at the scab running down his knife arm. "But I'm pretty much healed, thanks to your medkit, Scarface. And I meant it when I said you'd have free run of this place. It's intended for kzinti, not humans. High time I took your lifeboat over those force walls to Newduvai."

"Boots will miss you," said Kit.

Locklear smiled, recalling the other kzin female he'd released from stasis in a very pregnant condition. According to Kit, a kzin mother would not emerge from her birthing creche until the eyes of her twins had opened—another week, at least. "Give her my love," he said, and swilled the last of his stew.

"A pity you will not do that yourself," Kit sighed.

"Milady." Scarface became, for the moment, every inch a Graf-Commander. "Would you ask me to *ch'rowl* a human female?" He waited for Kit to control her mixed expression. "Then please be silent on the subject. Locklear is a warrior who knows what he fights for."

Locklear yawned. "There's an old song that says, 'Ain't gonna study war no more,' and a slogan that goes, 'Make love, not war.' "

Kit stood up with a fetching twitch of her tail. "I believe our leader has spoken, milord," she purred.

Locklear watched them swaying together into the night, and his parting call was plaintive. "Just try and keep it down, okay? A fellow needs his sleep."

The kzin lifeboat was over ten meters long, well-armed and furnished with emergency rations. In accord with their handshake armistice, Scarface had given flight instructions to his human pupil after disabling the hyperwave portion of its comm set. He had given no instructions on armament because Locklear, a peaceable man, saw no further use for anything larger than a sidearm. Neither of them could do much to make the lifeboat seating comfortable for Locklear, who was small even by human standards in an acceleration couch meant for a two-hundred-kilo kzin.

Locklear paused in the air lock in midmorning and raised one arm in a universal peace sign. Scarface returned it. "I'll call you now and then, if those force walls don't stop the signal," Locklear called. "If you let your other kzinti out of stasis, call and tell me how it works out."

"Keep your tail dry, Rockear," Kit called, perhaps forgetting he lacked that appendage—a compliment, of sorts.

"Will do," he called back as the air lock swung shut. Moments later, he brought the little craft to life and, cursing the cradle-rock motion that branded him a novice, urged the lifeboat into the yellow sky of Kzersatz.

Locklear made one pass, a "goodbye sweep," high above the region with its yellow and orange vegetation, taking care to stay well inside the frostline that defined those invisible force walls. He spotted the cave from the still-flattened grass where Kit had herded the awakened animals from the crypt and their sleep of forty thousand years, then steepened his climb and used aero boost to begin his trajectory. No telling whether the force walls stopped suddenly, but he did not want to find out by plowing into the damned things. It was enough to know they stopped below orbital height, and that he could toss the lifeboat from Kzersatz to Newduvai in a low-energy ballistic arc.

And he knew enough to conserve energy in the craft's main accumulators because one day, when the damned stupid Man-Kzin War was over, he'd need that energy to jump from Zoo to some part of known space. Unless, he amended silently, somebody found Zoo first. The war might already be over, and certainly the warlike kzinti must have the coordinates of Zoo . . .

Then he was at the top of his trajectory, seeing the planetary curvature of Zoo, noting the tiny satellite sunlets that bathed hundred-mile-diameter regions in light, realizing that a warship could condemn any one of those circular regions to death with one well-placed shot against its synthetic, automated little sun. He was already past the circular force walls now, and felt an enormous temptation to slow the ship by main accumulator energy. A good pilot could lower that lifeboat down between the walls of those force cylinders, in the hard vacuum between compounds. Outsiders might be lurking there, idly studying the specimens through invisible walls.

But Locklear was no expert with a kzin lifeboat, not yet, and he had to use his wristcomp to translate the warning on the console screen. He set the wing extensions just in time to avoid heavy buffeting, thankful that he had not needed orbital speed to manage his brief trajectory. He bobbled a maneuver once, twice, then felt the drag of Newduvai's atmosphere on the lifeboat and gave the lifting surfaces full extension. He put the craft into a shallow bank to starboard, keeping the vast circular frostline far to portside, and punched in an autopilot instruction. Only then did he dare to turn his gaze down on Newduvai.

Like Kzersatz it boasted a big lake, but this one glinted in a sun heartbreakingly like Earth's. A rugged jumble of cliffs soared into cloud at one side of the region, and green hills mounded above plains of mottled hues: tan, brown, green, Oh, God, all that green! He'd forgotten, in the saffron of Kzersatz, how much he missed the emerald of grass, the blue of sky, the darker dusty green of Earth forests. For it was, in every respect, perfectly Earthlike. He wiped his misting eyes, grinned at himself for such foolishness, and eased the lifeboat down to a lazy circular course that kept him two thousand meters above the terrain. If the builders of Zoo were consistent, one of those shallow creekbeds would begin not in a marshy meadow but in a horizontal shaft. And there he would find—he dared not think it through any further.

After his first complete circuit of Newduvai, he knew it had no herds of animals. No birds dotted the lakeshore; no bugs whacked his viewport. A dozen streams meandered and leapt down from the frostline where clouds dumped their moisture against cold encircling force walls. One stream ended in a second small lake with no obvious outlet, but none of the creeks or dry washes began with a cave.

Mindful of his clumsiness in this alien craft, Locklear set it down in soft sand where a dry wash delta met the kidney-shaped lake. After further consulting between his wristcomp and the ship's computer, he punched in his most important queries and listened to the ship cool while its sensors analyzed Newduvai.

Gravity: Earth normal. Atmosphere, solar flux, and temperature: all Earth normal. "And not a critter in sight," he told the cabin walls. In a burst of insight, he asked the computer to list anything that might be a health hazard to a kzin. If man and kzin could make steaks of each other, they probably should fear the same pathogens. The computer took its time, but its most fearsome finding was of tetanus in the dust.

He waited no longer, thrusting at the air lock in his hurry, filling his lungs with a rich soup of odors, and found his eyes brimming again as he stepped onto a little piece of Earth. Smells, he reflected, really got you back to basics. Scents of cedar, of dust, of grasses and yes, of wildflowers. Just like home—yet, in some skinprickling way, not quite.

Locklear sat down on the sand then, with an earthlike sunlet baking his back from a turquoise sky, and he wept. Outsiders or not, any bunch that could engineer a piece of home on the rim of known space couldn't be all bad.

He was tasting the lake water's very faint brackishness when, in a process that took less than a minute, the sunlight dimmed and was gone. "But it's only noontime," he protested, and then laughed at himself and made a notation on his wristcomp, using its faint light to guide him back to the air lock.

As with Kzersatz, he saw no stars; and then he realized that the position of Newduvai's sun had been halfway to the horizon when—almost as it happened on Kzersatz—the daily ration of sunlight was quenched. Why should Newduvai's sun keep the same time as that of Kzersatz? It didn't; nor did it wink off as suddenly as that of Kzersatz.

He activated the still-functioning local mode of the lifeboat's comm set, intending to pass his findings on to Scarface. No response. Scarface's handset was an allband unit; perhaps some wavelength could bounce off of debris from the kzin cruiser scuttled in orbit—but Locklear knew that was a slender hope, and soon it seemed no hope at all. He spent the longest few hours of his life then, turning floodlights on the lake in the forlorn hope of seeing a fish leap, and with the vague fear that a tyrannosaur might pay him a social call. But no matter where he turned the lights he saw no gleam of eyes, and the sand was innocent of any tracks. Sleep would not come until he began to address the problem of the stasis crypt in logical ways.

Locklear came up from his seat with a bound, facing a sun that brightened as he watched. His wristcomp said not quite twelve hours had passed since the sunlet dimmed. His belly said it was late. His memory said yes, by God, there was one likely plan for locating that horizontal shaft: fly very near the frostline and scan every dark cranny that was two hundred meters or so inside the force walls. On Kzersatz, the stasis crypt had ended exactly beneath the frostline, perhaps a portal for those who'd built Zoo. And the front entrance had been two hundred meters inside the force walls.

He lifted the lifeboat slowly, ignoring hunger pangs, beginning to plot a rough map of Newduvai on the computer screen because he did not know how to make the computer do it for him. Soon, he passed a dry plateau with date palms growing in its declivities and followed the ship's shadow to more fertile soil. Near frostline, he set the aeroturbine reactor just above idle and, moving briskly a hundred meters above the ground, began a careful scan of the terrain because he was not expert enough with kzin computers to automate the search.

After three hours he had covered more than half of his sweep around Newduvai, past semidesert and grassy fields to pine-dotted mountain slopes, and the lifeboat's reactor coolant was overheating from the slow pace. Locklear set the craft down nicely near that smaller mountain lake, chopped all power systems, and headed for scrubby trees in the near distance. Scattered among the pines were cedar and small oak. Nearer stood tall poplar and chestnut, invaded by wild grape with immature fruit. But nearest of all, the reason for his landing here, were gnarled little pear trees and, amid wild shoots of rank growth, trees laden with small ripe plums. He wolfed them down until juice dripped from his chin, washed in the lake, and then found the pears unripe. No matter: he'd seen dates, grapes, and chestnut, which suggested a model of some Mediterranean region. After identifying juniper, oleander and honeysuckle, he sent his wristcomp scurrying through its megabytes and narrowed his opinion of the area: a surrogate slice of Asia Minor.

He might have sat on sunwarmed stones until dark, lulled by this sensation of being, somehow, back home without a care. But then he glanced far across the lower hills and saw, proceeding slowly across a parched desert plateau many miles distant, a whirlwind with its whiplike curve and bloom of dust where it touched the soil.

"Uh-huh! That's how you reseed plants without insect vectors," he said aloud to the builders of Zoo. "But whirlwinds don't make honey, and they'll sting anyway. Hell, even *I* can play god better than that," he said, and bore a pocketful of plums into the lifeboat, filled once more with the itch to find the cave that might not even exist on Newduvai.

But it was there, all right. Locklear saw it only because of the perfect arc of obsidian, gleaming through a tangle of brush that had grown around the cave mouth.

He made a botch of the landing because he was trembling with anticipation. A corner of his mind kept warning him not to assume everything here was the same as on Kzersatz, so Locklear stopped just outside that brush-choked entrance. His *wtsai* blade made short work of the brush, revealing a polished floor. He strode forward, *wtsai* in one hand, his big kzin sidearm in the other, to the now-familiar luminous film that flickered, several meters inside the cave mouth, across an obsidian portal. He thrust his blade through the film and saw, as he had expected to see, stronger light flash behind the portal. Then he stepped through and stopped, listening.

He might have been back in the Kzersatz crypt: a quiet so deep his own breathing made echoes; the long obsidian central passage, with nine branches on each side, ending in a frost-covered force wall that filled the passageway. And the clear plastic containers ranked in the side passages were of three sizes on smooth metal bases, as expected. But Locklear took one look at the nearest specimen, spinning slowly in its stasis cage, and knew that here the resemblance to Kzersatz ended forever.

The monster lay in something like a fetal crouch, tumbling slowly in response to the grav polarizer as it had been doing for many thousands of years. It was black, with great forward-curving horns and heavy shoulders, and when released—*if* anyone dared, he amended—it would stand six feet at the shoulder. Locklear figured its weight at a ton. Some European zoologists had once tried to breed cattle back to this brute, but with scant success, and Locklear had not seen so much as a sketch of it since his undergrad work. It was a bull aurochs, a beast which had survived on Earth into historic times; and counting the cows, Locklear realized there were over forty of them.

No point in kidding himself about his priorities. Locklear walked past the stasized camels and gerbils, hurried faster beyond small horses and cheetahs and bats, began to trot as he ran to the next passage past lions and hares and grouse, and was sprinting as he passed whole schools of fish (without water? Why the hell not? They were in stasis, he reminded himself—) in their respective containers. He was out of breath by the time he dashed between specimens of reindeer and saw the monkeys.

NO! A mistake any kzin might have made, but: "How could I play such a shameful joke on myself?" They were in fetal curls, and some of them boasted a lot of body hair. And each of them, Locklear realized, was human.

In a kind of reverence he studied them all, careful to avoid touching the metal bases which, on Kzersatz, opened the cages and released the specimens. Narrowheaded and swarthy they were, no taller than he, with heavy brow ridges and high cheekbones. Noses like prizefighters; forearms like blacksmiths; and some had pendulous mammaries and a few had—had—

"Tits," he breathed. "There's a difference! Thank you, God."

Men and women like these had first been studied in a river valley near old Düsseldorf, hardy folk who had preceded modern humans on Earth and, in all probability, had intermarried with them until forty or fifty thousand years before. Locklear, rubbing at the gooseflesh on his arms, began to study each of the stasized nudes with great care. He would need every possible advantage because they would be disoriented, perhaps even furious, when they waked. And the last thing Locklear needed was to start off on the wrong foot with a frenzied Neanderthaler.

Only an idiot would release a mob of Neanderthal hunters into a tiny world without taking steps to protect endangered game animals. The killing of a dozen deer might doom the rest of that species to slow extinction here. On the other hand, Locklear might have released all the animals and waited for a season or more. But certain of the young women in stasis were not exactly repellent, and he did not intend to wait a year before making their acquaintance. Besides, his notes on a Neanderthal community could make him famous on a dozen worlds, and Locklear was anxious to get on with it.

His second option was to wake the people and guide them, by force if necessary, outside to fruits and grains. But each of them would see those stasized animals, probably as meat on the hoof, and might not respond to his demands. It was beyond belief that any of them would speak a language he knew. Then it struck him that he already knew how to disassemble a stasis cage, and that he had as much time as he needed. With a longing glance backward, Locklear retraced his steps to the lifeboat and started looking for something with wheels.

But kzin lifeboats do not carry cargo dollies, and the sun of Newduvai had dimmed before he found a way to remove the wheeled carriage below the reactor's heat exchanger unit. Evidently the unit needed replacement often enough that kzin engineers installed a carriage with it. That being so, Locklear decided not to use the lifeboat's reactor any more than he had to.

He worked until hunger and aching muscles drove him to

the cabin, where he cut slices of bricklike kzin rations and ate plums for dessert. But before he fell asleep, Locklear made some decisions that might save his hide. The lifeboat must be hidden away from inquisitive savage fingers; he would even camouflage the stasis crypt so that those savages would not know what lay inside; and it was absolutely crucial that he present himself as a shaman of great power. Without a few tawdry magics, he might not be able to distance himself as an observer; might even be challenged to combat by some strong male. And Locklear remembered those hornlike fingernails and bulging muscles all too well. He saw no sense in shooting a man, even a Neanderthal, merely to prove a point that could be made in peaceable ways.

He spent over a week preparing his hardware. His trials on Kzersatz had taught him how, when all you've got is a hammer, the whole world is a nail; and that you must hammer out a few other tools as soon as possible. He soon found the lifeboat's military toolbox complete with wire, pistol-grip arc welder, and motorized drill.

He took time off to gather fruit and to let his frustrations drain away. It was hard not to throw rocks at the sky when he commanded a state-of-the-art kzin craft, yet could not cannibalize much of it for the things he needed. "Maybe I should release a dog from stasis so I could kick it," he told himself aloud, while attaching an oak branch as a wagon tongue for the wheeled carriage. But lacking any other game, he figured, the dog would probably attack before he did.

Then he used oak staves to lever a cage base up, with flat stones as blocks, and eased his makeshift wagon beneath. The doe inside was heavy with young. Most likely, she would retreat far from him before bearing her fawns, and he knew what to do with the tuneable grav polarizer below that cage. Soon the clear plastic container sat gleaming in the sun, and Locklear poked hard at the base before retreating to the cave mouth.

As on Kzersatz, the container levered up, the red doe sank to the cage base, and the base slid forward. A moment later the creature moved, stood with lovely slender limbs shaking, and then saw him waving an oak stave. She reached grassy turf in one graceful bound and sped off with leaps he watched in admiration. Then, feeling somehow more lonely as the doe vanished, he sighed and disconnected the plastic container, then set about taking the entire cage to pieces. Already experienced with these gadgets, he would need at least two of the grav polarizer units before he could move stasized specimens outside with ease.

Disconnected from the stasis unit, a polarizer toroid with its power source and wiring could be tuned to lift varied loads; for example, a container housing a school of fish. The main thing was to avoid tipping it, which Locklear managed by wiring the polarizer securely to the underside of his wheeled carriage. Another hour saw him tugging his burden to the air lock, where he wrestled that entire, still-functioning cageful of fish inside. The fish, he saw, had sucking mouths meant for bottom-feeding on vegetable trash. They looked rather like carp or tilapia. Raising the lifeboat with great care, he eased toward the big lake some miles distant. It was no great trick to dump the squirming mass of life from the air lock port into the lake from a height of two meters, and then he celebrated by landing near the first laden fig tree he saw. Munching and lazing in the sun, he decided that his fortunes were looking up. But then, Locklear had been wrong before . . .

He knew that his next steps must be planned carefully. Before hiding the kzin craft away he must duplicate the airboat he had built on Kzersatz. After an exhaustive search—meanwhile mapping Newduvai's major features—he felled and stripped slender pines, hauling them in the lifeboat to his favorite spot near the small mountain lake. By now he had found a temporary spot in a barren cleft near frostline to hide the lifeboat itself, and began by stripping off its medium-caliber beam weapons from extension struts. The strut skins were attached by long screws, which Locklear saved. The weapon wiring came in handy, too, as he began fitting the raftlike platform of his airboat together. When he realized that the lifeboat's slings and emergency seats could be stripped for a fabric sail, he began to feel a familiar excitement.

This airboat was larger than his first, with its single sail and swiveling double-pole keel for balance. With wires for rigging, he could hunker down just behind the mast and operate the gravity control vernier through a slot in the flat deck. He could carry over two hundred kilos of ballast, the mass of a stasis cage with a human specimen inside, far from the crypt before setting that specimen free. "I'll have to carry the cage back, of course. Who knows what trouble a savage might create, fiddling with a stasis cage?" He snorted at himself;

he'd almost said "monkeying," and it was dangerous to assume he was smarter than these ancient people. But wasn't he, really? If Neanderthalers had died out on Earth, they must have been inferior in some way. Well, he was sure as hell going to find out.

If his new airboat was larger than the first, it was also more unwieldy. He used it to ferry logs to his cabin site at the small lake, cursing his need to tack in the light breezes, wishing he had a better propulsion system, for over a week before the solution hit him.

At the time he was debating the release of more animals. The mammoths, he promised himself, would come last. No wonder the builders of Newduvai had left them nearest the crypt entrance! Their cage tops would each make a dandy greenhouse and their grav polarizers would lift tons. *Or push tons.*

"Some things don't change," he told himself, laughing aloud. "I was dumb on Kzersatz and I've been dumb here." So he released the hares, gerbils, grouse and some other species of bird with beaks meant for crunching seeds. He promptly installed their grav units around his airboat seat for propulsion, removing the mast and keel poles for reuse as cabin roof beams. That was the day Locklear nearly killed himself caroming off the lake's surface at sixty miles an hour, whooping like a fool. Now the homemade craft was no longer a boat; it was a scooter, and would scoot with an extra fifty kilos of cargo.

It might have been elation with the sporty performance of his scooter that made him so optimistic, failing to remember that you have to kill pessimists, but optimists do it themselves. The log cabin, five meters square with fireplace and frond-thatched shed roof, needed only a pallet of sling fabric and fragrant boughs beneath. A *big* pallet, he decided. It had been Kit who taught him that he should have food and shelter ready before waking strangers in strange lands. He had figs and apricot slices drying, kzin rations for the strong of tooth, and kzin-sized drinking vessels from the lifeboat. He moved a few more items, including a clever kzin memory pad with electronic stylus and screen, from lifeboat to cabin, then attached a ten-meter cable harness from the scooter to the lifeboat's overhead weapon pylon.

It was only necessary then to set the scooter's bottom grav unit to slight buoyancy, and to pilot the kzin lifeboat very slowly, towing the scooter.

The cleft where he landed had become a soggy meadow from icemelt near the frostline high on Newduvai's perimeter, protected on one side by the towering force wall and on the other by jagged basalt. The lifeboat could not be seen from below, and if his first aerial visitors were kzinti, they'd have to fly dangerously near that force wall before they saw it. He sealed the lifeboat and then hauled the scooter down hand over hand, puffing with exertion, letting the scooter bounce harmlessly off the lifeboat's hull as he clambered aboard. Then he cast off and twiddled with those grav unit verniers until the wind whistled in his ears en route to the stasis crypt. He was already expert at modifying stasis units, and he would have lots of them to play with. If he had to protect himself from a wild woman, he could hardly wish for anything better.

He trundled the crystal cage into sunlight still wondering if he'd chosen the right—specimen? Subject? "Woman, dammit; woman!" He was trying to wear too many hats, he knew, with the one labeled "lecher" perched on top. He landed the scooter near his cabin, placed bowls of fruit and water nearby, and pressed the cage baseplate, retreating beyond his offerings.

She sank to the cage floor but only shifted position, still asleep, the breeze moving strands of chestnut hair at her cheeks. She was small and muscular, her breasts firm and immature, pubic hair sparse, limbs slender and marked with scratches; and yes, he realized as he moved nearer, she had a forty-thousand-year-old zit on her little chin. Easily the best-looking choice in the crypt, not yet fully developed into the Neanderthal body shape, she seemed capable of sleep in any position and was snoring lightly to prove it.

A genuine teen-ager, he mused, grinning. Aloud he said, "Okay, Lolita, up and at 'em." She stirred; a hand reached up as if tugging at an invisible blanket. "You'll miss the school shuttle," he said louder. It had never failed back on Earth with his sister.

It didn't fail here, either. She waked slowly, blinking as she sat up in lithe, nude, heartbreaking innocence. But her yawn snapped in two as she focused on him, and her pantomime of snatching a stone and hurling it at Locklear was convincing enough to make him duck. She leaped away scrabbling for real stones, and between her screams and her clods, all in Locklear's direction, she seemed to be trying to cover herself.

He retreated, but not far enough, and grabbed a chunk of

dirt only after taking one clod on his thigh. He threatened a toss of his own, whereupon she ducked behind the cage, watching him warily.

Well, it wouldn't matter what he said, so long as he said it calmly. His tone and gestures would have to serve. "You're a real little shit before breakfast, Lolita," he said, smiling, tossing his clod gently toward the bowls.

She saw the food then, frowning. His open hands and strained smile invited her to the food, and she moved toward it still holding clods ready. Wolfing plums, she paused to gape as he pulled a plum from a pocket and began to eat. "Never seen pockets, hm? Stick around, little girl, I'll show you lots of interesting things." The humor didn't work, even on himself; and at his first step toward her she ran like a deer.

Every time he pointed to himself and said his name, she screamed something brief. She moved around the area, checking out the cabin, draping a vine over her breasts, and after an hour Locklear gave up. He'd made a latchcord for the cabin door, so she couldn't do much harm. She watched from fifty meters distance with great wondering brown eyes as he waved, lifted the scooter, and sped away with her cage and a new idea.

An hour later he returned with a second cage, cursing as he saw Lolita trying to smash his cabin window with an oak stave. The clear plastic, of cage material, was tough stuff and he laughed as the scooter settled nearby, pretending he didn't itch to whack her rump. She began a litany of stone-age curses, then, as she saw the new cage and its occupant. Locklear actually had to mount the scooter and chase her off before she would quit pelting him with anything she could throw.

He made the same preparations as before, this time with shreds of smelly kzin rations as well, and stood leaning against the cage for long moments, facing Lolita, who lurked fifty meters away, to make his point. The young woman revolving slowly inside the cage was at his mercy. Then he pressed the baseplate, turned his back as the plastic levered upward, and strode off a few paces with a sigh. This one was a Neanderthal and no mistake: curves a little too broad to be exciting, massive forearms and calves, pug nose, considerable body hair. *Nice tits, though. Stop it, fool!*

The young woman stirred, sat up, looked around, then let her big jaw drop comically as she stared at Locklear, whose smile was a very rickety construction. She cocked her head at him, impassive, an instant before he spoke.

"You're no beauty, lady, so maybe you won't throw rocks at *me.* Too late for breakfast," he continued in his sweetest tones and a pointing finger. "How about lunch?"

She saw the bowls. Slowly, with caution and surprising grace, she stepped from the scooter's deck still eyeing him without smile or frown. Then she squatted to inspect the food, knees apart, facing him, and Locklear grew faint at the sight. He looked away quickly, flushing, aware that she continued to stare at him while sampling human and kzin rations with big strong teeth and wrinklings of her nose that made her oddly attractive. *More attractive. Why the hell doesn't she cover up or something?*

He pulled another plum from a pocket, and this magic drew a smile from her as they ate. He realized she was through eating when she wiped sticky fingers in her straight black hair, and stepped back by reflex as she stepped toward him. She stopped, with a puzzled inclination of her head, and smiled at him. That was when he stood his ground and let her approach. He had hoped for something like this, so the watching Lolita could see that he meant no harm.

When the woman stood within arm's length of him she stopped. He put a hand on his breast. "Me Locklear, you Jane," he said.

"(Something,)" she said. Maybe *Kh-roofeh.*

He was going to try saying it himself when she startled him into a wave of actual physical weakness. With eyes half-closed, she cupped her full breasts in both hands and smiled. He looked at her erect nipples, feeling the rush of blood to his face, and showed her his hands in a broad helpless shrug. Whereupon, she took his hands and placed them on her breasts, and now her big black eyes were not those of a savage Neanderthal but a sultry smiling Levantine woman who knew how to make a point. Two points.

Three points, as he felt a rising response and knew her hands were seeking that rise, hands that had never known velcrolok closures yet seemed to have an intelligence of their own. His whole body was tingling now as he caressed her, and when her hands found that fabric closure, she shared a fresh smile with him, and tried to pull him down on the ground with her.

So he took her hands in his and walked her to the cabin.

She "hmm"ed when he pulled the latchcord loop to open the door, and "ahh"ed when she saw the big pallet, and then offered those swarthy full breasts again and put her face against the hollow of his throat, and toyed inside his velcrolok closure until he astonished her by pulling his entire flight suit off, and offered her body in ways simple and sophisticated, and Locklear accepted all the offers he could, and made a few of his own, all of which she accepted expertly.

He had his first sensation of something eerie, something just below his awareness, as he lay inert on his back bathed in honest sweat, his partner lying facedown more or less across him like one stick abandoned across another stick after both had been rubbed to kindle a blaze. He saw a movement at his window and knew it was Lolita, peering silently in. He sighed.

His partner sighed too, and turned toward the window with a quick, vexed burst of some command. The face disappeared.

He chuckled, "Did you hear the little devil, or smell her?" Actually, his partner had more of the *eau de sweatsock* perfume than Lolita did; now more pronounced than ever. He didn't care. If the past half-hour had been any omen, he might never care again.

She stretched then, and sat up, dragging a heel that was rough as a rasp across his calf. Her heavy ragged nails had scratched him, and he was oily from God knew what mixture of greases in her long hair. He didn't give a damn about that either, reflecting that a man should allow a few squeaks in the hinges of the pearly gates.

She said something then, softly, with that tilt of her head that suggested inquiry. "Locklear," he replied, tapping his chest again.

Her look was somehow pitying then, as she repeated her phrase, placing one hand on her head, the other on his.

"Oh yeah, you're my girl and I'm your guy," he said, nodding, placing his hands on hers.

She sat quite still for a moment, her eyes sad on his. Then, delighting him, she placed one hand on his breast and managed a passable, "Loch-leah."

He grinned and nodded, then cocked his head and placed a hand between her (wonderful!) breasts. No homecoming queen, but dynamite in deep shadows . . .

He paid more attention as she said, approximately, "Ch'roof'h," and when he repeated it she laughed, closing her eyes with downcast chin. *A big chin, a really whopping big one to be honest about it,* and then he caught her gaze, not angry but perhaps reproachful, and again he felt the passage of something like a cold breeze through his awareness.

She rubbed his gooseflesh down for him, responding to his "ahh"s, and presently she astonished him again by beginning to query him on the names of things. Locklear knew that he could thoroughly confuse her if he insisted on perfectly grammatical tenses, cases, and syntax. He tried to keep it simple, and soon learned that "head down, eyes shut" was the same as a negative headshake. "Chin elevated, smiling" was the same as a nod—and now he realized he'd seen her giving him yesses that way from the first moment she awoke. A smile or a frown was the same for her as for him—but that heads-up smile was a definite gesture.

She drew him outside again presently, studying the terrain with lively curiosity, miming actions and listening as he provided words, responding with words of her own.

The name he gave her was, in part, because it was faintly like the one she'd offered; and in part because she seemed willing to learn his ways while revealing ancient ways of her own. He named her "Ruth." Locklear felt crestfallen when, by midafternoon, he realized Ruth was learning his language much faster than he was learning hers. And then, as he glanced over her shoulder to see little Lolita creeping nearer, he began to understand why.

Ruth turned quickly, with a shouted command and warning gestures, and Lolita dropped the sharpened stick she'd been carrying. Locklear knew beyond doubt that Lolita had made no sound in her approach. There was only one explanation that would fit all his data: Ruth unafraid of him from the first; offering herself as if she knew his desires; keeping track of Lolita without looking; and her uncanny speed in learning his language.

And that moment when she'd placed her hand on his head, with an inquiry that was somehow pitying. Now he copied her gesture with one hand on his own head, the other on hers, and lowered his head, eyes shut. "No," he said. "Locklear, no telepath. Ruth, yes?"

"Ruth, yes." She pointed to Lolita then. "No—telpat."

She needed another ten minutes of pantomime, attending to his words and obviously to his thoughts as he spoke them, to get her point across. Ruth was a "gentle," but like Locklear himself, Lolita was a "new."

—∾— —∾— —∾—

When darkness came to Newduvai, Lolita got chummier in a hurry, complaining until Ruth let her into the cabin. Despite that, Ruth didn't seem to like the girl much and accepted Locklear's name for her, shortening it to "Loli." Ruth spoke to her in their common tongue, not so much guttural as throaty, and Locklear had a strong impression that they were old acquaintances. Either of them could tend a fire expertly, and both were wary of the light from his kzin memory screen until they found that it would not singe a curious finger.

Locklear was bothered on two counts by Loli's insistence on taking pieces of kzin plastic film to make a bikini suit: first because Ruth plainly thought it silly, and second because the kid was more appealing with it than she was when stark naked. At least the job kept Loli silently occupied, listening and watching as Locklear got on with the business of talking with Ruth.

Their major breakthrough for the evening came when Locklear got the ideas of past and future, "before" and "soon," across to Ruth. Her telepathy was evidently the key to her quick grasp of his language; yet it seemed to work better with emotional states than with abstract ideas, and she grew upset when Loli became angry with her own first clumsy efforts at making her panties fit. Clearly, Ruth was a lady who liked her harmony.

For Ruth was, despite her rude looks, a lady—when she wasn't in the sack. Even so, when at last Ruth had seen to Loli's comfort with spare fabric and Locklear snapped off the light, he felt inviting hands on him again. "No thanks," he said, chuckling, patting her shoulder, even though he wanted her again. And Ruth *knew* he did, judging from her sly insistence.

"No. Loli here," he said finally, and felt Ruth shrug as if to say it didn't matter. Maybe it didn't matter to Neanderthals, but—"Soon," he promised, and shared a hug with Ruth before they fell asleep.

During the ensuing week, he learned much. For one thing, he learned that Loli was a chronic pain in the backside. She ate like a kzin warrior. She liked to see if things would break. She liked to spy. She interfered with Locklear's pace during his afternoon "naps" with Ruth by whacking on the door with sticks and stones, until he swore he would " . . . hit Loli soon."

But Ruth would not hear of that. "Hit Loli, same hit Ruth head. Locklear like hit Ruth head?"

But one afternoon, when she saw Locklear studying her with friendly intensity, Ruth spoke to Loli at some length. The girl picked up her short spear and, crooning her happiness, loped off into the forest. Ruth turned to Locklear smiling. "Loli find fruitwater, soon Ruth make fruitfood." A few minutes of miming showed that she had promised to make some kind of dessert, if Loli could find a beehive for honey.

Locklear had seen beehives in stasis, but explained that there were very few animals loose on Newduvai, and no hurtbugs.

"No hurtbugs? Loli no find, long time. Good," Ruth replied firmly, and led him by the hand into their cabin, and "good" was the operative word.

On his next trip to the crypt, Locklear needed all day for his solitary work. He might put it off forever, but it was clear by now that he must populate Newduvai with game before he released their most fearsome predators. The little horses needed only to see daylight before galloping off. Camels were quicker still, and the deer bounded off like golf balls down a freeway. The predators would simply have to wait until the herds were larger, and the day was over before he could rig grav polarizers to trundle mammoths to the mouth of the crypt. His last job of the day was his most troublesome, releasing small cages of bees near groves of fruit trees and wildflowers.

Locklear and Ruth managed to convey a lot with only a few hundred words, though some of those words had to do multiple duty while Ruth expanded her vocabulary. When she said "new," for example, it often carried a stigma. Neanderthals, he decided, were very conservative folk, and they sensed a lie before you told it. If Ruth was any measure, they also had little aptitude for math. She understood one and two and many. She understood "none," but not as a number. If there wasn't any, she conveyed to him, why try to count it? She had him there.

Eventually, between food-gathering forays, he used pebbles and sketches to tell Ruth of the many, many other animals and people he could bring to the scene. She was no sketch artist; in fact, she insisted, women were not supposed to draw things—especially huntthings. Ah, he said, magics were only for men? Yes, she said, then mystified him with pantomimes of sleep and pain. That was for men, too, and food-gathering was for women.

He pursued the mystery, sketching with the kzin memo

screen. At last, when she pretended to cut her throat with his *wtsai* knife, he understood, and added the word "kill" to her vocabulary. Men hunted and killed.

Dry-mouthed, he asked, "Man like kill Locklear?"

Now it was her turn to be mystified. "No kill. Why kill magic man?"

Because, he replied, "Locklear like Ruth, one-two other man like Ruth. Kill Locklear for Ruth?"

He had never seen her laugh aloud, but he saw it now, the big teeth gleaming, breasts shaking with merriment. "Locklear like Ruth, good. Many man like Ruth, good."

He was silent for a long time, fighting the temptation to tell her that many men liking Ruth was *not* good. Then: "Ruth like many man?"

She had learned to nod by now, and did it happily.

The next five minutes were troubled ones for Locklear. Ruth did not seem to understand monogamy in any form. Apparently, everybody took potluck in the sex department and was free to accept or reject. Some people were simply more popular than others. "Many man like Ruth," she said. "Many, many, many . . ."

"Okay, for Christ's sake, I get the idea," he exploded, and again he saw that look of sadness—or perhaps pain. "Locklear see, Ruth popular with man."

It seemed to be their first quarrel. Tentatively, she said, "Locklear popular with woman."

"No. Little popular with woman."

"Much popular with Ruth," she said, and began to rub his shoulders. That was the day she asked him about her appearance, and he responded the best way he could. She thought it silly to trim her strong, useful nails; sillier to wash her hair. Still, she did it, and he claimed she was pretty, and she knew he lied.

When it occurred to him to ask how he could look nice for her, Ruth said, "Locklear pretty now." But he never thought to wonder if *she* might be lying.

Whatever Ruth said about women and hunting, it did not seem to apply to Loli. While aloft in the scooter one day to study distribution of the animals, Locklear saw the girl chasing a hare across a meadow. She was no slouch with a short spear and nailed the hare on her second toss, dispatching it with a stone after a brief struggle. He lowered the scooter very, very slowly, watching her tear at the animal, disgusted when he realized she was eating it raw.

She saw his shadow when the scooter was hovering very near, and sat there blushing, looking at him with the innards of the hare across her lap.

She understood few of his words—or seemed to, at the cabin—but his tone was clear enough. "You couldn't share it, you little bastard. No, you sneak out here and stuff yourself." She began to suck her thumb, pouting. Then perhaps Loli realized the boss must be placated; she tried a smile on her blood-streaked face and held her grisly trophy out.

"No. Ruth. Give to Ruth," he scowled, pointing toward the cabin. She elevated her chin and smiled, and he flew off grumbling. He couldn't much blame the kid; kzin rations and fruit were getting pretty tiresome, and the gruel Ruth made from grain wasn't all that exciting without bits of meat. It was going to be rougher on the animals when he woke the men.

And why wake them at all? You've got it good here, he reminded himself in Sequence Umpteen of his private dialogue. *You have your own little world and a harem of one, and you know when her period comes so you know when not to play. And one of these days, Loli will be a knockout, 1 suspect. A much niftier dish than poor Ruth, who doesn't know what a skag she'd be in modern society, thank God.*

Moments like this made him squirm. Setting Ruth's looks aside, he had no complaint, not even about the country itself. *Not much seasonal change, no dangerous animals unless you want to release them, certainly none of the most dangerous animal of all.* Except for kzinti, of course. One on one, they were meaner predators than men—even Neanderthal savages.

"That's why I have to release 'em," he said to the wind. "If a fully-manned kzin ship comes, I'll need an army." He no longer kidded himself about scholarship and the sociology of *homo neanderthalensis,* which was strictly a secondary item. It was sobering to look yourself over and see self-interest riding you like a hunchback. So he flew directly to the crypt and spent the balance of the day releasing the whoppers: aurochs and bison, which didn't make him sweat much, and a half-dozen mammoths, which did.

A mammoth, he found, was a flighty beast not given to confrontations. He could set one shambling off with a shout, its trunk high like a periscope tasting the breeze. Every one of them turned into the wind and disappeared toward the frostline, and now the crypt held only its most dangerous creatures.

He returned to the cabin perilously late, the sun of Newduvai dying while he was still a hundred meters from the wisp of smoke rising from the cabin. He landed blind near the cabin, very slowly but with a jolt, and saw the faint gleam of the kzin light leap from the cabin window. Ruth might not have a head for figures, but she'd seen him snap that light on fifty times. *And she must've sensed my panic. I wonder how far off she can do that. . . .*

Ruth already had succulent broiled haunches of Loli's hare, keeping them warm over coals, and it wrenched his heart as he saw she was drooling as she waited for him. He wiped the corner of her mouth, kissed her anyhow, and sat at the rough pole table while she brought his supper. Loli had obviously eaten, and watched him as if fearful that he would order her outside.

Hauling mammoths, even with a grav polarizer, is exhausting work. After finishing off a leg of hare, and falling asleep at the table, Locklear was only half-aware when Ruth picked him up and carried him to their pallet as easily as she would have carried a child.

The next day, he had Ruth convey to Loli that she was not to hunt without permission. Then, with less difficulty than he'd expected, he sketched and quizzed her about the food of a Neanderthal tribe. Yes, they hunted everything: bugs to mammoths, it was all protein; but chiefly they gathered roots, grains, and fruits.

That made sense. Why risk getting killed hunting when tubers didn't fight back? He posed his big question then. If he brought a tribe to Newduvai (this brought a smile of anticipation to her broad face), and forbade them to hunt without his permission, would they obey?

Gentles might, she said. New people, such as Loli, were less obedient. She tried to explain why, conveying something about telepathy and hunting, until he waved the question aside. If he showed her sleeping gentles, would she tell him which ones were good? Oh yes, she said, adding a phrase she knew he liked: "No problem."

But it took him an hour to get Ruth on the scooter. That stuff was all very well for great magic men, she implied, but women's magics were more prosaic. After a few minutes idling just above the turf, he sped up, and she liked that fine. Then he slowed and lifted the scooter a bit. By noon, he was cruising fast as they surveyed groups of aurochs, solitary gazelles, and skittish horses from high above. It was she, sampling the wind with her nose, who directed him higher and then pointed out a mammoth, a huge specimen using its tusks to find roots.

He watched the huge animal briefly, estimating how many square miles a mammoth needed to feed, and then made a decision that saddened him. Earth had kept right on turning when the last mammoths disappeared. Newduvai could not afford many of them, ripping up foliage by the roots. Perhaps the Outsiders didn't care about that, but Locklear did. If you had to start sawing off links in your food chain, best if you started at the top. And he didn't want to pursue that thought by himself. At the very top was man. And kzin. It was the kind of thing he'd like to discuss with Scarface, but he'd made two trips to the lifeboat without a peep from its all-band comm set.

Finally, he flew to the crypt and set his little craft down nearby, reassuring Ruth as they walked inside. She paused for flight when she saw the rest of the mammoths, slowly tumbling inside their cages. "Much, much, much magic," she said, and patted him with great confidence.

But it was the sight of forty Neanderthals in stasis that really affected Ruth. Her face twisted with remorse, she turned from the nearest cage and faced Locklear with tears streaming down her cheeks. "Locklear kill?"

"No, no! Sleep," he insisted, miming it.

She was not convinced. "No sleeptalk," she protested, placing a hand on her head and pointing toward the rugged male nearby. And doubtless she was right; in stasis you didn't even dream.

"Before, Locklear take Ruth from little house," he said, tapping the cage, and then she remembered, and wanted to take the man out then and there. Instead, he got her help in moving the cage onto his improvised dolly and outside to the scooter.

They were halfway to the cabin and a thousand feet up on the heavily-laden scooter when Ruth somehow struck the cage base with her foot. Locklear saw the transparent plastic begin to rise, shouted, and nearly turned the scooter on its side as he leaped to slam the plastic down.

"Good God! You nearly let a wild man loose on a goddamn

raft, a thousand feet in the air," he raged, and saw her cringe, holding her head in both hands. "Okay, Ruth. Okay, no problem," he continued more slowly, and pointed at the cage base. "Ruth no hit little house more. Locklear hit, soon."

They remained silent until they landed, and Locklear had time to review Newduvai's first in-flight airline emergency. Ruth had not feared a beating. No, it was his own panic that had punished her. That figured: a kzin telepath sometimes suffered when someone nearby was suffering.

He brought food and water from the cabin, placed it near the scooter, then paused before pressing the cage base. "Ruth: gentle man talk in head same Ruth talk in head?"

"Yes, all gentles talk in head." She saw what he was getting at. "Ruth talk to man, say Locklear much, much good magic man."

He pointed again at the man, a muscular young specimen who, without so much body hair, might have excited little comment at a collegiate wrestling match. "Ruth friend of man?"

She blushed as she replied: "Yes. Friend long time."

"That's what I was afraid of," he muttered with a heavy sigh, pressed the baseplate, and then stepped back several paces, nearly bumping into the curious Loli.

The man's eyes flicked open. Locklear could see the heavy muscles tense, yet the man moved only his eyes, looking from him to Ruth, then to him again. When he did move, it was as though he'd been playing possum for forty thousand years, and his movements were as oddly graceful as Ruth's. He held up both hands, smiling, and it was obvious that some silent message had passed between them.

Locklear advanced with the same posture. A flat touch of hands, and then the man turned to Ruth with a burst of throaty speech. He was no taller than Locklear, but immensely more heavily boned and muscled. He stood as erect as any man, unconcerned in his nakedness, and after a double handclasp with Ruth he made a smiling motion toward her breasts.

Again, Locklear saw the deeper color of flushing over her face and, after a head-down gesture of negation, she said something while staring at the young man's face. Puzzled, he glanced at Locklear with a comical half-smile, and Locklear tried to avoid looking at the man's budding erection. He told the man his name, and got a reply, but as usual Locklear gave him a name that seemed appropriate. He called him "Minuteman."

After a quick meal of fruit and water, Ruth did the translating. From the first, Minuteman accepted the fact that Locklear was one of the "new" people. After Locklear's demonstrations with the kzin memo screen and a levitation of the scooter, Minuteman gave him more physical space, perhaps a sign of deference. Or perhaps wariness; time would tell.

Though Loli showed no fear of Minuteman, she spoke little to him and kept her distance—with an egg-sized stone in her little fist at all times. Minuteman treated Loli as a guest might treat an unwelcome pet. *Oh yes,* thought Locklear, *he knows her, all righty. . . .*

The hunt, Locklear claimed, was a celebration to welcome Minuteman, but he had an ulterior motive. He made his point to Ruth, who chattered and gestured and, no doubt, silently communed with Minuteman for long moments. It would be necessary for Minuteman to accompany Locklear on the scooter, but without Ruth if they were to lug any sizeable game back to the cabin.

When Ruth stopped, Minuteman said something more. "Yes, no problem," Ruth said then.

Minuteman, his facial scars writhing as he grinned, managed, "Yef, no pobbem," and laughed when Locklear did. *Amazing how fast these people adapt,* Locklear thought. *He wakes up on a strange planet, and an hour later he's right at home. A wonderful trusting kind of innocence; even childlike.* Then Locklear decided to see just how far that trust went, and gestured for Minuteman to sit down on the scooter after he wrestled the empty stasis cage to the ground.

Soon they were scudding along just above the trees at a pace guaranteed to scare the hell out of any sensible Neanderthal, Minuteman desperately trying to make a show of confidence in the leadership of this suicidal shaman, and Locklear was satisfied on two counts, with one count yet to come. First, the scooter's pace near trees was enough to make Minuteman hold on for dear life. Second, the young Neanderthal would view Locklear's easy mastery of the scooter as perhaps the very greatest of magics—and maybe Minuteman would pass that datum on, when the time came.

The third item was a shame, really, but it had to be done. A shaman without the power of ultimate punishment might be seen as expendable, and Locklear had to show that power. He showed it after passing over specimens of aurochs and horse, both noted with delight by Minuteman.

The goat had been grazing not far from three does until he saw the scooter swoop near. He was an old codger, probably driven off by the younger buck nearby, and Locklear recalled that the gestation period for goats was only five months—and besides, he told himself the Outsiders could be pretty dumb in some matters. You didn't need twenty bucks for twenty does.

All of the animals bounded toward a rocky slope, and Minuteman watched them as Locklear maneuvered, forcing the old buck to turn back time and again. When at last the buck turned to face them, Locklear brought the scooter down, moving straight toward the hapless old fellow. Minuteman did not turn toward Locklear until he heard the report of the kzin sidearm which Locklear held in both hands, and by that time the scooter was only a man's height above the rocks.

At the report, the buck slammed backward, stumbling, shot in the breast. Minuteman ducked away from the sound of the shot, seeing Locklear with the sidearm, and then began to shout. Locklear let the scooter settle but Minuteman did not wait, leaping down, rushing at the old buck, which still kicked in its death agony.

By the time Locklear had the scooter resting on the slope, Minuteman was tearing at the buck's throat with his teeth, trying to dodge flinty hooves, the powerful arms locked around his prey. In thirty seconds the buck's eyes were glazing and its movements grew more feeble by the moment. Locklear put away the sidearm, feeling his stomach churn. Minuteman was drinking the animal's blood; sucking it, in fact, in a kind of frenzy.

When at last he sat up, Minuteman began to massage his temples with bloody fingers—perhaps a ritual, Locklear decided. The young Neanderthal's gaze at Locklear was not pleasant, though he was suitably impressed by the invisible spear that had noisily smashed a man-sized goat off its feet leaving nothing more than a tiny hole in the animal's breast. Locklear went through a pantomime of shooting, and Minuteman gestured his "yes." Together, they placed the heavy carcass on the scooter and returned to the cabin. Minuteman seemed oddly subdued for a hunter who had just chewed a victim's throat open.

Locklear guffawed at what he saw at the cabin: in the cage so recently vacated by Minuteman was Loli, revolving in the slow dance of stasis. Ruth explained, "Loli like little house, like sleep. Ruth like for Loli sleep. Many like for Loli sleep long time," she added darkly.

It was Ruth who butchered the animal with the *wtsai,* while talking with Minuteman. Locklear watched smugly, noting the absence of flies. Damned if he was going to release those from their cages, nor the mosquitoes, locusts and other pests which lay with the predators in the crypt. Why would any god worth his salt pester a planet with flies, anyhow? The butterflies might be worth the trouble.

He was still ruminating on these matters when Ruth handed him the *wtsai* and entered the cabin silently. She seemed preoccupied, and Minuteman had wandered off toward the oaks so, just to be sociable, he said, "Minuteman see Locklear kill with magic. Minuteman like?"

She built a smoky fire, stretching skewers of stringy meat above the smoke, before answering. "No good, talk bad to magic man."

"It's okay, Ruth. Talk true to Locklear."

She propped the cabin door open to adjust the draft, then sat down beside him. "Minuteman feel bad. Locklear no kill meat fast, meat hurt long time. Meat feel much, much bad, so Minuteman feel much bad before kill meat. Locklear new person, no feel bad. Loli no feel bad. Minuteman no want hunt with Locklear."

As she attended to the barbecue and Locklear continued to ferret out more of this mystery, he grew more chastened. Neanderthal boys, learning to kill for food, began with animals that did not have a highly developed nervous system. Because when the animal felt pain, all the gentles nearby felt some of it too, especially women and girls. Neanderthal hunt teams were all-male affairs, and they learned every trick of stealth and quick kills because a clumsy kill meant a slow one. Minuteman had known that, lacking a club, he himself would feel the least pain if the goat bled to death quickly.

And large animals? You dug pit traps and visited them from a distance, or drove your prey off a distant cliff if you could. Neanderthal telepathy did not work much beyond twenty meters. The hunter who approached a wounded animal to pierce its throat with a spear was very brave, or very hungry. Or he was one of the new people, perfectly capable of irritating or even fighting a gentle without feeling the slightest psychic pain. The gentle Neanderthal, of course, was not protected against the new person's reflected pain. No wonder Ruth took care of Loli without liking her much!

He asked if Loli was the first "new" Ruth had seen. No, she said, but the only one they had allowed in the tribe. A hunt team had found her wandering alone, terrified and hungry, when she was only as high as a man's leg. Why hadn't the hunters run away? They had, Ruth said, but even then Loli had been quick on her feet. Rather than feel her gnawing fear and hunger on the perimeter of their camp, they had taken her in. And had regretted it ever since, ". . . long time. Long, long, long time!"

Locklear knew that he had gained a crucial insight; a Neanderthal behaved gently because it was in his own best interests. It was, at least, until modern Cro-Magnon man appeared without the blessing, and the curse, of telepathy.

Ruth's first telepathic greeting to the waking Minuteman had warned that he was in the presence of a great shaman, a "new" but nonetheless a good man. Minuteman had been so glad to see Ruth that he had proposed a brief roll in the grass, which involved great pleasure to participants—and it was expected that the audience could share their joy by telepathy. But Ruth knew better than that, reminding her friend that Locklear was not telepathic. Besides, she had the strongest kind of intuition that Locklear did not want to see her enjoying any other man. Peculiar, even bizarre; but new people were hard to figure. . . .

It was clear now, why Ruth's word "new" seemed to have an unpleasant side. New people were savage people. *So much for labels,* Locklear told himself. *Modern man is the real savage!*

Ruth took Loli out of stasis for supper, perhaps to share in the girl's pleasure at such a feast. Through Ruth, Locklear explained to Minuteman that he regretted giving pain to his guest. He would be happy to let gentles do the hunting, but all animals belonged to Locklear. No animals must be hunted without prior permission. Minuteman was agreeable, especially with a mouthful of succulent goat rib in his big lantern jaws. Tonight, Minuteman could share the cabin. Tomorrow he must choose a site for a camp, for Locklear would soon bring many, many more gentles.

Locklear fell asleep slowly, no thanks to the ache in his jaws. The others had wolfed down that barbecued goat as if it had been well-aged porterhouse, but he had been able to choke only a little of it down after endless chewing because, savory taste or not, that old goat had been tough as a kzin's knuckles.

He wondered how Kit and Scarface were getting along, on the other side of those force walls. He really ought to fire up the lifeboat and visit them soon. Just as soon as he got things going here. With his mind-bending discovery of the truly gentle nature of Neanderthals, he was feeling very optimistic about the future. And modestly hungry. And very, very sleepy.

Minuteman spent two days quartering the vast circular expanse of Newduvai while Locklear piloted the Scooter. In the process, he picked up a smatter of modern words though it was Ruth, in the evenings, who straightened out misunderstandings. Minuteman's clear choice for a major encampment was beside Newduvai's big lake, near the point where a stream joined the "big water." The site was a day's walk from the cabin, and Minuteman stressed that his choice might not be the choice of tribal elders. Besides, gentles tended to wander from season to season.

Though tempted by his power to command, Locklear decided against using it unless absolutely necessary. He would release them all and let them sort out their world, with the exception of excess hunting or tribal warfare. That didn't seem likely, but: "Ruth," he asked after the second day of recon, "see all people in little houses in cave?"

"Yes," she said firmly. "Many many in tribe of Minuteman and Ruth. Many many in other tribe."

But "many many" could mean a dozen or less. "Ruth see all in other tribe before?"

"Many times," she assured him. "Others give killstones, Ruth tribe give food."

"You trade with them," he said. After she had studied his face a moment, she agreed. He persisted: "Bad trades? Problem?"

"No problem," she said. "Trade one, two man or woman sometime, before big fire."

He asked about that, of course, and got an answer to a question he hadn't thought to ask. Ruth's last memory before waking on Newduvai—and Minuteman's too—was of the great fire that had driven several tribes to the base of a cliff. There, with trees bursting into flame nearby, the men had gathered around their women and children, beginning their song to welcome death. It was at that moment when the Outsiders must have put them in stasis and whisked them off to the rim of Known Space.

Almost an ethical decision, Locklear admitted. *Almost.* "No little gentles in cave," he reminded Ruth. "Locklear much sorry."

"No good, think of little gentles," she said glumly. And with that, they passed to matters of tribal leadership. The old men generally led, though an old woman might have followers. It seemed a loose kind of democracy and, when some faction disagreed, they could simply move out—perhaps no farther than a short walk away.

Locklear soon learned why the gentles tended to stay close: "Big, bad animals eat gentles," Ruth said. "New people take food, kill gentles," she added. Lions, wolves, bears—and modern man—were their reasons for safety in numbers.

Ruth and Minuteman had both seen much of Newduvai from the air by now. To check his own conclusions, Locklear said, "Plenty food for many people. Plenty for many, many, many people?"

"Plenty," said Ruth, "for all people in little houses; no problem." Locklear ended the session on that note and Minuteman, perhaps with some silent urging from Ruth, chose to sleep outside.

Again, Locklear had a trouble getting to sleep, even after a half-hour of delightful tussle with the willing, homely, gentle Ruth. He could hardly wait for morning and his great social experiment.

His work would have gone much faster with Minuteman's muscular help, but Locklear wanted to share the crypt's secrets with as few as possible. The lake site was only fifteen minutes from the crypt by scooter, and there were no predators to attack a stasis cage, so Locklear transported the gentles by twos and left them in their cages, cursing his rotten time-management. It soon was obvious that the job would take two days and he'd set his heart on results now, now, now!

He was setting the scooter down near his cabin when Minuteman shot from the doorway, began to lope off, and then turned, approaching Locklear with the biggest, ugliest smile he could manage. He chattered away with all the innocence of a ferret in a birdhouse, his maleness in repose but rather large for that innocence. And wet.

Ruth waved from the cabin doorway.

"Right," Locklear snarled, too exhausted to let his anger kindle to white-hot fury. "Minuteman, I named you well. Your pants would be down, if you had any. Ahh, the hell with it."

Loli was asleep in her cage, and Minuteman found employment elsewhere as Locklear ate chopped goat, grapes, and gruel. He did not look at Ruth, even when she sat near him as he chewed.

Finally he walked to the pallet, looking from it to Ruth, shook his head and then lay down.

Ruth cocked her head in that way she had. "Like Ruth stay at fire?"

"I don't give a good shit. Yes, Ruth stay at fire. Good." Some perversity made him want her, but it was not as strong as his need for sleep. And rejecting her might be a kind of punishment, he thought sleepily. . . .

Late the next afternoon, Locklear completed his airlift and returned to the cabin. He could see Minuteman sitting disconsolate, chin in hands, at the edge of the clearing. Apparently, no one had seen fit to take Loli from stasis. He couldn't blame them much. Actually, he thought as he entered the cabin, he had no logical reason to blame them for anything. They enjoyed each other according to their own tradition, and he was out of step with it. *Damn right, and I don't know if I could ever get in step.*

He called Minuteman in. "Many, many gentles at big water," he said. "No big bad meat hurt gentles. Like see gentles now?" Minuteman wanted to very much. So did Ruth. He urged them onto the scooter and handed Ruth her woven basket full of dried apricots, giving both hindquarters of the goat to Minuteman without comment. Soon they were flitting above conifers and poplars, and then Ruth saw the dozens of cages glistening beside the lake.

"Gentles, gentles," she exclaimed, and began to weep. Locklear found himself angry at her pleasure, the anger of a wronged spouse, and set the scooter down abruptly some distance from the stasis cages.

Minuteman was off and running instantly. Ruth disembarked, turned, held a hand out. "Locklear like wake gentles? Ruth tell gentles, Locklear good, much good magics."

"Tell 'em anything you like," he barked, "after you screw 'em all!"

In the distance, Minuteman was capering around the cages,

shouting in glee. After a moment, Ruth said, "Ruth like go back with Locklear."

"The hell you will! No, Ruth like push-push with many gentles. Locklear no like." And he twisted a vernier hard, the scooter lifting quickly.

Plaintively, growing faint on the breeze: "Ruth hurt in head. Like Locklear much . . ." And whatever else she said was lost.

He returned to the hidden kzin lifeboat, hating the idea of the silent cabin, and monitored the comm set for hours. It availed him nothing, but its boring repetitions eventually put him to sleep.

For the next week, Locklear worked like a man demented. He used a stasis cage, as he had on Kzersatz, to store his remaining few hunks of smoked goat. He flew surveillance over the new encampment, so high that no one would spot him, which meant that he could see little of interest, beyond the fact that they were building huts of bundled grass and some dark substance, perhaps mud. The stasis cages lay in disarray; he must retrieve them soon.

It was pure luck that he spotted a half-dozen deer one morning, a half-day's walk from the encampment, running as though from a predator. Presently, hovering beyond big chestnut trees, he saw them: men, patiently herding their prey toward an arroyo. He grinned to himself and waited until a rise of ground would cover his maneuver. Then he swooped low behind the deer, swerving from side to side to group them, yelping and growling until he was hoarse. By that time, the deer had put a mile between themselves and their real pursuers.

No better time than now to get a few things straight. Locklear swept the scooter toward the encampment at a stately pace, circling twice, hearing thin shouts as the Neanderthals noted his approach. He watched them carefully, one hand checking his kzin sidearm. They might be gentle but a few already carried spears and they were, after all, experts at the quick kill. He let the scooter hover at knee height, a constant reminder of his great magics, and noted the stir he made as the scooter glided silently to a stop at the edge of the camp.

He saw Ruth and Minuteman emerge from one of the dozen beehive-shaped, grass-and-wattle huts. No, it wasn't Ruth; he admitted with chagrin that they all looked very much alike. The women paused first, and then he did spot Ruth, waving at him, a few steps nearer. The men moved nearer, falling silent now, laying their new spears and stone axes down as if by prearrangement. They stopped a few paces ahead of the women.

An older male, almost covered in curly gray hair, continued to advance using a spear—no, it was only a long walking staff—to aid him. He too stopped, with a glance over his shoulder, and then Locklear saw a bald old fellow with a withered leg hobbling past the younger men. Both of the oldsters advanced together then, full of years and dignity without a stitch of clothes. The gray man might have been sixty, with a little potbelly and knobby joints suggesting arthritis. The cripple was perhaps ten years younger but stringy and meatless, and his right thigh had been hideously smashed a long time before. His right leg was inches too short, and his left hip seemed disfigured from years of walking to compensate.

Locklear knew he needed Ruth now, but feared to risk violating some taboo so soon. "Locklear," he said, showing empty hands, then tapping his breast.

The two old men cocked their heads in a parody of Ruth's familiar gesture, then the curly one began to speak. Of course it was all gibberish, but the walking staff lay on the ground now and their hands were empty.

Wondering how much they would understand telepathically, Locklear spoke with enough volume for Ruth to hear. "Gentles hunt meat in hills," he said. "Locklear no like." He was not smiling.

The old men used brief phrases to each other, and then the crippled one turned toward the huts. Ruth began to walk forward, smiling wistfully at Locklear as she stopped next to the cripple.

She waited to hear a few words from each man, and then faced Locklear. "All one tribe now, two leaders," she said. "Skywater and Shortleg happy to see great shaman who save all from big fire. Ruth happy see Locklear too," she added softly.

He told her about the men hunting deer, and that it must stop; they must make do without meat for awhile. She translated. The old men conferred, and their gesture for "no" was the same as Ruth's. They replied through Ruth that young men had always hunted, and always would.

He told them that the animals were his, and they must not

take what belonged to another. The old men said they could see that he felt in his head the animals were his, but no one owned the great mother land, and no one could own her children. They felt much bad for him. He was a very, very great shaman, but not so good at telling gentles how to live.

With great care, having chosen the names Cloud and Gimp for the old fellows, he explained that if many animals were killed, soon there would be no more. One day when many little animals were born, he would let them hunt the older ones.

The gist of their reply was this: Locklear obviously thought he was right, but they were older and therefore wiser. And because they had never run out of game no matter how much they killed, they *never could* run out of game. If it hadn't already happened, it wouldn't ever happen.

Abruptly, Locklear motioned to Cloud and had Ruth translate: he could prove the scarcity of game if Cloud would ride the scooter as Ruth and Minuteman had ridden it.

Much silent discussion and some out loud. Then old Cloud climbed aboard and in a moment, the scooter was above the trees.

From a mile up, they could identify most of the game animals, especially herd beasts in open plains. There weren't many to see. "No babies at all," Locklear said, trying to make gestures for "small." "Cloud, gentles *must* wait until babies are born." The old fellow seemed to understand Locklear's thoughts well enough, and spoke a bit of gibberish, but his head gesture was a Neanderthal "no."

Locklear, furious now, used the verniers with abandon. The scooter fled across parched arroyo and broken hill, closer to the ground and now so fast that Locklear himself began to feel nervous. Old Cloud sensed his unease, grasping handholds with gnarled knuckles and hunkering down, and Locklear knew a savage elation. *Serve the old bastard right if I splattered him all over Newduvai.* And then he saw the old man staring at his eyes, and knew that the thought had been received.

"No, I won't do it," he said. But a part of him had wanted to; *still* wanted to out of sheer frustration. Cloud's face was a rigid mask of fear, big teeth showing, and Locklear slowed the scooter as he approached the encampment again.

Cloud did not wait for the vehicle to settle, but debarked as fast as painful old joints would permit and stood facing his followers without a sound.

After a moment, with dozens of Neanderthals staring in stunned silence, they all turned their backs, a wave of moans rising from every throat.

Ruth hesitated, but she too faced away from Locklear.

"Ruth! No hurt Cloud. Locklear no like hurt gentles."

The moans continued as Cloud strode away. "Locklear need to talk to Ruth!" And then as the entire tribe began to walk away, he raised his voice: "No hurt gentles, Ruth!"

She stopped, but would not look at him as she replied. "Cloud say new people hurt gentles and not know. Locklear hurt Cloud before, want kill Cloud. Locklear go soon soon," she finished in a sob. Suddenly, then, she was running to catch the others.

Some of the men were groping for spears now. Locklear did not wait to see what they might do with them. A half-hour later he was using the dolly in the crypt, ranking cage upon cage just inside the obscuring film. With several lion cages stacked like bricks at the entrance, no sensible Neanderthal would go a step further. Later, he could use disassembled stasis units as booby traps as he had done on Kzersatz. But it was nearly dark when he finished, and Locklear was hurrying. Now, for the first time ever on Newduvai, he felt gooseflesh when he thought of camping in the open.

For days, he considered a return to Kzersatz in the lifeboat, meanwhile improving the cabin with Loli's help. He got that help very simply, by refusing to let her sleep in her stasis cage unless she did help. Loli was very bright, and learned his language quickly because she could not rely on telepathy. Operating on the sour-grape theory, he told himself that Ruth had been mud-fence ugly; he hadn't felt any real affection for a Neanderthal bimbo. Not *really* . . .

He managed to ignore Loli's budding charms by reminding himself that she was no more than twelve or so, and gradually she began to trust him. He wondered how much that trust would suffer if she found he was taking her from stasis only on the days he needed help.

As the days faded into weeks, the cabin became a two-room affair with a connecting passage for firewood and storage. Loli, after endless scraping and soaking of the stiff goathide in acorn water, fashioned herself a one-piece garment. She taught Locklear how repeated boiling turned acorns into edible nuts, and wove mats of plaited grass for the cabin.

He let her roam in search of small game once a week until the day she returned empty-handed. He was cutting hinge material of stainless steel from a stasis cage with Kzin shears at the time, and smiled. "Don't feel bad, Loli. There's plenty of meat in storage." The more he used complete sentences, the more she seemed to be picking up the lingo.

She shrugged, picking at a scab on one of her hard little feet. "Loli not hunt. Gentles hunt Loli." She read his stare correctly. "Gentles not try to hurt Loli; this many follow and hide," she said, holding up four fingers and making a comical pantomime of a stealthy hunter.

He held up four fingers. "Four," he reminded her. "Did they follow you here?"

"Maybe want to follow Loli here," she said, grinning. "Loli think much. Loli go far far—"

"Very far," he corrected.

"Very far to dry place, gentles no follow feet there. Loli hide, run very far where gentles not see. Come back to Locklear."

Yes, they'd have trouble tracking her through those desert patches, he realized, and she could've doubled back unseen in the arroyos. Or she might have been followed after all. "Loli is smart," he said, patting her shoulder, "but gentles are smart too. Gentles maybe want to hurt Locklear."

"Gentles cover big holes, spears in holes, come back, maybe find kill animal. Maybe kill Locklear."

Yeah, they'd do it that way. Or maybe set a fire to burn him out of the cabin. "Loli, would you feel bad if the gentles killed me?"

In her vast innocence, Loli thought about it before answering. "Little while, yes. Loli don't like to live alone. Gentles alltime like to play," she said, with a bump-and-grind routine so outrageous that he burst out laughing. "Locklear don't trade food for play," she added, making it obvious that Neanderthal men *did.*

"Not until Loli is older," he said with brutal honesty.

"Loli is a woman," she said, pouting as though he had slandered her.

To shift away from this dangerous topic he said, "Yes, and you can help me make this place safe from gentles." That was the day he began teaching the girl how to disassemble cages for their most potent parts, the grav polarizers and stasis units.

They burned off the surrounding ground cover bit by bit during the nights to avoid telltale smoke, and Loli assured him that Neanderthals never ventured from camp on nights as dark as Newduvai's. Sooner or later, he knew, they were bound to discover his little homestead and he intended to make it a place of terrifying magics.

As luck would have it, he had over two months to prepare before a far more potent new magic thundered across the sky of Newduvai.

Locklear swallowed hard the day he heard that long roll of synthetic thunder, recognizing it for what it was. He had told Loli about the kzinti, and now he warned her that they might be near, and saw her coltish legs flash into the forest as he sent the scooter scudding close to the ground toward the heights where his lifeboat was hidden. He would need only one close look to identify a kzin ship.

Dismounting near the lifeboat, peering past an outcrop and shivering because he was so near the cold force walls, he saw a foreshortened dot hovering near Newduvai's big lake. Winks of light streaked downward from it; he counted five shots before the ship ceased firing, and knew that its target had to be the big encampment of gentles.

"If only I had those beam cannons I took apart," he growled, unconsciously taking the side of the Neanderthals as tendrils of smoke fingered the sky. But he had removed the weapon pylon mounts long before. He released a long-held breath as the ship dwindled to a dot in the sky, hunching his shoulders, wondering how he could have been so naive as to forswear war altogether. Killing was a bitter draught, yet not half so bitter as dying.

The ship disappeared. Ten minutes later he saw it again, making the kind of circular sweep used for cartography, and this time it passed only a mile distant, and he gasped—for it was not a kzin ship. The little cruiser escort bore Interworld Commission markings.

"The goddamn tabbies must have taken one of ours," he muttered to himself, and cursed as he saw the ship break off its sweep. No question about it: they were hovering very near his cabin.

Locklear could not fight from the lifeboat, but at least he had plenty of spare magazines for his kzin sidearm in the lifeboat's lockers. He crammed his pockets with spares, expecting to see smoke roiling from his homestead as he began to skulk his scooter low toward home. His little vehicle would not bulk large on radar. And the tabbies might not realize how soon it grew dark on Newduvai. Maybe he could even the odds a little by landing near enough to snipe by the light of his burning cabin. He sneaked the last two hundred meters afoot, already steeling himself for the sight of a burning cabin.

But the cabin was not burning. And the kzinti were not pillaging because, he saw with utter disbelief, the armed crew surrounding his cabin was human. He had already stood erect when it occurred to him that humans had been known to defect in previous wars—and he was carrying a kzin weapon. He placed the sidearm and spare magazines beneath a stone overhang. Then Locklear strode out of the forest rubber-legged, too weak with relief to be angry at the firing on the village.

The first man to see him was a rawboned, ruddy private with the height of a belter. He brought his assault rifle to bear on Locklear, then snapped it to "port arms." Three others spun as the big belter shouted, "Gomulka! We've got one!"

A big fireplug of a man, wearing sergeant's stripes, whirled and moved away from a cabin window, motioning a smaller man beneath the other window to stay put. Striding toward the belter, he used the heavy bellow of command. "Parker, escort him in! Schmidt, watch the perimeter."

The belter trotted toward Locklear while an athletic specimen with a yellow crew cut moved out to watch the forest where Locklear had emerged. Locklear took the belter's free hand and shook it repeatedly. They walked to the cabin together, and the rest of the group relaxed visibly to see Locklear all but capering in his delight. Two other armed figures appeared from across the clearing, one with curves too lush to be male, and Locklear invited them all in with, "There are no kzinti on this piece of the planet; welcome to Newduvai."

Leaning, sitting, they all found their ease in Locklear's room, and their gazes were as curious as Locklear's own. He noted the varied shoulder patches: We Made It, Jinx, Wunderland. The woman, wearing the bars of a lieutenant, was evidently a Flatlander like himself. Commander Curt Stockton wore a Canyon patch, standing wiry and erect beside the woman, with pale gray eyes that missed nothing.

"I was captured by a kzin ship," Locklear explained, "and marooned. But I suppose that's all in the records; I call the planet 'Zoo' because I think the Outsiders designed it with that in mind."

"We had these coordinates, and something vague about prison compounds, from translations of kzin records," Stockton replied. "You must know a lot about this Zoo place by now."

"A fair amount. Listen, I saw you firing on a village near the big lake an hour ago. You mustn't do it again, Commander. Those people are real Earth Neanderthals, probably the only ones in the entire galaxy."

The blocky sergeant, David Gomulka, slid his gaze to lock on Stockton's and shrugged big sloping shoulders. The woman, a close-cropped brunette whose cinched belt advertised her charms, gave Locklear a brilliant smile and sat down on his pallet. "I'm Grace Agostinho; Lieutenant, Manaus Intelligence Corps, Earth. Forgive our manners, Mr. Locklear, we've been in heavy fighting along the Rim and this isn't exactly what we expected to find."

"Me neither," Locklear smiled, then turned serious. "I hope you didn't destroy that village."

"Sorry about that," Stockton said. "We may have caused a few casualties when we opened fire on those huts. I ordered the firing stopped as soon as I saw they weren't kzinti. But don't look so glum, Locklear; it's not as if they were human."

"Damn right they are," Locklear insisted. "As you'll soon find out, if we can get their trust again. I've even taught a few of 'em some of our language. And that's not all. But hey, I'm dying of curiosity without any news from outside. Is the war over?"

Commander Stockton coughed lightly for attention and the others seemed as attentive as Locklear. "It looks good around the core worlds, but in the Rim sectors it's still anybody's war." He jerked a thumb toward the two-hundred-ton craft, twice the length of a kzin lifeboat, that rested on its repulsor jacks at the edge of the clearing with its own small pinnace clinging to its back. "The *Anthony Wayne* is the kind of cruiser escort they don't mind turning over to small combat teams like mine. The big brass gave us this mission after we captured some kzinti files from a tabby dreadnought. Not as good as R & R back home, but we're glad of the break." Stockton's grin was infectious.

"I haven't had time to set up a distillery," Locklear said, "or I'd offer you drinks on the house."

"A man could get parched here," said a swarthy little private.

"Good idea, Gazho. You're detailed to get some medicinal brandy from the med stores," said Stockton.

As the private hurried out, Locklear said, "You could probably let the rest of the crew out to stretch their legs, you know. Not much to guard against on Newduvai."

"What you see is all there is," said a compact private with high cheekbones and a Crashlander medic patch. Locklear had not heard him speak before. Softly accented, laconic; almost a scholar's diction. But that's what you might expect of a military medic.

Stockton's quick gaze riveted the man as if to say, "that's enough." To Locklear he nodded. "Meet Soichiro Lee; an intern before the war. Has a tendency to act as if a combat team is a democratic outfit but," his glance toward Lee was amused now, "he's a good sawbones. Anyhow, the *Wayne* can take care of herself. We've set her auto defenses for voice recognition when the hatch is closed, so don't go wandering closer than ten meters without one of us. And if one of those hairy apes throws a rock at her, she might just burn him for his troubles."

Locklear nodded. "A crew of seven; that's pretty thin."

Stockton, carefully: "You want to expand on that?"

Locklear: "I mean, you've got your crew pretty thinly spread. The tabbies have the same problem, though. The bunch that marooned me here had only four members."

Sergeant Gomulka exhaled heavily, catching Stockton's glance. "Commander, with your permission: Locklear here might have some ideas about those tabby records."

"Umm. Yeah, I suppose," with some reluctance. "Locklear, apparently the kzinti felt there was some valuable secret, a weapon maybe, here on Zoo. They intended to return for it. Any idea what it was?"

Locklear laughed aloud. "Probably it was me. It ought to be the whole bleeding planet," he said. "If you stand near the force wall and look hard, you can see what looks like a piece of the Kzin homeworld close to this one. You can't imagine the secrets the other compounds might have. For starters, the life forms I found in stasis had been here forty thousand years, near as I can tell, before I released 'em."

"*You* released them?"

"Maybe I shouldn't have, but—" He glanced shyly toward Lieutenant Agostinho. "I got pretty lonesome."

"Anyone would," she said, and her smile was more than understanding.

Gomulka rumbled in evident disgust, "Why would a lot of walking fossils be important to the tabby war effort?"

"They probably wouldn't," Locklear admitted. "And anyhow, I didn't find the specimens until after the kzinti left." He could not say exactly why, but this did not seem the time to regale them with his adventures on Kzersatz. Something just beyond the tip of his awareness was flashing like a caution signal.

Now Gomulka looked at his commander. "So that's not what we're looking for," he said. "Maybe it's not on this Newduvai dump. Maybe next door?"

"Maybe. We'll take it one dump at a time," said Stockton, and turned as the swarthy private popped into the cabin. "Ah. I trust the Armagnac didn't insult your palate on the way, Nathan," he said.

Nathan Gazho looked at the bottle's broken seal, then began to distribute nested plastic cups, his breath already laced with his quick nip of the brandy. "You don't miss much," he grumbled.

But I'm missing something, Locklear thought as he touched his half-filled cup to that of the sloe-eyed, languorous lieutenant. *Slack discipline? But combat troops probably ignore the spit and polish. Except for this hotsy who keeps looking at me as if we shared a secret, they've all got the hand calluses and haircuts of shock troops. No, it's something else . . .*

He told himself it was reluctance to make himself a hero; and next he told himself they wouldn't believe him anyway. And then he admitted that he wasn't sure exactly why, but he would tell them nothing about his victory on Kzersatz unless they asked. *Maybe because I suspect they'd round up poor Scarface, maybe hunt him down and shoot him like a mad dog no matter what I said. Yeah, that's reason enough. But something else, too.*

Night fell, with its almost audible thump, while they emptied the Armagnac. Locklear explained his scholarly fear that the gentles were likely to kill off animals that no other ethologist had ever studied on the hoof; mentioned Ruth and Minuteman as well; and decided to say nothing about Loli to these hardbitten troops. Anse Parker, the gangling belter, kept bringing the topic back to the tantalizingly vague secret mentioned in kzin files. Parker, Locklear decided, thought himself subtle but managed only to be transparently cunning.

Austin Schmidt, the wide-shouldered blond, had little capacity for Armagnac and kept toasting the day when " . . . all this crap is history and I'm a man of means," singing that refrain from an old barracks ballad in a surprisingly sweet tenor. Locklear could not warm up to Nathan Gazho, whose gaze took inventory of every item in the cabin. The man's expensive wristcomp and pinky ring mismatched him like earrings on a weasel.

David Gomulka was all noncom, though, with a veteran's gift for controlling men and a sure hand in measuring booze. If the two officers felt any unease when he called them "Curt" and "Grace," they managed to avoid showing it. Gomulka spun out the tale of his first hand-to-hand engagement against a kzin penetration team with details that proved he knew how the tabbies fought. Locklear wanted to say, "That's right; that's how it is," but only nodded.

It was late in the evening when the commander cut short their speculations on Zoo, stood up, snapped the belt flash from its ring and flicked it experimentally. "We could all use some sleep," he decided, with the smile of a young father at his men, some of whom were older than he. "Mr. Locklear, we have more than enough room. Please be our guest in the *Anthony Wayne* tonight."

Locklear, thinking that Loli might steal back to the cabin if she were somewhere nearby, said, "I appreciate it, Commander, but I'm right at home here. Really."

A nod, and a reflective gnawing of Stockton's lower lip. "I'm responsible for you now, Locklear. God knows what those Neanderthals might do, now that we've set fire to their nests."

"But—" The men were stretching out their kinks, paying silent but close attention to the interchange.

"I must insist. I don't want to put it in terms of command, but I *am* the local sheriff here now, so to speak." The engaging grin again. "Come on, Locklear, think of it as repaying your hospitality. Nothing's certain in this place, and—" his last phrase bringing soft chuckles from Gomulka, "they'd throw me in the brig if I let anything happen to you now."

The taciturn Parker led the way, and Locklear smiled in the darkness thinking how Loli might wonder at the intensely bright, intensely magical beams that bobbed toward the ship. After Parker called out his name and a long number, the ship's hatch steps dropped at their feet and Locklear knew the reassurance of climbing into an Interworld ship with its familiar smells, whines and beeps.

Parker and Schmidt were loudly in favor of a nightcap, but Stockton's, "Not a good idea, David," to the sergeant was met with a nod and barked commands by Gomulka. Grace Agostinho made a similar offer to Locklear.

"Thanks anyway. You know what I'd really like?"

"Probably," she said, with a pursed-lipped smile.

He was blushing as he said, "Ham sandwiches. Beer. A slice of thrillcake," and nodded quickly when she hauled a frozen shrimp teriyaki from their food lockers. When it popped from the radioven, he sat near the ship's bridge to eat it, idly noting a few dark foodstains on the bridge linolamat and listening to Grace tell of small news from home. The Amazon dam, a new "mustsee" holo musical, a controversial cure for the common cold; the kind of tremendous trifles that cemented friendships.

She left him briefly while he chased scraps on his plate, and by the time she returned most of the crew had secured their pneumatic cubicle doors. "It's always satisfying to feed a man with an appetite," said Grace, smiling at his clean plate as she slid it into the galley scrubber. "I'll see you're fed well on the *Wayne.*" With hands on her hips, she said, "Well: Private Schmidt has sentry duty. He'll show you to your quarters."

He took her hand, thanked her, and nodded to the slightly wavering Schmidt, who led the way back toward the ship's engine room. He did not look back but, from the sound of it, Grace entered a cubicle where two men were arguing in subdued tones.

Schmidt showed him to the rearmost cubicle but not the rearmost dozen bunks. Those, he saw, were ranked inside a cage of duralloy with no privacy whatever. Dark crusted stains spotted the floor inside and outside the cage. A fax sheet lay in the passageway. When Locklear glanced toward it, the private saw it, tried to hide a startled response, and then essayed a drunken grin.

"Gotta have a tight ship," said Schmidt, banging his head on the duralloy as he retrieved the fax and balled it up with one hand. He tossed the wadded fax into a flush-mounted waste receptacle, slid the cubicle door open for Locklear, and managed a passable salute. "Have a good one, pal. You know how to adjust your rubberlady?"

Locklear saw that the mattresses of the two bunks were standard models with adjustable inflation and webbing. "No problem," he replied, and slid the door closed. He washed up at the tiny inset sink, used the urinal slot below it, and surveyed his clothes after removing them. They'd all seen better days. Maybe he could wangle some new ones. He was sleepier than he'd thought, and adjusted his rubberlady for a soft setting, and was asleep within moments.

He did not know how long it was before he found himself sitting bolt-upright in darkness. He knew what was wrong, now: *everything.* It might be possible for a little escort ship to plunder records from a derelict mile-long kzin battleship. It was barely possible that the same craft would be sent to check on some big kzin secret—*but not without at least a cruiser, if the kzinti might be heading for Zoo.*

He rubbed a trickle of sweat as it counted his ribs. He didn't have to be a military buff to know that ordinary privates do not have access to medical lockers, and the commander had told Gazho to get that brandy from med stores. Right; and all those motley shoulder patches didn't add up to a picked combat crew, either. And one more thing: even in his half-blotted condition, Schmidt had snatched that fax sheet up as though it was evidence against him. Maybe it was . . .

He waved the overhead lamp on, grabbed his ratty flight suit, and slid his cubicle door open. If anyone asked, he was looking for a cleaner unit for his togs.

A low thrum of the ship's sleeping hydraulics; a slightly louder buzz of someone sleeping, most likely Schmidt while on sentry duty. *Not much discipline at all. I wonder just how much commanding Stockton really does.* Locklear stepped into the passageway, moved several paces, and eased his free hand into the waste receptacle slot. Then he thrust the fax wad into his dirty flight suit and padded silently back, cursing the sigh of his door. A moment later he was colder than before.

The fax was labeled, "PRISONER RIGHTS AND PRIVILEGES," and had been signed by some Provost Marshal—or a doctor, to judge from its illegibility. He'd bet anything that fax had fallen, or had been torn, from those duralloy bars. Rust-colored crusty stains on the floor; a similar stain near the ship's bridge; but no obvious damage to the ship from kzin weapons.

It took all his courage to go into the passageway again, flight suit in hand, and replace the wadded fax sheet where he'd found it. And the door seemed much louder this time, almost a sob instead of a sigh.

Locklear felt like sobbing too. He lay on his rubberlady in the dark, thinking about it. A hundred scenarios might explain some of the facts, but only one matched them all:

the *Anthony Wayne* had been a prisoner ship, but now the prisoners were calling themselves "commander" and "sergeant," and the real crew of the *Anthony Wayne* had made those stains inside the ship with their blood.

He wanted to shout it, but demanded it silently: *So why would a handful of deserters fly to Zoo?* Before he fell at last into a troubled sleep, he had asked it again and again, and the answer was always the same: somehow, one of them had learned of the kzin records and hoped to find Zoo's secret before either side did.

These people would be deadly to anyone who knew their secret. And almost certainly, they'd never buy the truth, that Locklear himself was the secret because the kzinti had been so sure he was an Interworld agent.

Locklear awoke with a sensation of dread, then a brief upsurge of joy at sleeping in modern accommodations, and then he remembered his conclusions in the middle of the night, and his optimism fell off and broke.

To mend it, he decided to smile with the innocence of a Candide and plan his tactics. If he could get to the kzin lifeboat, he might steer it like a slow battering ram and disable the *Anthony Wayne.* Or they might blow him to flinders in midair—and what if his fears were wrong, and despite all evidence this combat team was genuine? In any case, disabling the ship meant marooning the whole lot of them together. It wasn't a plan calculated to lengthen his life expectancy; maybe he would think of another.

The crew was already bustling around with breakfasts when he emerged, and yes, he could use the ship's cleaning unit for his clothes. When he asked for spare clothing, Soichiro Lee was first to deny it to him. "Our spares are still—contaminated from a previous engagement," he explained, with a meaningful look toward Gomulka.

I bet they are, with blood, Locklear told himself as he scooped his synthesized eggs and bacon. Their uniforms all seemed to fit well. Probably their own, he decided. The stylized winged gun on Gomulka's patch said he could fly gunships. Lee might be a medic, and the sensuous Grace might be a real intelligence officer—and all could be renegades.

Stockton watched him eat, friendly as ever, arms folded and relaxed. "Gomulka and Gazho did a recon in our pinnace at dawn," he said, sucking a tooth. "Seems your apemen are already rebuilding at another site; a terrace at this end of the lake. A lot closer to us."

"I wish you could think of them as people," Locklear said. "They're not terribly bright, but they don't swing on vines."

Chuckling: "Bright enough to be nuisances, perhaps try and burn us out if they find the ship here," Stockton said. "Maybe bright enough to know what it is the tabbies found here. You said they can talk a little. Well, you can help us interrogate 'em."

"They aren't too happy with me," Locklear admitted as Gomulka sat down with steaming coffee. "But I'll try on one condition."

Gomulka's voice carried a rumble of barely hidden threat. "Conditions? You're talking to your commander, Locklear."

"It's a very simple one," Locklear said softly. "No more killing or threatening these people. They call themselves 'gentles,' and they are. The New Smithson, or half the Interworld University branches, would give a year's budget to study them alive."

Grace Agostinho had been working at a map terminal, but evidently with an ear open to their negotiations. As Stockton and Gomulka gazed at each other in silent surmise, she took the few steps to sit beside Locklear, her hip warm against his. "You're an ethologist. Tell me, what could the kzinti do with these gentles?"

Locklear nodded, sipped coffee, and finally said, "I'm not sure. Study them hoping for insights into the underlying psychology of modern humans, maybe."

Stockton said, "But you said the tabbies don't know about them."

"True; at least I don't see how they could. But you asked. I can't believe the gentles would know what you're after, but if you have to ask them, of course I'll help."

Stockton said it was necessary, and appointed Lee acting corporal at the cabin as he filled most of the pinnace's jumpseats with himself, Locklear, Agostinho, Gomulka, and the lank Parker. The little craft sat on downsloping delta wings that ordinarily nested against the *Wayne*'s hull, and had intakes for gas-reactor jets. "Newest piece of hardware we have," Stockton said, patting the pilot's console. It was Gomulka, however, who took the controls.

Locklear suggested that they approach very slowly, with hands visibly up and empty, as they settled the pinnace near the beginnings of a new gentles campsite. The gentles, including their women, all rushed for primitive lances but did not flee, and Anse Parker was the only one carrying an obvious weapon as the pinnace's canopy swung back. Locklear stepped forward, talking and smiling, with Parker at their backs. He saw Ruth waiting for old Gimp, and said he was much happy to see her, which was an understatement. Minuteman, too, had survived the firing on their village.

Cloud had not. Ruth told him so immediately. "Locklear make many deaths to gentles," she accused. Behind her, some of the gentles stared with faces that were anything but gentle. "Gentles not like talk to Locklear, he says. Go now. Please," she added, one of the last words he'd taught her, and she said it with urgency. Her glance toward Grace Agostinho was interested, not hostile but perhaps pitying.

Locklear moved away from the others, farther from the glaring Gimp. "More new people come," he called from a distance, pleading. "Think gentles big, bad animals. Stop when they see gentles; much much sorry. Locklear say not hurt gentles more."

With her head cocked sideways, Ruth seemed to be testing his mind for lies. She spoke with Gimp, whose face registered a deep sadness and, perhaps, some confusion as well. Locklear could hear a buzz of low conversation between Stockton nearby and Gomulka, who still sat at the pinnace controls.

"Locklear think good, but bad things happen," Ruth said at last. "Kill Cloud, many more. Gentles not like fight. Locklear know this," she said, almost crying now. "Please go!"

Gomulka came out of the pinnace with his sidearm drawn, and Locklear turned toward him, aghast. "No shooting! You promised," he reminded Stockton.

But: "We'll have to bring the ape-woman with the old man," Stockton said grimly, not liking it but determined. Gomulka stood quietly, the big sloping shoulders hunched.

Stockton said, "This is an explosive situation, Locklear. We must take those two for interrogation. Have the woman tell them we won't hurt them unless their people try to hunt us."

Then, as Locklear froze in horrified anger, Gomulka bellowed, *"Tell 'em!"*

Locklear did it and Ruth began to call in their language to the assembled throng. Then, at Gomulka's command, Parker ran forward to grasp the pathetic old Gimp by the arm, standing more than a head taller than the Neanderthal. That was the moment when Minuteman, who must have understood only a little of their parley, leaped weaponless at the big belter.

Parker swept a contemptuous arm at the little fellow's reach, but let out a howl as Minuteman, with those blacksmith arms of his, wrenched that arm as one would wave a stick.

The report was shattering, with echoes slapping off the lake, and Locklear whirled to see Gomulka's two-handed aim with the projectile sidearm. "No! Goddammit, these are human beings," he screamed, rushing toward the fallen Minuteman, falling on his knees, placing one hand over the little fellow's breast as if to stop the blood that was pumping from it. The gentles panicked at the thunder from Gomulka's weapon, and began to run.

Minuteman's throat pulse still throbbed, but he was in deep shock from the heavy projectile and his pulse died as Locklear watched helpless. Parker was already clubbing old Gimp with his rifle-butt and Gomulka, his sidearm out of sight, grabbed Ruth as she tried to interfere. The big man might as well have walked into a train wreck while the train was still moving.

Grace Agostinho seemed to know she was no fighter, retreating into the pinnace. Stockton, whipping the ornamental braid from his epaulets, began to fashion nooses as he moved to help Parker, whose left arm was half-useless. Locklear came to his feet, saw Gomulka's big fist smash at Ruth's temple, and dived into the fray with one arm locked around Gomulka's bull neck, trying to haul him off-balance. Both of Ruth's hands grappled with Gomulka's now, and Locklear saw that she was slowly overpowering him while her big teeth sought his throat, only the whites of her eyes showing. It was the last thing Locklear would see for awhile, as someone raced up behind him.

He awoke to a gentle touch and the chill of antiseptic spray behind his right ear, and focused on the real concern mirrored on Stockton's face. He lay in the room he had built for Loli, Soichiro Lee kneeling beside him, while Ruth and Gimp huddled as far as they could get into a corner. Stockton held a standard issue parabellum, arms folded, not pointing the weapon but keeping it in evidence. "Only a mild concussion," Lee murmured to the commander.

"You with us again, Locklear?" Stockton got a nod in response, motioned for Lee to leave, and sighed. "I'm truly sorry about all this, but you were interfering with a military operation. Gomulka is—he has a lot of experience, and a good commander would be stupid to ignore his suggestions."

Locklear was barely wise enough to avoid saying that Gomulka did more commanding than Stockton did. Pushing himself up, blinking from the headache that split his skull like an axe, he said, "I need some air."

"You'll have to get it right here," Stockton said, "because I can't—won't let you out. Consider yourself under arrest. Behave yourself and that could change." With that, he shouldered the woven mat aside and his slow footsteps echoed down the connecting corridor to the other room.

Without a door directly to the outside, he would have to run down that corridor where armed yahoos waited. Digging out would make noise and might take hours. Locklear slid down against the cabin wall, head in hands. When he opened them again he saw that poor old Gimp seemed comatose, but Ruth was looking at him intently. "I wanted to be friend of all gentles," he sighed.

"Yes. Gentles know," she replied softly. "New people with gentles not good. Stok-Tun not want hurt, but others not care about gentles. Ruth hear in head," she added, with a palm against the top of her head.

"Ruth must not tell," Locklear insisted. "New people maybe kill if they know gentles hear that way."

She gave him a very modern nod, and even in that hopelessly homely face, her shy smile held a certain beauty. "Locklear help Ruth fight. Ruth like Locklear much, much; even if Locklear is—new."

"Ruth, 'new' means 'ugly,' doesn't it? New, new," he repeated, screwing his face into a hideous caricature, making claws of his hands, snarling in exaggerated mimicry.

He heard voices raised in muffled excitement in the other room, and Ruth's head was cocked again momentarily. "Ugly?" She made faces, too. "Part yes. New means not same as before but also ugly, maybe bad."

"All the gentles considered me the ugly man. Yes?"

"Yes," she replied sadly. "Ruth not care. Like ugly man if good man, too."

"And you knew I thought you were, uh . . ."

"Ugly? Yes. Ruth try and fix before."

"I know," he said, miserable. "Locklear like Ruth for that and many, many more things."

Quickly, as boots stamped in the corridor, she said, "Big

problem. New people not think Locklear tell truth. New woman—"

Schmidt's rifle barrel moved the mat aside and he let it do his gesturing to Locklear. "On your feet, buddy, you've got some explaining to do."

Locklear got up carefully so his head would not roll off his shoulders. Stumbling toward the doorway he said to Ruth: "What about new woman?"

"Much, much new in head. Ruth feel sorry," she called as Locklear moved toward the other room.

They were all crowded in, and seven pairs of eyes were intent on Locklear. Grace's gaze held a liquid warmth but he saw nothing warmer than icicles in any other face. Gomulka and Stockton sat on the benches facing him across his crude table like judges at a trial. Locklear did not have to be told to stand before them.

Gomulka reached down at his own feet and grunted with effort, and the toolbox crashed down on the table. His voice was not its usual command timbre, but menacingly soft. "Gazho noticed this was all tabby stuff," he said.

"Part of an honorable trade," Locklear said, dry-mouthed. "I could have killed a kzin and didn't."

"They trade you a fucking LIFEBOAT, too?"

Those goddamn pinnace sorties of his! The light of righteous fury snapped in the big man's face, but Locklear stared back. "Matter of fact, yes. The kzin is a cat of his word, sergeant."

"Enough of your bullshit, I want the truth!"

Now Locklear shifted his gaze to Stockton. "I'm telling it. Enough of your bullshit, too. How did your bunch of bozos get out of the brig, Stockton?"

Parker blurted, "How the hell did—" before Gomulka spun on his bench with a silent glare. Parker blushed and swallowed.

"We're asking the questions, Locklear. The tabbies must've left you a girlfriend, too," Stockton said quietly. "Lee and Schmidt both saw some little hotsy queen of the jungle out near the perimeter while we were gone. Make no mistake, they'll hunt her down and there's nothing I can say to stop them."

"Why not, if you're a commander?"

Stockton flushed angrily, with a glance at Gomulka that was not kind. "That's my problem, not yours. Look, you want some straight talk, and here it is: Agostinho has seen the goddamned translations from a tabby dreadnought, and there *is* something on this godforsaken place they think is important, and we were in this Rim sector when—when we got into some problems, and she told me. I'm an officer, I really am, believe what you like. But we have to find whatever the hell there is on Zoo."

"So you can plea-bargain after your mutiny?"

"That's ENOUGH," Gomulka bellowed. "You're a little too cute for your own good, Locklear. But if you're ever gonna get off this ball of dirt, it'll be after you help us find what the tabbies are after."

"It's me," Locklear said simply. "I've already told you."

Silent consternation, followed by disbelief. "And what the fuck are you," Gomulka spat.

"Not much, I admit. But as I told you, they captured me and got the idea I knew more about the Rim sectors than I do."

"How much kzinshit do you think I'll swallow?" Gomulka was standing, now, advancing around the table toward his captive. Curt Stockton shut his eyes and sighed his helplessness.

Locklear was wondering if he could grab anything from the toolbox when a voice of sweet reason stopped Gomulka. "Brutality hasn't solved anything here yet," said Grace Agostinho. "I'd like to talk to Locklear alone." Gomulka stopped, glared at her, then back at Locklear. "I can't do any worse than you have, David," she added to the fuming sergeant.

Beckoning, she walked to the doorway and Gazho made sure his rifle muzzle grated on Locklear's ribs as the ethologist followed her outside. She said, "Do I have your honorable parole? Bear in mind that even if you try to run, they'll soon have you and the girl who's running loose, too. They've already destroyed some kind of flying raft; yours, I take it," she smiled.

Damn, hell, shit, and blast! "Mine. I won't run, Grace. Besides, you've got a parabellum."

"Remember that," she said, and began to stroll toward the trees while the cabin erupted with argument. Locklear vented more silent damns and hells; she wasn't leading him anywhere near his hidden kzin sidearm.

Grace Agostinho, surprisingly, first asked about Loli. She seemed amused to learn he had waked the girl first, and that he'd regretted it at his leisure. Gradually, her questions segued to answers. "Discipline on a warship can be vicious," she mused as if to herself. "Curt Stockton was—is a career officer, but it's his view that there must be limits to discipline. His own commander was a hard man, and—"

"Jesus Christ; you're saying he mutinied like Fletcher Christian?"

"That's not entirely wrong," she said, now very feminine as they moved into a glade, out of sight of the cabin. "David Gomulka is a rougher sort, a man of some limited ideas but more of action. I'm afraid Curt filled David with ideas that, ah, . . ."

"Stockton started a boulder downhill and can't stop it," Locklear said. "Not the first time a man of ideas has started something he can't control. How'd you get into this mess?"

"An affair of the heart; I'd rather not talk about it . . . When I'm drawn to a man, . . . well, I tend to show it," she said, and preened her hair for him as she leaned against a fallen tree. "You must tell them what they want to know, my dear. These are desperate men, in desperate trouble."

Locklear saw the promise in those huge dark eyes and gazed into them. "I swear to you, the kzinti thought I was some kind of Interworld agent, but they dropped me on Zoo for safekeeping."

"And were you?" Softly, softly, catchee monkey . . .

"Good God, no! I'm an—"

"Ethologist. I heard it. But the kzin suspicion does seem reasonable, doesn't it?"

"I guess, if you're paranoid." *God, but this is one seductive lieutenant.*

"Which means that David and Curt could sell you to the kzinti for safe passage, if I let them," she said, moving toward him, her hands pulling apart the closures on his flight suit. "But I don't think that's the secret, and I don't think *you* think so. You're a fascinating man, and I don't know when I've been so attracted to anyone. Is this so awful of me?"

He knew damned well how powerfully persuasive a woman like Grace could be with that voluptuous willowy sexuality of hers. And he remembered Ruth's warning, and believed it. But he would rather drown in honey than in vinegar, and when she turned her face upward, he found her mouth with his, and willingly let her lust kindle his own.

Presently, lying on forest humus and watching Grace comb her hair clean with her fingers, Locklear's breathing slowed. He inventoried her charms as she shrugged into her flight suit again; returned her impudent smile; began to readjust his togs. "If this be torture," he declaimed like an actor, "make the most of it."

"Up to the standards of your local ladies?"

"Oh yes," he said fervently, knowing it was only a small lie. "But I'm not sure I understand why you offered."

She squatted becomingly on her knees, brushing at his clothing. "You're very attractive," she said. "And mysterious. And if you'll help us, Locklear, I promise to plumb your mysteries as much as you like—and vice versa."

"An offer I can't refuse, Grace. But I don't know how I can do more than I have already."

Her frown held little anger; more of perplexity. "But I've told you, my dear: we must have that kzin secret."

"And you didn't believe what I said."

Her secret smile again, teasing: "Really, darling, you must give me some credit. I *am* in the intelligence corps."

He did see a flash of irritation cross her face this time as he laughed. "Grace, this is crazy," he said, still grinning. "It may be absurd that the kzinti thought I was an agent, but it's true. I think the planet itself is a mind-boggling discovery, and I said so first thing off. Other than that, what can I say?"

"I'm sorry you're going to be this way about it," she said with the pout of a nubile teenager, then hitched up the sidearm on her belt as if to remind him of it.

She's sure something, he thought as they strode back to his clearing. *If I had any secret to hide, could she get it out of me with this kind of attention? Maybe—but she's all technique and no real passion. Exactly the girl you want to bring home to your friendly regimental combat team.*

Grace motioned him into the cabin without a word and, as Schmidt sent him into the room with Ruth and the old man, he saw both Gomulka and Stockton leave the cabin with Grace. *I don't think she has affairs of the heart,* he reflected with a wry smile. *Affairs of the glands beyond counting, but maybe no heart to lose. Or no character?*

He sat down near Ruth, who was sitting with Gimp's head in her lap, and sighed. "Ruth much smart about new woman. Locklear see now," he said and, gently, kissed the homely face.

The crew had a late lunch but brought none for their captives, and Locklear was taken to his judges in the afternoon.

He saw hammocks slung in his room, evidence that the crew intended to stay awhile. Stockton, as usual, began as pleasantly as he could. "Locklear, since you're not on Agostinho's list of known intelligence assets in the Rim sectors, then maybe we've been peering at the wrong side of the coin."

"That's what I told the tabbies," Locklear said.

"Now we're getting somewhere. Actually, you're a kzin agent; right?"

Locklear stared, then tried not to laugh. "Oh, Jesus, Stockton! Why would they drop me here, in that case?"

Evidently, Stockton's pleasant side was loosely attached under trying circumstances. He flushed angrily. "You tell us."

"You can find out damned fast by turning me over to Interworld authorities," Locklear reminded him.

"And if you turn out to be a plugged nickel," Gomulka snarled, "you're home free and we're in deep shit. No, I don't think we will, little man. We'll do anything we have to do to get the facts out of you. If it takes shooting hostages, we will."

Locklear switched his gaze to the bedeviled Stockton and saw no help there. At this point, a few lies might help the gentles. "A real officer, are you? Shoot these poor savages? Go ahead, actually you might be doing me a favor. You can see they hate my guts! The only reason they didn't kill me today is that they think I'm one of you, and they're scared to. Every one you knock off, or chase off, is just one less who's out to tan my hide."

Gomulka, slyly: "So how'd you say you got that tabby ship?"

Locklear: "On Kzersatz. Call it grand theft, I don't give a damn." Knowing they would explore Kzersatz sooner or later, he said, "The tabbies probably thought I hightailed it for the Interworld fleet but I could barely fly the thing. I was lucky to get down here in one piece."

Stockton's chin jerked up. "Do you mean there's a kzin force right across those force walls?"

"There was; I took care of them myself."

Gomulka stood up now. "Sure you did. I never heard such jizm in twenty years of barracks brags. Grace, you never did like a lot of hollering and blood. Go to the ship." Without a word, and with the same liquid gaze she would turn on Locklear—and perhaps on anyone else—she nodded and walked out.

As Gomulka reached for his captive, Locklear grabbed for

the heavy toolbox. That little hand welder would ruin a man's entire afternoon. Gomulka nodded, and suddenly Locklear felt his arms gripped from behind by Schmidt's big hands. He brought both feet up, kicked hard against the table, and as the table flew into the faces of Stockton and Gomulka, Schmidt found himself propelled backward against the cabin wall.

Shouting, cursing, they overpowered Locklear at last, hauling the top of his flight suit down so that its arms could be tied into a sort of straitjacket. Breathing hard, Gomulka issued his final backhand slap toward Locklear's mouth. Locklear ducked, then spat into the big man's face.

Wiping spittle away with his sleeve, Gomulka muttered, "Curt, we gotta soften this guy up."

Stockton pointed to the scars on Locklear's upper body. "You know, I don't think he softens very well, David. Ask yourself whether you think it's useful, or whether you just want to do it."

It was another of those ideas Gomulka seemed to value greatly because he had so few of his own. "Well goddammit, what would you do?"

"Coercion may work, but not this kind." Studying the silent Locklear in the grip of three men, he came near smiling. "Maybe give him a comm set and drop him among the Neanderthals. When he's good and ready to talk, we rescue him."

A murmur among the men, and a snicker from Gazho. To prove he did have occasional ideas, Gomulka replied, "Maybe. Or better, maybe drop him next door on Kzinkatz or whatever the fuck he calls it." His eyes slid slowly to Locklear.

To Locklear, who was licking a trickle of blood from his upper lip, the suggestion did not register for a count of two beats. When it did, he needed a third beat to make the right response. Eyes wide, he screamed.

"Yeah," said Nathan Gazho.

"Yeah, right," came the chorus.

Locklear struggled, but not too hard. "My God! They'll— They EAT people, Stockton!"

"Well, it looks like a voice vote, Curt," Gomulka drawled, very pleased with his idea, then turned to Locklear. "But that's democracy for you. You'll have a nice comm set and you can call us when you're ready. Just don't forget the story about the boy who cried 'wolf'. But when you call, Locklear—" the big sergeant's voice was low and almost pleasant "—be ready to deal."

~ ~ ~

Locklear felt a wild impulse, as Gomulka shoved him into the pinnace, to beg, "Please, Br'er Fox, don't throw me in the briar patch!" He thrashed a bit and let his eyes roll convincingly until Parker, with a choke hold, pacified him half-unconscious.

If he had any doubts that the pinnace was orbit-rated, Locklear lost them as he watched Gomulka at work. Parker sat with the captive though Lee, beside Gomulka, faced a console. The three pirates negotiated a three-way bet on how much time would pass before Locklear begged to be picked up. His comm set, roughly shoved into his ear with its button switch, had fresh batteries but Lee reminded him again that they would be returning only once to bail him out. The pinnace, a lovely little craft, arced up to orbital height and, with only its transparent canopy between him and hard vac, Locklear found real fear added to his pretense. After pitchover, tiny bursts of light at the wingtips steadied the pinnace as it began its reentry over the saffron jungles of Kzersatz.

Because of its different schedule, the tiny programmed sunlet of Kzersatz was only an hour into its morning. "Keep one eye on your sweep screen," Gomulka said as the roar of deceleration died away.

"I am," Lee replied grimly. "Locklear, if we get jumped by a tabby ship I'll put a burst right into your guts, first thing."

As Locklear made a show of moaning and straining at his bonds, Gomulka banked the pinnace for its mapping sweep. Presently, Lee's infrared scanners flashed an overlay on his screen and Gomulka nodded, but finished the sweep. Then, by manual control, he slowed the little craft and brought it at a leisurely pace to the IR blips, a mile or so above the alien veldt. Lee brought the screen's video to high magnification.

Anse Parker saw what Locklear saw. "Only a few tabbies, huh? And you took care of 'em, huh? You son of a bitch!" He glared at the scene, where a dozen kzinti moved unaware amid half-buried huts and cooking fires, and swatted Locklear across the back of his head with an open hand. "Looks like they've gone native," Parker went on. "Hey, Gomulka: they'll be candy for us."

"I noticed," Gomulka replied. "You know what? If we bag 'em now, we're helping this little shit. We can come back any time we like, maybe have ourselves a tabby-hunt."

"Yeah; show 'em what it's like," Lee snickered, "after they've had their manhunt."

Locklear groaned for effect. *A village ready-made in only a few months! Scarface didn't waste any time getting his own primitives out of stasis. I hope to God he doesn't show up looking glad to see me.* To avoid that possibility he pleaded, "Aren't you going to give me a running chance?"

"Sure we are," Gomulka laughed. "Tabbies will pick up your scent anyway. Be on you like flies on a turd." The pinnace flew on, unseen from far below, Lee bringing up the video now and then. Once he said, "Can't figure out what they're hunting in that field. If I didn't know kzinti were strict carnivores I'd say they were farming."

Locklear knew that primitive kzinti ate vegetables as well, and so did their meat animals; but he kept his silence. It hadn't even occurred to these piratical deserters that the kzinti below might be as prehistoric as Neanderthalers. Good; let them think they understood the kzinti! *But nobody knows 'em like 1 do,* he thought. It was an arrogance he would recall with bitterness very, very soon.

Gomulka set the pinnace down with practiced ease behind a stone escarpment and Parker, his gaze nervously sweeping the jungle, used his gun barrel to urge Locklear out of the craft.

Soichiro Lee's gentle smile did not match his final words: "If you manage to hide out here, just remember we'll pick up your little girlfriend before long. Probably a better piece of snatch than the Manaus machine," he went on, despite a sudden glare from Gomulka. "How long do you want us to use her, asshole? Think about it," he winked, and the canopy's "thunk" muffled the guffaws of Anse Parker.

Locklear raced away as the pinnace lifted, making it look good. They had tossed Br'er Rabbit into his personal briar patch, never suspecting he might have friends here.

He was thankful that the village lay downhill as he began his one athletic specialty, long-distance jogging, because he could once again feel the synthetic gravity of Kzersatz tugging at his body. He judged that he was a two-hour trot from the village and paced himself carefully, walking and resting now and then. And planning.

As soon as Scarface learned the facts, they could set a trap for the returning pinnace. And then, with captives of his own, Locklear could negotiate with Stockton. It was clear by now that Curt Stockton considered himself a leader of virtue—because he was a man of ideas. David Gomulka was a man of action without many important ideas, the perfect model of a playground bully long after graduation.

And Stockton? He would've been the kind of clever kid who decided early that violence was an inferior way to do things, because he wasn't very good at it himself. Instead, he'd enlist a Gomulka to stand nearby while the clever kid tried to beat you up with words; debate you to death. And if that finally failed, he could always sigh, and walk away leaving the bully to do his dirty work, and imagine that his own hands were clean.

But Kzersatz was a whole 'nother playground, with different rules. Locklear smiled at the thought and jogged on.

An hour later he heard the beast crashing in panic through orange ferns before he saw it, and realized that it was pursued only when he spied a young male flashing with sinuous efficiency behind.

No one ever made friends with a kzin by interrupting its hunt, so Locklear stood motionless among palmferns and watched. The prey reminded him of a pygmy tyrannosaur, almost the height of a man but with teeth meant for grazing on foliage. The kzin bounded nearer, disdaining the *wtsai* knife at his belt, and screamed only as he leaped for the kill.

The prey's armored hide and thrashing tail made the struggle interesting, but the issue was never in doubt. A kzin warrior was trained to hunt, to kill, and to eat that kill, from kittenhood. The roars of the lizard dwindled to a hissing gurgle; the tail and the powerful legs stilled. Only after the kzin vented his victory scream and ripped into his prey did Locklear step into the clearing made by flattened ferns.

Hands up and empty, Locklear called in Kzin, "The kzin is a mighty hunter!" To speak in Kzin, one needed a good falsetto and plenty of spit. Locklear's command was fair, but the young kzin reacted as though the man had spouted fire and brimstone. He paused only long enough to snatch up his kill, a good hundred kilos, before bounding off at top speed.

Crestfallen, Locklear trotted toward the village again. He wondered now if Scarface and Kit, the mate Locklear had freed for him, had failed to speak of mankind to the ancient kzin tribe. In any case, they would surely respond to his use of their language until he could get Scarface's help. Perhaps the young male had simply raced away to bring the good news.

And perhaps, he decided a half-hour later, he himself was the biggest fool in Known Space or beyond it. They had ringed him before he knew it, padding silently through foliage the same mottled yellows and oranges as their fur. Then, almost simultaneously, he saw several great tigerish shapes disengage from their camouflage ahead of him, and heard the scream as one leapt upon him from behind.

Bowled over by the rush, feeling hot breath and fangs at his throat, Locklear moved only his eyes. His attacker might have been the same one he surprised while hunting, and he felt needle-tipped claws through his flight suit.

Then Locklear did the only things he could: kept his temper, swallowed his terror, and repeated his first greeting: "The kzin is a mighty hunter."

He saw, striding forward, an old kzin with ornate bandolier straps. The oldster called to the others, "It is true, the beast speaks the Hero's Tongue! It is as I prophesied." Then, to the young attacker, "Stand away at the ready," and Locklear felt like breathing again.

"I am Locklear, who first waked members of your clan from age-long sleep," he said in that ancient dialect he'd learned from Kit. "I come in friendship. May I rise?"

A contemptuous gesture and, as Locklear stood up, a worse remark. "Then you are the beast that lay with a palace *prret,* a courtesan. We have heard. You will win no friends here."

A cold tendril marched down Locklear's spine. "May I speak with my friends? The kzinti have things to fear, but I am not among them."

More laughter. "The Rockear beast thinks it is fearsome," said the young male, his ear-umbrellas twitching in merriment.

"I come to ask help, and to offer it," Locklear said evenly.

"The priesthood knows enough of your help. Come," said the older one. And that is how Locklear was marched into a village of prehistoric kzinti, ringed by hostile predators twice his size.

His reception party was all-male, its members staring at him in frank curiosity while prodding him to the village. They finally left him in an open area surrounded by huts with his hands tied, a leather collar around his neck, the collar linked by a short braided rope to a hefty stake. When he squatted on the turf, he noticed the soil was torn by hooves here and there. Dark stains and an abattoir odor said the place was used for butchering animals. The curious gazes of passing females said he was only a strange animal to them. The disappearance of the males into the largest of the semi-submerged huts suggested that he had furnished the village with something worth a town meeting.

At last the meeting broke up, kzin males striding from the hut toward him, a half-dozen of the oldest emerging last, each with a four-fingered paw tucked into his bandolier belt. Prominent scars across the breasts of these few were all exactly similar; some kind of self-torture ritual, Locklear guessed. Last of all with the ritual scars was the old one he'd spoken with, and this one had *both* paws tucked into his belt. *Got it; the higher your status, the less you need to keep your hands ready, or to hurry.*

The old devil was enjoying all this ceremony, and so were the other big shots. Standing in clearly-separated rings behind them were the other males with a few females, then the other females, evidently the entire tribe. Locklear spotted a few kzinti whose expressions and ear-umbrellas said they were either sick or unhappy, but all played their obedient parts.

Standing before him, the oldster reached out and raked Locklear's face with what seemed to be only a ceremonial insult. It brought welts to his cheek anyway. The oldster spoke for all to hear. "You began the tribe's awakening, and for that we promise a quick kill."

"I waked several kzinti, who promised me honor," Locklear managed to say.

"Traitors? They have no friends here. So *you*—have no friends here," said the old kzin with pompous dignity. "This the priesthood has decided."

"You are the leader?"

"First among equals," said the high priest with a smirk that said he believed in no equals.

"While this tribe slept," Locklear said loudly, hoping to gain some support, "a mighty kzin warrior came here. I call him Scarface. I return in peace to see him, and to warn you that others who look like me may soon return. They wish you harm, but I do not. Would you take me to Scarface?"

He could not decipher the murmurs, but he knew amusement when he saw it. The high priest stepped forward, untied the rope, handed it to the nearest of the husky males who stood behind the priests. "He would see the mighty hunter who had new ideas," he said. "Take him to see that hero, so that he will fully appreciate the situation. Then bring him back to the ceremony post."

With that, the high priest turned his back and followed by the other priests, walked away. The dozens of other kzinti hurried off, carefully avoiding any backward glances. Locklear said, to the huge specimen tugging on his neck rope, "I cannot walk quickly with hands behind my back."

"Then you must learn," rumbled the big kzin, and lashed out with a foot that propelled Locklear forward. *I think he pulled that punch,* Locklear thought. *Kept his claws retracted, at least.* The kzin led him silently from the village and along a path until hidden by foliage. Then, "You are the Rockear," he said, slowing. "I am (something as unpronounceable as most kzin names)," he added, neither friendly nor unfriendly. He began untying Locklear's hands with, "I must kill you if you run, and I will. But I am no priest," he said, as if that explained his willingness to ease a captive's walking.

"You are a stalwart," Locklear said. "May I call you that?"

"As long as you can," the big kzin said, leading the way again. "I voted to my priest to let you live, and teach us. So did most heroes of my group."

Uh-huh; they have priests instead of senators. But this smells like the old American system before direct elections. "Your priest is not bound to vote as you say?" A derisive snort was his answer, and he persisted. "Do you vote your priests in?"

"Yes. For life," said Stalwart, explaining everything.

"So they pretend to listen, but they do as they like," Locklear said.

A grunt, perhaps of admission or of scorn. "It was always thus," said Stalwart, and found that Locklear could trot, now. Another half-hour found them moving across a broad veldt, and Locklear saw the scars of a grass fire before he realized he was in familiar surroundings. Stalwart led the way to a rise and then stopped, pointing toward the jungle. "There," he said, "is your scarfaced friend."

Locklear looked in vain, then back at Stalwart. "He must be blending in with the ferns. You people do that very—"

"The highest tree. What remains of him is there."

And then Locklear saw the flying creatures he had called "batowls," tiny mites at a distance of two hundred meters, picking at tatters of something that hung in a net from the highest tree in the region. "Oh, my God! Won't he die there?"

"He is dead already. He underwent the long ceremony," said Stalwart, "many days past, with wounds that killed slowly."

Locklear's glare was incriminating: "I suppose you voted against that, too?"

"That, and the sacrifice of the palace *prret* in days past," said the kzin.

Blinking away tears, for Scarface had truly been a cat of his word, Locklear said, "Those *prret*. One of them was Scarface's mate when I left. Is she—up there, too?"

For what it was worth, the big kzin could not meet his gaze. "Drowning is the dishonorable punishment for females," he said, pointing back toward Kzersatz's long shallow lake. "The priesthood never avoids tradition, and she lies beneath the water. Another *prret* with kittens was permitted to rejoin the tribe. She chose to be shunned instead. Now and then, we see her. It is treason to speak against the priesthood, and I will not."

Locklear squeezed his eyes shut; blinked; turned away from the hideous sight hanging from that distant tree as scavengers picked at its bones. "And I hoped to help your tribe! A pox on all your houses," he said to no one in particular. He did not speak to the kzin again, but they did not hurry as Stalwart led the way back to the village.

The only speaking Locklear did was to the comm set in his ear, shoving its pushbutton switch. The kzin looked back at him in curiosity once or twice, but now he was speaking Interworld, and perhaps Stalwart thought he was singing a death song.

In a way, it was true—though not a song of his own death, if he could help it. "Locklear calling the *Anthony Wayne,*" he said, and paused.

He heard the voice of Grace Agostinho reply, "Recording."

"They've caught me already, and they intend to kill me. I don't much like you bastards, but at least you're human. I don't care how many of the male tabbies you bag; when they start torturing me I won't be any further use to you."

Again, Grace's voice replied in his ear: "Recording."

Now with a terrible suspicion, Locklear said, "Is anybody there? If you're monitoring me live, say 'monitoring.' "

His comm set, in Grace's voice, only said, "Recording."

Locklear flicked off the switch and began to walk even more slowly, until Stalwart tugged hard on the leash. Any kzin who cared to look, as they reentered the village, would have seen a little man bereft of hope. He did not complain when Stalwart retied his hands, nor even when another kzin marched him away and fairly flung him into a tiny hut near the edge of the village. Eventually they flung a bloody hunk of some recent kill into his hut, but it was raw and, with his hands tied behind him, he could not have held it to his mouth.

Nor could he toggle his comm set, assuming it would carry past the roof thatch. He had not said he would be in the village, and they would very likely kill him along with everybody else in the village when they came. *If* they came.

He felt as though he would drown in cold waves of despair. A vicious priesthood had killed his friends and, even if he escaped for a time, he would be hunted down by the galaxy's most pitiless hunters. And if his own kind rescued him, they might cheerfully beat him to death trying to learn a secret he had already divulged. And even the gentle Neanderthalers hated him, now.

Why not just give up? I don't know why, he admitted to himself, and began to search for something to help him fray the thongs at his wrists. He finally chose a rough-barked post, sitting down in front of it and staring toward the kzin male whose lower legs he could see beneath the door matting.

He rubbed until his wrists were as raw as that meat lying in the dust before him. Then he rubbed until his muscles refused to continue, his arms cramping horribly. By that time it was dark, and he kept falling into an exhausted, fitful sleep, starting to scratch at his bonds every time a cramp woke him. The fifth time he awoke, it was to the sounds of scratching again. And a soft, distant call outside, which his guard answered just as softly. It took Locklear a moment to realize that those scratching noises were not being made by *him.*

The scratching became louder, filling him with a dread of the unknown in the utter blackness of the Kzersatz night. Then he heard a scrabble of clods tumbling to the earthen floor. Low, urgent, in the fitz-rowr of a female kzin: "Rockear, quickly! Help widen this hole!"

He wanted to shout, remembering Boots, the new mother of two who had scorned her tribe; but he whispered hoarsely: "Boots?"

An even more familiar voice than that of Boots. "She is entertaining your guard. Hurry!"

"Kit! I can't, my hands are tied," he groaned. "Kit, they said you were drowned."

"Idiots," said the familiar voice, panting as she worked. A very faint glow preceded the indomitable Kit, who had a modern kzin beltpac and used its glowlamp for brief moments. Without slowing her frantic pace, she said softly, "They built a walkway into the lake and—dropped me from it. But my mate, your friend Scarface, knew what they intended. He told me to breathe—many times just before I fell. With all the stones—weighting me down, I simply walked on the bottom, between the pilings—and untied the stones beneath the planks near shore. Idiots," she said again, grunting as her fearsome claws ripped away another chunk of Kzersatz soil. Then, "Poor Rockear," she said, seeing him writhe toward her.

In another minute, with the glowlamp doused, Locklear heard the growling curses of Kit's passage into the hut. She'd said females were good tunnelers, but not until now had he realized just how good. The nearest cover must be a good ten meters away . . . "Jesus, don't bite my hand, Kit," he begged, feeling her fangs and the heat of her breath against his savaged wrists. A moment later he felt a flash of white-hot pain through his shoulders as his hands came free. He'd been cramped up so long it hurt to move freely. "Well, by God it'll just have to hurt," he said aloud to himself, and flexed his arms, groaning.

"I suppose you must hold to my tail," she said. He felt the long, wondrously luxuriant tail whisk across his chest and because it was totally dark, did as she told him. Nothing short of true and abiding friendship, he knew, would provoke her into such manhandling of her glorious, her sensual, her fundamental tail.

They scrambled past mounds of soft dirt until Locklear felt cool night air on his face. "You may quit insulting my tail now," Kit growled. "We must wait inside this tunnel awhile. You take this: I do not use it well."

He felt the cold competence of the object in his hand and exulted as he recognized it as a modem kzin sidearm. Crawling near with his face at her shoulder, he said, "How'd you know exactly where I was?"

"Your little long-talker, of course. We could hear you moaning and panting in there, and the magic tools of my mate located you."

But I didn't have it turned on. Ohhh-no; I didn't KNOW it was turned on! The goddamned thing is transmitting all the time . . . He decided to score one for Stockton's people, and dug the comm set from his ear. Still in the tunnel, it wouldn't transmit well until he moved outside. Crush it? Bury it? Instead, he snapped the magazine from the sidearm and, after removing its ammunition, found that the tiny comm set would fit inside. Completely enclosed by metal, the comm set would transmit no more until he chose.

He got all but three of the rounds back in the magazine, cursing every sound he made, and then moved next to Kit again. "They showed me what they did to Scarface. I can't tell you how sorry I am, Kit. He was my friend, and they will pay for it."

"Oh, yes, they will pay," she hissed softly. "Make no mistake, he is still your friend."

A thrill of energy raced from the base of his skull down his arms and legs. "You're telling me he's alive?"

As if to save her the trouble of a reply, a male kzin called softly from no more than three paces away: "Milady; do we have him?"

"Yes," Kit replied.

"Scarface! Thank God you're—"

"Not now," said the one-time warship commander. "Follow quietly."

Having slept near Kit for many weeks, Locklear recognized her steam-kettle hiss as a sufferer's sigh. "I know your nose is hopeless at following a spoor, Rockear. But try not to pull me completely apart this time." Again he felt that long bushy tail pass across his breast, but this time he tried to grip it more gently as they sped off into the night.

Sitting deep in a cave with rough furniture and booby-trapped tunnels, Locklear wolfed stew under the light of a kzin glowlamp. He had slightly scandalized Kit with a hug, then did the same to Boots as the young mother entered the cave without her kittens. The guard would never be trusted to guard anything again, said the towering Scarface, but that rescue tunnel was proof that a kzin had helped. Now they'd be looking for Boots, thinking she had done more than lure a guard thirty meters away.

Locklear told his tale of success, failure, and capture by human pirates as he finished eating, then asked for an update of the Kzersatz problem. Kit, it turned out, had warned Scarface against taking the priests from stasis but one of the devout and not entirely bright males they woke had done the deed anyway.

Scarface, with his small hidden cache of modern equipment, had expected to lead; had he not been Tzak-Commander, once upon a time? The priests had seemed to agree—long enough to make sure they could coerce enough followers. It seemed, said Scarface, that ancient kzin priests hadn't the slightest compunctions about lying, unlike modern kzinti. He had tried repeatedly to call Locklear with his all-band comm set, without success. Depending on long custom, demanding that tradition take precedence over new ways, the priests had engineered the capture of Scarface and Kit in a hook-net, the kind of cruel device that tore at the victim's flesh at the slightest movement.

Villagers had spent days in building that walkway out over a shallowly sloping lake, a labor of loathing for kzinti, who hated to soak in water. Once it was extended to the point where the water was four meters deep, the rough-hewn dock made an obvious reminder of ceremonial murder to any female who might try, as Kit and Boots had done ages before, to liberate herself from the ritual prostitution of yore.

And then, as additional mental torture, they told their bound captives what to expect, and made Scarface watch as Kit was thrown into the lake. Boots, watching in horror from afar, had then watched the torture and disposal of Scarface. She was amazed when Kit appeared at her birthing bower, having seen her disappear with great stones into deep water. The next day, Kit had killed a big ruminant, climbing that tree at night to recover her mate and placing half of her kill in the net.

"My medkit did the rest," Scarface said, pointing to ugly scar tissue at several places on his big torso. "These scum have never seen anyone recover from deep body punctures. Antibiotics can be magic, if you stretch a point."

Locklear mused silently on their predicament for long minutes. Then: "Boots, you can't afford to hang around near the village anymore. You'll have to hide your kittens and—"

"They have my kittens," said Boots, with a glitter of pure hate in her eyes. "They will be cared for as long as I do not disturb the villagers."

"Who told you that?"

"The high priest," she said, mewling pitifully as she saw the glance of doubt pass between Locklear and Scarface. The priests were accomplished liars.

"We'd best get them back soon," Locklear suggested. "Are you sure this cave is secure?"

Scarface took him halfway out one tunnel and, using the glowlamp, showed him a trap of horrifying simplicity. It was a grav polarizer unit from one of the biggest cages, buried just beneath the tunnel floor with a switch hidden to one side. If you reached to the side carefully and turned the switch off, that hidden grav unit wouldn't hurl you against the roof of the tunnel as you walked over it. If you didn't, it did. Simple. Terrible. "I like it," Locklear smiled. "Any more tricks I'd better know before I plaster myself over your ceiling?"

There were, and Scarface showed them to him. "But the least energy expended, the least noise and alarm to do the job, the best. Instead of polarizers, we might bury some stasis units outside, perhaps at the entrance to their meeting hut. Then we catch those *kshat* priests, and use the lying scum for target practice."

"Good idea, and we may be able to improve on it. How many units here in the cave?"

That was the problem; two stasis units taken from cages were not enough. They needed more from the crypt, said Locklear.

"They destroyed that little airboat you left me, but I built a better one," Scarface said with a flicker of humor from his ears.

"So did I. Put a bunch of polarizers on it to push yourself around and ignored the sail, didn't you?" He saw Scarface's assent and winked.

"Two units might work if we trap the priests one by one," Scarface hazarded. "But they've been meddling in the crypt. We might have to fight our way in. And you . . ." he hesitated.

"And I have fought better kzinti before, and here I stand," Locklear said simply.

"That you do." They gripped hands, and then went back to set up their raid on the crypt. The night was almost done.

When surrendering, Scarface had told Locklear nothing of his equipment cache. With two sidearms he could have made life interesting for a man; interesting and short. But his word had been his bond, and now Locklear was damned glad to have the stuff.

They left the females to guard the cave. Flitting low across the veldt toward the stasis crypt with Scarface at his scooter controls, they planned their tactics. "I wonder why you didn't start shooting those priests the minute you were back on your feet," Locklear said over the whistle of breeze in their faces.

"The kittens," Scarface explained. "I might kill one or two priests before the cowards hid and sent innocent fools to be shot, but they are perfectly capable of hanging a kitten in the village until I gave myself up. And I did not dare raid the crypt for stasis units without a warrior to back me up."

"And I'll have to do." Locklear grinned.

"You will." Scarface grinned back; a typical kzin grin, all business, no pleasure.

They settled the scooter near the ice-rimmed force wall and moved according to plan, making haste slowly to avoid the slightest sound, the huge kzin's head swathed in a bandage of leaves that suggested a wound while—with luck—hiding his identity for a few crucial seconds.

Watching the kzin warrior's muscular body slide among weeds and rocks, Locklear realized that Scarface was still not fully recovered from his ordeal. *He made his move before he was ready because of me, and I'm not even a kzin. Wish I thought I could match that kind of commitment,* Locklear mused as he took his place in front of Scarface at the crypt entrance. His sidearm was in his hand. Scarface had sworn the priests had no idea what the weapon was and, with this kind of ploy, Locklear prayed he was right. Scarface gripped Locklear by the neck then, but gently, and they marched in together expecting to meet a guard just inside the entrance.

No guard. No sound at all—and then a distant hollow slam, as of a great box closing. They split up then, moving down each side corridor, returning to the main shaft silently, exploring side corridors again. After four of these forays, they knew that no one would be at their backs.

Locklear was peering into the fifth when, glancing back, he saw Scarface's gesture of caution. Scuffing steps down the side passage, a mumble in Kzin, then silence. Then Scarface resumed his hold on his friend's neck and, after one mutual glance of worry, shoved Locklear into the side passage.

"Ho, see the beast I captured," Scarface called, his voice booming in the wide passage, prompting exclamations from two surprised kzin males.

Stasis cages lay in disarray, some open, some with transparent tops ripped off. One kzin, with the breast scars and bandoliers of a priest, hopped off the cage he used as a seat, and placed a hand on the butt of his sharp *wtsai.* The other bore scabs on his breast and wore no bandolier. He had been tinkering with the innards of a small stasis cage, but whirled, jaw agape.

"It must have escaped after we left, yesterday," said the priest, looking at the "captive," then with fresh curiosity at Scarface. "And who are—"

At that instant, Locklear saw what levitated, spinning, inside one of the medium-sized cages; spinning almost too fast to identify. But Locklear knew what it had to be, and while the priest was staring hard at Scarface, the little man lost control.

His cry was in Interworld, not Kzin: "You filthy bastard!" Before the priest could react, a roundhouse right with the massive barrel of a kzin pistol took away both upper and lower incisors from the left side of his mouth. Caught this suddenly, even a two-hundred-kilo kzin could be sent reeling from the blow, and as the priest reeled to his right, Locklear kicked hard at his backside.

Scarface clubbed at the second kzin, the corridor ringing with snarls and zaps of warrior rage. Locklear did not even notice, leaping on the back of the fallen priest, hacking with his gun barrel until the *wtsai* flew from a smashed hand, kicking down with all his might against the back of the priest's head. The priest, at least twice Locklear's bulk, had lived a life much too soft, for far too long. He rolled over, eyes wide not in fear but in anger at this outrage from a puny beast. It is barely possible that fear might have worked.

The priest caught Locklear's boot in a mouthful of broken teeth, not seeing the sidearm as it swung at his temple. The thump was like an iron bar against a melon, the priest falling limp as suddenly as if some switch had been thrown.

Sobbing, Locklear dropped the pistol, grabbed handfuls of ear on each side, and pounded the priest's head against cruel obsidian until he felt a heavy grip on his shoulder.

"He is dead, Locklear. Save your strength," Scarface advised. As Locklear recovered his weapon and stumbled to his feet, he was shaking uncontrollably. "You must hate our kind more than I thought," Scarface added, studying Locklear oddly.

"He wasn't your kind. I would kill a man for the same crime," Locklear said in fury, glaring at the second kzin who squatted, bloody-faced, in a corner holding a forearm with an extra elbow in it. Then Locklear rushed to open the cage the priest had been watching.

The top levered back, and its occupant sank to the cage floor without moving. Scarface screamed his rage, turning toward the injured captive. "You experiment on tiny kittens? Shall we do the same to you now?"

Locklear, his tears flowing freely, lifted the tiny kzin kitten—a male—in hands that were tender, holding it to his breast. "It's breathing," he said. "A miracle, after getting the centrifuge treatment in a cage meant for something far bigger."

"Before I kill you, do something honorable," Scarface said to the wounded one. "Tell me where the other kitten is."

The captive pointed toward the end of the passage. "I am only an acolyte," he muttered. "I did not enjoy following orders."

Locklear sped along the cages and, at last, found Boot's female kitten revolving slowly in a cage of the proper size. He realized from the prominence of the tiny ribs that the kitten would cry for milk when it waked. *If* it waked. "Is she still alive?"

"Yes," the acolyte called back. "I am glad this happened. I can die with a less-troubled conscience."

After a hurried agreement and some rough questioning, they gave the acolyte a choice. He climbed into a cage hidden behind others at the end of another corridor and was soon revolving in stasis. The kittens went into one small cage. Working feverishly against the time when another enemy might walk into the crypt, they disassembled several more stasis cages and toted the working parts to the scooter, then added the kitten cage and, barely, levitated the scooter with its heavy load.

An hour later, Scarface bore the precious cage into the cave and Locklear, following with an armload of parts, heard the anguish of Boots. "They'll hear you from a hundred meters," he cautioned as Boots gathered the mewing, emaciated kittens in her arms.

They feared at first that her milk would no longer flow but presently, from where Boots had crept into the darkness, Kit returned. "They are suckling. Do not expect her to be much help from now on," Kit said.

Scarface checked the magazine of his sidearm. "One priest has paid. There is no reason why I cannot extract full payment from the others now," he said.

"Yes, there is," Locklear replied, his fingers flying with hand tools from the cache. "Before you can get 'em all, they'll send devout fools to be killed while they escape. You said so yourself. Scarface, I don't want innocent kzin blood on my hands! But after my old promise to Boots, I saw what that maniac was doing and—let's just say *my* honor was at stake." He knew that any modern kzin commander would understand that. Setting down the wiring tool, he shuddered and waited until he could speak without a tremor in his voice. "If you'll help me get the wiring rigged for these stasis units, we can hide them in the right spot and take the entire bloody priesthood in one pile."

"All at once? I should like to know how," said Kit, counting the few units that lay around them.

"Well, I'll tell you how," said Locklear, his eyes bright with fervor. They heard him out, and then their faces glowed with the same zeal.

When their traps lay ready for emplacement, they slept while Kit kept watch. Long after dark, as Boots lay nearby cradling her kittens, Kit waked the others and served a cold broth. "You take a terrible chance, flying in the dark," she reminded them.

"We will move slowly," Scarface promised, "and the village fires shed enough light for me to land. Too bad about the senses of inferior species," he said, his ear umbrellas rising with his joke.

"How would you like a nice cold bath, tabby?" Locklear's question was mild, but it held an edge.

"Only monkeys *need* to bathe," said the kzin, still amused. Together they carried their hardware outside and, by the light of a glowlamp, loaded the scooter while Kit watched for any telltale glow of eyes in the distance.

After a hurried nuzzle from Kit, Scarface brought the scooter up swiftly, switching the glowlamp to its pinpoint setting and using it as seldom as possible. Their forward motion was so slow that, on the two occasions when they blundered into the tops of towering fernpalms, they jettisoned nothing more than soft curses. An hour later, Scarface maneuvered them over a light yellow strip that became a heavily trodden path and began to follow that path by brief glowlamp flashes. The village, they knew, would eventually come into view.

It was Locklear who said, "Off to your right."

"The village fires? I saw them minutes ago."

"Oh shut up, supercat," Locklear grumped. "So where's our drop zone?"

"Near," was the reply, and Locklear felt their little craft swing to the side. At the pace of a weed seed, the scooter wafted down until Scarface, with one leg hanging through the viewslot of his craft, spat a short, nasty phrase. One quick flash of the lamp guided him to a level landing spot and then, with admirable panache, Scarface let the scooter settle without a creak.

If they were surprised now, only Scarface could pilot his scooter with any hope of getting them both away. Locklear grabbed one of the devices they had prepared and, feeling his way with only his feet, walked until he felt a rise of turf. Then he retraced his steps, vented a heavy sigh, and began the emplacement.

Ten minutes later he felt his way back to the scooter, tapping twice on one of its planks to avoid getting his head bitten off by an all-too-ready Scarface. "So far, so good," Locklear judged.

"This had better work," Scarface muttered.

"Tell me about it," said the retreating Locklear, grunting with a pair of stasis toroids. After the stasis units were all in place, Locklear rested at the scooter before creeping off again, this time with the glowlamp and a very sloppy wiring harness.

When he returned for the last time, he virtually fell onto the scooter. "It's all there," he said, exhausted, rubbing wrists still raw from his brief captivity. Scarface found his bearings again, but it was another hour before he floated up an arroyo and then used the lamp for a landing light.

He bore the sleeping Locklear into the cave as a man might carry a child. Soon they both were snoring, and Locklear did not hear the sound that terrified the distant villagers in late morning.

Locklear's first hint that his plans were in shreds came with rough shaking by Scarface. "Wake up! The monkeys have declared war," were the first words he understood.

As they lay at the main cave entrance, they could see sweeps of the pinnace as it moved over the kzin village. Small energy beams lanced down several times, at targets too widely spaced to be the huts. "They're targeting whatever moves," Locklear ranted, pounding a fist on hard turf. "And I'll bet the priests are hiding!"

Scarface brought up his all-band set and let it scan. In moments, the voice of David Gomulka grated from the speaker.

" . . . Kill 'em all. Tell 'em, Locklear! And when they do let you go, you'd better be ready to talk; over."

"I can talk to 'em any time I like, you know," Locklear said to his friend. "The set they gave me may have a coded carrier wave."

"We must stop this terror raid," Scarface replied, "before they kill us all!"

Locklear stripped his sidearm magazine of its rounds and fingered the tiny ear set from its metal cage, screwing it into his ear. "Got me tied up," he said, trying to ignore the disgusted look from Scarface at this unseemly lie. "Are you receiving . . ."

"We'll home in on your signal," Gomulka cut in.

Locklear quickly shoved the tiny set back into the butt of his sidearm. "No, you won't," he muttered to himself. Turning to Scarface: "We've got to transmit from another place, or they'll triangulate on me."

Racing to the scooter, they fled to the arroyo and skimmed the veldt to another spot. Then, still moving, Locklear used the tiny set again. "Gomulka, they're moving me."

The sergeant, furiously: "Where the fuck—?"

Locklear: "If you're shooting, let the naked savages alone. The real tabbies are the ones with bandoliers, got it? Bag 'em if you can but the naked ones aren't combatants."

He put his little set away again but Scarface's unit, on "receive only," picked up the reply. "Your goddamn signal is shooting all over hell, Locklear. And whaddaya mean, not combatants? I've never had a chance to hunt tabbies like this. No little civilian shit is gonna tell us we can't teach 'em what it's like to be hunted! You got that, Locklear?"

They continued to monitor Gomulka, skating back near the cave until the scooter lay beneath spreading ferns. Fleeing into the safety of the cave, they agreed on a terrible necessity. "They intend to take ears and tails as trophies, or so they say," Locklear admitted. "You must find the most peaceable of your tribe, Boots, and bring them to the cave. They'll be cut down like so many vermin if you don't."

"No priests, and no acolytes," Scarface snarled. "Say nothing about us but you may warn them that no priest will leave this cave alive! That much, my honor requires."

"I understand," said Boots, whirling down one of the tunnels.

"And you and I," Scarface said to Locklear, "must lure that

damned monkeyship away from this area. We cannot let them see kzinti streaming in here."

In early afternoon, the scooter slid along rocky highlands before settling beneath a stone overhang. "The best cover for snipers on Kzersatz, Locklear. I kept my cache here, and I know every cranny and clearing. We just may trap that monkeyship, if I am clever enough at primitive skills."

"You want to trap them here? Nothing simpler," said Locklear, bringing out his tiny comm set.

But it was not to be so simple.

Locklear, lying in the open on his back with one hand under saffron vines, watched the pinnace thrum overhead. The clearing, ringed by tall fernpalms, was big enough for the *Anthony Wayne,* almost capacious for a pinnace. Locklear raised one hand in greeting as he counted four heads inside the canopy: Gomulka, Lee, Gazho, and Schmidt. Then he let his head fall back in pretended exhaustion, and waited.

In vain. The pinnace settled ten meters away, its engines still above idle, and the canopy levered up; but the deserter crew had beam rifles trained on the surrounding foliage and did not accept the bait. "They may be back soon," Locklear shouted in Interworld. He could hear the faint savage ripping at vegetation nearby, and wondered if they heard it, too. "Hurry!"

"Tell us now, asshole," Gomulka boomed, his voice coming both from the earpiece and the pinnace. "The secret, *now,* or we leave you for the tabbies!"

Locklear licked his lips, buying seconds. "It's— It's some kind of drive. The Outsiders built it here," he groaned, wondering feverishly what the devil his tongue was leading him into. He noted that Gazho and Lee had turned toward him now, their eyes blazing with greed. Schmidt, however, was studying the tallest fernpalm, and suddenly fired a thin line of fire slashing into its top, which was already shuddering.

"Not good enough, Locklear," Gomulka called. "We've got great drives already. Tell us where it is."

"In a cavern. Other side of—valley," Locklear said, taking his time. "Nobody has an—instantaneous drive but Outsiders," he finished.

A whoop of delight, then, from Gomulka, one second before that fernpalm began to topple. Schmidt was already watching it, and screamed a warning in time for the pilot to see the slender forest giant begin its agonizingly slow fall. Gomulka hit the panic button.

Too late. The pinnace, darting forward with its canopy still up, rose to meet the spreading top of the tree Scarface had cut using claws and fangs alone. As the pinnace was borne to the ground, its canopy twisting off its hinges, the swish of foliage and squeal of metal filled the air. Locklear leaped aside, rolling away.

Among the yells of consternation, Gomulka's was loudest. "Schmidt, you dumb fuck!"

"It was him," Schmidt yelled, coming upright again to train his rifle on Locklear—who fired first. If that slug had hit squarely, Schmidt would have been dead meat, but its passage along Schmidt's forearm left only a deep bloody crease.

Gomulka, every inch a warrior, let fly with his own sidearm though his nose was bleeding from the impact. But Locklear, now protected by another tree, returned the fire and saw a hole appear in the canopy next to the wide-staring eyes of Nathan Gazho.

When Scarface cut loose from thirty meters away, Gomulka made the right decision. Yelling commands, laying down a cover of fire first toward Locklear, then toward Scarface, he drove his team out of the immobile pinnace by sheer voice command while he peered past the armored lip of the cockpit.

Scarface's call, in Kzin, probably could not be understood by the others, but Locklear could not have agreed more. "Fight, run, fight again," came the snarling cry.

Five minutes later after racing downhill, Locklear dropped behind one end of a fallen log and grinned at Scarface, who lay at its other end. "Nice aim with that tree."

"I despise chewing vegetable matter," was the reply. "Do you think they can get that pinnace in operation again?"

"With safety interlocks? It won't move at more than a crawl until somebody repairs the—" but Locklear fell silent at a sudden gesture.

From uphill, a stealthy movement as Gomulka scuttled behind a hillock. Then to their right, another brief rush by Schmidt, who held his rifle one-handed now. This advance, basic to any team using projectile weapons, would soon overrun their quarry. The big blond was in the act of dropping behind a fern when Scarface's round caught him squarely in the breast, the rifle flying away, and Locklear saw answering fire send tendrils of smoke from his log. He was only a flicker behind

Scarface, firing blindly to force enemy heads down, as they bolted downhill again in good cover.

Twice more, during the next hour, they opened up at long range to slow Gomulka's team. At that range they had no success. Later, drawing nearer to the village, they lay behind stones at the lip of an arroyo. "With only three," Scarface said with satisfaction. "They are advancing more slowly."

"And we're wasting ammo," Locklear replied. "I have, uh, two eights and four rounds left. You?"

"Eight and seven. Not enough against beam rifles." The big kzin twisted, then, ear umbrellas cocked toward the village. He studied the sun's position, then came to some internal decision and handed over ten of his precious remaining rounds. "The brush in the arroyo's throat looks flimsy, Locklear, but I could crawl under its tops, so I know you can. Hold them up here, then retreat under the brushtops in the arroyo and wait at its mouth. With any luck I will reach you there."

The kzin warrior was already leaping toward the village. Locklear cried softly. "Where are you going?"

The reply was almost lost in the arroyo: "For reinforcements."

The sun had crept far across the sky of Kzersatz before Locklear saw movement again, and when he did it was nearly too late. A stone descended the arroyo, whacking another stone with the crack of bowling balls; Locklear realized that someone had already crossed the arroyo. Then he saw Soichiro Lee ease his rifle into sight. Lee simply had not spotted him.

Locklear took two-handed aim very slowly and fired three rounds, full-auto. The first impact puffed dirt into Lee's face so that Locklear did not see the others clearly. It was enough that Lee's head blossomed, snapping up and back so hard it jerked his torso, and the rifle clattered into the arroyo.

The call of alarm from Gazho was so near it spooked Locklear into firing blindly. Then he was bounding into the arroyo's throat, sliding into chest-high brush with spreading tops.

Late shadows were his friends as he waited, hoping one of the men would go for the beam rifle in plain sight. Now and then he sat up and lobbed a stone into brush not far from Lee's body. Twice, rifles scorched that brush. Locklear knew better than to fire back without a sure target while pinned in that ravine.

When they began sending heavy fire into the throat of the

arroyo, Locklear hoped they would exhaust their plenums, but saw a shimmer of heat and knew his cover could burn. He wriggled away downslope, past a trickle of water, careful to avoid shaking the brush. It was then that he heard the heavy reports of a kzin sidearm toward the village.

He nearly shot the rope-muscled kzin that sprang into the ravine before recognizing Scarface, but within a minute they had worked their way together. "Those *kshat* priests," Scarface panted, "have harangued a dozen others into chasing me. I killed one priest; the others are staying safely behind."

"So where are our reinforcements?"

"The dark will transform them."

"But we'll be caught between enemies," Locklear pointed out.

"Who will engage each other in darkness, a dozen fools against three monkeys."

"Two," Locklear corrected. But he saw the logic now, and when the sunlight winked out a few minutes later he was watching the stealthy movement of kzin acolytes along both lips of the arroyo.

Mouth close to Locklear's ear, Scarface said, "They will send someone up this watercourse. Move aside; my *wtsai* will deal with them quietly."

But when a military flare lit the upper reaches of the arroyo a few minutes later, they heard battle screams and suddenly, comically, two kzin warriors came bounding directly between Locklear and Scarface. Erect, heads above the brushtops, they leapt toward the action and were gone in a moment.

Following with one hand on a furry arm, Locklear stumbled blindly to the arroyo lip and sat down to watch. Spears and torches hurtled from one side of the upper ravine while thin energy bursts lanced out from the other. Blazing brush lent a flickering light as well, and at least three great kzin bodies surged across the arroyo toward their enemies.

"At times," Scarface said quietly as if to himself, "I think my species more valiant than stupid. But they do not even know their enemy, nor care."

"Same for those deserters," Locklear muttered, fascinated at the firefight his friend had provoked. "So how do we get back to the cave?"

"This way," Scarface said, tapping his nose, and set off with Locklear stumbling at his heels.

—~— —~— —~—

The cave seemed much smaller when crowded with a score of worried kzinti, but not for long. The moment they realized that Kit was missing, Scarface demanded to know why.

"Two acolytes entered," explained one male, and Locklear recognized him as the mild-tempered Stalwart. "They argued three idiots into helping take her back to the village before dark."

Locklear, in quiet fury: "No one stopped them?"

Stalwart pointed to bloody welts on his arms and neck, then at a female lying curled on a grassy pallet. "I had no help but her. She tried to offer herself instead."

And then Scarface saw that it was Boots who was hurt but nursing her kittens in silence, and no cave could have held his rage. Screaming, snarling, claws raking tails, he sent the entire pack of refugees pelting into the night, to return home as best they could. It was Locklear's idea to let Stalwart remain; he had, after all, shed his blood in their cause.

Scarface did not subside until he saw Locklear, with the kzin medkit, ministering to Boots. "A fine ally, but no expert in kzin medicine," he scolded, choosing different unguents.

Boots, shamed at having permitted acolytes in the cave, pointed out that the traps had been disarmed for the flow of refugees. "The priesthood will surely be back here soon," she added.

"Not before afternoon," Stalwart said. "They never mount ceremonies during darkness. If I am any judge, they will drown the beauteous *prret* at high noon."

Locklear: "Don't they ever learn?"

Boots: "No. They are the priesthood," she said as if explaining everything, and Stalwart agreed.

"All the same," Scarface said, "they might do a better job this time. You," he said to Stalwart; "could you get to the village and back here in darkness?"

"If I cannot, call me acolyte. You would learn what they intend for your mate?"

"Of course he must," Locklear said, walking with him toward the main entrance. "But call before you enter again. We are setting deadly traps for anyone who tries to return, and you may as well spread the word."

Stalwart moved off into darkness, sniffing the breeze, and Locklear went from place to place, switching on traps while Scarface tended Boots. This tender care from a kzin warrior might be explained as gratitude; even with her kittens, Boots had tried to substitute herself for Kit. Still, Locklear thought, there was more to it than that. He wondered about it until he fell asleep.

Twice during the night, they were roused by tremendous thumps and, once, a brief kzin snarl. Scarface returned each time licking blood from his arms. The second time he said to a bleary-eyed Locklear, "We can plug the entrances with corpses if these acolytes keep squashing themselves against our ceilings." The grav polarizer traps, it seemed, made excellent sentries.

Locklear did not know when Stalwart returned but, when he awoke, the young kzin was already speaking with Scarface. True to their rigid code, the priests fully intended to drown Kit again in a noon ceremony using heavier stones and, afterward, to lay siege to the cave.

"Let them; it will be empty," Scarface grunted. "Locklear, you have seen me pilot my little craft. I wonder . . ."

"Hardest part is getting around those deserters, if any," Locklear said. "I can cover a lot of ground when I'm fresh."

"Good. Can you navigate to where Boots had her birthing bower before noon?"

"If I can't, call me acolyte," Locklear said, smiling. He set off at a lope just after dawn, achingly alert. Anyone he met, now, would be a target.

After an hour, he was lost. He found his bearings from a promontory, loping longer, walking less, and was dizzy with fatigue when he climbed a low cliff to the overhang where Scarface had left his scooter. Breathing hard, he was lowering his rump to the scooter when the rifle butt whistled just over his head.

Nathan Gazho, who had located the scooter after scouring the area near the pinnace, felt fierce glee when he saw Locklear's approach. But he had not expected Locklear to drop so suddenly. He swung again as Locklear, almost as large as his opponent, darted in under the blow. Locklear grunted with the impact against his shoulder, caught the weapon by its barrel, and used it like a prybar with both hands though his left arm was growing numb. The rifle spun out of reach. As they struggled away from the ten-meter precipice, Gazho cursed—the first word by either man—and snatched his utility knife from its belt clasp, reeling back, his left forearm out. His crouch, the shifting of the knife, its extraordinary honed edge: marks of a man who had fought with knives before.

Locklear reached for the kzin sidearm but he had placed it in a left-hand pocket and now that hand was numb. Gazho darted forward in a swordsman's balestra, flicking the knife in a short arc as he passed. By that time Locklear had snatched his own *wtsai* from its sheath with his right hand. Gazho saw the long blade but did not flinch, and Locklear knew he was running out of time. Standing four paces away, he pump-faked twice as if to throw the knife. Gazho's protecting forearm flashed to the vertical at the same instant when Locklear leaped forward, hurling the *wtsai* as he squatted to grasp a stone of fist size.

Because Locklear was no knife-thrower, the weapon did not hit point-first; but the heavy handle caught Gazho squarely on the temple and, as he stumbled back, Locklear's stone splintered his jaw. Nathan Gazho's legs buckled and inertia carried him backward over the precipice, screaming.

Locklear heard the heavy thump as he was fumbling for his sidearm. From above, he could see the broken body twitching, and his single round from the sidearm was more kindness than revenge. Trembling, massaging his left arm, he collected his *wtsai* and the beam rifle before crawling onto the scooter. Not until he levitated the little craft and guided it ineptly down the mountainside did he notice the familiar fittings of the standard-issue rifle. It had been fully discharged during the firefight, thanks to Scarface's tactic.

Many weeks before—it seemed a geologic age by now—Locklear had found Boots' private bower by accident. The little cave was hidden behind a low waterfall near the mouth of a shallow ravine, and once he had located that ravine from the air it was only a matter of following it, keeping low enough to avoid being seen from the kzin village. The sun was almost directly overhead as Locklear approached the rendezvous. If he'd cut it too close . . .

Scarface waved him down near the falls and sprang onto the scooter before it could settle. "Let me fly it," he snarled, shoving Locklear aside in a way that suggested a kzin on the edge of self-control. The scooter lunged forward and, as he hung on, Locklear told of Gazho's death.

"It will not matter," Scarface replied as he piloted the scooter higher, squinting toward the village, "if my mate dies this day." Then his predator's eyesight picked out the horrifying details, and he began to gnash his teeth in uncontrollable fury.

When they were within a kilometer of the village, Locklear

could see what had pushed his friend beyond sanity. While most of the villagers stood back as if to distance themselves from this pomp and circumstance, the remaining acolytes bore a bound, struggling burden toward the lakeshore. Behind them marched the bandoliered priests, arms waving beribboned lances. They were chanting, a cacophony like metal chaff thrown into a power transformer, and Locklear shuddered.

Even at top speed, they would not arrive until that procession reached the walkway to deep water; and Kit, her limbs bound together with great stones for weights, would not be able to escape this time. "We'll have to go in after her," Locklear called into the wind.

"I cannot swim," cried Scarface, his eyes slitted.

"I can," said Locklear, taking great breaths to hoard oxygen. As he positioned himself for the leap, his friend began to fire his sidearm.

As the scooter swept lower and slower, one kzin priest crumpled. The rest saw the scooter and exhorted the acolytes forward. The hapless Kit was flung without further ceremony into deep water but, as he was leaping feet-first off the scooter, Locklear saw that she had spotted him. As he slammed into deep water, he could hear the full-automatic thunder of Scarface's weapon.

Misjudging his leap, Locklear let inertia carry him before striking out forward and down. His left arm was only at half-strength but the weight of his weapons helped carry him to the sandy bottom. Eyes open, he struggled to the one darker mass looming ahead.

But it was only a small boulder. Feeling the prickles of oxygen starvation across his back and scalp, he swiveled, kicking hard—and felt one foot strike something like fur. He wheeled, ignoring the demands of his lungs, wresting his *wtsai* out with one hand as he felt for cordage with the other. Three ferocious slices, and those cords were severed. He dropped the knife—the same weapon Kit herself had once dulled, then resharpened for him—and pushed off from the bottom in desperation.

He broke the surface, gasped twice, and saw a wide-eyed priest fling a lance in his direction. By sheer dumb luck, it missed, and after a last deep inhalation Locklear kicked toward the bottom again.

The last thing a wise man would do is locate a drowning tigress in deep water, but that is what Locklear did. Kit, no swimmer, literally climbed up his sodden flightsuit, forcing him into an underwater somersault, fine sand stinging his eyes. The next moment he was struggling toward the light again, disoriented and panicky.

He broke the surface, swam to a piling at the end of the walkway, and tried to hyperventilate for another hopeless foray after Kit. Then, between gasps, he heard a spitting cough echo in the space between the water's surface and the underside of the walkway. "Kit!" He swam forward, seeing her frightened gaze and her formidable claws locked into those rough planks, and patted her shoulder. Above them, someone was raising kzin hell. "Stay here," he commanded, and kicked off toward the shallows.

He waded with his sidearm drawn. What he saw on the walkway was abundant proof that the priesthood truly did not seem to learn very fast.

Five bodies sprawled where they had been shot, bleeding on the planks near deep water, but more of them lay curled on the planks within a few paces of the shore, piled atop one another. One last acolyte stood on the walkway, staring over the curled bodies. He was staring at Scarface, who stood on dry land with his own long *wtsai* held before him, snarling a challenge with eyes that held the light of madness. Then, despite what he had seen happen a half-dozen times in moments, the acolyte screamed and leaped.

Losing consciousness in midair, the acolyte fell heavily across his fellows and drew into a foetal crouch, as all the others had done when crossing the last six meters of planking toward shore. Those units Locklear had placed beneath the planks in darkness had kept three-ton herbivores in stasis, and worked even better on kzinti. They'd known damned well the priesthood would be using the walkway again sooner or later; but they'd had no idea it would be *this* soon.

Scarface did not seem entirely sane again until he saw Kit wading from the water. Then he clasped his mate to him, ignoring the wetness he so despised. Asked how he managed to trip the gangswitch, Scarface replied, "You had told me it was on the inside of that piling, and those idiots did not try to stop me from wading to it."

"I noticed you were wet," said Locklear, smiling. "Sorry about that."

"I shall be wetter with blood presently," Scarface said with a grim look toward the pile of inert sleepers.

Locklear, aghast, opened his mouth.

But Kit placed her hand over it. "Rockear, I know you, and I know my mate. It is not your way but this is Kzersatz. Did you see what they did to the captive they took last night?"

"Big man, short black hair? His name is Gomulka."

"His name is meat. What they left of him hangs from a post yonder."

"Oh my God," Locklear mumbled, swallowing hard. "But—look, just don't ask me to help execute anyone in stasis."

"Indeed." Scarface stood, stretched, and walked toward the piled bodies. "You may want to take a brief walk, Locklear," he said, picking up a discarded lance twice his length. "This is kzin business, not monkey business." But he did not understand why, as Locklear strode away, the little man was laughing ruefully at the choice of words.

Locklear's arm was well enough, after two days, to let him dive for his *wtsai* while kzinti villagers watched in curiosity—and perhaps in distaste. By that time they had buried their dead in a common plot and, with the help of Stalwart, begun to repair the pinnace's canopy holes and twisted hinges. The little hand-welder would have sped the job greatly but, Locklear promised, "We'll get it back. If we don't hit first, there'll be a stolen warship overhead with enough clout to fry us all."

Scarface had to agree. As the warrior who had overthrown the earlier regime, he now held not only the rights, but also the responsibilities of leading his people. Lounging on grassy beds in the village's meeting hut on the third night, they slurped hot stew and made plans. "Only the two of us can make that raid, you know," said the big kzin.

"I was thinking of volunteers," said Locklear, who knew very well that Scarface would honor his wish if he made it a demand.

"If we had time to train them," Scarface replied. "But that ship could be searching for the pinnace at any moment. Only you and I can pilot the pinnace so, if we are lost in battle, those volunteers will be stranded forever among hostile monk—hostiles," he amended. "Nor can they use modern weapons."

"Stalwart probably could, he's a natural mechanic. I know Kit can use a weapon—not that I want her along."

"For a better reason than you know," Scarface agreed, his ears winking across the fire at the somnolent Kit.

"He is trying to say I will soon bear his kittens, Rockear," Kit said. "And please do not take Boots' new mate away merely because he can work magics with his hands." She saw the surprise in Locklear's face. "How could you miss that? He fought those acolytes in the cave for Boots' sake."

"I, uh, guess I've been pretty busy," Locklear admitted.

"We will be busier if that warship strikes before we do," Scarface reminded him. "I suggest we go as soon as it is light."

Locklear sat bolt upright. "Damn! If they hadn't taken my wristcomp—I keep forgetting. The schedules of those little suns aren't in synch; it's probably daylight there now, and we can find out by idling the pinnace near the force walls. You can damned well see whether it's light there."

"I would rather go in darkness," Scarface complained, "if we could master those night-vision sensors in the pinnace."

"Maybe, in time. I flew the thing here to the village, didn't I?"

"In daylight, after a fashion," Scarface said in a friendly insult, and flicked his sidearm from its holster to check its magazine. "Would you like to fly it again, right now?"

Kit saw the little man fill his hand as he checked his own weapon, and marveled at a creature with the courage to show such puny teeth in such a feral grin. "I know you must go," she said as they turned toward the door, and nuzzled the throat of her mate. "But what do we do if you fail?"

"You expect enemies with the biggest ship you ever saw," Locklear said. "And you know how those stasis traps work. Just remember, those people have night sensors and they can burn you from a distance."

Scarface patted her firm belly once. "Take great care," he said, and strode into darkness.

The pinnace's controls were simple, and Locklear's only worry was the thin chorus of whistles: air, escaping from a canopy that was not quite perfectly sealed. He briefed Scarface yet again as their craft carried them over Newduvai, and piloted the pinnace so that its reentry thunder would roll gently, as far as possible from the *Anthony Wayne.*

It was late morning on Newduvai, and they could see the gleam of the *Wayne*'s hull from afar. Locklear slid the pinnace at a furtive pace, brushing spiny shrubs for the last few kilometers before landing in a small desert wadi. They pulled hinge pins from the canopy and hid them in the pinnace to make its theft tedious. Then, stuffing a roll of binder tape into his pocket, Locklear began to trot toward his clearing.

"I am a kitten again," Scarface rejoiced, fairly floating along in the reduced gravity of Newduvai. Then he slowed, nose twitching. "Not far," he warned.

Locklear nodded, moved cautiously ahead, and then sat behind a green thicket. Ahead lay the clearing with the warship and cabin, seeming little changed—but a heavy limb held the door shut as if to keep things in, not out. And Scarface noticed two mansized craters just outside the cabin's foundation logs. After ten minutes without sound or movement from the clearing, Scarface was ready to employ what he called the monkey ruse; not quite a lie, but certainly a misdirection.

"Patience," Locklear counseled. "I thought you tabbies were hunters."

"Hunters, yes; not skulkers."

"No wonder you lose wars," Locklear muttered. But after another half-hour in which they ghosted in deep cover around the clearing, he too was ready to move.

The massive kzin sighed, slid his *wtsai* to the rear and handed over his sidearm, then dutifully held his big pawlike hands out. Locklear wrapped the thin, bright red binder tape around his friend's wrists many times, then severed it with its special stylus. Scarface was certain he could bite it through until he tried. Then he was happy to let Locklear draw the stylus, with its chemical enabler, across the tape where the slit could not be seen. Then, hailing the clearing as he went, the little man drew his own *wtsai* and prodded his "prisoner" toward the cabin.

His neck crawling with premonition, Locklear stood five paces from the door and called again:

"Hello, the cabin!"

From inside, several female voices and then only one, which he knew very well: "Locklear go soon soon!"

"Ruth says that many times," he replied, half amused, though he knew somehow that this time she feared for him. "New people keep gentles inside?"

Scarface, standing uneasily, had his ear umbrellas moving fore and aft. He mumbled something as, from inside, Ruth said, "Ruth teach new talk to gentles, get food. No teach, no food," she explained with vast economy.

"I'll see about that," he called and then, in Kzin, "what was that, Scarface?"

Low but urgent: "Behind us, fool."

Locklear turned. Not twenty paces away, Anse Parker was moving forward as silently as he could and now the hatchway of the *Anthony Wayne* yawned open. Parker's rifle hung from its sling but his service parabellum was leveled, and he was smirking. "If this don't beat all: my prisoner has a prisoner," he drawled.

For a frozen instant, Locklear feared the deserter had spied the *wtsai* hanging above Scarface's backside—but the kzin's tail was erect, hiding the weapon. "Where are the others?" Locklear asked.

"Around. Pacifyin' the natives in that tabby lifeboat," Parker replied. "I'll ask you the same question, asshole."

The parabellum was not wavering. Locklear stepped away from his friend, who faced Parker so that the wrist tape was obvious. "Gomulka's boys are in trouble. Promised me amnesty if I'd come for help, and I brought a hostage," Locklear said.

Parker's movements were not fast, but so casual that Locklear was taken by surprise. The parabellum's short barrel whipped across his face, splitting his lip, bowling him over. Parker stood over him, sneering. "Buncha shit. If that happened, you'd hide out. You can tell a better one than that."

Locklear privately realized that Parker was right. And then Parker himself, who had turned half away from Scarface, made a discovery of his own. He discovered that, without moving one step, a kzin could reach out a long way to stick the point of a *wtsai* against a man's throat. Parker froze.

"If you shoot me, you are deader than chivalry," Locklear said, propping himself up on an elbow. "Toss the pistol away."

Parker, cursing, did so, looking at Scarface, finding his chance as the kzin glanced toward the weapon. Parker shied away with a sidelong leap, snatching for his slung rifle. And ignoring the leg of Locklear who tripped him nicely.

As his rifle tumbled into grass, Parker rolled to his feet and began sprinting for the warship two hundred meters away. Scarface outran him easily, then stationed himself in front of the warship's hatch. Locklear could not hear Parker's words, but his gestures toward the *wtsai* were clear: there ain't no justice.

Scarface understood. With that kzin grin that so many humans failed to understand, he tossed the *wtsai* near Parker's feet in pure contempt. Parker grabbed the knife and saw his enemy's face, howled in fear, then raced into the forest, Scarface bounding lazily behind.

Locklear knocked the limb away from his cabin door and found Ruth inside with three others, all young females. He embraced the homely Ruth with great joy. The other young Neanderthalers disappeared from the clearing in seconds but Ruth walked off with Locklear. He had already seen the spider grenades that lay with sensors outspread just outside the cabin's walls. Two gentles had already died trying to dig their way out, she said.

He tried to prepare Ruth for his ally's appearance but, when Scarface reappeared with his *wtsai,* she needed time to adjust. "I don't see any blood," was Locklear's comment.

"The blood of cowards is distasteful," was the kzin's wry response. "I believe you have my sidearm, friend Locklear."

They should have counted, said Locklear, on Stockton learning to fly the kzin lifeboat. But lacking heavy weapons, it might not complicate their capture strategy too much. As it happened, the capture was more absurd than complicated.

Stockton brought the lifeboat bumbling down in late afternoon almost in the same depressions the craft's jackpads had made previously, within fifty paces of the *Anthony Wayne.* He and the lissome Grace wore holstered pistols, stretching out their muscle kinks as they walked toward the bigger craft, unaware that they were being watched. "Anse; we're back," Stockton shouted. "Any word from Gomulka?"

Silence from the ship, though its hatch steps were down. Grace shrugged, then glanced at Locklear's cabin. "The door prop is down, Curt. He's trying to hump those animals again."

"Damn him," Stockton railed, and both turned toward the cabin. To Grace he complained, "If you were a better lay, he wouldn't always be—*good God!*"

The source of his alarm was a long blood-chilling, gut-wrenching scream. A kzin scream, the kind featured in horror holovision productions; and very, very near. "Battle stations, red alert, up ship," Stockton cried, bolting for the hatch.

Briefly, he had his pistol ready but had to grip it in his teeth as he reached for the hatch rails of the *Anthony Wayne.* For that one moment he almost resembled a piratical man of action, and that was the moment when he stopped, one foot on the top step, and Grace bumped her head against his rump as she fled up those steps.

"I don't think so," said Locklear softly. To Curt Stockton, the muzzle of that alien sidearm so near must have looked like a torpedo launcher. His face drained of color, the commander allowed Locklear to take the pistol from his trembling lips. "And Grace," Locklear went on, because he could not see her past Stockton's bulk, "I doubt if it's your style anyway, but don't give your pistol a second thought. That kzin you heard? Well, they're out there behind you, but they aren't in here. Toss your parabellum away and I'll let you in."

Late the next afternoon they finished walling up the crypt on Newduvai, with a small work force of willing hands recruited by Ruth. As the little group of gentles filed away down the hillside, Scarface nodded toward the rubble-choked entrance. "I still believe we should have executed those two, Locklear."

"I know you do. But they'll keep in stasis for as long as the war lasts, and on Newduvai—well, Ruth's people agree with me that there's been enough killing." Locklear turned his back on the crypt and Ruth moved to his side, still wary of the huge alien whose speech sounded like the sizzle of fat on a skewer.

"Your ways are strange," said the kzin, as they walked toward the nearby pinnace. "I know something of Interworld beauty standards. As long as you want that female lieutenant alive, it seems to me you would keep her, um, available."

"Grace Agostinho's beauty is all on the outside. And there's a girl hiding somewhere on Newduvai that those deserters never did catch. In a few years she'll be—well, you'll meet her someday." Locklear put an arm around Ruth's waist and grinned. "The truth is, Ruth thinks *I'm* pretty funny-looking, but some things you can learn to overlook."

At the clearing, Ruth hopped from the pinnace first. "Ruth will fix place nice, like before," she promised, and walked to the cabin.

"She's learning Interworld fast," Locklear said proudly. "Her telepathy helps—in a lot of ways. Scarface, do you realize that her people may be the most tremendous discovery of modern times? And the irony of it! The empathy these people share probably helped isolate them from the modern humans that came from their own gene pool. Yet their kind of empathy might be the only viable future for us." He sighed and stepped to the turf. "Sometimes I wonder whether I want to be found."

Standing beside the pinnace, they gazed at the *Anthony Wayne.* Scarface said, "With that warship, you could do the finding."

Locklear assessed the longing in the face of the big kzin. "I know how you feel about piloting, Scarface. But you must accept that I can't let you have any craft more advanced than your scooter back on Kzersatz."

"But—surely, the pinnace or my own lifeboat?"

"You see that?" Locklear pointed toward the forest.

Scarface looked dutifully away, then back, and when he saw the sidearm pointing at his breast, a look of terrible loss crossed his face. "I see that I will never understand you," he growled, clasping his hands behind his head. "And I see that you still doubt my honor."

Locklear forced him to lean against the pinnace, arms behind his back, and secured his hands with binder tape. "Sorry, but I have to do this," he said. "Now get back in the pinnace. I'm taking you to Kzersatz."

"But I would have—"

"Don't say it," Locklear demanded. "Don't tell me what you want, and don't remind me of your honor, goddammit! Look here, I *know* you don't lie. And what if the next ship here is another kzin ship? You won't lie to them either, your bloody honor won't let you. They'll find you sitting pretty on Kzersatz, right?"

Teetering off-balance as he climbed into the pinnace without using his arms, Scarface still glowered. But after a moment he admitted, "Correct."

"They won't court-martial you, Scarface. Because a lying, sneaking monkey pulled a gun on you, tied you up, and sent you back to prison. I'm telling you here and now, I see Kzersatz as a prison and every tabby on this planet will be locked up there for the duration of the war!" With that, Locklear sealed the canopy and made a quick check of the console readouts. He reached across to adjust the inertia-reel harness of his companion, then shrugged into his own. "You have no choice, and no tabby telepath can ever claim you did. *Now* do you understand?"

The big kzin was looking below as the forest dropped away, but Locklear could see his ears forming the kzin equivalent of a smile. "No wonder you win wars," said Scarface.

The Children's Hour

by Jerry Pournelle
& S.M. Stirling

Prologue

The kzin floated motionless in the bubble of space. The yacht *Boundless-Ranger* was orbiting beyond the circle of Wunderland's moons, and the planet obscured the disk of Alpha Centauri; Beta was a brighter point of light. All around him the stars shone, glorious and chill, multihued. He was utterly relaxed; the points of his claws showed slightly, and the pink tip of his tongue. Long ago he had mastered the impulse to draw back from vertigo, uncoupling the conscious mind and accepting the endless falling, forever and ever. . . .

A small chiming brought him gradually back to selfhood. "Hrrrr," he muttered, suddenly conscious of dry throat and nose. The bubble was retracting into the personal spacecraft; he oriented himself and landed lightly as the chamber switched to opaque and Kzin-normal gravity. Twice that of Wunderland, about a fifth more than that of Earth, home of the great enemies.

"Arrrgg."

The dispenser opened and he took out a flat dish of chilled cream, lapping gratefully. A human observer would have found him very catlike at that moment, like some great orange-red tiger hunched over the beautiful subtle curve of the saucer. A closer examination would have shown endless differences of detail, the full-torso sheathing of flexible ribs, naked pink tail, the eyes round-pupiled and huge and golden. Most important of all, the four-digit hands with a fully opposable thumb, like a black leather glove; that and the long braincase that swept back from the heavy brow-ridges above the blunt muzzle.

Claws scratched at the door; he recognized the mellow but elderly scent.

"Enter," he said.

The kzin who stepped through was ancient, his face seamed by a ridge of scar that tracked through his right eye and left it milky-white and blind.

"Recline, Conservor-of-the-Patriarchal-Past," he said. "Will you take refreshment?"

"I touch nose, honored Chuut-Riit," the familiar gravelly voice said.

The younger kzin fetched a jug of heated milk and bourbon from the dispenser, and a fresh saucer. The two reclined in silence for long minutes. As always, Chuut-Riit felt the slightest prickling of unease, despite their long familiarity. Conservor had served his Sire before him, and helped to tutor the Riit siblings. Yet still there was an unkzin quality to the ancient priest-sage-counselor . . . a Hero strove all his life to win a full Name, to become a patriarch and sire a heroic Line. Here was one who had attained that and then renounced it of his own will, to follow wisdom purely for the sake of kzinkind. Rare and not quite canny; such a kzintosh was *dedicated.* The word he thought was from the Old Faith; sacrifices had been *dedicated,* in the days when kzinti fought with swords of wood and volcanic glass.

"What have you learned?" Conservor said at last.

"Hrrr. That which is difficult to express," Chuut-Riit muttered.

"Yet you seem calmer."

"Yes. There was risk in the course of study you set me." Chuut-Riit's hardy soul shuddered slightly. The human . . . *fictions*, that was the term . . . had been disturbing. Alien to the point of incomprehensibility at one moment, mind-wrackingly kzinlike the next. "I begin to integrate the insights, though."

"Excellent. The soul of the true Conquest Hero is strong through flexibility, like the steel of a fine sword—not the rigidity of stone, which shatters beneath stress."

"Arreowg. Yes. Yet . . . my mind does not return to all its accustomed patterns." He brooded, twitching out his batwing ears. "Contemplating the stars, I am oppressed by their magnitude. Is the universe not merely greater than we imagine, but greater than we *can* imagine? We seek the Infinite Hunt, to shape all that is to the will of kzinkind. Yet is this a delusion imposed by our genes, our nature?" His pelt quivered as skin rippled in a shudder.

"Such thoughts are the food of leadership," Conservor said. "Only the lowly may keep all sixteen claws dug firmly in the earth. Ever since the outer universe came to Homeworld, such as you have been driven to feed on strange game and follow unknown scents."

"Hrrrr." He flicked his tail-tip, bringing the discussion back to more immediate matters. "At least, I think that now my understanding of the humans becomes more intuitive. It would be valuable if others could undertake this course of meditation and knowledge-stalking as well. Traat-Admiral, perhaps?"

Conservor flared his whiskers in agreement. "To a limited extent. As much as his spirit—a strong one—can bear. Too long has the expansion of our hunting grounds waited here, unable to encompass Sol, fettering the spirit of kzin. Whatever is necessary must be done."

"Rrrrr. Agreed. Yet . . . yet there are times, my teacher, when I think that our conquest of the humans may be as much a lurker-by-water threat as their open resistance."

Chapter 1

"We want you to kill a kzin," the general said.

Captain Jonah Matthieson blinked. *Is this some sort of flatlander idea of a joke?* he thought.

"Well . . . that's more or less what I've been doing," the Sol-Belter said, running a hand down the short-cropped black crest that was his concession to military dress codes. He was a tall man even for a Belter, slim, with slanted green eyes.

The general sighed and lit another cheroot. "Display. A-7, schematic," he said. The rear wall of the office lit with a display of hashmarked columns; Jonah studied it for a moment and decided it represented the duration and intensity of a kzin attack: number of ships, weapons, comparative casualties.

"Time sequence, phased," the senior officer continued. The computer obliged, superimposing four separate mats.

"That," he said, "is the record of the four fleets the kzin have sent since they took Wunderland and the Alpha Centauri system, forty-two years ago. Notice anything?"

Jonah shrugged: "We're losing." The war with the felinoid aliens had been going on since before his birth, since humanity's first contact with them, sixty years before. Interstellar warfare at sublight speeds was a game for the patient.

"Fucking brilliant, Captain!" General Early was a short man, even for a Terran: black, balding, carrying a weight of muscle that was almost obscene to someone raised in low gravity; he looked to be in early middle age, which, depending on how much he cared about appearances, might mean anything up to a century and a half these days. With a visible effort, he controlled himself.

"Yeah, we're losing. Their fleets have been getting bigger and their weapons are getting better. We've made some improvements too, but not as fast as they have."

Jonah nodded. There wasn't any need to say anything.

"What do you think I did before the war?" the general demanded.

"I have no idea, sir."

"Sure you do. ARM bureaucrat, like all the other generals," Early said. The ARM was the UN's enforcement arm, and supervised—mainly suppressed, before the kzin had arrived—technology of all types. "Well, I was. But I also taught military history in the ARM academy. Damn near the only Terran left who paid any attention to the subject."

"Oh."

"Right. We weren't ready for wars, any of us. Terrans didn't believe in them. Belters didn't either; too damned independent. Well, the goddam pussies do."

"Yes sir." *Goddam,* he thought. *This joker is older than I thought*. It had been a long time since many in the Sol system took a deity's name in vain.

"Right. Everyone knows that. Now *think* about it. We're facing a race of carnivores with a unified interstellar government of completely unknown size, organized for war. They started ahead of us, and now they've had Wunderland and its belt for better than a generation. If nothing else, at this rate they can eventually swamp us with numbers. Just one set of multimegatonners getting through to Earth . . ."

He puffed on the cigar with short, vicious breaths. Jonah shivered inside himself at the thought: all those people, dependent on a single life-support system. . . . He wondered how flatlanders had ever stood it. Why, a single asteroid impact . . . The Belt was less vulnerable. Too much delta vee required to match the wildly varying vectors of its scores of thousands of rocks, its targets weaker individually but vastly more numerous and scattered.

He forced his mind back to the man before him, gagging slightly on the smell of the tobacco. *How does he get away with that on shipboard?* For that matter, the habit had almost died out; it must have been revived since the pussies came, like so many archaic customs.

Like war and armies, the Belter thought sardonically. The branch-of-service flashes on the shoulder of the flatlander's coverall were not ones he recognized. Of course, there were

18 billion people in the solar system, and most of them seemed to be wearing some sort of uniform these days; flatlanders particularly, they loved playing dress-up. *Comes of having nothing useful to do most of their lives,* he thought. *Except wear uniforms and collect knickknacks.* There was a truly odd one on the flatlander's desk, a weird-looking pyramid with an eye in it, topped by a tiny cross.

"So every time it gets harder. First time was bad enough, but they really underestimated us. Did the next time, too, but not so badly. They're getting better all the time. This last one—that was bad." General Early pointedly eyed the ribbons on Jonah's chest. Two Comets, and the unit citation his squadron of Darts had earned when they destroyed a kzin fighter-base ship.

"As you know. You saw some of that. What you didn't see was the big picture—because we censored it, even from our military units. Captain, they nearly broke us. Because *we* underestimated *them.* This time they didn't just 'shriek and leap.' They came in tricky, fooled us completely when they looked like retreating . . . and we know why."

He spoke to the computer again, and the rear wall turned to holo image. A woman in lieutenant's stripes, but with the same branch-badges as the general. Tall and slender, paler-skinned than most, and muscular in the fashion of low-gravity types who exercise. When she spoke it was in Belter dialect.

"The subject's name was Esteban Cheung Jagrannath," the woman said. The screen split, and a battered-looking individual appeared beside her; Jonah's eye picked out the glisten of sealant over artificial skin, the dying-rummy pattern of burst blood vessels from explosive decompression, the mangy look of someone given accelerated marrow treatments for radiation overdose. *That is one sorry-looking son of a bitch.* "He claims to have been born in Tiamat, in the Serpent Swarm of Wunderland, twenty-five subjective years ago."

Now I recognize the accent, Jonah thought. The lieutenant's English had a guttural overtone despite the crisp Belter vowels; the Belters who migrated to the asteroids of Alpha Centauri talked that way. Wunderlander influence.

"Subject is a power-systems specialist, drafted into the kzin service as a crewman on a corvette tender"—the blue eyes looked down to a readout below the pickup's line of sight "—called—" Something followed in the snarling hiss-spit of the Hero's Tongue.

"Roughly translated, the *Bounteous-Mother's-Teats*. *Tits* took a near-miss from a radiation-pulse bomb right toward the end. The kzin captain didn't have time to self-destruct; the bridge took most of the blast. She was a big mother"—the general blinked, snorted—"so a few of the repair crew survived, like this gonzo. All humans, as were most of the technical staff. A few nonhuman, nonkzin species as well, but they were all killed. Pity."

Jonah and the flatlander both nodded in unconscious union. The kzin empire was big, hostile, not interested in negotiation, and contained many subject species and planets; and that was about the limit of human knowledge. Not much background information had been included in the computers of the previous fleets, and very little of that survived; vessels too badly damaged for their crews to self-destruct before capture usually held little beyond wreckage.

The general spoke again: "Gracie, fast forward to the main point." The holo-recording blurred ahead. "Captain, you can review at your leisure. It's all important background, but for now—" He signed, and the recording returned to normal speed.

" . . . the new kzin commander arrived three years before they left. His name's Chuut-Riit, which indicates a close relation to the . . . Patriarch, that's as close as we've been able to get. Apparently, his first command was to delay the departure of the fleet." A thin smile. "Chuut-Riit's not just related to their panjandrum; he's an author, of sorts. Two works on strategy: *Logistical Preparation as the Key to Victory in War* and *Conquest Through the Defensive Offensive.*"

Jonah shaped a soundless whistle. *Not your typical kzin. If we have any idea of what a typical kzin is like. We've met their warriors, coming our way behind beams and bombs.*

The lieutenant's image was agreeing with him. "The pussies find him a little eccentric, as well; according to the subject, gossip had it that he fought a whole series of duels, starting almost the moment he arrived and held a staff conference. The new directives included a pretty massive increase in the support infrastructure to go with the fleet. Meanwhile, he ordered a complete changeover in tactics, especially to ensure that accurate reports of the fighting got back to Wunderland."

The flatlander general cut off the scene with a wave. "So." He folded his hands and leaned forward, the yellowish whites of his eyes glittering in lights that must be kept deliberately low. "We are in trouble, Captain. So far we've beaten off the pussies because we're a lot closer to our main sources of supply, and because they're . . . predictable. Adequate tacticians, but with little strategic sense, even less than we had at first, despite the Long Peace. The analysts say that indicates they've never come across much in the way of significant opposition before. If they had they'd have learned from it like they are—damn it!—from us.

"In fact, what little intelligence information we've got, a lot of it from prisoners taken with the Fourth Fleet, backs that up; the kzin just don't have much experience of war."

Jonah blinked. "Not what you'd assume," he said carefully.

A choppy nod. "Yep. Surprises you, eh? Me, too."

General Early puffed delicately on his cigar. "Oh, they're aggressive enough. Almost insanely so, barely gregarious enough to maintain a civilization. Ritualized conflict to the death is a central institution of theirs. Some of the xenologists swear they must have gotten their technology from somebody else, that this culture they've got could barely rise above the hunter-gatherer stage on its own.

"In any event; they're wedded to a style of attack that's almost pitifully straightforward." He looked thoughtfully at the wet chewed end of his cigar and selected another from the sealed humidor.

"And as far as we can tell, they have only one society, one social system, one religion, and one state. That fits in with some other clues we've gotten. The kzin species has been united for a long time—millennia. They have a longer continuous history than any human culture." Another puff. "They're curiously genetically uniform, too. We know more about their biology than their beliefs, more corpses than live prisoners. Less variation than you'd expect; large numbers of them seem to be siblings."

Jonah stirred. "Well, this is all very interesting, General, but—"

"—what's it got to do with you?" The flatlander leaned forward again, tapping paired thumbs together. "This Chuut-Riit is a first-class menace. You see, we're losing those advantages I mentioned. The kzin have been shipping additional force into the Wunderland system in relays, not so much weapons as knocked-down industrial plants and personnel; furthermore, they've got the locals well organized. It's a fully industrialized economy, with an Earth-type planet and an asteroid belt richer than Sol's; the population's much lower—hundreds of millions instead of nearly twenty billion—but that doesn't matter much."

Jonah nodded in his turn. With ample energy and raw materials, the geometric-increase potential of automated machinery could build a war-making capacity in a single generation, given the knowledge and skills the kzin inner sphere could supply. Faster than that, if a few crucial administrators and technicians were imported too. Earth's witless hordes were of little help to Sol's military effort, a drain on resources, and not even useful as cannon fodder in a conflict largely fought in space.

"So now they're in a position to outproduce us. We have to keep our advantages in operational efficiency."

"You play chess with good chessplayers, you get good," the Belter said.

"No. It's academic whether the pussies are more or less intelligent than we. What's intelligence, anyway? But we've proven experimentally that they're culturally and genetically less flexible. Man, when this war started we were absolute pacifists, we hadn't had so much as a riot in three centuries. We even censored history so that the majority didn't know there had ever been wars! That was less than a century ago, less than a single lifetime, and look at what we've done since. The pussies are only just now starting to smarten up about us."

"This Chuut-Riit sounds as if he's, oh shit. Sir."

A wide white grin. "Exactly. An exceptionally able rat-cat, and they're less prone to either genius or stupidity than we are. In a position to knock sense into their heads. He has to go."

The Earther stood and began striding back and forth behind the desk, gesturing with the cigar. Something more than the stink made Jonah's stomach clench.

"Covert operations is another thing we've had to reinvent, just lately. We need somebody who's good with spacecraft . . . a Belter, because the ones who settled the Serpent Swarm belt of Wunderland have stayed closer to the ancestral stock than the Wunderlanders downside. A good combat man, who's proved himself capable of taking on kzin hand-to-hand. And someone who's good with computer systems, because our informants tell us that is the skill most in demand by the kzin on Wunderland itself."

The general halted and stabbed toward Jonah with the hand that held the stub of burning weeds. "Last but not least, someone with contacts in the Alpha Centauri system."

Jonah felt a wave of relief. A little relief, because the general was still grinning at him.

"Sir, I've never left—"

An upraised hand halted him. "Lieutenant Raines?" A woman came in and saluted smartly, first the general and then Jonah; he recognized her from the holo report. "I'd like you to meet Captain Matthieson."

☆ ☆ ☆

"Hrrrr," the cub crooned, plastering itself to the ground.

Chuut-Riit, Scion of the Patriarch, kzinti overlord of the Wunderland system, Grand Admiral of the Conquest Fleet; pulled on the string.

The clump of feathers dragged through the long grass, and the young kzin crept after it on all fours, belly flat to the ground. The grass was Terran, as alien to Wunderland as the felinoids, and bright green; the brown-spotted orange of the cub's fur showed clearly as be snaked through the meter-high stems. Eyes flared wide, pupils swallowing amber-yellow iris, and the young kzin screamed and leaped.

"Huufff!" it exclaimed, as Chuut-Riit's hand made the lure blur out from underneath the pounce.

"Sire!" it mewled complainingly, sprawled on its belly. The fur went flat as the adult kzinti picked it up by the scruff of the neck; reflex made the cub's limbs splay out stiffly.

"You made a noise, youngling," Chuut-Riit said, leaning forward to lick his son's ears in affectionate admonishment "You'll never catch your prey that way." His nostrils flared, taking in the pleasant scent of healthy youngster.

"Sorry, Sire," the cub said, abashed. His head pivoted; a dozen of his brothers were rioting up from the copse of trees in the valley below, where the guards and aircars were parked. They showed as ripples in the long grass of the hillside, with bursts of orange movement as cubs soared up in leaps after the white glitter of butterflies, or just for the sake of movement. They could leap ten meters or more, in this gravity; Wunderland was only about half Kzin-normal, less than two-thirds of Earth's pull.

"Gertrude-nurse!" Chuut-Riit called.

A Wunderlander woman came puffing up, dressed in a white uniform with body-apron and gloves of tough synthetic. Chuut-Riit extended the cub at the end of one tree-thick arm.

"Yes, Chuut-Riit," the nurse said; a kzin with a full Name was never addressed by title, of course. "Come along, now, young master," the nurse said, in a passable imitation of the Hero's Tongue. House servants were allowed to speak it, as a special favor. "Dinner-time."

The God alone knows what sort of accent the young will learn, Chuut-Riit thought, amused.

"Eat?" The cub made a throaty rumble. "*Want* to eat, Gertrude-human." The kzin dropped into Wunderlander. "Is it good? Is it warm and salty? Will there be cream?"

"Certainly not," Gertrude said with mock severity. Her charge bounced up as his father released him, wrapping arms and legs and long pink prehensile tail around the human, pressing his muzzle to her chest and purring.

"Dinner! Dinner!" the other cubs chorused as they arrived on the hilltop; they made a hasty obeisance to Chuut-Riit and the other adults, then followed the nurse downslope, walking upright and making little bounds of excitement, their tails held rigid. "Dinner!"

"I caught a mouse, it tasted funny."

"Gertrude-human, Funny-Spots ate a bug!"

"I did not, I spit it out. Liar, tie a knot in your tail!"

The two quarreling youngsters flew together and rolled down ahead of the others in a ball, play-fighting. Chuut-Riit rippled his whiskers, and the fur on his blunt-muzzled face moved in the kzinti equivalent of a chuckle as he rejoined the group at the kill. Traat-Admiral was there, his closest supporter; Conservor-of-the-Patriarchal-Past, holy and ancient; and Staff-Officer, most promising of the inner-world youngsters who had come with him from homeworld. The kill was a fine young buffalo bull, and had even given them something of a fight before they brought it down beneath a tall native toshborg tree. The kzinti males were all in high good humor, panting slightly as they lolled, occasionally worrying a mouthful free from the carcass.

"A fine lot of youngsters," Conservor said, a little wistfully; such as he maintained no harem, although they were privileged to sire offspring on the mates of others at ritual intervals. "Very well-behaved for their age."

Chuut-Riit threw himself down and pulled a flask out of his hunter's pack, pouring it into broad shallow bowls the others held out. The strong minty-herb scent of the liquor filled the air, along with the pleasant scent of fresh-killed meat, grass, trees. The Viceroyal hunting preserve sprawled over hundreds of kilometers of rich land, and the signs of agriculture had almost vanished in the generation since the conquest. It was a mixed landscape, the varying shades of green from Terra, native Wunderlander reddish-gold, and here and there a spot of kzin orange. The animals were likewise diverse: squat thickset armored beasts from homeworld, tall spindly local forms like stick-figures from a cartoon, Earth-creatures halfway between.

We fit in as well as anything, Chuut-Riit thought. *More, since we own it.* The kzinti lay sprawled on their bellies, their quarter-ton of stocky muscle and dense bone relaxed into the grass. Bat-wing ears were fully extended and lips were loosened from fangs in fellowship; all here were old friends, and sharing a kill built trust at a level deeper even than that.

The kzinti governor sank his fangs into a haunch, rearing back and shaking his head until a two-kilo gobbet pulled loose. He threw back his head to bolt it—kzinti teeth were designed for ripping and tearing, not chewing—and extended the claws on one four-digit hand to pick bits of gristle from his teeth.

"Rrrrr, yes, they're promising," he said, nodding to the boil of cubs around the table where the human nurse was cutting chunks of rib from a porker. "The local servants are very good with infants, if you select carefully."

"Some kzintosh is very glad of that!" Staff-Officer joked, making a playful-protective grab at his crotch.

The others bristled in mock-fear-amusement. Kzinti females were useless for child-rearing beyond the nursing stage, being subsapient and speechless; the traditional caregiver for youngsters was a gelded male. Such were usually very docile, and without hope for offspring of their own tended to identify with any cubs they were exposed to. Still, it was a little distasteful to modern sensibilities; one of the many conveniences of alien slaves was their suitability for such work. Humans were very useful. . . .

"Speaking of which, Traat-Admiral, tell me again of your protégé's pet."

Traat-Admiral lapped at his cup for an instant longer and belched. "Yiao-Captain. He swears this human of his has found an astronomical anomaly worth investigating." A sideways flick of the head, a kzin shrug. "I sent him to that ancestor-forsaken outpost in . . . urrrr, Skogarna, to test his patience." The word was slightly derogatory, in the Hero's Tongue . . . but among Chuut-Riit's entourage they were working to change that.

"Good hunting up there," Staff-Officer said brashly, then touched his nose in a patently insincere apology when the older males gave him a glare.

"Chhrrrup. As you say. Worth dispatching a *Swift Hunter* to investigate, at least . . . which brings us to the accelerated Solward surveillance."

"To receive quickly the news of the Fourth Fleet's triumphant leap upon the humans?" Conservor asked.

The tip of his tail twitched. The others could sniff the dusty scent of irony. For that matter, it would be better than a decade before the news returned; worst-case analysis and political realities both demanded that the years ahead be spent readying a Fifth Fleet.

A part of Chuut-Riit's good humor left him. Moodily, he drew his *wtsai* and used the pommel of the knife to crack a thighbone.

"Grrf," he muttered; sucking marrow. His own tail thumped the ground. "I await inconclusive results at best." They all winced slightly. *Four* fleets; and the home system of the monkeys was still resisting the Eternal Pack. Chuut-Riit's power here was still new, still shaky; it had been necessary to ship most of those who resented a homeworld prince as governor off with the Fourth Fleet. Since they also constituted the core of policy resistance to his more cautious strategy, that had considerable political merit as well.

"No, it is possible that the wild humans will attempt some countermeasure. What, I cannot guess—they still have not made extensive use of gravity polarizer technology, which means we control interstellar space—but my nose is dry when I consider the time we have left them for thought. A decade for each attack . . . They are tricky prey, these hairless tree-swingers."

☆ ☆ ☆

"God, what have you done to her?" Jonah asked, as they grabbed stanchions and halted by the viewport nearest his ship.

The observation corridor outside the central graving dock of the base-asteroid was a luxury, but then, with a multimega-ton mass to work with and unlimited energy, the Sol-system military could afford that type of extravagance. Take a nickel-iron rock. Drill a hole down the center with bomb-pumped lasers. Put a spin on the resulting tube, and rig large mirrors with the object at their focal points; the sun is dim beyond the orbit of Mars, but in zero-G you can build big mirrors *big*. The nickel-iron pipe heats, glows, turns soft as taffy, swells outward evenly like cotton candy at a fair; cooling, it leaves a huge open space surrounded by a thick shell of metal-rich rock. Robots drill the tunnels and corridors, humans and robots install the power sources, life-support, gravity polarizers . . .

An enlisted crewman bounced by them horizontal to their plane of reference, sketching a sloppy salute as he twisted, hit the corner feetfirst, and rebounded away. The air had the cool clean tang that Belters grew up with, and an industrial-tasting underlay of ozone and hot metal: the seals inside UNSN base Gibraltar were adequate for health but not up to Belt civilian standards. Even while he hung motionless and watched the technicians gutting his ship, some remote corner of Jonah's mind noted that again. Flatlanders had a nerve-wracking tendency to make-do solutions.

My ship, he thought.

UNSN *Catskinner* hung in the vacuum chamber, surrounded by the flitting shapes of spacesuited repair workers, compu-waldos, and robots; torches blinked blue-white, and a haze of detached fittings hinted the haste of the work. Beneath it the basic shape of the Dart-class attack boat showed, a massive fusion-power unit, tiny life-support bubble, and the asymmetric fringe of weapons and sensors designed for deep-space operation.

"What have you done to her?" Jonah said again.

"Made modifications, Captain," Raines replied. "The basic drive and armament systems are unaltered."

Jonah nodded grudgingly. He could see the clustered grips for the spike-pods, featureless egg-shaped ovoids, that were the basic weapon for light vessels, a one-megaton bomb pumping an X-ray laser. In battle they would spread out like the wings of a raptor, a pattern thousands of kilometers wide slaved to the computers in the control pod; and the other weapons, fixed lasers, ball-bearing scatterers, railguns, particle-beam projectors, the antennae for stealthing and beam-deflection fields.

Unconsciously, the pilot's hands twitched; his reflexes and memory were back in the crashcouch, fingers moving infinitesimally in the lightfield gloves, holos feeding data into his eyes. Dodging with fusion-powered feet, striking with missile fists, his Darts locked with the kzinti *Vengeful Slashers* in a dance of battle that was as much like zero-G ballet as anything else. . . .

"What modifications?" he asked.

"Grappling points for attachment to a ramscoop ship.

Battleship class, technically, although she's a one-off, experimental; they're calling her the *Yamamoto*. The plan is that we ride piggyback, and she goes through the Wunderland system at high Tau, accelerating all the way from here to Alpha Centauri, and drops us off on the way. They won't have much time to prepare, at those speeds."

The ship would be on the heels of the wave-front announcing its arrival. She called up data on her beltcomp, and he examined it. His lips shaped a silent whistle; *big* tanks of onboard hydrogen, and initial boost from half the launch-lasers in the solar system. There was going to be a *lot* of energy behind the *Yamamoto*. For that matter, the fields a ramscooper used to collect interstellar matter were supposed to be fatal to higher life forms.

Lucky it's just us sods in uniform, then, he thought sardonically, continuing aloud: "Great. And just how are we supposed to stop?" At .90 light, things started to get really strange. Particles of interstellar hydrogen began acting like cosmic rays. . . .

"Oh, that's simple," Raines said. For the first time in their brief acquaintance, she smiled. *Damn, she's good looking,* Jonah thought with mild surprise. *Better than good. How could I not notice?*

"We ram ourselves into the sun," she continued.

Several billion years before, there had been a species of sophonts with a peculiar ability. They called themselves (as nearly as humans could reproduce the sound) the thrint; others knew them as Slavers. The ability amounted to an absolutely irresistible form of telepathic hypnosis, evolved as a hunting aid in an ecosystem where most animals advanced enough to have a spinal cord were at least mildly telepathic; this was a low-probability development, but in a universe as large as ours anything possible will occur sooner or later. On their native world, thrintun could give a subtle prod to a prey-animal, enough to tip its decision to come down to the waterhole. The thrint evolved intelligence, as an additional advantage. After all, their prey had millions of years to develop resistance.

Then a spaceship landed on the thrint homeworld. Its crew immediately became slaves; absolutely obedient, absolutely trustworthy, willing and enthusiastic slaves. Operating on nervous systems that had not evolved in an environment saturated with the Power, any thrint could control dozens of sophonts. With the amplifiers that slave-technicians developed, a thrint could control an entire planet. Slaves industrialized a culture in the hunting-band stage, in a single generation. Controlled by the Power, slaves built an interstellar empire covering most of a galaxy.

Slaves did everything, because the thrint had never been a *very* intelligent species, and once loose with the Power they had no need to think. Eventually they met, and thought they had enslaved, a very clever race indeed, the tnuctipun. The revolt that eventually followed resulted in the extermination of every tool-using sentient in the Galaxy, but before it did the tnuctipun made some remarkable things. . . .

"A Slaver stasis field?" he said. Despite himself, awe showed in his voice. One such field had been discovered on Earth, then lost, one more on a human-explored world. Three centuries of study had found no slightest clue concerning their operating principles; they were as incomprehensible as a molecular-distortion battery would have been to Thomas Edison. Monkey-see monkey-do copies had been made, each taking more time and expense than the *Gibraltar*, and so far exactly two had functioned. One was supposedly guarding UNSN headquarters, wherever that was.

"Uh-mmm, give the captain a big cigar, right the first time."

Jonah shuddered, remembering the flatlander's smoke. "No, thanks."

"Too right, Captain. Just a figure of speech."

"Call me Jonah. We're going to be camped enough on this trip without poking rank-elbows in each other's ribs."

"Jonah. The *Yamamoto* skims through the system, throwing rocks." At .90 of *c*, missiles needed no warheads. The kinetic energies involved made the impacts as destructive as antimatter. "We go in as an offcourse rock. Course corrections, then on with the stasis field, go ballistic, use the outer layer of the sun for braking down to orbital speeds."

Nothing outside its surface could affect the contents of a Slaver field; let the path of the *Catskinner* stray too far inward and they would spend the rest of the lifespan of the universe at the center of Alpha Centauri's sun, in a single instant of frozen time. For that matter, the stasis field would probably survive the re-contraction of the primal monobloc and its explosion into a new cosmic cycle. . . . He forced his mind away from the prospect.

"And we're putting in a Class-VII computer system."

Jonah raised a brow. Class-VII systems were consciousness-level; they also went irredeemably insane sometime between six months and a year after activation, as did any artificial entity complex enough to be aware of being aware.

"Our . . . mission won't take any longer than that, and it's worth it." A shrug. "Look, why don't we hit a cafeteria and talk some more. Really talk, you're going to have briefings running out of every orifice before long, but that isn't the same."

Jonah sighed, and stopped thinking of ways out of the role for which he had been "volunteered." This was too big to be dodged, far and away too big. Two stasis fields in the whole Sol system; one guarding United Nations Space Navy HQ, the other on his ship. His ship, a Dart-Commander like ten thousand or so others, until this week. How many Class-VII computers? Nobody built consciousness-level systems anymore, except occasionally for research; it simply wasn't cost-effective. Build them much more intelligent than humans and they went non-comp almost at once; a human-level machine gave you a sentient with a six-month lifespan that could do arithmetic in its head. Ordinary computers could do the math, and for thinking people were much cheaper. It was a dead-end technology, like direct interfacing between human neural systems and computers. And they had revived it, for a special purpose mission.

"Shit," Jonah mumbled, as they came to a lock and reoriented themselves feet-down. There was a gravity warning strobing beside it; they pushed through the air-screen curtain and into the dragging acceleration of a one-G field. The crewfolk about them were mostly flatlander now, relaxed in the murderous weight that crushed their frames lifelong.

"Naacht wh'r?" Ingrid asked. In Wunderlander, but the Sol-Belter did not have to know that bastard offspring of Danish and Plattdeutsch to sense the meaning.

"I just realized . . . hell, I just realized how important this must all be. If the high command were willing to put that much effort into this, willing to sacrifice half of our most precious military asset, throw in a computer that costs more than this base complete with crew . . . then they must have put at least equal effort into searching for just the right pilot. There's simply no point in trying to get out of it. Tanj. I need a drink."

☆ ☆ ☆

"Take your grass-eater stink out of my air!" Chuut-Riit shrieked. He was standing, looking twice his size as his orange-red pelt bottled out, teeth exposed in what an uninformed human might have mistaken for a grin, naked pink tail lashing. The reference to smell was purely metaphorical, since the conversation was 'cast. Which was as well, he was pouring aggression-pheromones into the air at a rate that would have made a roomful of adult male kzin nervous to the point of lost control.

The holo images on the wall before him laid themselves belly-down on the decking of their ship and crinkled their ears, their fur lying flat in propitiation.

"Leave the recordings and flee, devourers of your own kittens!" screamed the kzinti governor of the Alpha Centauri system. The Hero's Tongue is remarkably rich in expressive insults. *"Roll in your own shit and mate with sthondats!"* The wall blanked, and a light blinked in one corner as the data was packed through the link into his private files.

Chuut-Riit's fur smoothed as he strode around the great chamber. It stood open to the sky, beneath a near-invisible dome that kept the scant rain of this area off the kudlotlin-hide rugs. They were priceless imports from the home world; the stuffed matched pair of Chunquen on a granite pedestal were souvenirs acquired during the pacification of that world. He looked at them, soothing his eyes with the memory-taste of a successful hunt, at other mementos. Wild smells drifted in over thin walls that were crystal-enclosed sandwiches of circuitry; in the distance something squalled hungrily. The palace-preserve-fortress of a planetary governor, governor of the richest world to be conquered by kzin in living memory. Richest in wealth, richest in honor . . . if the next attack on the human homeworld was something more than a fifth disaster.

"Secretariat," he rasped. The wall lit.

A human looked from a desk, stood and came to attention. "Henrietta," the kzin began, "hold my calls for the rest of the day. I've just gotten the final download on the Fourth Fleet fiasco, and I'm a little upset. Run it against my projections, will you?" Most of the worst-case scenarios he had run were quite close to the actual results; that did not make it much easier to bear.

"Yes, Chuut-Riit," he said—*No, God devour it, she, I've got to start remembering human females are sentient.* At least he could tell them apart without smelling them, now. Even distinguish between individuals of the same subspecies. *There are so many types of them!*

"I don't think you'll find major discrepancies."

"That bad?" the human said.

The expression was a closed curve of the lips; the locals had learned that baring their teeth at a kzin was not a good idea. Smile, Chuut-Riit reminded himself. Betokening amusement, or friendliness, or submission. *Which is it feeling?* Born after the Conquest Fleet arrived here. Reared from a cub in the governor's palace, superbly efficient . . . *but what does it think inside that ugly little head?*

"Worse, the ——"—he lapsed into the Hero's Tongue, since no human language was sufficient for what he felt about the Fourth Fleet's hapless Kfraksha-Admiral—"couldn't apply the strategy properly in circumstances beyond the calculated range of probable response."

It was impossible to set out too detailed a plan of campaign, when communication took over four years. His fur began to bristle again, and he controlled his reaction with a monumental effort of will. *I need to fight something,* he thought.

"Screen out all calls for the next sixteen hours, unless they're Code VI or above." A thought prompted at him. "Oh, It's your offspring's naming-day next week, isn't it?"

"Yes, Chuut-Riit." Henrietta had once told him that among pre-Conquest humans it had been a mark of deference to refer to a superior by title, and of familiarity to use names. His tail twitched. Extraordinary. Of course, humans all had names, without having to earn them. *In a sense, they're assigned names as we are rank titles,* he thought.

"Well, I'll drop by at the celebration for an hour or so and bring one of my cubs." That would be safe enough if closely supervised; most intelligent species had long infancies.

"We are honored, Chuut-Riit!" The human bowed, and the kzin waved a hand to break contact.

"Valuable," he muttered to himself, rising and pacing once more. Humans were the most valuable subject-species the kzin had yet acquired. *Or partially acquired,* he reminded himself. Most kzin nobles on Wunderland had large numbers of human servants and technicians about their estates, but few had gone as far as he in using their administrative talents.

"Fools," he said in the same undertone; his kzin peers knew his opinion of them, but it was still inadvisable to get into the habit of saying it aloud. "I am surrounded by fools." Humans fell into groups *naturally,* they thought organization. The remote ancestors of Kzin had hunted in small packs; the prehumans in much larger ones. *Stupidity to deny the evidence of senses and logic,* he thought with contempt. *These hairless monkeys have talents we lack.*

Most refused to admit that, as though it somehow diminished the Hero to grant a servant could do what the master could not. Idiocy. Chuut-Riit yawned, a pink, red, and white expanse of ridged palate, tongue, and fangs, his species's equivalent of a dismissive shrug. *Is it beneath the Hero to admit that a sword extends his claws, or a computer his mind?* With human patience and organizational talent at the service of the Heroes, there was *nothing* that they could not accomplish! Even monkey inquisitiveness was a trait not without merit, irritating though it could be.

He pulled his mind away from vistas of endless victory, a hunt ranging over whole spiral arms; that was a familiar vision, one that had driven him to intrigue and duel for this position. To use a tool effectively, you had to know its balance and heft, its strengths and weaknesses. Humans were more gregarious than kzin, more ready to identify with a leader-figure; but to elicit such cooperation, you had to know the symbol-systems that held power over them. *I must wear the mask they can see. Besides which, their young are . . . what is their word? Cute. I will select the cub carefully, one just weaned, and stuff it full of meat first. That will be safest.*

Chuut-Riit intended to take his offspring, the best of them, with him to Earth, after the conquest. Early exposure to humans would give them an intuitive grasp of the animals that he could only simulate through careful study. With a fully domesticated human species at their disposal, his sons' sons' sons could even aspire to . . . no, unthinkable. And not necessary to think of it; that was generations away.

Besides that, it would take a great deal of time to tame the humans properly. Useful already, but far too wild, too undependable, too varied. A millennium of culling might be necessary before they were fully shaped to the purpose.

☆ ☆ ☆

" . . . didn't just bull in," Lieutenant Raines was saying, as she followed the third aquavit with a beer chaser. Jonah sipped more cautiously at his, thinking that the asymmetry of nearly pure alcohol and lager was typically Wunderlander.

"Only it wasn't caution—the pussies just didn't want to mess the place up and weren't expecting much resistance. Rightly so."

Jonah restrained himself from patting her hand as she scowled into her beer. It was dim in their nook, and the gravity was Wunderland-standard, .61 Earth. The initial refugees from the Alpha Centauri system had been mostly planetsiders, and from the dominant Danish-Dutch-German-Balt ethnic group. They had grown even more clannish in the generation since, which showed in the tall ceramic steins along the walls, plastic wainscoting that made a valiant attempt to imitate fumed oak, and a human bartender in wooden shoes, lederhosen, and a beard clipped closer on one side than the other.

The drinks slipped up out of the center of the table, of course.

"That was, teufel, three years ago, my time. We'd had some warning, of course, once the UN started masering what the crew of the *Angel's Pencil* found on the wreckage of that kzin ship. Plenty of singleships, and any reaction drive's a weapon; couple of big boost-lasers. But"—a shrug—"you know how it was back then."

"Before my time, Lieutenant," Jonah said, then cursed himself as he saw her wince. Raines had been born nearly three quarters of a century ago, even if her private duration included only two and a half decades of it.

"Ingrid, if you're going to be Jonah instead of Captain Matthiesson. Time—I keep forgetting, my head remembers but my gut forgets . . . Well, we just weren't set up to think in terms of war, that was ancient history. We held them off for nearly six months, though. Long enough to refit the three slowships in orbit and give them emergency boost; I think the pussies didn't catch up and blast us simply because they didn't give a damn. They couldn't decelerate us and get the ships back . . . arrogant sons of . . ." Another of those broad urchin grins. "Well, bitches isn't quite appropriate, is it?"

Jonah laughed outright. "You were in Munchen when the kzin arrived?"

"No, I'd been studying at the Scholarium there, software design philosophy, but I was on sabbatical in Vallburg with two friends of mine, working out some, ah, personal problems."

The bartender with the unevenly forked beard was nearly as attenuated as a Belter, but he had the disturbingly mobile ears of a pure-bred Wunderland *herrenmann*, and they were pricked forward. Alpha Centauri's only habitable planet has a thin atmosphere; the original settlers have adapted, and keen hearing is common among them. Jonah smiled at the man and stabbed a finger for a privacy screen. It flickered into the air across the outlet of the booth, and the refugee saloonkeeper went back to polishing a mug.

"That'd be, hmmm, Claude Montferrat-Palme and Harold Yarthkin-Schotmann?"

Raines nodded, moodily drawing a design on the tabletop with a forefinger dipped in the dark beer. "Yes . . . teufel, they're both of them in their fifties now, getting on for middle-aged." A sigh. "Look . . . Harold's a—hmmm, hard to explain to a Sol-Belter, or even someone from the Serpent Swarm who hasn't spent a lot of time dirtside. His father was a Herrenmann, one of the Nineteen Families, senior line. His mother wasn't married to him."

"Oh," Jonah said, racking his memory. History had never been an interest of his, and his generation had been brought up to the War, anyway. "Problems with wills and inheritances and suchlike?"

"You know what a bastard is?"

"Sure. Someone you don't like, such as for example that flatlander bastard who assigned me to this." He raised his stein in salute. "Though I'm fast becoming resigned to it, Ingrid."

She half-smiled in absent-minded acknowledgment, her mind 4.3 light-years and four decades away. "It means he got an expensive education, a nice little nest-egg settled on him . . . and that he'd never, never be allowed past the front door of the Yarthkin-Schotmanns' family schloss. Lucky to be allowed to use the name. An embarrassment."

"Might eat at a man," Jonah said.

"Like a little kzin in the guts. Especially when he grew enough to realize why his father only came for occasional visits; and then that his half-siblings didn't have half his brains or drive and didn't need them either. It drove him, he had to do everything twice as fast and twice as good, take crazy risks . . . made him a bit of a bastard in the Sol sense of the word too, spines like a pincodillo, sense of humor that could flay a gruntfish."

"And Montferrat-Palme?"

"Claude? Now, he was Herrenmann all through; younger son of a younger son, poor as an Amish dirt-farmer, and . . ." A laugh. "You had to meet Claude to understand him. I think he got serious about me mostly because I kept turning him down—it was a new experience and drove him crazy. And Harold he halfway liked and halfway enjoyed needling . . ."

☆ ☆ ☆

Municipal Director of Internal Affairs Claude Montferrat-Palme adjusted his cape and looked up at the luminous letters that floated disembodied ten centimeters from the smooth brown brick of the building in front of him.

HAROLD'S TERRAN BAR, it read. A WORLD ON ITS OWN. Below, in smaller letters: HUMANS ONLY.

Ah, Harold, he thought. Always the one for a piece of useless melodrama. As if kzin would be likely to frequent this section of Old Munchen, or wish to enter a human entertainment spot if they did, or as if they could be stopped if by some fluke of probability they did end up down here.

His escort stirred, looking around nervously. The Karl-Jorge Avenue was dark, most of its glowstrips long ago stolen or simply spray-painted in the random vandalism that breeds in lives fueled by purposeless anger. It was fairly clean, because the kzin insisted on that, and the four-story brick buildings were solid enough, because the early settlers had built well. Brick and concrete and cobbled streets glimmered faintly, still damp from the afternoon's rain; loud wailing music echoed from open windows, and there would have been groups of idle-looking youths loitering on the front steps of the tenements, if the car had not had Munchen Polezi plates.

Baha'i, he thought, mentally snapping his fingers. He was tall, even for a Herrenmann, with one side of his face cleanshaven and the other a close-trimmed brown beard cut to a foppish point; the plain blue uniform and circular brimmed cap of the city police emphasized the deep-chested greyhound build. *This was a Baha'i neighborhood.*

"You may go," he said to the guards. "I will call for the car."

"Sir," the sergeant said, the guide-cone of her stunner waving about uncertainly. Helmet and nightsight goggles made her eyes unreadable. " 'Tis iz a rough district."

"I am aware of that, Sergeant. Also that Harold's place is a known underworld hangout. Assignment to my headquarters squad is a promotion; please do not assume that it entitles you to doubt my judgment." *Or you may find yourself back walking a beat, without such opportunities for income-enhancement,* went unspoken between them. He ignored her salute and walked up the two low stairs.

The door recognized him, read retinas and encephalograph patterns, slid open. The coal-black doorman was as tall as the police officer and twice as broad, with highly-illegal impact armor underneath the white coat and bow tie of Harold's Terran Bar. The impassive smoky eyes above the ritually scarred cheeks gave him a polite once-over, an equally polite and empty bow.

"Pleased to see you here again, *Herrenmann* Montferrat-Palme," he said.

You grafting ratcat-loving collaborationist son of a bitch. Montferrat added the unspoken portion himself. *And I love you too.*

Harold's Terran Bar was a historical revival, and therefore less out of place on Wunderland than it would have been in the Sol system. Once through the vestibule's inner bead-curtain doorway Montferrat could see most of the smoke-hazed main room, a raised platform in a C around the sunken dance-floor and the long bar. Strictly human-service here, which was less of an affectation now than it had been when the place opened, twenty years ago. Machinery was dearer than it used to be, and human labor much cheaper, particularly since refugees began pouring into Munchen from a countryside increasingly preempted for kzin estates. Not to mention those displaced by strip-mining . . .

"Good evening, Claude."

He started; it was always disconcerting, how quietly Harold moved. There at his elbow now, expressionless blue eyes. Face that should have been ugly, big-nosed with a thick lower lip and drooping eyelids. He was . . . what, sixty-three now? Just going grizzled at the temples, which was an affectation or a sign that his income didn't stretch to really first-class geriatric treatments. Short, barrel-chested; what sort of genetic mismatch had produced that build from a *Herrenmann* father and a Belter mother?

"Looking me over for signs of impending dissolution, Claude?" Harold said, steering him toward his usual table and snapping his fingers for a waiter. "It'll be a while yet."

Perhaps not so long, Montferrat thought, looking at the pouches beneath his eyes. That could be stress . . . or Harold could be *really* skimping on the geriatrics. *They become more expensive every year. The kzin don't care . . . there are people dying of old age at seventy, now, and not just Amish. Shut up, Claude, you hypocrite. Nothing you can do about it.*

"You will outlast me, old friend."

"A case of cynical apathy wearing better than cynical corruption?" Harold asked, seating himself across from the police chief.

Montferrat pulled a cigarette case from his jacket's inner pocket and snapped it open with a flick of the wrist. It was plain white gold, from Earth, with a Paris jeweler's initials inside the frame and a date two centuries old, one of his few inheritances from his parents . . . Harold took the proffered cigarette.

"You will join me in a schnapps?" Montferrat said.

"Claude, you've been asking that question for twenty years, and I've been saying no for twenty years. I don't drink with the paying customers."

Yarthkin leaned back, let smoke trickle through his nostrils. The liquor arrived, and a plateful of grilled things that resembled shrimp about as much as a lemur resembled a man, apart from being dark-green and having far too many eyes. "Now, didn't my bribe arrive on time?"

Montferrat winced. "Harold, Harold, will you never learn to phrase these things politely?" He peeled the translucent shell back from one of the grumblies, snapped off the head between thumb and forefinger and dipped it in the sauce. "Exquisite . . ." he breathed, after the first bite, and chased it down with a swallow of schnapps. "Bribes? Merely a token recompense, when out of the goodness of my heart and in memory of old friendship, I secure licenses, produce permits, contacts with owners of estates and fishing boats—"

"—so you can have a first-rate place to guzzle—"

"—I allow this questionable establishment to flourish, risking my position, despite the, shall we say, *dubious* characters known to frequent it—"

"—because it makes a convenient listening post and you get a lot of, *shall we say,* lucrative contacts."

They looked at each other coolly for a moment, and then Montferrat laughed. "Harold, perhaps the real reason I allow this den of iniquity to continue is that you're the only person who still has the audacity to deflate my hypocrisies."

Yarthkin nodded calmly. "Comes of knowing you when you were an idealistic patriot, Director. Like being in hospital together . . . Will you be gambling tonight, or did you come to pump me about the rumors?"

"Rumors?" Montferrat said mildly, shelling another grumbly.

"Of another kzin defeat. Two shiploads of our esteemed ratcat masters coming back with their fur singed."

"For *god's* sake!" Montferrat hissed, looking around.

"No bugs," Yarthkin continued. "Not even by your ambitious assistants. They offered a hefty sweetener, but I wouldn't want to see them in your office. They don't stay bought."

Montferrat smoothed his mustache. "Well, the kzin do seem to have a rather lax attitude toward security at times," he said. *Mostly, they don't realize how strong the human desire to get together and chatter is,* he mused.

"Then there's the rumor about a flatlander counterstrike," Yarthkin continued.

Montferrat raised a brow and cocked his mobile *Herrenmann* ears forward. "Not becoming a believer in the myth of liberation, I hope," he drawled.

Yarthkin waved the hand that held the cigarette, leaving a trail of blue smoke. "I did my bit for liberation. Got left at the altar, as I recall, and took the amnesty," he said. His face had become even more blank, merely the slightest hint of a sardonic curve to the lips. "Now I'm just an innkeeper. What goes on outside these walls is no business of mine." A pause. "It is yours, of course, Director. People know the ratcats got their whiskers pasted back, for the fourth time. They're encouraged . . . also desperate. The kzin will be stepping up the war effort, which means they'll be putting more pressure on us. Not to mention that they're breeding faster than ever."

Montferrat nodded with a frown. Battle casualties made little difference to a kzin population; their nonsentient females were held in harems by a small minority of males, in any event. Heavy losses meant the lands and mates of the dead passing to the survivors . . . and more young males thrown out of the nest, looking for lands and a Name of their own. And kzin took up a *lot* of space; they weighed in at a quarter-ton each, and they were pure carnivores. Nor would they eat synthesized meat except on board a military spaceship. There were still fewer than a hundred thousand in the Wunderland system, and more than twenty times that many humans, and even so it was getting crowded.

"More 'flighters crowding into Munchen every day," Yarthkin continued in that carefully neutral tone.

Refugees. Munchen had been a small town within their own lifetimes; the original settlers of Wunderland had been a close-knit coterie of plutocrats, looking for elbow room. Limited industrialization, even in the Serpent Swarm, and rather little on the planetary surface. Huge domains staked out by the Nineteen Families and their descendants; later immigrants had fitted into the cracks of the pattern, as tenants, or carving out smallholdings on the fringes of the settled zone. Many of them were ethnic or religious separatists anyway.

Until the kzin came. Kzin nobles expected vast territories for their own polygamous households, and naturally seized the best and most-developed acreages. Some of the human landworkers stayed to labor for new masters, but many more were displaced. Or eaten, if they objected.

Forced-draft industrialization in Munchen and the other towns; kzin did not live in cities, and cared little for the social consequences. Their planets had always been sparsely settled, and they had developed the gravity polarizer early in their history, hence they mined their asteroid belts but put little industry in space. Refugees flooding in, to work in industries that produced war matériel for the kzin fleets, not housing or consumer-goods for human use . . .

"It must be a bonanza for you, selling exit-permits to the Swarm," Harold continued. Outside the base-asteroid of Tiamat, the Belters were much more loosely controlled than the groundside population. "And exemptions from military call-up."

Montferrat smiled and leaned back, following the schnapps with lager. "There must be regulations," he said reasonably. "The Swarm cannot absorb all the would-be immigrants. Nor can Wunderland afford to lose the labor of all who would like to leave. The kzin demand technicians, and we cannot refuse; the burden must be allocated."

"Nor can you afford to pass up the palm-greasing and the, ach, *romantic* possibilities—" Yarthkin began.

"Alert! Alert! Emergency broadcast!" The mirror behind the long bar flashed from reflective to broadcast, and the smoky gloom of the bar's main hall erupted in shouted questions and screams.

The strobing pattern of light settled into the civil-defense blazon, and the unmistakable precision of an artificial voice. "All civilians are to remain in their residences. Emergency and security personnel to their duty stations, repeat, emergency and security personnel to their—"

A blast of static and white noise loud enough to send hands to ears, before the system's emergency overrides cut in. When reception returned the broadcast was two-dimensional, a space-armored figure reading from a screenprompt over the receiver. The noise in Harold's Terran Bar sank to shocked silence at the sight of the human shape of the combat armor, the blue-and-white UN sigil on its chest.

"—o all citizens of the Alpha Centauri system," the Terran was saying. In Wunderlander, but with a thick accent that could not handle the gutturals. "Evacuate areas of military or industrial importance *immediately.* Repeat, *immediately.* The United Nations Space Command is attacking kzinti military and industrial targets in the Alpha Centauri system. Evacuate areas—" The broadcast began again, but the screen split to show the same message in English and two more of the planet's principal languages. The door burst open and a squad of Munchen Polezi burst through.

"Scheisse!" Montferrat shouted, rising. He froze as the receiver in his uniform cap began hissing and snarling override-transmission in the Hero's Tongue. Yarthkin relaxed and smiled as the policeman sprinted for the exit. He cocked one eye towards the ceiling and silently flourished Montferrat's last glass of schnapps before sending it down with a snap of his wrist.

☆ ☆ ☆

"Weird," Jonah Matthieson muttered, looking at the redshifted cone of light ahead of them. *Better this way.* This way he didn't have to think of what they were going to do when they arrived. He had been a singleship pilot before doing his military service; the Belt still needed miners. You could do software design anywhere there was a computer system, of course, and miners had a *lot* of spare time. His reflexes were a pilot's, and they included a strong inhibition against high-speed intercept trajectories.

This was going to be the highest-speed intercept of all time.

The forward end of the pilot's cabin was very simple, a hemisphere of smooth synthetic. For that matter, the rest of the cabin was quite basic as well; two padded crashcouches, which was one more than normal, an autodoc, an autochef, and rather basic sanitary facilities. That left just enough room to move—in zero gravity. Right now they were under one-G acceleration, crushingly uncomfortable. They had been under one-G for weeks, subjective time; the *Yamamoto* was being run to flatlander specifications.

"Compensate," Ingrid said. The view swam back, the blue

stars ahead and the dim red behind turning to the normal variation of colors. The dual-sun Centauri system was dead ahead, looking uncomfortably close. "We're making good time. It took thirty years coming back on the slowboat, but the *Yamamoto*'s going to put us near Wunderland in five point seven. Objective, that is. Probably right on the heels of the pussy scouts."

Jonah nodded, looking ahead at the innocuous twinned stars. His hands were in the control-gloves of his couch, but the pressure-sensors and lightfields were off, of course. There had been very little to do in the month-subjective since they left the orbit of Pluto. Accelerated learning with RNA boosters, and he could now speak as much of the Hero's Tongue as Ingrid—enough to understand it. Kzin evidently didn't like their slaves to speak much of it; they weren't worthy. He could also talk Belter-English with the accent of the Serpent Swarm, Wunderland's dominant language, and the five or six other tongues prevalent in the many ethnic enclaves . . . sometimes he found himself dreaming in Pahlavi or Croat or Amish *Pletterdeisz.* It wasn't going to be a long trip; with the gravity polarizer and the big orbital lasers to push them up to ramscoop speeds, and no limit on the acceleration their compensators could handle . . .

We must be nipping the heels of photons by now, he thought. Speeds only robot ships had achieved before, with experimental fields supposedly keeping the killing torrent of secondary radiation out. . . .

"Tell me some more about Wunderland," he said. Neither of them were fidgeting. Belters didn't; this sort of cramped environment had been normal for their people since the settlement of the Sol-system Belt three centuries before. It was the thought of how they were going to *stop* that had his nerves twisting.

I've already briefed you twenty times," she replied, with something of a snap in the tone. Military formality wore thin pretty quickly in close quarters like this. "All the first-hand stuff is fifty-six years out of date, and the nine-year-old material's in the computer. You're just bored."

No, I'm just scared shitless. "Well, talking would be better than nothing. Spending a month strapped to this thing is even more monotonous than being a rockjack You were right, I'm bored."

"And scared."

He looked around. She was lying with her hands behind her head, grinning at him.

"I'm scared too. The offswitch is exterior to the surface of the effect." It had to be; time did not pass inside a stasis field.

"The designers were pretty sure it'd work."

"I'm sure of only two things, Jonah."

"Which are?"

"Well, the *first* one is that the designers aren't going to be diving into the photosphere of a sun at point-nine lights."

"Oh." That had occurred to him too. On the other hand, it really was easier to be objective when your life wasn't on the line . . . and in any case, it would be quick. "What's the other thing?"

Her smile grew wider, and she undid the collar-catch of her uniform. "Even in a gravity field, there's *one* thing I want to experience again before possible death."

☆ ☆ ☆

"Overview, schematic, trajectory," Traat-Admiral commanded. The big semicircle of the kzinti dreadnought's bridge was dim-lit by the blue and red glow of screens and telltales, crackly with the ozone scents of alerted kzintosh; *Throat-Ripper* was preparing for action.

Spray-fans appeared on the big circular display-screen below his crash couch. Traat-Admiral's fangs glinted wet as he considered them. The ship would pass fairly near Wunderland, and quite near Alpha Centauri itself. Slingshot effect was modest with something moving at such speeds, but . . . ah, yes. The other two suns of this cluster would also help. Still, it would be a long time before that vessel headed back towards the Sol system, if indeed that was their aim.

What forsaken-of-ancestors trick is this? he wondered. Then: *Were those Kfraksha-Admiral's last thoughts?*

He shook off the mood. "Identification?"

"Definitely a ramscoop vessel, Dominant One," Riesu-Fleet-Operations said. "Estimated speed is approximately .9071 *c*. In the 1600 kilokzinmass range."

About the mass of a light cruiser, then. His whiskers ruffled. Quite a weight to get up to such a respectable fraction of *c*, when you did not have the gravity polarizer. On the other paw, the humans used very powerful launch-boost lasers—useful as weapons, too, which had been an unanticipated disaster for the kzinti fleets—and by now they might *have* the gravity polarizer. Polarizer-drive vessels could get up to about .8 *c* if they were willing to spend the energy, and that was well above ramscoop initial speeds.

"Hrrr. That is considerably above the mass-range of the robot vessels the humans used"—for scouting new systems and carrying small freight loads over interstellar distances. They used big slowboats at .3 *c* for colonization and passenger traffic. "Fleet positions, tactical."

The screen changed, showing the positions of his squadrons, stingfighter carriers and dreadnoughts, destroyers and cruisers. Most were still crawling across the disk of the Alpha Centauri system, boosting from their ready stations near replenishment asteroids or in orbit around Wunderland itself. He scowled; the human probe was damnably well stealthed for something moving that fast, and there had been little time. His own personal dreadnought and battle-group were thirty AU outside the outermost planet, beginning to accelerate back in toward the star. The problem was that no sane being moved at interstellar speeds this close to high concentrations of matter, which put the enemy vessel in an entirely different energy envelope.

We must strike in passing, he thought; he could feel the claws slide out of the black-leather-glove shapes of his hands, pricking against the rests in the gloves of his space armor.

"Dominant One," Riesu-Fleet-Operations said. The tone in his voice and a sudden waft of spoiled-ginger scent brought Traat-Admiral's ears folding back into combat position, and his tongue lapped across his nose instinctively. "Separation . . . No, it's not breaking up . . . We're getting relay from the outer-system drone sentinels, Traat-Admiral. The human ship is launching."

"Launching what?"

"Traat-Admiral . . . ahhh. Projectiles of various sorts. Continuous launch. None over one-tenth kzinfist mass." About twenty grams, in human measurements—but stealthing could be in use, hiding much larger objects in the clutter. "Some are buckshot arrays, others slugs. Spectroscopic analysis indicates most are of nickel-iron composition. Magnetic flux. The human ship is using magnetic launchers of very great power for initial guidance."

Traat-Admiral's fur went flat, then fluffed out to stand erect all over his body.

"Trajectories!" he screamed.

"Ereaauuuu—" the officer mewled, then pulled himself

together. "Dominant One, intersection trajectories for the planet itself and the following installations—"

Alarm klaxons began to screech. Traat-Admiral ignored them and reached for his communicator. Chuut-Riit was not going to be happy, when he learned of how the humans replied to the Fourth Fleet.

Chuut-Riit had told him that some humans were worthy of respect. He was beginning to believe it.

☆ ☆ ☆

Raines and Jonah commanded the front screen to stop mimicking a control board; beyond a certain level fear-adrenaline was an anti-aphrodisiac. Now the upper half was an unmodified view of the Alpha Centauri system; the lower was a battle schematic, dots and graphs and probability-curves like bundles of fuzzy sticks. The *Yamamoto* was going to cross the disk of the Wunderland system in subjective minutes, mere hours even by outside clocks, with her ramscoop fields spreading a corona around her deadly to any life-form with a nervous system, and the fusion flare a sword behind her half a parsec long, fed by the fantastically rich gas-field that surrounded a star. Nothing but beam-weapons stood a chance of catching her, and even messages were going to take prodigies of computing power to unscramble. Her own weapons were quite simple: iron eggs. Velocity equals mass; when they intercepted their targets, the results would be in the megaton-yield range.

Jonah's lips skinned back from his teeth, and the hair struggled to raise itself along his spine. *Plains ape reflex,* he thought, smelling the rank odor of fight/flight sweat trickling down his flanks. *Your genes think they're about to tackle a Cape buffalo with a thighbone club.* His fingers pressed the inside of the chair seat in a complex pattern.

"Responding," said the computer in its usual husky contralto.

Was it imagination that there was more inflection in it? Conscious computer, but not a human consciousness. Memory and instincts designed by humans . . . free will, unless he or Ingrid used the override keys. Unless the high command had left sleeper drives. Perhaps not so much free will; a computer would see the path most likely to succeed and follow it. How would it be to know that you were a made thing, and doomed to encysted madness in six months or less? Nobody had ever been able to learn why. He had speculated to himself that it was a matter of time; to a consciousness that could think in nanoseconds, that could govern its own sensory input, what would be the point of remaining linked to a refractory cosmos? It could make its own universe, and have it last forever in a few milliseconds. Perhaps that was why humans who linked directly to a computer system of any size went catatonic as well. . . .

"Detection. Neutronic and electromagnetic-range sensors." The ship's system was linked to the hugely powerful but subconscious level machines of the *Yamamoto*. "Point sources."

Rubies sprang out across the battle map, and they moved as he watched, swelling up on either side and pivoting in relation to each other. A quick glimpse at the fire-bright point source of Alpha Centauri in the upper screen showed a perceptible disk, swelling as he watched. Jonah's skin crawled at the sight; this was like ancient history, air and sea battles out of Earth's past. He was used to maneuvers that lasted hours or days, matching relative velocities while the planets moved *slowly* and the sun might as well be a fixed point at the center of the universe . . . perhaps when gravity polarizers were small and cheap enough to fit in Dart-class boats, it would all be like this.

"The pussies have the system pretty well covered," he said.

"And the Swarm's Belters," Ingrid replied. Jonah turned his head, slowly, at the sound of her voice. Shocked, he saw a glistening in her eyes.

"Home . . ." she whispered. Then more decisively: "Identification, human-range sensors, discrete."

Half the rubies flickered for a few seconds. Ingrid continued to Jonah: "This is a messy system; more of its mass in asteroids and assorted junk than yours. Belters use more deep-radar and don't rely on telescopes as much. The pussies couldn't have changed that much; they'd cripple the Swarm's economy and destroy its value to them." Slowly. "That's the big station on Tiamat. They've got a garrison there, it's a major shipbuilding center, was even"—she swallowed—"fifty years ago. Those others are bubbleworlds . . . More detectors on Wunderland than there used to be, and in close orbit. At the poles, and that looks like a military-geosynchronous setup."

"Enemy action. Laser and particle-beam weapons." Nothing they could do about that. "Enemy vessels are detonating high-yield fusion weapons on our anticipated trajectory."

Attempting to overload the ramscoop, and unlikely to succeed unless they had something tailored for it, like cesium gas bombs. The UNSN had done theoretical studies, but the pussies were unlikely to have anything on hand. This trick was not in their book, and they were rather inflexible in tactics.

Of course, if they *did* have something, the *Yamamoto* would become a rather dangerous slug of high-velocity gas in nanoseconds. *Catskinner* might very well survive, if the stasis field kicked in quickly enough . . . in which case her passengers would spend the next several thousand years in stasis, waiting for just the right target to slow them down.

"Home," Ingrid said, very softly.

Jonah thought briefly what it would be like to return to the Sol-Belt after fifty years. Nearly a third of the average lifetime, longer than Jonah had been alive. What it *would* be like, if he ever got home. The *Yamamoto* could expect to see Sol again in twenty years objective, allowing time to pass through the Alpha Centauri system, decelerate and work back up to a respectable Tau value. The plan-in-theory was for him and Ingrid to accomplish their mission and then boost the *Catskinner* out in the direction of Sol, turn on the stasis field again and wait to be picked up by UNSN craft.

About as likely as doing it by putting our heads between our knees and spitting hard, he thought sardonically.

"Ships," the computer said in its dispassionate tone. "Movement. Status, probable class and dispersal cones."

Color-coded lines blinking over the tactical map. Columns of print scrolling down one margin, coded velocities and key-data; hypnotic training triggered bursts into their minds, crystalline shards of fact, faster than conscious recall. Jonah whistled.

"Loaded for bandersnatch," he said. There were a *lot* of warships spraying out from bases and holding-orbits, and that was not counting those too small for the *Yamamoto*'s detection systems: their own speed would be degrading signal drastically. Between the ramscoop fields, their velocity, and normal shielding, there was very little that could touch the ramscooper, but the kzin were certainly going to try.

"Aggressive bastards," he said, keeping his eyes firmly fixed on the tactical display. Getting in the way of the *Yamamoto* took courage, individually and on the part of their commander. Nobody had used a ramscoop ship like this before; the kzin had never developed a Bussard-type drive; they had had the gravity polarizer for a long time, and it had aborted work on reaction jet systems. But they must have made staff studies, and they would know what they were facing. Which was something more in the nature of a large-scale cosmic event than a ship. Mass equals velocity: by now the *Yamamoto* had the effective bulk of a medium-sized moon, moving only a tenth slower than a laser beam.

That reminded him of what the *Catskinner* would be doing shortly—and the Dart did not have anything *like* the scale of protection the ramscoop warship did. Even a micrometeorite . . . Alpha Centauri was a black disk edged by fire in the upper half of the screen.

"Projectiles away," the computer said. Nothing physical, but another inverted cone of trajectories splayed out from the path of the *Yamamoto.* Highly polished chrome-tungsten-steel alloy slugs, which had spent the trip from Sol riding grapnel-fields in the *Yamamoto*'s wake. Others were clusters of small shot, or balloons, to transmit energy to fragile targets; at these speeds, a slug could punch through a ship without slowing enough to do more than leave a small glowing hole through the structure. Wildly varying albedos, from fully-stealthed to deliberately reflective; the *Catskinner* was going to be rather conspicuous when the Slaver stasis field's impenetrable surface went on. Now the warship's magnetics were twitching the kinetic-energy weapons out in sprays and clusters, at velocities that would send them across the Wunderland system in hours. It would take the firepower of a heavy cruiser to significantly damage one, and there were a *lot* of them. Iron was cheap, and the *Yamamoto* grossly overpowered.

"You know, we ought to have done this before," Jonah said. The sun-disk filled the upper screen, then snapped down several sizes as the computer reduced the field. A sphere, floating in the wild arching discharges and coronas of a G-type sun. "We could have used ramrobots. Or the pussies could have copied our designs and done it to us."

"Nope," Ingrid said. She coughed, and he wondered if her eyes were locking on the sphere again as it clicked down to a size that would fit the upper screen. "Ramscoop fields. Think about it."

"Oh." When you put it that way, he could think of about a half-dozen ways to destabilize one; drop, oh, ultracompressed radon into it. Countermeasures . . . luckily, nothing the kzin were likely to have right on hand.

"For that matter," she continued, "throwing relativistic weapons around inside a solar system is a bad idea. If you want to keep it."

"Impact," the computer said helpfully. An asteroid winked,

the tactical screen's way of showing an expanding sphere of plasma: nickel-iron, oxygen, nitrogen, carbon-compounds, some of the latter kzin and humans and children and their pet budgies.

"You have to aim at stationary targets," Ingrid was saying. "The things that war is supposed to be about seizing. It's as insane as fighting a planetside war with fusion weapons and no effective defense. Only possible once."

"Once would be enough, if we knew where the kzin home system was." For a vengeful moment he imagined robot ships falling into a sun from infinite distances, scores of light-years of acceleration at hundreds of G's, their own masses raised to near-stellar proportions. "No. Then again, no."

"I'm glad you said that," Ingrid replied. Softly: "I wonder what it's like, for them out there."

"Interesting," Jonah said tightly. "At the very least, interesting."

Chapter 2

"Please, keep calm," Harold Yarthkin-Schotmann said, for the fourth time. "For Finagle's sake, *sit down and shut up!*"

This one seemed to sink in, or perhaps the remaining patrons were getting tired of running around in circles and shouting. The staff were all at their posts, or preventing the paying customers from hitting each other or breaking anything expensive. Several of them had police-model stunners under their dinner jackets, like his; hideous illegal, hence quite difficult to square. Not through Claude—he was quite conscientious about avoiding things that would seriously annoy the ratcats—but there were plenty lower down the totem pole who lacked his gentlemanly sense of their own long-term interests.

Everyone was watching the screen behind the bar again; the UNSN announcement was off the air, but the Munchen news service was slapping in random readouts from all over the planet. For once the collaborationist government was too busy to follow their natural instincts and keep everyone in the dark, and the kzin had never given much of a damn; the only thing *they* cared about was behavior, propaganda be damned.

The flatlander warship was still headed insystem; from the look of things they were going to use the sun for as much of a course-alteration as possible. He could feel rusty spaceman's reflexes creaking into action. That was a perfectly sensible ploy; ramscoop ships were *not* easy to turn. Even at their speeds, you couldn't use the interstellar medium to bank; turning meant applying lateral thrust, and it would be easier to decelerate, turn and work back up to high Tau. Unless you could use a gravitational sling, like a kid on roller-skates going hell-for-leather down a street and then slapping a hand on a lamppost—and even a star's gravity was pretty feeble at those speeds.

He raised his glass to the sometime mirror behind the bar. It was showing a scene from the south polar zone. Kzin were stuck with Wunderland's light gravity, but they preferred a cooler, drier climate than humans. The first impact had looked like a line of light drawn down from heaven to earth, and the shockwave flipped the robot camera into a spin that had probably ended on hard, cold ground. Yarthkin grinned, and snapped his fingers for coffee.

"With a sandwich, sweetheart," he told the waitress. "Heavy on the mustard." He loosened his archaic tie and watched flickershots of boiling dust-clouds crawling with networks of purple-white lightning. Closer, into canyons of night seething up out of red-shot blackness. That must be molten rock; something had punched right through into the magma.

"Sam." The man at the musicomp looked up from trailing his fingers across the keyboard; it was configured for piano tonight. An archaism, like the whole setup. Popular, as more and more fled in fantasy what could not be avoided in reality, back into a history that was at least human. Of course, Wunderlanders were prone to that; the planet had been a patchwork of refugees from an increasingly homogenized and technophile Earth anyway. *I've spent a generation cashing in on a nostalgia boom,* Yarthkin thought wryly. *Was that because I had foresight, or was I one of the first victims?*

"Sir?" Sam was Krio, like McAndrews the doorman, although he had never gone the whole route and taken warrior scars. Just as tough in a fight, though. He'd been enrolled in the Sensor-Effector program at the Scholarium, been a gunner with Yarthkin in the brief war in space, and they had been together in the hills. And he had come along when Yarthkin took the amnesty, too. Even more of a wizard with the keys than he had been with a jizzer or a strakaker or a ratchet knife.

"Play something appropriate, Sam. 'Stormy Weather.' "

The musician's face lit with a vast white grin, and he launched into the ancient tune with a will, even singing his own version, translated into Wunderlander. Yarthkin murmured into his lapel to turn down the hysterical commentary from the screen, still babbling about dastardly attacks and massive casualties.

It took a man back. Humans were dying out there, but so were ratcats . . . *Here's looking at you,* he thought to the hypothetical crew of the *Yamamoto.* Possibly nothing more than recordings and sensor-effector mechanisms, but he doubted it.

"Stormy weather for sure," he said softly to himself. Megatons of dust and water vapor were being pumped into the atmosphere. "Bad for the crops." Though there would be a harvest from this, yes indeed. *I could have been on that ship,* he thought to himself, with a sudden flare of murderous anger. *I was good enough. There are probably Wunderlanders aboard her; those slowships got through. If I hadn't been left sucking vacuum at the airlock, it could have been me out there!*

"But not Ingrid," he whispered to himself. "The bitch wouldn't have the guts." Sam was looking at him; it had been a long time since the memory of the last days came back. With a practiced effort of will he shoved it deeper below the threshold of consciousness and produced the same mocking smile that had faced the world for most of his adult life.

"I wonder how our esteemed ratcat masters are taking it," he said. "Been a while since the ones here've had to lap out of the same saucer as us lowlife monkey-boys. I'd like to see it, I truly would."

☆ ☆ ☆

" . . . estimate probability of successful interception at less than one-fifth," the figure in the screen said. "*Vengeance-Fang* and *Rampant-Slayer* do not respond to signals. *Lurker-At-Waterholes* continues to accelerate at right angles to the ecliptic. We must assume they were struck by the ramscoop fields."

The governor watched closely; the slight bristle of whiskers and rapid open-shut flare of wet black nostrils was a sign of intense frustration.

"You have leapt well, Traat-Admiral," Chuut-Riit said formally. "Break off pursuit. The distant shadow-watchers would have their chance."

A good tactician, Traat-Admiral; if he had come from a better family, he would have a double name by now. *Would* have a double name, when Earth was conquered, a name, and vast wealth. One percent of all the product of the new conquest for life, since he was to be in supreme military command of the Fifth Fleet. That would make him founder of a Noble Line, his bones in a worship shrine for a thousand generations; Chuut-Riit had hinted that he would send several of his daughters to the admiral's harem, letting him mingle his blood with that of the Patriarch.

"Chuut-Riit, are we to let the . . . the . . . omnivores escape unscathed?" The admiral's ears were quivering with the effort required to keep them out at parade-rest.

A rumble came from the space-armored figures that bulked in the dim orange light behind the flotilla commandant. *Good,* the planetary governor thought. *They are not daunted.*

"Your bloodlust is commendable, Traat-Admiral, but the fact remains that the human ship is traveling at velocities which render it . . . It is at a different point on the energy gradient, Traat-Admiral."

"We can pursue as it leaves the system!"

"In ships designed to travel at point-eight lightspeed? From behind? Remember the Human Lesson. That is a *very* effective reaction drive they are using."

A deep ticking sound came from his throat, and Traat-Admiral's ears laid back instinctively. The thought of trying to maneuver past that planetary-length sword of nuclear fire . . .

Chuut-Riit paused to let the thought sink home before continuing: "This has been a startling tactic. We assumed that possession of the gravity polarizer would lead the humans to neglect further development of their so-efficient reaction drives, as we had done; *hr'rrearow t'chssseee mearowet'aatrurrte,* this-does-not-follow. We must prepare countermeasures, investigate the possibility of ramscoop interstellar missiles . . . At least they did not strike at this system's sun, or drop a really large mass into the planetary gravity well."

The fur of the kzin on *Throat-Ripper*'s bridge lay flat, sculpting the bone-and-muscle planes of their faces.

"Indeed, Chuut-Riit," Traat-Admiral said fervently.

"A series of polarizer-driven missiles, with laser-cannon boost, deployed ready to destabilize ramscoop fields . . . In any case, you are ordered to break off action, assist with emergency rescue efforts, detach two units with interstellar capacity to shadow the intruder until it leaves the immediate vicinity. Waste no more Heroes in futility; instead, we must repair the damage and redouble our preparations for the next attack on Sol."

"As you command, Chuut-Riit, although it goes against the grain to let the leaf-eating monkeys escape, when the Fifth Fleet is so near completion."

The governor rose, letting his weight forward on hands whose claws slid free. He restrained any further display of impatience. *I must teach him to think. To think correctly, he must be allowed to make errors.*

"Its departure has already been delayed. Will losing further units in fruitless pursuit speed the repairs and modifications which must be made? Attend to your orders!"

"At once, Chuut-Riit!"

The governor held himself impressively immobile until the screen blanked. Then he turned and leaped with a tearing shriek over the nearest wall, out into the unnatural storm and darkness. A half-hour later he returned, meditatively picking bits of hide and bone from between his teeth with a thumb-claw. His pelt was plastered flat with mud, leaves, and blood, and a thorned branch had cut a bleeding trough across his sloping forehead. The screens were still flicking between various disasters, each one worse than the last.

"Any emergency calls?" he asked mildly.

"None at the priority levels you established," the computer replied.

"Murmeroumph," he said, opening his mouth wide into the killing gape to get at an irritating fragment between two of the back shearing teeth. "Staff."

One wall turned to the ordered bustle of the household's management centrum. "Ah, Henrietta," he said in Wunderlander. "You have that preliminary summary ready?"

The human swallowed and averted her eyes from the bits of *something* that the kzin was flicking from his fangs and muzzle. The others behind her were looking drawn and tense as well, but no signs of panic. *If I could recognize them,* the kzin thought. *They panic differently.* A Hero overcome with terror either fled, striking out at anything in his path, or went into mindless berserker frenzy.

Berserker, he mused thoughtfully. The concept was fascinating; reading of it had convinced him that kzin and humankind were enough alike to cooperate effectively.

"Yes, Chuut-Riit," she was saying. "Installations Seven, Three, and Twelve in the north polar zone have been effectively destroyed, loss of industrial function in the seventy-five to eighty percent range. Over ninety percent at Six, the main fusion generator destabilized in the pulse from a near-miss." Ionization effects had been quite spectacular. "Casualties in the range of five thousand Heroes, thirty thousand humans. Four major orbital facilities hit, but there was less collateral damage there, of course, and more near-misses." No air to transmit blast in space. "Reports from the asteroid belt still coming in."

"Merrower," he said, meditatively. Kzin government was heavily decentralized; the average Hero did not make a good bureaucrat, that was work for slaves and computers. A governor was expected to confine himself to policy decisions. Still . . . "Have my personal spaceship prepared for lift. I will be doing a tour."

Henrietta hesitated. "Ah, noble Chuut-Riit, the feral humans will be active, with defense functions thrown out of order."

She was far too experienced to mistake Chuut-Riit's expression for a smile.

"Markham and his gang? I hope they do, Henrietta, I sincerely hope they do." He relaxed. "I'll view the reports from here. Send in the groomers; my pelt must be fit to be seen." A pause. "And replacements for one of the bull buffalo in the holding pen."

The kzin threw himself down on the pillow behind his desk, massive head propped with its chin on the stone surface of the workspace. Grooming would help him think. Humans were so good at it . . . and blowdryers, blowdryers alone were worth the trouble of conquering them.

☆ ☆ ☆

"Prepare for separation," the computer said. The upper field of the *Catskinner*'s screen was a crawling slow-motion curve of orange and yellow and darker spots; the battle schematic showed the last few slugs dropping away from the *Yamamoto,* using the gravity of the sun to whip around and curve out toward targets in a different quarter of the ecliptic plane. More than a few were deliberately misaimed, headed for catastrophic destruction in Alpha Centauri's photosphere as camouflage.

It can't be getting hotter, he thought.

"Gottdamn, it's hot," Ingrid said. "I'm swine-sweating."

Thanks, he thought, refraining from speaking aloud with a savage effort. "Purely psychosomatic," he grated.

"There's one thing I regret," Ingrid continued.

"What's that?"

"That we're not going to be able to *see* what happens when the *Catskinner* and those slugs make a high-Tau transit of the sun's outer envelope," she said.

Jonah felt a smile crease the rigid sweat-slick muscles of his face. The consequences had been extrapolated, but only roughly. At the very least, there would be solar-flare effects like nothing this system had ever witnessed before, enough to foul up every receptor pointed this way. "It would be interesting, at that."

"Prepare for separation," the computer continued. "Five seconds and counting."

One. Ingrid had crossed herself just before the field went on. Astonishing. There were worse people to be crammed into a Dart with for a month, even among the more interesting half of the human race.

Two. They were probably going to be closer to an active star than any other human beings had ever been and survived to tell the tale. Provided they survived, of course.

Three. His grandparents had considered emigrating to the Wunderland system; he remembered them complaining about how the Belt had been then, everything regulated and taxed to death, and psychists hovering to resanitize your mind as soon as you came in from a prospecting trip. If that'd happened, *he* might have ended up as a conscript technician with the Fourth Fleet.

Four. Or a guerrilla: the prisoners had mentioned activity by "feral humans." Jonah bared his teeth in an expression a kzin would have had no trouble at all understanding. *I intend to remain very feral indeed. The kzin may have done us a favor; we were well on the way to turning ourselves into sheep when they arrived. If I'm going to be a monkey, I'll be a big, mean baboon, by choice.*

Five. Ingrid was right, it was a pity they wouldn't be able to see it.

"Personally, I just wish that ARM bastard who volunteered me for this was here—"

—discontinuity—

"Ready for separation, sir," the computer said.

Buford Early grunted. He was alone in the corvette's control room; none of the others had wanted to come out of deepsleep just to sit helplessly and watch their fate decided by chance.

"The kzinti aren't the ones who should be called pussies," he said. Early chuckled softly, enjoying a pun not one human in ten million would have appreciated. Patterns of sunlight crawled across his face from the screens; the *Inner Ring* was built inside the hull of a captured kzinti corvette, but the UNSN—and the ARM—had stuffed her full of surprises. "I don't know what the youth of today is coming to."

At that he laughed outright; he had been born into a family of the . . . even mentally, he decided not to specify . . . secret path. Born a long, *long* time ago, longer even than the creaking quasi-androids of the Struldbrug Club would have believed; there were geriatric technologies that the ARM and its masters guarded as closely as the weapons and destabilizing inventions people knew about.

Damn, but I'm glad the Long Peace is over, he mused. It had been far too long, whatever the uppermost leadership thought, although of course he had backed the policy. Besides, there was no real fun in being master in the Country of the Cows; Earthers had gotten just plain boring, however docile.

"Boring this isn't, no jive," he said, watching the disk of Alpha Centauri grow. "About—"

—discontinuity—

"Greow-Captain, there is an anomaly in the last projectile!"

"They are all anomalies, Sensor-Operator!" The commander did not move his eyes from the schematic before his face, but his tone held conviction that the humans had used irritatingly nonstandard weapons solely to annoy and humiliate him. Behind his back, the other two kzin exchanged glances and moved expressive ears.

The *Slasher*-class armed scout held three crewkzin in its delta-shaped control chamber: the commander forward and the Sensor and Weapons operators behind him to either side. There were three small screens instead of the single larger divisible one a human boat of the same size would have had, and many more manually activated controls. Kzin had broader-range senses than humans, faster reflexes, and they trusted cybernetic systems rather less. They had also had gravity control almost from the beginning of spaceflight; a failure serious enough to immobilize the crew usually destroyed the vessel.

"Simply tell me," the kzin commander said, "if our particle-beam is driving it down." The cooling system was whining audibly as it pumped energy into its central tank of degenerate matter, and still the cabin was furnace-hot and dry, full of the wild odors of fear and blood that the habitation-system poured out in combat conditions. The ship shuddered and banged as it plunged in a curve that was not quite suicidally close to the outer envelope of the sun.

Before Greow-Captain a stepped-down image showed the darkened curve of the gas envelope, and the gouting coriolis-driven plumes as the human projectiles plowed their way through plasma. Shocks of discharge arched between them as they drew away from the kzin craft above, away from the beams that sought to tumble them down into denser layers where even their velocity would not protect them. Or at least throw them enough off course that they would recede harmlessly into interstellar space. The light from the holo-screen crawled in iridescent streamers across the flared scarlet synthetic of the kzin's helmet and the huge lambent eyes; the whole corona of Alpha Centauri was writhing, flowers of nuclear fire, a thunder of forces beyond the understanding of human or kzinkind.

The two Operators were uneasily conscious that Greow-Captain felt neither awe nor the slightest hint of fear. Not because he was more than normally courageous for a young male kzin, but because he was utterly indifferent to everything but how this would look on his record. Another uneasy glance went between them. Younger sons of nobles were notoriously anxious to earn full Names at record ages, and Greow-Captain had complained long and bitterly when their squadron was not assigned to the Fourth Fleet. Operational efficiency might suffer.

They knew better than to complain openly, of course. Whatever the state of his wits, there was *nothing* wrong with Greow-Captain's reflexes, and he already had an imposing collection of kzin-ear dueling trophies.

"Greow-Captain, the anomaly is greater than a variance in reflectivity," the Sensor-Operator yowled. Half his instruments were useless in the flux of energetic particles that were sheeting off the *Slasher*'s screens. He *hoped* they were being deflected; as a lowly Sensor-Operator he had not had a chance to breed—not so much as a sniff of kzinrret fur since they carried him mewling from the teats of his mother to the training creche. "The projectile is not absorbing the quanta of our beam as the previous one did, nor is its surface ablating. And its trajectory is incompatible with the shape of the others; this is larger, less dense, and moving" . . . a pause of less than a second to query the computer . . . "moving as if its outer shell were absolutely frictionless and reflective, Greow-Captain. Should this not be reported?"

Reporting would mean retreat, out to where a message-maser

could punch through the chaotic broad-spectrum noise of an injured star's bellow.

"Do my Heroes refuse to follow into danger?" Greow-Captain snarled.

"Lead us, Greow-Captain!" Put that way, they had no choice; which was why a sensible officer would never have put it that way. Both Operators silently cursed the better diet and personal-combat training available to offspring of a noble's household. It had been a *long* time since kzin met an enemy capable of exercising greater selective pressure than their own social system. His very scent was intimidating, overflowing with the ketones of a fresh-meat diet.

"Weapons-Operator, shift your aim to the region of compressed gases directly ahead of our target, all energy weapons. I am taking us down and accelerating past red-line." With a little luck, he could ignite the superheated and compressed monatomic hydrogen directly ahead of the projectile, and let the multimega-ton explosion flip it up or down off the ballistic trajectory the humans had launched it on.

Muffled howls and spitting sounds came from the workstations behind him; the thin black lips wrinkled back more fully from his fangs, and slender lines of saliva drooled down past the open neckring of his suit. *Warren-dwellers,* he thought, as the *Slasher* lurched and swooped.

His hands darted over the controls, prompting the machin-ery that was throwing it about at hundreds of accelerations. *Vatach hunters.* The little quasi-rodents were all lower-caste kzin could get in the way of live meat. Although the anomaly was interesting, and he would report noticing it to Khurut-Squadron-Captain. *I will show them how a true hunter—*

The input from the kzin boat's weapons was barely a fraction of the kinetic energy the *Catskinner* was shedding into the gases that slowed it, but that was just enough. Enough to set off chain-reaction fusion in a sizable volume around the invulnerably-protected human vessel. The kzin craft was far enough away for the wave-front to arrive before the killing blow:

"—shield overload, loss of directional *hhnrrreaw—*"

The Sensor-Operator shrieked and burned as induction-arcs crashed through his position. Weapons-Operator was screaming the hiss of a nursing kitten as his claws slashed at the useless controls.

Greow-Captain's last fractional second was spent in a cry

as well, but his was of pure rage. The *Slasher*'s fusion-bottle destabilized at almost the same nanosecond as her shields went down and the gravity control vanished; an imperceptible instant later only a mass-spectroscope could have told the location as atoms of carbon and iron scattered through the hot plasma of the inner solar wind.

—discontinuity—

"Shit," Jonah said, with quiet conviction. "Report. *And stabilize that view.*" The streaking pinwheel in the exterior-view screen slowed and halted, but the control surface beside it continued to show the *Catskinner* twirling end-over-end at a rate that would have pasted them both as a thin reddish film over the interior without the compensation fields. Gravity polarizers were a wonderful invention, and he was very glad humans had mastered them, but they were nerve-wracking.

The screen split down the middle as Ingrid began establishing their possible paths.

"We are," the computer said, "traveling twice as fast as our projected velocity at switchoff, and on a path twenty-five degrees further to the solar north." A pause. "We are still, you will note, in the plane of the ecliptic."

"Thank Finagle for small favors," Jonah muttered, working his hands in the control gloves. The *Catskinner* was running on her accumulators, the fusion reactor and its so-detectable neutrino flux shut down.

"Jonah," Ingrid said. "Take a look." A corner of the screen lit, showing the surface of the sun and a gigantic pillar of flare reaching out in their wake like the tongue of a hungry fire-elemental. "The pussies are burning up the communications spectra, yowling about losing scout-boats. They had them down low and dirty, trying to throw the slugs that went into the photosphere with us off-course."

"Lovely," the man muttered. *So much for quietly matching velocities with Wunderland while the commnet is still down.* To the computer: "What's ahead of us?"

"For approximately twenty-three point six light-years, nothing."

"What do you mean, nothing?"

"Hard vacuum, micrometeorites, interstellar dust, possible spacecraft, bodies too small or nonradiating to be detected, superstrings, shadowmatter—"

"Shut up!" he snarled. "Can we brake?"

"Yes. Unfortunately, this will require several hours of thrust and exhaust our onboard fuel reserves."

"And put up a fucking great sign, *'Hurrah, we're back'* for every pussy in the system," he grated. Ingrid touched him on the arm.

"Wait, I have an idea. . . . Is there anything substantial in our way, that we could reach with less of a burn?"

"Several asteroids, Lieutenant Raines. Uninhabited."

"What's the status of our stasis-controller?"

A pause. "Still . . . I must confess, I am surprised." The computer sounded surprised that it could be. "Still functional, Lieutenant Raines."

Jonah winced. "Are you thinking what I think you're thinking?" he said plaintively. *"Another* collision?"

Ingrid shrugged. "Right now, it'll be less noticeable than a long burn. Computer, will it work?"

"Ninety-seven percent chance of achieving a stable Swarm orbit. The risk of emitting infrared and visible-light signals is unquantifiable. The field switch will *probably* continue to function, Lieutenant Raines."

"It should, it's covered in neutronium." She turned her head to Jonah. "Well?"

He sighed. "Offhand, I can't think of a better solution. When you can't think of a better solution than a high-speed collision with a rock, something's wrong with your thinking, but I can't think of what would be better to think . . . What do *you* think?"

"That an *unshielded* collision with a rock might be better than another month imprisoned with your sense of humor. . . . Gott, all those fish puns . . ."

"Computer, prepare for minimal burn. Any distinguishing characteristics of those rocks?"

"One largely silicate, one eighty-three percent nickel-iron with traces of—"

"Spare me. The nickel-iron, it's denser and less likely to break up. Prepare for minimal burn."

"I have so prepared, on the orders of Lieutenant Raines."

Jonah opened his mouth, then frowned. "Wait a minute. Why is it always *Lieutenant Raines*? You're a damned sight more respectful of *her*."

Ingrid buffed her fingernails. "While you were briefing up on Wunderland and the Swarm . . . I was helping the team that programmed our tin friend."

☆ ☆ ☆

"Are you sure?"

The radar operator held her temper in check with an effort. She had not been part of the *Nietzsche*'s crew long, but more than long enough to learn that you did not back-talk Herrenmann Ulf Reichstein-Markham. *Bastard's as arrogant as a kzin himself,* she thought resentfully.

"Yes, sir. It's definitely heading our way since that microburn. Overpowered thruster, unusual spectrum, and unless it's unmanned they have a gravity polarizer. Two hundred G's, they pulled."

The guerrilla commander nodded thoughtfully. "Then it is either kzin, which is unlikely in the extreme since they do not use reaction drives on any of their standard vessels, or . . ."

"And, sir, it's cool. Hardly radiating at all, when the fusion plant's off. If we weren't close and didn't know where to look . . . granted, this isn't a military sensor, but I doubt the ratcats have seen him."

Markham's long face drew into an expression of disapproval. "They are called kzin, soldier. I will tolerate no vulgarities in my command."

Bastard. "Yessir."

The man was tugging at his asymmetric beard. "Evacuate the asteroid. It will be interesting to see how they decelerate, perhaps some gravitic effect . . . and even more interesting to find out what those fat cowards in the Sol system think they are doing."

☆ ☆ ☆

"Prepare for stasis," the computer said.

"How?" Ingrid and Jonah asked in unison. The rock came closer, tumbling, half a kilometer on a side, falling forever in a slow silent spiral. Closer . . .

"Interesting," the computer said. "There is a ship adjacent."

"What?" Jonah said. His fingers slid into the control gloves like snakes fleeing a mongoose, then froze. It was too late, and they were committed.

"Very well stealthed." A pause, and the asteroid grew in the wall before them, filling it from end to end.

Tin-brained idiot's a sadist, Jonah thought.

"And the asteroid is an artifact. Well hidden as well, but at this range my semi-passive systems can pick up a tunnel complex and shut-down power system. Life support on maintenance. Twelve seconds to impact."

"Is anybody there?" Jonah barked.

"Negative, Jonah. The ship is occupied; I scan twinned fusion drives, and hull-mounted weaponry, concealed as part of the grappling apparatus. X-ray lasers, possible rail-guns. Two of the cargo bays have dropslots that would be of appropriate size for kzin light-seeker missiles. Eight seconds to impact."

"Put us into combat mode," the Sol-Belter snapped. "Prepare for emergency stabilization as soon as the stasis field is off. Warm for boost. Ingrid, if we're going to talk you'll probably be better able to convince them of our—"

—discontinuity—

"—bona fides."

The ripping-cloth sound of the gravity polarizer hummed louder and louder, and there was a wobble felt more as a subliminal tugging at the inner ear, as the system strained to stop a spin as rapid as a gyroscope's. The asteroid was fragments glowing a dull orange-red streaked with dark slag, receding; the *Catskinner* was moving backward under twenty G's, her laser-pods star-fishing out and railguns humming with maximum charge.

"Alive again," Jonah breathed, feeling the response under his fingertips. The wall ahead had divided into a dozen panels, schematics of information, stresses, possibilities; the central was the exterior view. "Tightbeam signal, identify yourselves."

"Sent. Receiving signal also tightbeam." A pause. "Obsolete hailing pattern. Requesting identification."

"Request video, same pattern."

The screen flickered twice, and an off-right panel lit with a furious bearded face, tightly contained fury, in a face no older than his own, less than thirty; beard close-shaven on one side, pointed on the right, yellow-blond and wiry, like the close-cropped mat on the narrow skull; pale narrow eyes, mobile ears, long-nosed with a prominent bony chin beneath the carefully cultivated goatee. Behind him a control-chamber that was like the one in the Belter museum back at Ceres, an early-model independent miner—but modified, crammed with jury-rigged systems of which many were marked in the squiggles-and-angles kzin script; crammed with people as well, some of them in armored spacesuits. An improvised warship, then. Most of the crew were in neatly tailored gray skinsuits, with a design of a phoenix on their chests.

"Explain yourzelfs," the man said, with a slight guttural overtone to his Belter English, enough to mark him as one born speaking Wunderlander.

"UNSN *Catskinner,* Captain Jonah Matthieson commanding, Lieutenant Raines as second. Presently," he added dryly, "on detached duty. As representative of the human armed forces, I require your cooperation."

"Cooperation!" That was one of the spacesuited figures behind the Wunderlander, a tall man with hair cut in the Belter crest, and adorned with small silver bells. "You fucker, you just missiled my bloody base and a year's takings!"

"We didn't missile it, we just rammed into it," Jonah said. "Takings? What are these people, pirates?"

"Calm yourzelf, McAllistaire," the Wunderlander said. His eyes had narrowed slightly at the Sol-Belter's words, and his ears cocked forward. "Permit self-introduction, Hauptmann Matthieson. Commandant Ulf Reichstein-Markham, at your zerfice. Commandant in the Free Wunderland navy, zat is. My, ahh, coworker here is an independent entrepreneur who iss pleazed to cooperate wit' the naval forces."

"Goddam you, Markham, that was a year's profits yours and mine both. Shop the bastard to the ratcats, *now.* We could get a pardon out of it, easy. Hell, you could get that piece of dirt back on Wunderland you're always on about."

The self-proclaimed Commandant held up a hand palm-forward to Jonah and turned to speak to the owner of the ex-asteroid. "You try my patience, McAllistaire. Zilence."

"Silence yourself, dirtsider. I—"

"—am now dispensable." Markham's finger tapped the console. Stunners hummed in the guerrilla ship, and the figures not in gray crumpled.

The Commandant turned to a figure offscreen. "Strip zem of all useful equipment and space zem," he said casually. Turning to the screen again, with a slight smile. "It is true, you haff cost us valuable matériel . . . You will understant, a clandestine war requires unort'odox measures, Captain. Ve are forced sometimes to requisition goods, as the Free Wunderland government cannot levy ordinary taxes, and it iss necessary to exchange these for vital supplies vit t'ose not of our cause." A more genuine smile. "As an officer ant a chentelman, you vill appreciate the relief of no lonker having to deal vit this schweinerie."

Ingrid spoke softly to the computer, and another portion

of the screen switched to an exterior view of the Free Wunderland ship. An airlock door swung open, and figures spewed out into vacuum with a puff of vapor; some struggled and thrashed for nearly a minute. Another murmur, and a green line drew itself around the figure of Markham. *Stress-reading,* Jonah reminded himself. *Pupil-dilation monitoring. I should have thought of that. Interesting: he thinks he's telling the truth.*

One of the gray-clad figures gave a dry retch at her console. "Control yourzelf, soldier," Markham snapped. To the screen: "Wit' all the troubles, the kzin are unlikely to have noticed your, ah, sudden deceleration." The green line remained. "Still, ve should establish vectors to a less conspicuous spot. Then I can offer you the hozpitality of the *Nietzsche,* and we can discuss your mission and how I may assist you at leisure." The green line flickered, shaded to green-blue. Mental reservations.

Not on board your ship, that's for sure, Jonah thought, smiling into the steely fanatic's gaze in the screen. "By all means," he murmured.

☆ ☆ ☆

" . . . zo, as you can imagine, we are anxious to take advantage of your actions," Markham was saying. The control chamber of the *Catskinner* was crowded with him and the three "advisors" he had insisted on; all three looked wirecord-tough, and all had stripped to usefully lumpy coveralls. And they all had something of the outer-orbit chill of Markham's expression.

"To raid kzin outposts while they're off-balance?" Ingrid said. Markham gave her a quick glance down the eagle sweep of his nose.

"You vill understand, wit' improvised equipment it is not always pozzible to attack the kzin directly," he said to Jonah, pointedly ignoring the junior officer. "As the great military t'inker Clausewitz said, the role of a guerrilla is to avoid strength and attack weakness. Ve undertake to sabotage their operations by dizrupting commerce, and to aid ze groundside partisans wit' intelligence and supplies as often as pozzible."

Translated, you hijack ships and bung the crews out the airlock when it isn't an unmanned cargo pod, all for the Greater Good. Finagle's ghost, this is one scary bastard. Luckily, I know some things he doesn't.

"And the late unlamented McAllistaire?"

A frown. "Vell, unfortunately, not all are as devoted to the Cause as might be hoped. In terms of realpolitik, it iss to be eggspected, particularly of the common folk when so many of deir superiors haff decided that collaboration wit' the kzin is an unavoidable necessity." The faded blue eyes blinked at him. "Not an unreasonable supposition, when Earth has abandoned us—until now . . . Zo, of the ones willing to help, many are merely the lawless and corrupt. Motivated by money; vell, if one must shovel manure, one uses a pitchfork."

Jonah smiled and nodded, grasping the meaning if not the agricultural metaphor. *And the end justifies the means. My cheeks are starting to hurt.* "Well, I have my mission to perform. On a need-to-know basis, let's just say that Lieutenant Raines and I have to get to Wunderland, preferably to a city. With cover identities, currency, and instructions to the underground there to assist us, if it's safe enough to contact."

"Vell." Markham seemed lost in thought for moments. "I do not believe ve can expect a fleet from Earth. They would have followed on the heels of the so-effective attack, and such would be impossible to hide. You are an afterthought." Decision, and a mouth drawn into a cold line. "You must tell me of this mission before scarce resources are devoted to it."

"Impossible. This whole attack was to get Ingri—the lieutenant and me to Wunderland." Jonah cursed himself for the slip, saw Markham's ears twitch slightly. His mouth was dry, and he could feel his vision focusing and narrowing, bringing the aquiline features of the guerrilla chieftain into closer view.

"Zo. This I seriously doubt. But ve haff become adept at finding answers, even some kzin haff ve persuaded." The three "aides" drew their weapons, smooth and fast; two stunners and some sort of homemade dart-thrower. "You vill answer. Pozzibly, if the answers come quickly and wizzout damage, I vill let you proceed and giff you the help you require. This ship vill be of extreme use to the Cause, vhatever the bankers and merchants of Earth, who have done for us nothing in fifty years of fighting, intended. Ve who haff fought the kzin vit' our bare hands, while Earth did nothing, nothing . . ."

Markham pulled himself back to self-command. "If it is inadvisable to assist you, you may join my crew or die." His eyes, flatly dispassionate, turned to Ingrid. "You are from zis system. You also vill speak, and then join or . . . no, there is always a market for workable bodies, if the mind is first removed. Search them thoroughly and take them across to the *Nietzsche* in a bubble." A sign to his followers. "The first thing you must learn, is that I am not to be lied to."

"I don't doubt it," Jonah drawled, lying back in his crash-couch. "But you can't take this ship."

"Ah." Markham smiled again. "Codes. You vill furnish them."

"The ship," Ingrid said, considering her fingertips, "has a mind of its own. You may test it."

The Wunderlander snorted. "A zelf-aware computer? Impozzible. Laboratory curiosities."

"Now that," the computer said, "could be considered an insult, Landholder Ulf Reichstein-Markham." The weapons of Markham's companions were suddenly thrown away with stifled curses and cries of pain. "Induction fields . . . Your error, sir. Spaceships in this benighted vicinity may be metal shells with various systems tacked on, but *I* am an organism. *And you are in my intestines.*"

Markham crossed his arms. "You are two to our four, and in the same environment, so no gases or other such may be used. You vill tell me the control codes for this machine eventually; it is easy to make such a device mimic certain functions of sentience. Better for you if you come quietly."

"Landholder Markham, I grow annoyed with you," the computer said. "Furthermore, consider that your knowledge of cybernetics is fifty years out of date, and that the kzin are a technologically conservative people with no particular gift for information systems. Watch."

A railgun yapped through the hull, and there was a bright flare on the flank of the stubby toroid of Markham's ship. A voice babbled from the handset at his belt, and the view in the screen swooped crazily as the *Catskinner* dodged.

"That was your main screen generator," the computer continued. "You are now open to energy weapons. Need I remind you that this ship carries more than thirty parasite-rider X-ray lasers, pumped by one-megaton bombs? Do we need to alert the kzin to our presence?"

There was a sheen of sweat on Markham's face. "I haff perhaps been somevhat hasty," he said flatly. No nonsentient computer could have been given this degree of initiative. "A fault of youth, as mein mutter is saying." His accent had become thicker. "As chentlemen, we may come to some agreement."

"Or we can barter like merchants," Jonah said, with malice aforethought. Out of the corner of his eye, he saw Ingrid flash an "O" with her fingers. "Is he telling the truth?"

"To within ninety-seven percent of probability," the computer said. "From pupil, skin-conductivity, encephalographic and other evidence." Markham hid his start quite well. "I suggest the bargaining commence. Commandant Reichstein-Markham, you would also be well advised not to . . . engage in falsehoods."

☆ ☆ ☆

"You are not on the datarecord of vessels detached for this duty," the kzin in the forward screen said.

Buford Early watched carefully as the readouts beside the catlike face formed themselves into a bar-graph; *worry, generalized anxiety,* and *belief.* Not as good as the readings on humans—ARM computer technology was as good as telepathy on that, and far more reliable—but enough. Around him the four-person combat crew tensed at their consoles, although at this range reaction to any attack would have to be largely cybernetic. The control chamber was very quiet, and the air had a neutral pine-scented coolness that leached out the smell of fear-sweat. They were a long way from home, and going into harm's way.

"Ktrodni-Stkaa has ordered me to observe and report upon the efficiency with which these operations are carried out," he said; the computer would translate that into the Hero's Tongue, adding a kzin image and appropriate body language. The *Inner Circle*'s stealthing included an ability to broadcast energies which duplicated the electromagnetic and neutrino signatures of a kzinti corvette.

The kzin officer's muzzle jerked toward the screen and the round pupils of his eyes flared wide. *Hostility. Aggressive intent,* the computer indicated silently.

"This is not Ktrodni-Stkaa's sector!" the kzin snarled. Literally; lines of saliva trailed from the thin black lips as they peeled back from the inch-long ivory daggers of the fangs. Early felt tiny hairs crawling along his spine, as instincts remembered ancestors who had fought lions with spears.

Early shrugged. Formal lines of authority in the kzinti armed forces seemed to be surprisingly loose; the prestige of individual chieftains mattered a good deal more, and the networks of patronage and blood kinship. And it was not at all uncommon for a high-ranking, full-name kzin to jump the chain of command and send personal representatives to the site of an important action. Ktrodni-Stkaa seemed to be about fourth from the top in the kzinti military hierarchy, to judge from the broadcast monitoring they had been able to do, and a locally-born opponent of Chuut-Riit.

"Report on your progress," he went on, insultingly refusing to give his own name or ask the other kzin's.

"You may monitor," the alien replied.

Receiving dataflow, the computer added.

The kzinti ships were floating near an industrial habitat, an elongated cylinder that had been spun for gravity, with a crazy quilt of life-bubbles and fabricator frameworks spun out for kilometers on either side. There had been a rough order to it, before the missiles from the *Yamamoto* struck. Those had been ballonets and string-wire; broad surfaces worked well in vacuum and transferred energy more readily to the target. The main spin-habitat was tumbling now, peeled open along its long axis; many of the other components were drifting away, with their connecting lattices and pipelines severed as if by giant flying cheesecutters. Two kzinti corvettes hung near, with space-armored figures flitting about; they were much like the one the *Inner Mind* had been rebuilt from. A troop-transport must be loading with refugees from the emergency bubbles, and a human-built self-propelled graving dock had been brought for heavy repair work.

Which will be needed, Early reflected; the strikes would have lasted microseconds, but the damage was comprehensive. Frozen air glittered in the blind unmerciful light, particles of water-ice and ores and metal mists, of blood and bone. The close-ups showed bodies drifting amid the wrecked fabricators and processing machines, and doubtless the habitat had been a refuge for children and pregnant mothers, as was common in the Sol-belt. Certain things required gravity, and he doubted the kzinti had spread gravity polarizers around wholesale.

A pity, he thought coldly, a little surprised at his own lack of emotion. You could not live as long as he had, in the service to which he had been born, without becoming detached. *What is necessary, must be done.*

"Why are you wasting efforts here?" he said harshly, watching the growling response of the kzin to the computer's arrogant synthesis. "Most of the equipment"—the facility had manufactured fission-triggers, superconductors, and degenerate-matter energy storage devices—"seems to be in good order and salvage can wait." The machine provided his false image with the ripple of fur, ears, tail that provided an analogue of a chuckle. "And the meat will keep."

"If you sthondat-groomers can't be of use, get out of the

way!" the kzin screamed. *Extreme hostility,* the computer warned. *Intent to initiate violence.* "We're doing emergency rescue work here."

"Your leader's concern for monkeys is touching," Early sneered.

"These are valuable and loyal slaves, personal property of the Patriarchal clan," the other said. "Evacuate the vicinity."

"I order you to depart for work of higher priority," Early rasped. "Co-ordinates follow."

"I defecate upon your co-ordinates and leave it unburied!" the kzin howled. "I am here under direct orders of the Vice-regal Staff!"

"I convey the orders of Ktrodni-Stkaa."

"Then Ktrodni-Stkaa is a vatach-sucking fool—"

A beam stabbed out from the kzin vessel, deliberately aimed to miss. The torrent of fire that followed from the *Inner Circle* was aimed to kill, and did so very effectively. The ships had been at zero relative velocity and within a few hundred thousand kilometers, rare conditions for space combat. Precisely-aimed laser and neutral-particle beams from the camouflaged human vessel stabbed into the kzinti corvettes like superheated icepicks. Metal and synthetic sublimed and gouted out in asymmetric jets of plasma. The warships tumbled; the kzin officer's face was driven into the visual pickup of his screen, a fractional second of horrified surprise before flesh smeared over the crystal. That screen went black, but the exterior pickup showed two brief new stars as fusion warheads detonated point-blank.

"Computer," Early said. "Broadcast to the survivors"—most of the kzinti crews had been doing EVA rescue work—"that we were acting under Ktrodni-Stkaa's orders, and that Chuut-Riit's vessels initiated hostilities. Oh, and hole that transport—gut her passenger compartments."

"Sir!" One of the others, turning a sweat-sheened face to Early. "Sir, there are humans aboard that transport."

"Exactly," Early said with chill satisfaction, as the big wedge-shaped craft blossomed fragments of hull panel and began to tumble slowly. "Son, we're here to stir up Resistance activity, among other things. You should read more history." A quasi-pornographic activity, even now that the restrictions of the Long Peace had been lifted. "Our friend Chuut-Riit is a sensible, rational—Finagle, even humane, by kzin standards—pussy. The absolute last thing we want; we want the kzin to be as horrible and brutal as possible, and if they won't do the atrocities themselves we'll tanjit do it ourselves and blame them. Besides stoking up dissension within enemy ranks, of course."

He leaned back. *Divide et impera,* he thought. The ARM's true motto, and the Brotherhood's—with the added proviso that you did it without anyone realizing who was to blame.

He grinned; an almost kzinlike expression. *Naive, that's what these pussies are.*

☆ ☆ ☆

Chuut-Riit always enjoyed visiting the quarters of his male offspring.

"What will it be this time?" he wondered, as he passed the outer guards. The household troopers drew claws before their eyes in salute, faceless in impact-armor and goggled helmets, the beam-rifles ready in their hands. He paced past the surveillance cameras, the detector pods, the death-casters, and the mines; then past the inner guards at their consoles, humans raised in the household under the supervision of his personal retainers.

The retainers were males grown old in the Riit family's service; there had always been those willing to exchange the uncertain rewards of competition for a secure place, maintenance, and the odd female. Ordinary kzin were not to be trusted in so sensitive a position, of course, but these were families which had served the Riit clan for generation after generation. There was a natural culling effect; those too ambitious left for the Patriarchy's military and the slim chance of advancement, those too timid were not given opportunity to breed.

Perhaps a pity that such cannot be used outside the household, Chuut-Riit thought. Competition for rank was far too intense and personal for that, of course.

He walked past the modern sections, and into an area that was pure Old Kzin; maze-walls of reddish sandstone with twisted spines of wrought-iron on their tops, the tips glistening razor-edged. Fortress-architecture from a world older than this, more massive, colder and drier; from a planet harsh enough that a plains carnivore had changed its ways, put to different use an upright posture designed to place its head above savannah grass, grasping paws evolved to climb rock. Here the modern features were reclusive, hidden in wall and buttress. The door was a hammered slab graven with the faces of night-hunting beasts, between towers five times the height of a kzin. The air smelled of wet rock and the raked sand of the gardens.

Chuut-Riit put his hand on the black metal of the outer portal, stopped. His ears pivoted, and he blinked; out of the corner of his eye he saw a pair of tufted eyebrows glancing through the thick twisted metal on the rim of the ten-meter battlement. *Why, the little sthondats,* he thought affectionately. *They managed to put it together out of reach of the holo pickups.*

The adult put his hand to the door again, keying the locking sequence, then bounded backward four times his own length from a standing start. Even under the lighter gravity of Wunderland, it was a creditable feat. And necessary, for the massive panels rang and toppled as the rope-swung boulder slammed forward. The children had hung two cables from either tower, with the rock at the point of the V and a third rope to draw it back. As the doors bounced wide he saw the blade they had driven into the apex of the egg-shaped granite rock, long and barbed and polished to a wicked point.

Kittens, he thought. *Always going for the dramatic.* If that thing had struck him or the doors under its impetus, there would have been no need of a blade. *Watching too many historical adventure holos.*

"Errorowwww!" he shrieked in mock-rage, bounding through the shattered portal and into the interior court, halting atop the kzin-high boulder. A round dozen of his older sons were grouped behind the rock, standing in a defensive clump and glaring at him; the crackly scent of their excitement and fear made the fur bristle along his spine. He glared until they dropped their eyes, continued it until they went down on their stomachs, rubbed their chins along the ground and then rolled over for a symbolic exposure of the stomach.

"Congratulations," he said. "That was the closest you've gotten. Who was in charge?"

More guilty sidelong glances among the adolescent males crouching among their discarded pull-rope, and then a lanky youngster with platter-sized feet and hands came squatting-erect. His fur was in the proper flat posture, but the naked pink of his tail still twitched stiffly.

"I was," he said, keeping his eyes formally down. "Honored Sire Chuut-Riit," he added, at the adult's warning rumble.

"Now, youngling, what did you learn from your first attempt?"

"That no one among us is your match, Honored Sire

Chuut-Riit," the kitten said. Uneasy ripples went over the black-striped orange of his pelt.

"And what have you learned from this attempt?"

"That all of us together are no match for you, Honored Sire Chuut-Riit," the striped youth said.

"That we didn't locate all of the cameras," another muttered. "You idiot, Spotty." That to one of his siblings; they snarled at each other from their crouches, hissing past bared fangs and making striking motions with unsheathed claws.

"No, you did, cubs," Chuut-Riit said. "I presume you stole the ropes and tools from the workshop, prepared the boulder in the ravine in the next courtyard, then rushed to set it all up between the time I cleared the last gatehouse and my arrival?"

Uneasy nods. He held his ears and tail stiffly, letting his whiskers quiver slightly and holding in the rush of love and pride he felt, more delicious than milk heated with bourbon. *Look at them!* he thought. At an age when most young kzin were helpless prisoners of instinct and hormone, wasting their strength ripping each other up or making fruitless direct attacks on their sires, or demanding to be allowed to join the Patriarchy's service *at once* to win a Name and household of their own . . . *his* get had learned to *cooperate* and use their minds!

"Ah, Honored Sire Chuut-Riit, we set the ropes up beforehand, but made it look as if we were using them for tumbling practice," the one the others called Spotty said. Some of them glared at him, and the adult raised his hand again.

"No, no, I am *moderately* pleased." A pause. "You did not hope to take over my official position if you had disposed of me?"

"No, Honored Sire Chuut-Riit," the tall leader said. There had been a time when any kzin's holdings were the prize of the victor in a duel, and the dueling rules were interpreted more leniently for a young subadult. Everyone had a sentimental streak for a successful youngster; every male kzin remembered the intolerable stress of being physically mature but remaining under dominance as a child.

Still, these days affairs were handled in a more civilized manner. Only the Patriarchy could award military and political office. And this mass assassination attempt was . . . unorthodox, to say the least. Outside the rules more because of its rarity than because of formal disapproval. . . .

A vigorous toss of the head. "Oh, no, Honored Sire Chuut-Riit. We had an agreement to divide the private possessions. The lands and the, ah, females." Passing their own mothers to half-siblings, of course. "Then we wouldn't each have so much we'd get too many challenges, and we'd agreed to help each other against outsiders," the leader of the plot finished virtuously.

"Fatuous young scoundrels," Chuut-Riit said. His eyes narrowed dangerously. "You haven't been communicating outside the household, have you?" he snarled.

"Oh, *no,* Honored Sire Chuut-Riit!"

"Word of honor! May we die nameless if we should do such a thing!"

The adult nodded, satisfied that good family feeling had prevailed. "Well, as I said, I am somewhat pleased. If you have been keeping up with your lessons. Is there anything you wish?"

"Fresh meat, Honored Sire Chuut-Riit," the spotted one said. The adult could have told him by the scent, of course. A kzin never forgot another's personal odor; that was one reason why names were less necessary among their species. "The reconstituted stuff from the dispensers is always . . . so . . . *quiet.*"

Chuut-Riit hid his amusement. Young Heroes-to-be were always kept on an inadequate diet, to increase their aggressiveness. A matter for careful gauging, since too much hunger would drive them into mindless cannibalistic frenzy.

"And couldn't we have the human servants back? They were nice." Vigorous gestures of assent. Another added: "They told good stories. I miss my Clothidal-human."

"Silence!" Chuut-Riit roared. The youngsters flattened stomach and chin to the ground again. "Not until you can be trusted not to injure them. How many times do I have to tell you, it's dishonorable to attack household servants! You are getting to be big enough to hurt them easily; until you learn self-control, you will have to make do with machines."

This time all of them turned and glared at a mottled youngster in the rear of their group; there were half-healed scars over his head and shoulders. "It bared its *teeth* at me," he said sulkily. "All I did was swipe at it. How was I supposed to know it would die?" A chorus of rumbles, and this time several of the covert kicks and clawstrikes landed.

"Enough," Chuut-Riit said after a moment. *Good, they have even learned how to discipline each other as a unit.* "I will consider it, when all of you can pass a test on the interpretation of human expressions and body-language." He drew himself up. "In the meantime, within the next two eight-days, there will be a formal hunt and meeting in the Patriarch's Preserve; kzinti homeworld game, the best Earth animals, and even some feral-human outlaws, perhaps!"

He could smell their excitement increase, a mane-crinkling musky odor not unmixed with the sour whiff of fear. Such a hunt was not without danger for adolescents, being a good opportunity for hostile adults to cull a few of a hated rival's offspring with no possibility of blame. *They will be in less danger than most,* Chuut-Riit thought judiciously. *In fact, they may run across a few of my subordinates' get and mob them. Good.*

"And if we do well, afterwards a feast and a visit to the Sterile Ones." That had them all quiveringly alert, their tails held rigid and tongues lolling; nonbearing females were kept as a rare privilege for Heroes whose accomplishments were not *quite* deserving of a mate of their own. Very rare for kits still in the household to be granted such, but Chuut-Riit thought it past time to admit that modern society demanded a prolonged adolescence. The days when a male kit could be given a spear, a knife, a rope, and a bag of salt and kicked out the front gate at puberty were long gone. Those were the wild, wandering years in the old days, when survival challenges used up the superabundant energies. Now they must be spent learning history, technology, xenology, none of which burned off the gland-juices saturating flesh and brain.

He jumped down amid his sons, and they pressed around him, purring throatily with adoration and fear and respect; his presence and the failure of their plot had reestablished his personal dominance unambiguously, and there was no danger from them for now. Chuut-Riit basked in their worship, feeling the rough caress of their tongues on his fur and scratching behind their ears. *Together,* he thought. *Together we will do wonders.*

Chapter 3

Dreaming, Harold Yarthkin-Schotmann twitched. Sweat ran down his stubbled bulldog face, and his fingers dug into the sodden sheets. It had been—

Crack. Crack.

Pulses of orange-purple light went by overhead. Ahead of them the building where the aircar was hidden exploded. The air was pitch-black, stars hidden by the smoke of burning buildings, air full of a chemical reek. It rasped at the inside of his throat, and he coughed savagely as they went to ground and he slapped down the hunting goggles. Green-tinted brightness replaced the black, and he raised his head to peer back over the rim of the shattered house. Overhead the scorched yellow leaves of the jacaranda tree rustled.

"Scheisse," he muttered in awe. Half of Munchen seemed to be burning, the ruddy light glittering off the unnatural waves of the Donau river.

"Von Sydow, Hashami, get a hundred meters or so west and take overwatch on our route. Mogger, spread the rest out. Wait for my word," Harold snapped. The half-dozen others melted back into the rubble of the low stone-block houses that had lined this street, the half-dozen who were left out of the thirty who had been with them yesterday.

Sam Ogun grunted beside him, shifting the burden of the makeshift antitank rocket in his arms. Everything was makeshift. . . . "Anything, Claude?" he said.

"Spaceport's still holding out," he said, fiddling with the keyboard of the communicator unit. "And the Ritterhaus. Not for long. We make it in half an hour or we don't make it."

"Why they still letting launches go on?" Sam wondered.

"I think they're playing with us," Harold said. *God, I'm tired.* At least there were no civilians around here . . . Most of them had gone bush, gone to ground outside town, when the ratcats landed. Nobody had known what to do; no human had fought a war for three hundred-odd years.

At least we weren't completely domesticated, like the flatlanders. Wunderland still had the odd bandit, and a riot now and then. The Families maintained a ghost of a martial tradition as well . . . *We knew enough to take the* Angel's Pencil *warning seriously.* The *Angel* had been the first human ship to contact the kzinti, and had survived by a miracle. Back in the Sol system, the ARM had suppressed the news—suppressed the fact that the first aliens humans had encountered traveled in warships. Wunderland had had a year to prepare, although most of it was spent reinventing the wheel.

"Much good it did us, oh *scheisse,*" he muttered.

A vehicle was floating down the broad stone-block pavement of K. von Bulowstrasse. Some sort of gravity-control effect, too small for fusion-power, but massive, like a smoothly gleaming wedge of some dark material, bristled with the pickups of sensors and communications gear. From the sharply sloped front jutted a segmented tube. *Plasma gun,* he recognized from the sketchy briefings. The howling whine of its passage overrode the roar of flames, and gusts of smoke and dirt billowed sideways from under it. A wrecked groundcar spun away from a touch of the kzinti vehicle's bow, flipping end-over-end into the remains of an outdoor restaurant.

The others had frozen; he heard Claude whisper, very softly; "Why only one?"

Because it's more Finagle-fucked fun, *Claude,* Harold thought savagely. *Because they're* hunting *us.*

Don't miss, Sam. There was a taut grin on the black Krio's face as he raised the tube.

Crack. The hovertank had pivoted and fired a plasma-pulse into an intact house on the other side of the street and a few hundred meters down. Stone spalled away, burning white as it turned to lime; the front of the building rumbled down into the street, and the interior stood exposed. It was like a breakaway doll's house, kitchen and autochef, bedrooms upstairs with beds neatly made, all perfect and small for a moment before the floors fell in. Rubble cascaded into the street, snapping off trees. The vehicle pivoted again to aim its gun down the street, slid sideways and began circling the pile of broken stone and furniture.

"Now," Harold whispered.

Thup. The missile whooshed out of the tube, driven by magnetic coils. The kzin tank detected it, lost a vital half-second trying to bring its gun to bear before it was around the last of the stone. The hovertank's rear swung wide as its bow ground against rock, and the missile arrived overhead. A *bang* this time, a pancake of orange fire turning to a ball as the self-forging arrowhead of tungsten drove straight down into the upper deck of the war machine. It staggered, died, fell with an echoing clang to the road; hatches like gull-wings popped open on either side just behind the gun.

"Now!" Harold shouted.

His strakaker gave its high-pitched strangled scream, spitting out a stream of high-velocity pellets filled with liquid teflon. Four others did likewise. The two huge orange shapes were springing out of the tank, blurring fast. One staggered in midair, fell to the pavement with a thud audible even now; the other managed to recoil, but a long pink tail and short thick arm sprawled out, motionless. The hand flexed and then went limp, four digits like a big black leather glove, the claws glinting as they slid free a last time. Blood dripped, darker than human; on general principle he emptied the rest of the clip into the compartment, aiming where the body would be. Limb and tail jerked as the pellets jellied the corpse.

"Samedi bless, it worked," Sam Ogun said.

"Harry, we've got to *move,*" Claude Montferrat-Palme said. "They're still not trying for a matching orbit with the slowboat"—for some inscrutable alien reason the kzinti had not tried to stop anyone leaving the Alpha Centauri system; contempt, perhaps—"but it's the last shuttle and the last launch-window."

"Well, Ingrid's piloting," Harold said, forcing himself to grin. Suddenly the noise of fire and distant fighting seemed almost quiet.

"Von Sydow, Hashami," he called softly. "All clear?"

One of the other guerrillas raised her head to look for the scouts. It vanished in an almost-visible flicker of white light; beam-rifle, close range. The body stayed upright for a moment, then toppled backward like a tree. The screaming began a moment later, astonishingly loud; a month ago he would have sworn it came from something other than a human throat.

"Ratcat!" someone shouted; there was a scramble as they dove for new positions that gave cover to their rear. All but Sam. He came to his knees, raising his jazzer.

"Eat this!" he screamed, and the stubby-barreled weapon thumped twice, pitching out its bomblets.

"Follow me!" Harold yelled on the heels of the quick *crumpcrumpcrump* of their explosion; there was no *time* for a firefight. One more human died before they reached what had been a sunken garden behind the house, still screened by the wreckage of a pergola and a scarlet froth of bougainvillea. The broad muzzle of a beam rifle showed above; behind him Claude snapshot with his strakaker, tearing it out of the kzin's hands. Harold dove through the screen of withes and vines—

—and fell to his back as his feet slipped on flagstones running with blood. Human blood, mostly. Von Sydow and Hashami were here; Hashami's legs were missing, and her head. Von Sydow was still alive, but it looked as if something had bitten half his stomach out and then *pulled*.

Something had. It loomed over him, immense even for a kzin, two and a half meters. Infantry this time, synthetic impact-armor glittering where fragments and bullets had cut it, a bone-deep slash on the blunt muzzle running dark-red blood as it reached for him. Pain and hysteria made it disdain the other weapons clipped to its harness; artificial claws of density-enhanced steel glittered and snapped out on its gauntlets as it reached to pull his throat to that mouthful of fangs. His strakaker seemed fixed in honey as he strained to bring it around, finger closing spasmodically on the trigger plate. Pellets splashed on the impact-armor over the thing's belly, knocking it back. The weapon hissed empty. The kzin straightened with a grunting roar, and then it was coming at him again—

A whining buzz, and it stopped in its tracks. Then it fell, legs useless. Twirling and slashing with its claws even as it collapsed, but Sam danced back, poised as graceful as a matador, moved in with a chopping cut. Kzinti blood smoked away from the buzzing wire edges of his ratchet knife, spurted in hose-like jets from the alien's throat; the Krio thumbed the weapon off and clipped it back at his shoulder. Behind him a strakaker chittered once and von Sydow's gasping breath ceased.

"Come on, Mr. Yarthkin," he said, extending a hand. "Miss Raines is waiting."

—and Harold jerked awake.

"Hunh," he mumbled, shaking his head in the darkness, shaking away the nightmare and forty years. His teeth chattered on the glass he grabbed two-handed from the bedside stand; some of the verguuz slopped down the sides, its smell sharp and minty in the stale odors of his bedroom. Fire bloomed in his gut, giving him steadiness enough to palm on the lights. That had been a bad one, he hadn't had that one for more than a decade.

"But she wasn't waiting," he said quietly. The glass crashed against the wall. "She wasn't there at all."

☆ ☆ ☆

Interesting, Chuut-Riit thought, standing on the veranda of his staff-secretary's house and lapping at the gallon tub of half-melted vanilla ice cream in his hands. *Quite comely, in its way.*

In a very unkzin fashion. The senior staff quarters of his estate were laid out in a section of rolling hills, lawns and shrubs and eucalyptus trees, modest stone houses with high-pitched shingle roofs set among flowerbeds. A dozen or so of the adults who dwelt here were gathered at a discreet distance, down by the landing pad; he could smell their colognes and perfumes, the slightly mealy odor of human flesh beneath, a mechanical tang overlain with alien greenness and animals and . . . Yes, the children were coming back—preceded by the usual blast of sound. The kzin's ears folded themselves away at the jumbled high-pitched squealing, one of the less attractive qualities of young humans. Although there was a very kzinlike warbling mixed in among the monkeysounds. . . .

The giant ball of yarn bounced around the corner of the house and across the close-clipped grass of the lawn, bounding from side to side with the slight drifting wobble of .61 gravities, trailing floppy ends. A peacock fled shrieking from the toy and the shouting mob of youngsters that followed it; the bird's head was parallel to the ground and its feet pumped madly. Chuut-Riit sighed, finished the ice cream, and began licking his muzzle and fingers clean. Alpha Centauri was setting, casting bronze shadows over the creeper-grown stone around him, and it was time to go.

"Like this!" the young kzin leading the pack screamed, and leaped in a soaring arch, landing spreadeagled on the soft fuzzy surface of the ball. He was a youngster of five, all head and hands and feet, the fur of his pelt an electric orange with fading black spots, the infant mottling that a very few kzin kept into early youth. Several of the human youngsters made a valiant attempt to follow, but only one landed and clutched the strands, screaming delightedly. The others fell, one skinning a knee and bawling.

Chuut-Riit rose smoothly to his feet and bounced forward, scooping the crying infant up and stopping the ball with his other hand.

"You should be more careful, my son," he said to the kzin child in the Hero's Tongue. To the human: "Are you injured?"

"Mama!" the child wailed, twining its fists into his fur and burying its tear-and-snot-streaked face in his side.

"Errruumm," Chuut-Riit rumbled helplessly. *They are so fragile.* His nostrils flared as he bent over the tiny form, taking in the milky-sweat smell of distress and the slight metallic-salt odor of blood from its knee.

"Here is your mother," he continued as the human female scuttled up and began apologetically untwining the child.

"Here, take it," he rumbled, as she cuddled the infant. The woman gave it a brief inspection and looked up at the eight-foot orange height of the kzin.

"No harm done, just overexcited, Honored Chuut-Riit," she said. The kzin rumbled again, looked up at the guards standing by his flitter in the driveway, and laid back his ears; they became elaborately casual, examining the sky or the ground and controlling their expressions. He switched his glare back to his own offspring on top of the ball. The cub flattened itself apologetically, then whipped its head to one side as the human child clinging to the slope of the ball threw a loose length of yarn. Chuut-Riit wrenched his eyes from the fascinating thing and plucked his son into the air by the loose skin at the back of his neck.

"It is time to depart," he said. The young kzin had gone into an instinctive half-curl. He cast a hopeful glance over his shoulder at his father, sighed, and wrapped the limber pink length of his tail around the adult's massive forearm.

"Yes, Honored Sire Chuut-Riit," he said meekly, then brightened and waved at the clump of estate-worker children standing by the ball. "Good-bye," he called, waving a hand that seemed too large for his arm, and adding a cheerful parting yeowl in the Hero's Tongue. Literally translated it meant roughly *"drink blood and tear cattle into gobbets,"* but the adult trusted the sentiment would carry over the wording.

The human children jumped and waved in reply as Chuut-Riit carried his son over to the car and the clump of parents waiting there: Henrietta was in the center with her offspring by her side. *I think her posture indicates contentment,* he thought. *This visit confers much prestige among the other human servants.* Which was excellent; a good executive secretary was a treasure beyond price. Besides . . .

"That was fun, Father," the cub said. "Could I have another piece of cake?"

"Certainly not, you will be sick as it is," Chuut-Riit said decisively. Kzin were not quite the pure meat-eaters they claimed to be, and their normal diet contained the occasional sweet, but stuffing that much sugar-coated confection down on top of a stomach already full of good raw *ztirgor* was something the cub would regret soon. Ice cream, though . . . Why had nobody told him about ice cream before? Even better than bourbon-and-milk; he must begin to order in bulk.

"I must be leaving, Henrietta," Chuut-Riit said. "And young Ilge," he added, looking down at the offspring. It was an odd-looking specimen, only slightly over knee-high to him and with long braided head-pelt of an almost kzinlike orange; the bare skin of its face was dotted with markings of almost the same color. Remarkable. The one standing next to it was *black*—there was no end to their variety.

The cub wiggled in his grasp and looked down. "I hope you like your armadillo, Ilge," he said. Ilge looked down at the creature she had not released since the gift-giving ceremony and patted it again. A snout and beady eye appeared for a second, caught the scent of kzin, and disappeared back into an armored ball with a snap.

"They're lots of fun." Kzin children adored armadillos, and Chuut-Riit provided his with a steady supply, even if the shells made a mess once the cubs finally got them peeled.

"It's nice," she said solemnly.

"The ball of fiber was an excellent idea," Chuut-Riit added to Henrietta. "I must procure one for my other offspring."

"I thought it would be, Honored Chuut-Riit," the human replied, and the kzin blinked in bafflement at her amusement.

One of the guards was too obviously entertained by his commander's eccentricity. "Here," Chuut-Riit called as he walked through the small crowd of bowing humans. "Guard Trooper. Care for this infant as we fly, in the forward compartment. Care for him well."

The soldier blinked dubiously at the small bundle of chocolate-and-mud-stained fur that looked with eager interest at the fascinating complexities of his equipment, then slung his beam rifle and accepted the child with an unconscious bristling. Chuut-Riit gave the ear-and-tail twitch that was the kzin equivalent of sly amusement as he stepped into the passenger compartment and threw himself down on the cushions. There was a slight internal wobble as the car lifted, an expected retching sound and a yeowl of protest from the forward compartment.

The ventilators will be overloaded, the governor thought happily. *Now, about that report . . .*

☆ ☆ ☆

Tiamat was shabby. Coming in to dock on the rockjacker prospecting craft Markham had found for them it had looked the same, a little busier and more exterior lights; a spinning ironrock tube twenty kilometers across and sixty long, with ships of every description clustered at the docking yards at either end. More smelters and robofabricators hanging outside, more giant baggies of water ice and volatiles. But inside it was shabby, rundown.

That was Ingrid Raines's first thought: shabby. The hand-grips were worn, the vivid murals that covered the walls just in from the poles of the giant cylinder fading and grease-spotted. The constant subliminal rumble from the freighter docks was louder; nobody was bothering with the sonic baffles that damped the vibration of megatons of powdered ore, liquid metal, vacuum-separated refinates pouring into the network of pumptubes. Styles were more garish than she remembered, face-paint and tiger-striped oversuits; there was a quartet of police hanging spaced evenly around the entry corridor, toes hooked into rails and head in toward the center. Obstructing traffic, but nobody was going to object, not when the goldskins wore impact armor and powered endoskeletons, not when shockrods dangled negligently in their hands.

"Security's tight," Jonah murmured as they made flip-over and went feet-first into the stickyfield at the inward end of the passage. There was a familiar subjective click behind their eyes, and the corridor became a half-kilometer of hollow tower over their heads, filled with the up-and-down drift of people.

"Shut up," Ingrid muttered back. That had been no surprise; from what they'd been told the collaborationist government had reinvented the police state all by themselves in their enthusiasm. They went through the emergency pressure curtains, into the glare and blare of the inner corridors. Zero-G, here near the core of Tiamat, away from the rims that were under one-G. *Tigertown,* she thought. The resident kzin were low-status engineers and supervisors, or navy types: They liked heavy gravity; the pussies had never lived in space without gravity control. *Tigers,* she reminded herself. That was the official slang term. Ratcat if you wanted to be a little dangerous.

They turned into a narrow side corridor, what had been a residential section the last time she was here, transient's quarters around the lowgrav manufacturing sections of the core. Now it was lined on three sides by shops and small businesses, with the fourth spinward side playing down. Not that there was enough gravity to matter this close to the center of spin, but it was convenient. They slowed to a stroll, two more figures in plain rockjack innersuits, the form-fitting coverall everyone wore under vacuum armor. Conservative Belter stripcuts, backpacks with printseal locks to discourage pickpockets, and the black plastic hilts of ratchet knives.

Ingrid looked around her, acutely conscious of the hard shape nestling butt-down on her collarbone. Distortion battery, and a blade-shaped lozenge of wire; switch it on, and the magnetic field made it vibrate, very fast. Very sharp. She had been shocked when Markham's intelligence officer pushed them across the table to the UNSN operatives.

"Things are *that* bad?"

"The ratcats don't care," the officer had said. "Humans are forbidden any weapon that can kill at a distance. Only the collabo police can carry stunners, and the only thing the ratcats care about is that production keeps up. What sort of people do you think join the collabo goldskins? Social altruists? The only ordinary criminals they go after are the ones too poor or stupid to pay them off. When things get bad enough to foul up war production, they have a big sweep, and maybe catch some of the middling-level gangrunners and feed them to the ratcats. The big boys? The big boys *are* the police, or vice versa. That's the way it is, sweetheart."

Ingrid shivered, and Jonah put an arm around her waist as they walked in the glide-lift-glide of a stickyfield. "Changed a lot, hey?" he said.

She nodded. The booths were for the sort of small-scale industry that bigger firms contracted out; filing, hardcopy, genetic engineering of bacteria for process production of organics, all mixed in with cookshops and handicrafts and service trades of a thousand types. Holo displays flashed and glittered, strobing with all shades of the visible spectrum; music pounded and blared and crooned, styles she remembered and styles utterly strange and others that were revivals of modes six centuries old: Baroque and Classical and Jazz and Dojin-Go Punk and Meddlehoffer. People crowded the 'way, on the downside and wall-hopping between shops, and half the shops had private guards. The passersby were mostly planet-siders, some so recent you could see they had trouble handling low-G movement.

Many were ragged, openly dirty. *How can that happen?* she thought. Fusion-distilled water was usually cheap in a closed system. *Oh. Probably a monopoly.* And there were beggars, actual beggars with open sores on their skins or hands twisted with arthritis, things she had only seen in historical flats so old they were shot two-dimensional.

"Here it is," Jonah grunted. The eating-shop was directly above them; they switched off their shoes, waited for a clear space, and flipped up and over, slapping their hands onto the catch net outside the door. Inside, the place was clean, at least, with a globular free-fall kitchen and a human chef, and customers in dark pajama-like clothing floating with their knees crossed under stick-tables. Not Belters, too stocky and muscular; mostly heavily Oriental by bloodline, rare in the genetic stew of the Sol system but more common here.

Icy stares greeted them as they swung to a vacant booth and slid themselves in, their long legs tangling under the synthetic pineboard of the stick-table.

"It must be harder for you," Jonah said. "Your home."

She looked up at him with quick surprise. He was usually the archetypical rockjack, the stereotype asteroid prospector, quiet, bookish, self-sufficient, a man without twitches or mannerisms but capable of cutting loose on furlough—but perceptive, and rockjacks were not supposed to be good at people.

Well, he was a successful officer, too, she thought. *And they* do *have to be good at people.*

A waitress in some many-folded garment of black silk floated up to the privacy screen of their cubicle and reached a hand through to scratch at the post. Ingrid keyed the screen, and the woman's features snapped clear.

"Sorry, so sorry," she said. "This special place, not Belter food." There was a singsong accent to her English that Jonah did not recognize, but the underlying impatience and hostility came through the calm features.

He smiled at her and ran a hand over his crest. "But we were told the tekkamaki here is fine, the *oyabun* makes the best," he said. Ingrid could read the thought that followed: *Whatever the fuck that means.*

The frozen mask of the waitress's face could not alter, but the quick duck of her head was empty of the commonplace tension of a moment before. She returned quickly with bowls of soup and drinking straws; it was some sort of fish broth with onions and a strange musky undertaste. They drank in silence, waiting. *For what, the pussies to come and get us?* she thought. The *Catskinner*-computer had said Markham was on the level—but also that he was capable of utter treachery once he had convinced himself that Right was on his side, and that to Markham the only ultimate judge of Right was, guess who, the infallible Markham.

Gottdamned Herrenmann, she mused: going on fifty years objective, everything else in the system had collapsed into shit, and the arrogant lop-bearded bastards hadn't changed a bit. . . .

A man slid through the screen. Expensively nondescript dress, gray oversuit, and bowl-cut black hair. Hint of an expensive natural cologne. Infocomp at his waist, and the silver button of a reader-bonephone behind his ear. This was Markham's "independent entrepreneur." Spoken with tones of deepest contempt, more than a Herrenmann's usual disdain for business, so probably some type of criminal like McAllistaire. She kept a calm smile on her face as she studied the man, walling off the remembered sickness as the kicking doll-figures tumbled into space, bleeding from every orifice. Oriental, definitely; there were Sina and Nipponjin enclaves down on Wunderland, ethnic separatists like many of the early settlers. Not in the Serpent Swarm Belt, not when she left, Belters did not go in for racial taboos. Things had changed.

The quiet man smiled and produced three small drinking-bulbs. "Rice wine," he said. "Heated. An affectation, to be sure, but we are very traditional these days."

Pure Belter English, no hint of an accent. She called up training, looked for clues: in the hands, the skin around the eyes, the set of the mouth. Very little, no more than polite attention; this was a very calm man. Hard to tell even the age; if he was getting good geriatric care, anything from fifty minimum up to a hundred. Teufel, he could have been from Sol system himself, one of the last bunches of immigrants, and wouldn't *that* be a joke to end them all.

Silence stretched. The oriental sat and sipped at his hot sake and smiled; the two Belters followed suit, controlling their surprise at the varnish-in-the-throat taste.

At the last, Jonah spoke: "I'm Jonah. This is Ingrid. The man with gray eyes sent us for tekkamaki."

"Ah, our esteemed GVB," the man said. A deprecatory laugh and a slight wave of the fingers; the man had almost as few hand gestures as a Belter. "Gotz von Blerichgen, a little joke. Yes, I know the one you speak of. My name is Shigehero Hirose, and as you will have guessed, I am a hardened criminal of the worst sort." He ducked his head in a polite bow. Ingrid noticed his hands then, the left missing the little finger, and the edges of vividly-colored tattoos under the cuffs of his suit.

"And you," he continued to Jonah, "are sent not by our so-Aryan friend, but by the UNSN." A slight frown. "Your charming companion is perhaps of the same provenance, but from the Serpent Swarm originally."

Jonah and Ingrid remained silent. Another shrug. "In any case, according to our informants, you wish transportation to Wunderland and well-documented cover identities."

"If you're wondering how we can pay . . ." Jonah began. They had the best and most compact source of valuata the UN military had been able to provide.

"No, please. From our own resources, we will be glad to do this."

"Why?" Ingrid said, curious. "Criminals seem to be doing better now than they ever did in the old days."

Hirose smiled again, that bland expression that revealed nothing and never touched his eyes. "The young lady is as perceptive as she is ornamental." He took up his sake bulb and considered it. "My . . . association is a very old one. You might call us predators; we would prefer to think of it as a symbiotic relationship. We have endured many changes, many social and technological revolutions. But something is common to each: the desire to have something and yet to forbid it.

"Consider drugs and alcohol . . . or wirehead drouds. All

strictly forbidden at one time, legal another, but the demand continues. Instruction in martial arts, likewise. In our early days in *dai Nippon,* we performed services for feudal lords that their own code forbade. Later, the great corporations, the *zaibatsu,* found us convenient for dealing with recalcitrant shareholders and unions; we moved substances of various types across inconvenient national frontiers, liberated information selfishly stockpiled in closed data banks, recruited entertainers, provided banking services . . . invested our wealth wisely, and moved outward with humanity to the planets and the stars. Sometimes we have been so respectable that our affairs were beyond question; sometimes otherwise. A conservative faction undertook to found our branch in the Alpha Centauri system, but I assure you the . . . family businesses, clans if you will, still flourish in Sol system as well. Inconspicuously."

"That doesn't answer Ingrid's question," Jonah said bluntly. "This setup looks like hog heaven for you."

"Only in the short term. Which is enough to satisfy mere thugs, mere bandits such as a certain rockholder known as McAllistaire . . . You met this person? But consider: we are doing well for the same reason bacteria flourish in a dead body. The human polity of this system is dying, its social defenses disorganized, but the carnival of the carrion-eaters will be shortlived. We speak of the free humans and those in the direct service of the kzin, but to our masters we of the 'free' are slaves of the Patriarchy who have not yet been assigned individual owners. We are squeezed, tighter and tighter; eventually, there will be nothing but the households of kzin nobles. My association could perhaps survive such a situation; we are making preparations. Better by far to restore a functioning human system; our pickings would be less in the short term, more secure in the longer."

"And by helping us, you'll have a foot in both camps and come up smelling of roses whoever wins."

Hirose spread his hands. "It is true, the kzin have occasionally found themselves using our services." His smile became more genuine, and sharklike. "Nor are all, ah, Heroes, so incorruptible, so immune to the temptations of vice and profit, as they would like to believe.

"Enough." He produced a sealed packet and slid it across the table to them. "The documentation and credit is perfectly genuine. It will stand even against kzin scrutiny; our influence reaches far. I have no knowledge of what it contains, nor do

I wish to. You in turn have learned nothing from me that possible opponents do not already know, and know that I know, and I know that they know . . . but please, even if I cannot join you, do stay and enjoy this excellent restaurant's cuisine."

"Well . . ." Jonah palmed the folder. "It might be out of character, rockjacks in a fancy live-service place like this."

Shigehero Hirose halted, partway through the privacy screen. "You would do well to study local conditions a little more carefully, man-from-far-away. It has been a long time since autochefs and dispensers were cheaper than humans."

Shigehero Hirose sat back on his heels and sighed slightly. "Well, my dear?" he said.

His wife laid the bamboo strainer down on the tray and lifted the teacup in both hands. He accepted her unspoken rebuke and the teacup, raising it to his lips as he looked out the pavilion doors. Even the Association's wealth could not buy open space on Tiamat, but this was a reasonable facsimile. The graceful structure about them was dark varnished wood, sparely ornamented, carrying nothing but the low tray that held the tea service and a single chrysanthemum. Outside was a chamber of raked gravel and a few well-chosen rocks, and a quiet recirculating fountain. The air was sterile, though; no point in a chemical mockery of garden scents.

There are times when I regret accepting this post, he thought, sipping the tea and returning the cup with a ritual gesture of thanks. It was hard, not seeing green things except ones that grew in a tank. . . .

Of course, this was the post of honor and profit. Humans would remain half-free longer in the Serpent Swarm than on the surface of Wunderland, and so the Association was preparing its bolt-holes. Nothing must endanger that.

Enough, he told himself. *Put aside care.*

Much later, his wife sighed herself. "Worthless though my advice is, yet all possible precautions must be taken," she said, hands folded in her lap and eyes downcast.

Traditional to a fault, he thought; perhaps a bit excessive, seeing that she had a degree in biomechanics. Still . . .

"It would be inadvisable to endanger their mission excessively," he pointed out.

"Ah, very true. But maintaining our connections with the human government is still essential."

Essential and more difficult all the time. The kzinti pressed on their collaborationist tools more and more each year; they grew more desperate in turn. Originally many had been idealists of a sort, trying to protect the general populace as much as they could. Few of that sort were left, and the rest were beginning to eat each other like crabs in a bucket.

"Still . . . a vague rumor would be best, I think. We will use the fat man as our go-between; we can claim we were playing them along for more information if they are taken."

"My husband is wise," she said, bowing.

"And if the collaborationists grow desperate enough, they might offer rewards sufficient to justify sacrificing those two."

"Who are, after all, only *gaijin.* And on a mission which will do us little good even if it succeeds."

"Indeed, there are limits to altruism." They turned their faces to the garden and fell silent once more.

☆ ☆ ☆

"The inefficiency of you leaf-eaters is becoming intolerable," the kzin said.

Claude Montferrat-Palme bowed his head. *Don't stare. Never, never stare at a ratca—at a kzin.* "We do our best, Ktiir-Supervisor-of-Animals," he said.

The kzin superintendent of Munchen stopped its restless striding and stood close, smiling, its tail held stiffly beside one column-thick leg. Two and a half meters tall, a thickly padded cartoon-figure cat that might have looked funny in a holo, it grinned down at him with the direct gaze that was as much a threat display as the bared fangs.

"You play your monkey games of position and money, while the enemies of the Patriarchy scurry and bite in the underbrush." Its head swiveled toward the police chief's desk. "Scroll!"

Data began to move across the suddenly transparent surface, with a moving schematic of the Serpent Swarm; colors and symbols indicated feral-human attacks. Ships lost, outposts raided, automatic cargo containers hijacked . . .

"Comparative!" the kzin snapped. Graphs replaced the schematic. "Distribution!

"See," he continued. "Raids of every description have sprouted like fungus since the sthondat-spawned Sol-monkeys made their coward's passage through this system. With no discernible pattern. And even the lurkers in the mountains are slipping out to trouble the estates again."

"With respect, Ktiir-Supervisor-of-Animals, my sphere of

responsibility is the human population of this city. There has been little increase in feral activity here."

Claws rested centimeters from his eyes. "Because this city is the locus where feral-human packs dispose of their loot, exchange information and goods, meet and coordinate—paying their percentage to you! Yes, yes, we have heard your arguments that it is better for this activity to take place where our minions may monitor it, and they are logical enough—while we lack the number of Heroes necessary to reduce this system to true order and are preoccupied with the renewed offensive against Sol."

He mumbled under his breath, and Montferrat caught an uncomplimentary reference to Chuut-Riit.

The human bowed again. "Ktiir-Supervisor-of-Animals, most of the groups operating against the righteous rule of the Patriarchy are motivated by material gain; this is a characteristic of my species. They cooperate with the genuine rebels, but it is an alliance plagued by mistrust and mutual contempt; furthermore, the rebels themselves are as much a grouping of bands as a unified whole." *And were slowly dying out, until the UN demonstrated its reach so spectacularly. Now they'll have recruits in plenty again, and the bandits will want to draw the cloak of respectable Resistance over themselves.*

His mind cautiously edged toward a consideration of whether it was time to begin hedging *his* bets, and he forced it back. The kzin used telepaths periodically to check the basic loyalties of their senior servants. That was one reason he had never tried to reach the upper policy levels of the collaborationist government, that and . . . a wash of non-thought buried the speculation.

"Accordingly, if their activity increases, our sources of information increase likewise. Once the confusion of the, ah, passing raid dies down, we will be in a position to make further gains. Perhaps to trap some of the greater leaders, Markham or Hirose."

"And you will take your percentage of all these transactions," Ktiir-Supervisor-of-Animals said with heavy irony. "Remember that a trained monkey that loses its value may always serve as monkeymeat. Remember where your loyalties ultimately lie, in this insect-web of betrayals you fashion, slave."

Yes, thought Montferrat, dabbing at his forehead as the kzin left. *I must remember that carefully.*

"Collation," he said to his desk. "Attack activity." The

schematic returned. "Eliminate all post-*Yamamoto* raids that correlate with seventy-five percent MO mapping to pre-*Yamamoto* attacks."

A scattering, mostly directed toward borderline targets that had been too heavily protected for the makeshift boats of the Free Wunderland space-guerrillas, disconcertingly many of them on weapons-fabrication plants, with nearly as many seizing communications, stealthing, command-and-control components. Once those were passed along to the other asteroid lurkers, all hell was going to break lose. And gravity-polarization technology was becoming more and more widespread as well. The kzin had tried to keep it strictly for their own ships and for manufacturing use, but the principles were not too difficult, and the methods the Patriarchy introduced were heavily dependent on it.

"Now, correlate filtered attacks with past ten-year pattern for bandits Markham, McAllistaire, Finbogesson, Cheung, Latimer, Wu. Sequencing.

"Scheisse," he whispered. Markham, without a doubt: the man did everything by the book, and you could rewrite the manuscript by watching him. Now equipped with something whose general capacities were equivalent to a kzin Stalker, and proceeding in a methodical amplification of the sort of thing he had been doing before . . . Markham was the right sort for the Protracted Struggle, all right. He'd read his Mao and Styrikawsi and Laugidis, even if he gave Clausewitz all the credit.

"Code, *Till Eulenspiegel.* Lock previous analysis, non-redo, simulate other pattern if requested. Stop."

"Stop and locked," the desk said.

Montferrat relaxed. At least partly, the *Eulenspiegel* file was supposedly secure. Certainly none of his subordinates had it, or they would have gone to the ratcats with it long ago; there was more than enough in there to make him prime monkey-meat. He swallowed convulsively; as Police Chief of Munchen, he was obliged to screen the kzin hunts far too frequently. Straightening, he adjusted the lapels of his uniform and walked to the picture window that formed one wall of the office. Behind him stretched the sleek expanse of feathery down-dropper-pelt rugs over marble tile, the settees and loungers of pebbled but butter-soft okkaran hide. A Matisse and two Vorenagles on the walls, and a priceless Pierneef . . . he stopped at the long oak bar and poured himself a single glass of Maivin; that was permissible.

Interviews with the kzin Supervisor-of-Animals were always rather stressful. Montferrat sipped, looking down on the low-pitched tile roofs of Old Munchen: carefully restored since the fighting, whatever else went short. The sprawling shanty-suburbs and shoddy gimcrack factories of recent years were elsewhere. This ten-story view might almost be as he had known it as a student, the curving tree-lined streets that curled through the hills beside the broad blue waters of the Donau. Banked flowers beside the pedestrian ways, cafés, the honeygold quadrangles of the University, courtyarded homes built around expanses of greenery and fountains. Softly blooming frangipani and palms and gumblossom in the parks along the river; the gothic flamboyance of the Ritterhaus, where the Landholders had met in council before the kzin came. And the bronze grouping in the great square before it, the Nineteen Founders.

Memory rose before him, turning the hard daylight of afternoon to a soft summer's night; he was young again, arm in arm with Ingrid and Harold and a dozen of their friends, the new students' caps on their heads. They had come from the beercellar and hours of swaying song, the traditional graduation-night feast, and they were all a little merry. Not drunk, but happy and in love with all the world, a universe and a lifetime opening out before them. The three of them had led the scrambling mob up the granite steps of the plinth, to put their white-and-gold caps on the three highest sculpted heads, and they had ridden the bronze shoulders and waved to the sea of dancing, laughing young faces below. Fireworks had burst overhead, yellow and green . . . *Shut up,* he told himself. The present was what mattered. The UN raid had not been the simple smash-on-the wing affair it seemed, not at all.

"I knew it," he muttered. "It wasn't logical, they didn't do as much damage as they could have." The kzin had not thought so, but then, they had a predator's reflexes. They just did not think in terms of mass destruction; their approach to warfare was too pragmatic for that. Which was why their armament was so woefully lacking in planet-busting weapons: the thought of destroying valuable real estate did not occur to them. Montferrat had run his own projections: with weapons like that ramship, you could destabilize *stars.*

"And humans *do* think that way." So there must have been some other point to the raid, and not merely to get an effective ship to the Free Wunderlanders. Nothing overt, which left something clandestine. Intelligence work. Perhaps elsewhere in the system, pray *God* elsewhere in the system, not in his backyard. But it would be just as well . . .

He crossed to the desk. "Axelrod-Bauergartner," he said.

A holo of his second-in-command formed, seated at her desk. The meter-high image put down its coffee cup and straightened. "Yes, Chief?"

"I want redoubled surveillance on all entry-exit movements in the Greater Munchen area. *Everything,* top priority. Activate all our contacts, call in favors, lean on everybody we can lean on. I'll be sending you some data on deep-hook threads I've been developing among the hardcore ferals."

He saw her look of surprise; that was one of the holecards he used to keep his subordinates in order. *Poor Axelrod-Bauergartner,* he thought. *You want this job so much, and would do it so badly. I've held it for twenty years because I've got a sense of proportion; you'd be monkeymeat inside six months.*

"*Zum befhel,* Chief."

"Our esteemed superiors also wish evidence of our zeal. Get them some monkeymeat for the next hunt, nobody too crucial."

"I'll round up the usual suspects, Chief."

The door retracted, and a white-coated steward came in with a covered wheeled tray. Montferrat looked up, checking . . . yes, the chilled Bloemvin 2337, the heart-of-palm salad, the paté . . . "And for now, send in the exit-visa applicant, the one who was having the problems with the paperwork."

The projected figure grinned wickedly. "Oh, *her.* Right away, Chief." Montferrat flicked the transmission out of existence and rose, smoothing down his uniform jacket and flicking his mustaches into shape with a deft forefinger. *This job isn't* all *grief,* he mused happily.

"Recode *Till Eulenspiegel,*" Yarthkin said, leaning back. "Interesting speculation, Claude old *kamerat,*" he mused. The bucket chair creaked as he leaned back, putting his feet up on the cluttered desk. The remains of a cheese-and-mustard sandwich rested at his elbow, perched waveringly on a stack of printout. The office around him was a similar clutter, bookcases and safe and a single glowlight, a narrow cubicle at the alley-wall of the bar. Shabby and rundown and smelling of beer and old socks, except for the extremely up-to-date infosystem built into the archaic wooden desk; one of the reasons the office was so shabby was that nobody but

Ogreson was allowed in, and he was an indifferent housekeeper at best.

He lit a cigarette and blew a smoke ring at the ceiling. *Have to crank up my contacts,* he thought. *Activity's going to heat up systemwide, and there's no reason I shouldn't take advantage of it. Safety's sake, too: arse to the wall, ratcats over all. This wasn't all to get our heroic Herrenmann in the Swarm a new toy; that was just a side-effect, somehow.*

"Sam," he said, keying an old-fashioned manual toggle. "Get me Suuomalisen."

☆ ☆ ☆

"Finagle," Jonah muttered under his breath. Munchenport was solidly cordoned off, antiaircraft missiles and heavy beamers all around it, and the shuttle station had been moved out into open country. The station was a series of square extruded buildings and open spaces for the gravitic shuttles, mostly for freight; the passenger traffic was a sideline. "Security's tight."

Ingrid smiled at the guard and handed over their ident-cards. The man smiled back and fed them into the reader, waiting a few seconds while the machine read the data, scanned the two Belters for congruence, and consulted the central files.

"Clear," he said, and shifted into Wunderlander: "Enjoy your stay planetside. God knows, more trying to get off than on, what with casualties from the raid and all."

"Thank you," Jonah said; his command of the language was adequate, and his accent would pass among non-Belters. "It was pretty bad out in the Belt, too."

The lineup moving through the scanners in the opposite direction stretched hundreds of meters into the barnlike gloom of the terminal building. A few were obviously space-born returning home, but most were thicker-built, as those brought up under even as feeble a gravity as Wunderland's tended to be, families with crying children and string-tied parcels, or ragged-looking laborers. They smelled, of unwashed bodies and poverty, a peculiar sweet-sour odor blending with the machinery-and-synthetics smell of the building and the residual ozone of heavy power release. More raw material for the industries of the Serpent Swarm, attracted by the higher wages and the lighter hand of the kzin off-planet.

"Watch it," Ingrid said. The milling crowds silenced and parted as a trio of the felinoids walked through trailed by human servants with baggage on maglifters; Jonah caught snatches of the Hero's Tongue, technical jargon. They both wheeled at a sudden commotion. The guards were closing in on an emigrant at the head of the line, a man arguing furiously with the checker.

"It's right!" he screamed. "I paid good money for it, all we got for the farm, it's *right*!"

"Look, scheisskopf, the machine says there's no record of it. *Raus!* You're holding up the line."

"It's the right paper, let me through!" The man lunged, trying to vault the turnstile. The guard at the checker recoiled, shrieked as the would-be traveler slammed down his metal-edged carryall on her arm. The two agents could hear the wet crackle of broken bone even at five meters' distance, and then the madman's body disappeared behind a circle of helmeted heads, marked by the rise and fall of shockrods. The others in the line drew back, as if afraid of infection, and the police dragged the man off by his arms; the injured one followed, holding her splintered arm and kicking the semiconscious form with every other step.

"Monkeymeat, you're *monkeymeat,* shithead," she shrilled, and kicked him again. There was solid force behind the blow, and she grunted with the effort and winced as it jarred her arm.

"Tanj," Jonah said softly. The old curse: *there ain't no justice.*

"No, there isn't," Ingrid answered. "Come on, the railcar's waiting."

☆ ☆ ☆

"And the word from the Nippojen in Tiamat is that two important ferals will be coming through soon," Suuomalisen said.

Yarthkin leaned back, sipping at his coffee and considering him. Suuomalisen was fat, even by Wunderland standards, where the .61 standard gravity made it easy to carry extra tissue. His head was pink, egg-bald, with a beak of a nose over a slit mouth and a double chin; the round body was expensively covered in a suit of white natural silk with a conservative black cravat and onyx ring. The owner of Harold's Terran Bar waited patiently while his companion tucked a linen handkerchief into his collar and began eating: scrambled eggs with scallions, grilled wurst, smoked *kopjfissche,* biscuits.

"You set a marvelous table, my friend," the fat man said. They were alone in the dining nook; Harold's did not serve breakfast, except for the owner and staff. "Twice I have offered your cook a position in my Suuomalisen's Sauna, and twice she has refused. You must tell me your secret."

Acquaintance, not friend, Harold thought. *And my chef prefers to work for someone who lets her people quit if they want to.* Mildly: "From the Free Wunderland people? They've been doing better at getting through to the bands in the Jotunscarp recently."

"No, no, these are *special* somehow. Carrying special goods, something that will upset the ratcats very much. The tip was vague; I don't know if my source was not informed or whether the slant-eyed devils are just playing both ends against the middle again." A friendly leer. "If you could identify them for me, my friend, I'd be glad to share the police reward. Not from Montferrat, from lower down . . . strictly confidential, of course; I wouldn't want to cut into the income you get from those who think this is the safest place in town."

"Suuomalisen, has anyone ever told you what a toad you are?" Yarthkin said, butting out the cigarette in the cold remains of the coffee.

"Many times, many times! But a very *successful* toad."

The shrewd little eyes blinked at him. "Harold, my friend, it is a grief to me that you take such little advantage of this excellent base of operations. A fine profit source, and you have wonderful contacts; think of the use you could make of them! You should diversify, my friend. Into contracting, it is a natural with the suppliers you have. Then, with your gambling, you could bid for the lottery contracts—perhaps even get into Guild work!"

"I'll leave that to you, Suuomalisen. Your Sauna is a good 'base of operations'; me, I run a bar and some games in the back, and I put people together sometimes. That's all. The tree that grows too high attracts the attention of people with axes."

The fat man shook his head. "You independent entrepreneurs must learn to move with the times, and the time of the little man is past . . . Ah, well, I must be going."

Yarthkin nodded. "Thanks for the tip. I'll have Wendy send round a case of the kirsch. Good stuff, pre-War."

"Pre-War!" The fat man's eyes lit. "Generous, generous. Where do you get such stuff?"

From ex-affluent people who can't pay their gambling debts, Yarthkin thought. "You have to let me keep a few little secrets; little secrets for little men."

A laugh from the fat man. "And again, any time you wish to join my organization . . . or even just to sell Harold's Terran Bar, my offer stands. I'll even promise to keep on all your people; they make the ambience of the place anyway."

"No deal, Suuomalisen. Thanks for the consideration, though."

☆ ☆ ☆

Dripping, Jonah padded back out of the shower; at least here in Munchen, nobody was charging you a month's wages for hot water. Ingrid was standing at the window toweling her hair and letting the evening breeze dry the rest of her. The room was narrow, part of an old mansion split into the cubicles of a cheap transients' hotel; there were more luxurious places in easy walking distance, but they would be the haunt of the local elite. He joined her at the opening and put an arm around her shoulders. She sighed and looked down the sloping street to the rippled surface of the Donau and the traffic of sail-boats and barges. A metal planter creaked on chains below the window; it smelled of damp earth and half-dead flowers.

"This is the oldest section of Munchen," she said slowly. "There wasn't much else, when I was a student here. Five years ago, my time . . . and the buildings I knew are old and shabby . . . There must be a hundred thousand people living here now!"

He nodded, remembering the sprawling squatter-camps that surrounded the town. "We're going to have to act quickly," he said. "Those passes the *oyabun* got us are only good for two weeks."

"Right," she said with another sigh, turning from the window. Jonah watched with appreciation as she rummaged in their bags for a series of parts, assembling them into a featureless box and snapping it onto the bedside datachannel. "There are probably blocks on the public channels . . ." She turned her head. "Instead of standing there making the passing girls sigh, why not get some of the other gear put together?"

"Right." Weapons first. The UN had dug deep into the ARM's old stores, technology that was the confiscated product of centuries of perverted ingenuity. Jonah grinned. Like most Belters, he had always felt the ARM tended to err on the side of caution in their role as technological police. Opening their archives had been like pulling teeth, from what he heard, even with the kzin bearing down on Sol system in all their carnivorous splendor. *I bleed for them,* he thought. *I won't say from where.*

The killing-tools were simple: two light-pencils of the sort engineers carried, for sketching on screens. Which was actually what they were, and any examination would prove it, according to the ARM. The only difference was that if you twisted the cap, *so,* pressed down on the clip that held the pen in a pocket and pointed it at an organism with a spinal cord, the pen emitted a sharp yawping sound whereupon said being went into *grand mal* seizure. Range of up to fifty meters, cause of death, "he died." Jonah frowned. *On second thought, maybe the ARM was right about this one.*

"Tanj," Ingrid said.

"Problem?"

"No, just that you have to input your ID and pay a whopping great fee to access the commercial net—even allowing for the way this fake *krona* they've got has depreciated."

"We've got money."

"Sure, but we don't want to call *too* much attention to ourselves." She continued to tap the keys. "There, I'm past the standard blocks . . . confirming . . . Yah, it'd be a bad idea to ask about the security arrangements at you-know-who's place. It's probably flagged."

"Commercial services," Jonah said. "Want me to drive?"

"Not just yet. Right, I'll just look at the record of commercial subcontracts. Hmm. About what you'd expect." Ingrid frowned. "Standard goods delivered to a depot and picked up by kzin military transports; no joy there. Most of the services are provided by household servants, born on the estate; no joy there, either. Ahh, outside contractors; now that's interesting."

"What is?" Jonah said, stripping packets of what looked like hard candy out of the lining of a suitcase. Sonic grenades, but you had to spit them at the target.

"Our great and good Rin-Tin-Kzin has been buying info-systems and 'ware from human makers. And he's the only one who is; the ratcat armed forces order subcomponents to their own specs and assemble them in plants under their direct supervision. But not him."

She paused in thought. "It fits . . . limited number of system types, like an ascending series, with each step up a set increment of increased capacity over the one below. Nothing like our wild and woolly jungle of manufacturers. They're not used to nonstandardized goods; they make them uneasy."

"How does that 'fit'?"

"With what the xenologists were saying. The ratcats have

an old, old civilization—very stable. Like what the UN would have become in Sol system, with the psychists 'adjusting' everybody into peacefulness and the ARM suppressing dangerous technology—which is to say, *all* technology. A few hundred years down the road we'd be on, if the kzin hadn't come along and upset the trajectory."

"Maybe they do some good after all." Jonah finished checking the wire garrotes that lay coiled in the seams of their clothing, the tiny repeating blowgun with the poisoned darts, and the harmless-looking fulgurite plastic frames of their backpacks—you twisted *so* and it went soft as putty, with the buckle acting as detonator-timer.

"It fits with what we know about you-know-who, as well." The room had been very carefully swept, but there were a few precautions it did not hurt to take. Not mentioning names, for one; a robobugger could be set to conversations with key words in them. "Unconventional. Wonder why he has human infosystems installed, though? Ours aren't *that* much better. Can't be." Infosystems were a mature technology, long since pushed to the physical limits of quantum indeterminancy.

"Well, they're more versatile, even the obsolete stuff here on Wunderland. I think"—she tugged at an ear—"I think it may be the 'ware he's after, though. Ratcat 'ware is almost as stereotyped as their hardwiring."

Jonah nodded; software was a favorite cottage industry in human space, and there must be millions of hobbyists who spent their leisure time fiddling with one problem or another.

"So we just enter a bid?" he said, flopping back on the bed. He was muscular for a Belter, but even the .61 Wunderland gravity was tiring when there was no place to get away from it.

"Doubt it." Ingrid murmured to the system. "Finagle, no joy. It's handled through something called the Datamongers' Guild: 'A mutual benefit association of those involved in infosystem development and maintenance.' Gott knows what that is." A pause. "Whatever it is, there's no public info on how to join it. The contracts listed say you-know-who takes a random selection from their duty roster to do his maintenance work."

Ingrid sank back on one elbow. "We need a local contact," she said slowly. "Jonah . . . We both know why Intelligence picked me as your partner. I was the only one remotely qualified who might know . . . and I do."

"Which one?" he asked. She laughed bitterly.

"I'd have thought Claude, but he's . . . Jonah, I wouldn't have believed it!"

Jonah shrugged. "There's an underground surrender movement on Earth. Lots of flatlander quislings; and the pussies aren't even there yet. Why be surprised there are more here?"

"But Claude! Oh, well."

"So who else you got?"

She continued to tap at the console. "Not many. None. A lot of them are listed as dead in the year or two after I left. No cause of death, just dead . . ." Her face twisted.

Survivor guilt, Jonah thought. *Dangerous. Have to watch for that.*

"Except Harold."

"Can you trust him?"

"Look, we have two choices. Go to Harold, or try the underworld contacts. The known-unreliable underworld contacts."

"One of whom is your friend Harold."

She sighed. "Yes, but—well, that's a good sign, isn't it? That he's worked with the—with them, and against—"

"Maybe."

"And a bar is a good place to meet people."

And mostly you just can't wait to see him. A man who'll be twice your age while you're still young. Do you love him or hate him?

"I . . ." She paused and ran a hand over her hair. "I don't know; he just didn't make the rendezvous in time, they were closing in, and . . ." A shrug.

Jonah linked hands behind his head. "I still say it's damned iffy but I guess it's the best chance we have; I certainly don't want to give the gangsters another location to find us at. I guess it's the best chance we have. At least we'll be able to get a drink."

Chapter 4

"This is supposed to be a *Terran* bar?" Jonah asked dubiously. He lifted one of the greenish shrimpoids from the platter and clumsily shelled it, got a thin cut under his thumbnail, and sucked on it, cursing. There was a holo of a stick-thin girl with body paint dancing in a cage over the bar, and dancing couples and groups beneath it; most of the tables were cheek-to-jowl, and they had had to pay heavily for one with a shield, here overlooking the lower level of the club.

Ingrid ignored him, focusing on the knot in her stomach and the clammy feel of nervous sweat across her shoulders under the formal low-necked black jumpsuit. Harold's Terran Bar was crowded tonight, and the entrance-fee had been stiff. The *verguuz* was excellent, however, and she sipped cautiously, welcoming the familiar mint-sweet-*wham* taste. The imitations in the Sol system never quite measured up. Shuddering, she noticed that two Swarm-Belter types at the next table were knocking back shot glasses of it, and then following the liqueur with beer chasers, in a mixture of extravagance and reckless disregard for their digestions. The squarebuilt Krio at the musicomp was tinkling out something old-sounding, piano with muted saxophone undertones.

Gottdamn, but that takes me back.

Claude had had an enormous collection of classical music, expensively enhanced stuff originally recorded on Earth, some of it on hardcopy or analog disks. His grandfather had acquired it, one of the eccentricities that had ruined the Montferrat-Palme fortunes. A silver-chased ebony box as big as a man's head, with a marvelous projection system. All the ancient greats, Brahms and Mozart and Jagger and Armstrong . . . They had all spent hours up in his miserable little attic, knocking back cheap Maivin and playing *Eine Kleine Nachtmusik* or *Sympathy for the Devil* loud enough to bring hammering broomstick protests from the people below. . . .

Gottdamn, it is *him,* she thought, with a sudden flare of determination.

"Jonah," she said, laying a hand on his arm. "This is too public, and we can't just wait for him. It's . . . likely to be something of a shock, you know? That musician, I knew him back when too. I'll get him to call through directly, it'll be faster."

The Sol-Belter nodded tightly; she squeezed the forearm before she rose. In space or trying to penetrate an infosystem, rank and skill both made him the leader, but here the mission and his life were both dependent on her. On her contacts, decades old here, and severed in no friendly wise.

Ingrid moistened her lips; Sam had been on the edge of their circle of friends, and confronting him would be difficult enough, much less Harold . . . She wiped palms down her slacks and walked over to the musicomp; it was a handsome legged model in Svarterwood with a beautiful point resonator, and a damper field to ensure that nothing came from the area around it but the product of the keyboard.

"*G'tag,* Sam," she said, standing by one side of the Instrument. "Still picking them out, I see."

"Fra?" he said, looking up at her with the dignified politeness of a well-raised Krio country-boy. The face was familiar, but one side of it was immobile; she recognized the signs of a rushed reconstruction job, the type they did after severe nerve-damage in the surface tissues.

"Well, I haven't changed *that* much, Sam. Remember Graduation Night, and that singalong we all had by the Founders?"

His features changed, from the surface smoothness of a well-trained professional to a shock so profound that the living tissue went as rigid as the dead. "Fra Raines," he whispered. The skilled hands continued over the musicomp's surface, but the tune had changed without conscious intent. He winced and hesitated, but she put a hand on his shoulder.

"No, keep playing, Sam.

"Remember me and you
And you and me

Together forever
I can't see me lovin' nobody but you—
For all my life—"

The musician shook his head. "The boss doesn't like me to play that one, Fra Raines," he said. "It reminds him, well, you'd know."

"I know, Sam. But this is bigger than any of us, and it means we can't let the past sleep in its grave. Call him, tell him we're waiting."

"Mr. Yarthkin?" the voice asked.

He had been leaning a shoulder against one wall of the inner room, watching the roulette table. The smoke in here was even denser than by the front bar, and the ornamental fans made patterns and traceries through the blue mist. Walls were set for a space scene, a holo of Jupiter taken from near orbit on one side and Wunderland on the other. Beyond them the stars were hard glitters, pinpoints of colored light receding into infinity, infinitely out of reach. Yarthkin dropped his eyes to the table. The ventilation system was too good to carry the odor of the sweat that gleamed on the hungrily intent faces. . . .

Another escape, he thought. Like the religious revivals, and the nostalgia craze; even the feverish corruption and pursuit of wealth. A distraction.

"Herrenmann Yarthkin-Schotmann?" the voice asked again, and a hand touched his elbow.

He looked down, into a girl's face framed in a black kerchief. Repurified Amish, by the long drab dress. Well-to-do, by the excellent material; many of that sect were. Wunderland had never relied much on synthetic foods, and the Herrenmen estates had used the Amish extensively as subtenants. They had flourished, particularly since the kzin came and agricultural machinery grew still scarcer . . . That was ending now, of course.

"No *'Herrenmann,'* sweetheart," he said gently. She was obviously terrified, this would be a den of Satan by her folks' teaching. "Just Harold, or Mr. Yarthkin if you'd rather. What can I do for you?"

She clasped her gloved hands together, a frown on the delicately pretty features and a wisp of blond hair escaping from her scarf and bonnet. "Oh . . . I was wondering if you could give me some advice, please, Mr. Yarthkin. Everyone says you know what goes on in Munchen." He heard the horror in her voice as she named the city, probably from a lifetime of hearing it from the pulpit followed by "Whore of Babylon" or some such.

"Advice I provide free," he said neutrally. *Shut up,* he added to his mind. *There's thousands more in trouble just as bad as hers. None of your business.*

"Wilhelm and I," she began, and then halted to search for words. Yarthkin's eyes flicked up to a dark-clad young man with a fringe of beard around his face sitting at the roulette table. Sitting slumped, placing his chits with mechanical despair.

"Wilhelm and I, we lost the farm." She put a hand to her eyes. "It wasn't his fault, we both worked so hard . . . but the kzin, they took the estate where we were tenants and . . ."

Yarthkin nodded. Kzin took a *lot* of feeding. And they would not willingly eat grain-fed meat; they wanted lean range beasts. More kzin estates meant less work for humans, and what there was was in menial positions, not the big tenant holdings for mixed farming that the Herrenmen had preferred. Farmholders reduced to beggary, or to an outlaw existence that ended in a kzin hunt.

"Your church wouldn't help?" he said. The Amish were a close-knit breed.

"They found new positions for our workers, but the bishop, the bishop said Wilhelm . . . that there was no money to buy him a new tenancy, that he should humble himself and take work as a foreman and pray for forgiveness." Repurified Amish thought that worldly failure was punishment for sin. "Wilhelm, Wilhelm is a good man, I told him to listen to the bishop, but he cursed him to his face, and now we are shunned." She paused. "Things, things are very bad there now. It is no place to live or raise children, with food so scarce and many families crowded together."

"Sweetheart, this isn't a charitable institution," Yarthkin said warily.

"No, Mr. Yarthkin." She drew herself up and wrapped pride around herself like a cloak. "We had some money, we sold everything, the stock and tools. Swarm Agrobiotics offered Wilhelm and me a place—they are terraforming new farm-asteroids. With what they pay we could afford to buy a new tenancy after a few years." He nodded. The Swarm's population was growing by leaps and bounds, and it was cheaper to grow than synthesize, but skilled dirt-farmers were rare. "But we must be there soon, and there are so many difficulties with the papers."

Bribes, Yarthkin translated to himself.

"It takes so much more than we thought, and to live while we wait! Now we have not enough for the final clearance, and . . . and we know nothing but farming. The policeman told Wilhelm that we must have four thousand krona more, and we had less than a thousand. Nobody would lend more against his wages, not even the Sina moneylender, he just laughed and offered to . . . to sell me to . . . and Wilhelm hit him, and we had to pay more to the police. Now he gambles, it is the only way we might get the money, but of course he loses."

The house always wins, Yarthkin thought. The girl steeled herself and continued.

"The Herrenmann policeman—"

"Claude Montferrat-Palme?" Yarthkin inquired, nodding with his chin. The police chief was over at the baccarat tables with a glass of verguuz at his elbow, playing his usual cautiously skillful game.

"Yes," she whispered. "He told me that there was a way the papers could be approved." A silence. "I said nothing to Wilhelm, he is . . . very young, younger than me in some ways." The china-blue eyes turned to him. "Is this Herrenmann one who keeps his word?"

"Claude?" Yarthkin said. "Yes. A direct promise, yes; he'll keep the letter of it."

She gripped her hands tighter. "I do not know what to do," she said softly. "I must think."

She nodded jerkily to herself and moved off. Yarthkin threw the butt of his cigarette down for the floor to absorb and moved over to the roulette table. A smile quirked the corner of his mouth, and he picked up a handful of hundred-krona chips from in front of the croupier. *Stupid,* he thought to himself. *Oh, well, a man has to make a fool of himself occasionally.*

The Amishman had dropped his last chip and was waiting to lose it; he gulped at the drink at his elbow and loosened the tight collar of his jacket. *Probably seeing the Welfare Office ahead of him,* Yarthkin thought. These days, that meant a labor camp where the room-and-board charges were twice the theoretical wages . . . They would find something else for his wife to do. Yarthkin dropped his counter beside the young farmer's.

"I'm feeling lucky tonight, Tony," he said to the croupier. "Let's see it."

She raised one thin eyebrow, shrugged her shoulders under the sequins and spun the wheel. "Place your bets, gentlefolk, please." Impassively, she tossed the ball into the whirring circle of metal. "Number eight. Even, in the black."

The Amishman blinked down in astonishment as the croupier's ladle pushed his doubled stakes back toward him. Yarthkin reached out and gripped his wrist as the young man made an automatic motion toward the plaques. It was thick and springy with muscle, the arm of a man who had worked with his hands all his life, but Yarthkin had no difficulty stopping the motion.

"Let it ride," he said. "Play the black, I'll do the same."

Another spin, but the croupier's lips were compressed into a thin line; she was a professional, and hated a break in routine. "Place your bets . . . Black wins again, gentlefolk."

"Try twelve," Yarthkin said, shifting his own chip. "No, all of it."

"Place your bets . . . twelve wins, gentlefolk."

Glancing up, Yarthkin caught Montferrat's coldly furious eye, and grinned with an equal lack of warmth. At the next spin of the wheel he snapped his finger for the waiter and urged the younger man at his side to his feet, piling the chips on an emptied drink tray. "That's five thousand," Yarthkin said. "Why don't you cash them in and call it a night?"

Wilhelm paused, scrubbed his hands across his face, straightened his rumpled clothes. "Yes . . . Yes, thank you sir, perhaps I should." He looked down at the pile of chips, and Yarthkin could see his lips whiten with shock as the impact hit home. "I . . ."

The girl came to meet him, and gave Yarthkin a single glance through tear-starred lashes before the two left, clinging to each other. The owner of Harold's shrugged and pushed his own counters back to the pile before the croupier.

"How are we doing tonight, Tony?" he asked.

"About five thousand krona less well than we could have," she said sharply.

"We'll none of us starve," Yarthkin added mildly, and strolled over to the baccarat table. Montferrat glanced up sharply, but his anger had faded.

"You're a sentimental idiot, Harry," he said.

"Probably true, Claude," Yarthkin said, and took a plain

unlogoed credit chip from the inside pocket of his jacket. "The usual."

Montferrat palmed it and smoothed back his mustache with a finger. "Sometimes I think you indulge in these little quixotic gestures just to annoy me," he added, and dropped three cards from his hand. "Banco," he continued.

"Probably right there too, Claude," he said. "I'm relying on the fact that you're not an unmitigated scoundrel."

"Now I'm an honest man?"

"No, a scoundrel with mitigating factors . . . and I'm a sentimental idiot, as you mentioned." He stopped, listened abstractedly. "See you later; somebody wants to see me. Sam says it's important, and he isn't given to exaggeration."

The doors slid open and Yarthkin stepped into the main room, beside the north end of the long bar. The music was the first thing he heard, the jaunty remembered beat. Cold flushed over his skin, and the man he had been smiling and waving to flinched. That brought the owner of Harold's Terran Bar back to his duties; they were self-imposed, and limited to this building, but that did not mean they could be shirked. He moved with swift grace through the throng, shouting an occasional greeting over the surf-roar of voices, slapping a shoulder, shaking a hand, smiling. The smile was still on his face as he stepped up off the dance floor and through the muting field around the musicomp, but he could taste the acid and copper of his own rage at the back of his throat.

"I told you never to play that song again," he said coldly. *"We've been together a long time, Samuel Ogun, it'd be a pity to end a beautiful friendship this way."*

The musician keyed the instrument to continue without him and swiveled to face his employer. "Boss . . . Mr. Yarthkin, once you've talked to those two over at table three, you'll understand. Believe me."

Yarthkin nodded curtly and turned to the table. The two Belters were sitting close to the musicomp, with the shimmer of a privacy field around them, shrouding features as well as dulling voices. Yarthkin smoothed the lapels of his jacket and wove deftly between tables and servers as he approached, forcing his anger down into an inner cesspit where discarded emotions went. Sam was no fool, he must mean *something* by violating a standing order that old. He did not shake easy, either, and that had been plain to see on him. This should be interesting, at least; it was good to have a straightforward bargaining session ahead, after the embarrassing exhilaration of the incident in the gambling room. Money was a relaxing game to play; the rules were clear, victory and defeat a matter of counting the score and no embarrassing emotions. And these *might* be the ones with the special load that the rumors had told of. More profit and more enjoyment if they were. More danger, too, but a man had to take an occasional calculated risk. Otherwise, you might as well put a droud in your head and be done with it.

The man looked thirty and might be anything between that and seventy; tough-looking, without the physical softness that so many rockjacks got from a life spent in cramped zero-G spaceships. A conservative dark innersuit, much less gaudy than what most successful Swarmers wore these days, and an indefinably foreign look about the eyes. Yarthkin sat, pulled out a chair and looked over to study the woman's face. The world went black.

"Boss, are you all right?" There was a sharp hiss against his neck, and the sudden sharp-edged alertness of a stimshot. "Are you all right?"

"You," Yarthkin whispered, shaking the Krio's hand off his shoulder with a shrug. Ingrid's face hovered before him, unchanged, no, a little thinner, more tanned. But the *same,* not forty years different, the *same.* He could feel things moving in his head, like a mountain river he had seen on a spring hunting trip once. Cracks running across black ice, and the rock beneath his feet toning with the dark water's hidden power. "You." His voice went guttural, and his right hand went inside the dress jacket.

"Jonah, no!" Ingrid's hand shot out and slapped her companion's to the table. Yarthkin felt his mind stagger and broach back toward reality as the danger-prickle ran over his skin; that was probably *not* an engineer's light-pencil in the younger man's hand. He struggled for self-command, dropped his gun-hand back to the table.

"Well." What was there to say? "Long time, no see. Glad you could make it. The last time, you seemed to have a pressing appointment elsewhere. *I* showed up on time, and there the 'boat was, boosting like hell a couple of million klicks Solward. Me in a single ship with half a dozen kzin Slashers sniffing around."

Ingrid's face went chalk-white. "Let me explain—"

"Don't bother. Closed account." He paused, lit a cigarette, astonished at the steadiness of his own hands.

"Claude know you're here?"

"No, and it's best he doesn't."

"Sure. Let me guess. Now you're back, and Mr. Quick-Draw here with you, on some sort of UN skullbuggery, and need my help." He looked thoughtful. "Come to that, how did you get here?"

"Jonah Matthieson," the Sol-Belter said. "Yes. How we got here isn't important. We do need your help. Damned little we've gotten in this system that hasn't been bought and paid for, and half the time we've been sold out to the pussies even so."

"Pussies? Oh, the ratcats." He laughed, a little wildly. "So you haven't found legions of eager, idealistic volunteers ready to throw themselves into the jaws of the kzin to help you on your sacred mission, whatever it is. How *can* that be?"

Yarthkin's finger touched behind one ear, and the mirror behind the bar went screenmode. It showed an overgrown park, flicking between micropickups scattered wholesale through the vegetation. There had been lawns here once; now there was waist-high grass, Earth trees grown to scores of meters in the light gravity, native Wunderlander growths soaring on spidery trunks. The sound of panting breath, and a naked human came stumbling through the undergrowth. His legs and flanks were lashed and scratched by thorns and burrs. He reeled with exhaustion, feet pounding with careless heaviness; the eyes were flat and blank in the stubbled face, mouth dribbling. Behind him there was a flash of orange-red, alien among the cool greens of Earth, the tawny olives of Wunderland. A flash: two hundred kilos of sentient carnivore charging on all fours in a hunching rush that parted the long grass in an arrow of rippling wind. Not so much like a cat as a giant weasel, blurring, looming up behind the fleeing human in a wall of flesh, a wall that fell tipped with bright teeth and black claws.

The screaming began at once, sank to a bubbling sound and the wet tearing noises of feeding. Shouts of protest rose from the dance floor and the other tables, and the sound of someone vomiting into an expensive meal. Yarthkin touched the spot behind his ear and the screen switched back to mirror. The protests lasted longer, and the staff of Harold's went among the patrons to sooth with free drinks and apologies, murmurs.

Technical mistake, government override, here, let me fix that for you, gentlefolk . . .

"And that," Yarthkin said, "is a *good* reason why you're not going to be finding hordes beating down your door to volunteer. We've been living with that for *forty years,* you fool. While you in the Sol system sat fat and happy and safe."

Jonah leaned forward. "I'm here now, aren't I? Neither fat, nor very happy, and not at all safe right now. I was in two fleet actions, Mr. Yarthkin. Out of four. Earth's been fighting the kzin since I was old enough to vote, and we haven't lost so far. Been close a couple of times, but we haven't lost. We could have stayed home. Note we didn't. Ingrid and I are considerably less safe than you."

Ingrid and I, Yarthkin thought, looking at the faces, side by side. The *young* faces; at the Sol-Belter. *Hotshot pilot. Secret agent. All-round romantic hero, come to save us worthless pussy-whipped peons.* Tonight seemed to be a night for strong emotions, something he had been trying to unlearn. Now he felt hatred strong and thick, worse than anything he had ever felt for the kzin. Worse even than he had felt for himself, for a long time.

"So what do you need?"

"A way into the Datamongers' Guild, for a start."

Yarthkin looked thoughtful. "That's easy enough." He realized that Ingrid had been holding her breath. *Bad. She wants this bad. How bad?*

"And any other access to the—to networks."

"Networks. Sure. Networks. Any old networks, right? Want into Claude's system? Want to see his private files? What else would you like?"

"Hari—"

"I can do that, you know. Networks."

She didn't say anything.

"Help. You want help," he said slowly. "Well that leaves only one question." He poured himself a drink in Jonah's water glass, tossed it back. "What will you pay?"

"Anything we have. Anything you want."

"Anything?"

"Of course. When do you want me?"

"Ingrid—"

"Not your conversation, Belter. Get lost."

The club was dim, with the distinctive stale chill smell of tobacco and absent people that came in the hours just before dawn. Yarthkin sat at the table and sipped methodically at the verguuz; it was a shame to waste it on just getting drunk, but owning a bar did have *some* advantages. He took another swallow, letting the smooth sweet minty taste flow over his tongue, then breathing out as the cold fire ran back up his throat. A pull at the cigarette, one of the clove-scented ones well-to-do Baha'i smoked. *My, aren't we wallowing in sensual indulgence tonight.*

"Play," he said to the man at the musicomp. The Krio started and ran his fingers over the surface of the instrument, and the brassy complexities of Meddlehoffer lilted out into the deserted silence of the room.

"Not that," Yarthkin said, and knocked back the rest of the Verguuz. "You know what I want."

"No you don't," Sam said. "That's a *manti-manti mara,"* he continued, dropping back into his native tongue: a great stupidity. "What you want is to get drunk and manyamanya, smash something up. Go ahead, it's your bar."

"I said, *play it."* The musician shrugged, and began the ancient melody. The husky voice followed:

" . . . no matter what we say or do—"

A contralto joined it: *"So happy together."*

They both looked up with a start. Ingrid dropped into a chair across from Yarthkin, reached for the bottle and poured herself a glass.

"Isn't there enough for two?" she asked, raising a brow into his scowl. The musician rose, and Yarthkin waved him back.

"You don't have to leave, Sam."

"Do I have to stay? No? Then it's late, boss, and I'm going for bed. See you tomorrow."

"Where's the Sol-Belter?" Yarthkin asked. His voice was thickened but not slurred, and his hand was steady as he poured.

"In the belly of the whale . . . still working in your office." *And trying not to think about what we're doing. Or will be doing in a minute, if you're sober enough.* "That's a pretty impressive system you have there."

"Yeah. And I'm taking a hell of a chance letting you two use it."

"So are we."

"So are we all. Honorable men, all, all honorable men. And women. Honorable."

"Hari—"

"That's *Herr* Yarthkin to you, Lieutenant."

"If you let me explain—"

"Explain what?"

"Hari, the rendezvous time was fixed, and you didn't make it! We *had* to boost; there were hundreds of lives riding on it."

"Oh, no, Lieutenant Raines. The *ships* had to boost, and we had to keep the kzin off your backs as long as we could. Not every pilot had to go with them."

"Angers was dying, radiation sickness, puking her guts out. Flambard's nerve had gone, Finagle's sake, Hari, I was the best they had, and—" She stopped, looking at his face, slumped. "Long ago, long ago."

Not so long for you as for me, he thought. Her face was the same, not even noticeably aged. What was different? Where did the memory lie? *Unformed,* he thought. *She looks . . . younger than I remember. Not as much behind the eyes.*

"Long ago, kid. How'd you get here?"

"You wouldn't believe me if I told you."

"Probably I wouldn't. That raid—"

She nodded. "That raid. The whole reason for that raid was to get us here."

"For god's sake, why?"

"I can't tell you."

"It's part of the price, sweetheart."

"Literally, I can't," Ingrid said. "Post-hypnotic. Reinforced with— The psychists have some new tricks, Hari. I would literally die before I told you, or anyone else."

"Even if they're taking you apart?"

She nodded.

Harold thought about that for a moment and shuddered. "OK. It was a long time ago, and maybe—maybe you saw things I didn't see. You always were bigger on romantic causes than the rest of us." He stood.

She got to her feet and stood expectantly. "Where?"

"There's a bedroom upstairs."

She nodded. "I've—I've thought about this a lot."

"Not as much as I have. You haven't had as long."

She laughed. "That's right."

"So now I'm old—"

"No. Not old, Hari. Not old. Which way? The stairs over there?"

"Just a minute, kid. So. Assuming it works, whatever you have planned, what afterward?"

"Once it's done it doesn't matter."

"Tell that to a man under thirty. Women and we oldsters know better."

"Well, we brought a ship with us. Nice boat, the best the UN's making these days. Markham's keeping her for us, and then we'll do the guerrilla circuit afterwards."

"Markham? Ulf *Reichstein*-Markham?" An old enmity sharpened his tone, one less personal. "A legitimate bastard of a long line of bastards, who does his best to out-bastard them all. He'd cut your throat for six rounds of pistol ammunition, if he needed them."

"Didn't strike me as a bandit."

"Worse, a True Believer . . . and you can whistle in the wind for that ship."

She smiled. "That ship, you might say she has a mind of her own; really, we've got a hold on it."

Then you'll be off to the Swarm, Yarthkin thought. *Playing dodgem with the ratcats, you and that Jonah. Flirting with danger and living proud.* There was a taste of bile at the back of his mouth. Remembering the long slow years of defeat, strength crumbling away as one after another despaired; until nothing was left but the fanatics and the outlaws, a nuisance to the enemy and a deadly danger to their own people. What was honor, going on with the killing when it had all turned pointless and rancid, or taking the amnesty and picking up the pieces of life? *But not for you. You and Jonah, you'll win or go out in a blaze of glory. No dirty alliances and dirtier compromises and decisions with no good choices. The two of you have stolen my life.*

"Get out," he said. "Get the hell out."

"No." She took his hand and led him toward the stairs.

Chapter 5

Chuut-Riit shook his clawed fists in the air and screamed. *"I will have his ears! I will have his testicles for my cubs to eat! I will kill, kill, kill—"*

Someone bit his tail, hard. The kzinti governor leapt for the ceiling screeching, whirled, and landed in attack position; almost horizontal, with hands outstretched.

It was Conservor. Chuut-Riit halted his leap before it began, glaring murderously at the priest-counsellor. His calm was unkzin, only a slight quirking of eyebrow-tufts and whiskers indicating sympathetic amusement; his scent had the almost buttery flavor of complete relaxation. Yet of his own will Chuut-Riit was apprentice in the ways of the Conservors—unorthodox for a high noble, but not without precedent—and such tricks were among the teaching techniques.

"You must think before you attack, Chuut-Riit," Conservor said firmly. "You *must.* This I lay on you in the name of the God."

The younger kzin rose and began pacing; the inner sanctum was a five-meter square of sandstone block, with the abstract-looking sculptures and scent-markings of his ancestors standing in niches in the walls. Iron braziers wrought in the shape of crossed claws glowed, sending trails of incense to the high blackened beams of the ceiling. For the rest it was empty save for the low desk and three reclining cushions, with floors of sanded pine. Traat-Admiral occupied the third cushion, and *he* was quivering-eager for battle, ears folded away and gingery anger-smell rising from him.

"I cannot tolerate open flouting of my authority," Chuut-Riit said. He had forced enough relaxation that his tail lashed instead of standing out behind him like a rigid pink column of muscle. "What am I to do? Turn him loose in my harem? Invite him to urinate on the shrines?"

One arm slashed at the figures; some of them were so ancient that nostrils must flare to take their scent. He licked his nose and inhaled deeply with his mouth open. The smell of their strength and pride flowed into him, heartening and maddening at the same time.

"Ktrodni-Stkaa disclaims all responsibility for the destruction of the *Feud* and the *Severed-Vein,*" Conservor said. Traat-Admiral let his lips flutter against his fangs, derisive laughter.

"No," Conservor continued, making a palm-up gesture: *do not seize what you cannot hold.* "Ktrodni-Stkaa is . . . hasty. He is your enemy. He is not the best tactician in the fleets of the Great Pack. He is overproud of his blood. But he is a Hero; he would not engage in such deception against an honorable"—that was, kzinti—"foe."

"Unless he has decided that I am not *worthy* of honorable combat, because of my *cautious* ideas," Chuut-Riit said. He snarled, drooling slightly, fingers flexing as he imagined fangs grinding into bone as he brought up his rear feet and ripped and ripped and ripped . . .

"That is so," Conservor acknowledged with a ripple of his spinal fur. "Yet the balance of hard data could be construed to support his claim of noninvolvement. Is this not so?"

Traat-Admiral gave a grunting cough and licked angrily at his forearms for a moment. "The fur lies flat in that direction," he said grudgingly. "Few recordings survived the EMP of the engagement. They show only a corvette of the *Bone-Breaker* class, of which there are thousands. Data is insufficient for identification. With the damage to our systemwide surveillance net, we have no direct remote tracking of where it went. Perhaps it is as Ktrodni-Stkaa says"—Traat-Admiral's claws slid in, sign of unconscious distaste—"and an individual firebrand was responsible."

"Arreeoghw," Chuut-Riit said; he had stopped in mid-stride, his fur bottling out. "*Bone-Breaker* class—that is the older specification, is it not?"

The other two kzinti flexed thumbclaws in agreement; when Chuut-Riit had arrived two decades ago he had brought the latest designs from the inner worlds. Not that there had been great differences—warship design was a mature technology, like most within the Patriarchy—but there had been some refinements in weapons mountings.

"Many of those would have been dispatched with the Fourth Fleet," Chuut-Riit continued softly, musing. "Very many. According to the reports of the survivors, Kfraksha-Admiral lost a number of vessels relatively intact."

"Arrrh." Traat-Admiral came up on all fours, back arching. Conservor sank down fluidly, eyes seeking something beyond the walls.

"Arrrh," Traat-Admiral repeated. "The mass is low enough that the human ramscoop vessel could have included a corvette. But deceleration—the energy discharge— No corvette could carry enough fuel, not with the most efficient of polarizers. And a reaction-drive deceleration is ridiculous; such a discharge would have been a banner across the system for days."

Chuut-Riit licked meditatively at his wrist and smoothed his ears with it, fluttering them out for the soothing feel of cool air on the pink bare-skin membranes.

"Hrrrr. Doubtless correct. A thought, no more."

"Still," Conservor said. The two younger kzin started slightly. "Physics is not my specialty. Yet consider: we and the humans have been learning of each other, in the best of schools." War—nothing taught you a being's inwardness like fighting it. *"If* such a thing were possible, and *if* the humans had learned somewhat of us, would this not be a shrewd jugular-strike?"

"Not if we knew—arrrhhhg. Ktrodni-Stkaa."

"Yes." They were all imagining trying to convince that arrogance that mere monkeys were capable of playing on kzinti internal rivalries. Ktrodni-Stkaa barely acknowledged that humans existed, save when he was hungry.

"Still, it is unlikely," Traat-Admiral said, twitching the end of his tail.

"So is sentience," Conservor said. Silence dwelt for long moments. "Let us consider, and clear our minds."

All three sank into the hands-folded-under-chests posture of meditation and let their chins sink to the floor.

☆ ☆ ☆

"They've accepted our bid, Captain."

Jonah nodded stiffly. "Thank you, Lieutenant. Not that I'm surprised."

"No, sir."

Back in Sol system a thousand hackers had labored to produce advanced software they thought might be salable on

Wunderland. Most of it had been too advanced; they'd predicted a higher state of the art than Wunderland had retained, and the stuff wouldn't work on the ancient hardware. Even so, there was plenty that did work. It had only taken fifty days to make Jan Hardman and Lucy van den Berg moderately big names in the Datamongers' Guild. The computer records showed them as old timers, with a scattering of previous individual sales. They told everyone on the net that they owed their big success to teaming up.

Teaming up. A damned tough fifty days . . . Jonah looked unashamedly at Ingrid. "I admit you've improved Herr Yarthkin's disposition one whole hell of a lot, but do you have to look so tanj happy?"

"Capt—Jonah, I *am* happy."

"Yeah."

"I—Jonah, I'm sorry if it hurts you."

"Yeah. All right. Lieutenant. We've got work to do."

☆ ☆ ☆

"These are the same monkeys as before." The guards spoke in the Hero's Tongue. "The computer says they have access."

The kzin tapped a large button on the console, and the door lifted.

Jonah and Ingrid cringed and waited. The kzin sniffed, then led the way outside. Another kzin warrior followed, and two more fell in on either side. The routine had been the same the other two times they had been here.

This will be different. Maybe. Jonah pushed the thoughts away. Kzin weren't really telepathic, but they could sense excitement and smell fear. *Of course the fear's natural. They probably like that scent.*

Sunlight was failing behind evening clouds, and the air held a dank chill and the wild odors of storm-swept grassland. The two humans crossed the landing field between forms a third again their height, living walls of orange-red fur; claws slid out in unconscious reflex on the stocks of the giants' heavy beam rifles.

Jonah kept his eyes carefully down. It would be an unbearable irony if they were killed by mistake, victims of some overzealous kzin spooked by the upsurge in guerrilla activity. The attack of the *Yamamoto* had created the chaos that let them into Wunderland, but that same chaos just might kill them.

Doors slid aside, and they descended into chill corridors like a dreadnought's, surfaces laced with armored data conduits and the superconducting coil-complexes of field generators.

One of the kzin followed. "This way," he said, prodding Jonah's shoulder with the muzzle of his weapon. The light down here was reddish, frequencies adjusted to the aliens' convenience; the air was drier, colder than humans would have wished. And everything was too *big,* grips and stairs and doors adapted to a thick-bodied, short-legged race with the bulk of terrestrial gorillas.

They went through a chamber filled with computer consoles. This was as far as they'd been allowed the last two times. "Honored Governor Chuut-Riit is pleased with your work," the kzin officer said.

"We are honored," Ingrid replied.

"This way."

The kzin led them through another door. They stepped into an outsized elevator, dropped for a small eternity; when the door opened they were in another complex, this one with its own gravity polarizer set to Kzin normal. Their knees sagged, and they stepped through into another checkzone. The desire to gawk around was intolerable, but the gingery smell of kzin was enough to restrain them as they walked through a thick sliding door with the telltale slickness of density-enhanced matter. Jonah recognized the snouts of heavy remote-waldoed weapons up along the edges of the roof. Past that was another control room, a dozen kzin operators lying recumbent on spaceship-style swiveling couches before semicircular consoles. Their helmets were not the featureless wraparounds humans would have used; these had thin crystal facepieces, adjustable audio pickups, and cutouts for the ears. Not as efficient, but probably a psychological necessity. Kzin have keener senses than man, but are more vulnerable to claustrophobia, any sort of confinement that cuts off the flow of scent, sound, light.

Patience comes harder to them, too, Jonah thought. Ancestral kzin had chased their prey down in relays.

They penetrated still another set of armored doors to the ultimate sanctum. *At last!*

"Accomplish your work," the kzin said. "The inspector will arrive in six hours. Sanitary facilities are there."

Jonah exhaled a long breath as the alien left. Now there was only the featureless four-meter box of the control room; the walls were a neutral pearly white, ready to transmit visual data. The only console was a standup model modified with a pedestal so that humans could use it. Ingrid and he exchanged a wordless glance as they walked to it and began unpacking their own gear, snapping out the support tripod and sliding home the thin black lines of the data jacks.

A long pause, while their fingers played over the small black rectangles of their portable interfacing units; the only sound was a subliminal sough of ventilators and the faint natural chorus that the kzin always broadcast through the speakers of a closed installation; insects and the rustle of vegetation. Jonah felt a familiar narrowing, a focus of concentration more intense than sex or even combat, as the lines of a program-schematic sprang out on his unit.

"Finagle, talk about paranoids," he muttered. "See this freeze-function here?"

Ingrid's face was similarly intent, and the rushing flicker of the scroll-display on her unit gave her face a momentary look as of light through stained glass.

"Got it. Freeze."

"We're bypassed?"

"This is under our authorized codes. All right, these are the four major subsystems. See the physical channeling? The hardware won't accept config commands of more than 10K except through this channel we're at."

"Slow response, for a major system like this," he mused. The security locks were massive and complex, but a little cumbrous.

"It's the man-kzin hardware interfacing," Ingrid said. "I think. Their basic architecture's more synchronic. Betcha they never had an industrial-espionage problem . . . Hey, notice that?"

"Ahhhh. Interesting." Jonah kept his voice carefully phlegmatic. *Tricky kitty. Tricky indeed.* "Odd. This would be much harder to access through the original Hero system."

"Tanj, you're right," Ingrid said. She looked up with an urchin grin that blossomed with the pure delight of solving a software problem.

Jonah gave her a cautioning look.

Her face went back to a mask of concentration. "Clearly this was designed with security against *kzinti* in mind. See, here and here? That's why they've deliberately preserved the original human operating system on this—two of them—and used this patch-cocked integral translation chip here, see?"

"Right!" His fingers flew. "In fact, if analyzed with the original system as an integrating node and catchpoint . . . See?"

"Right. Murphy, but you'd have more luck wandering through a minefield blindfolded than trying to get at this from an exterior connection! There's nothing in the original stem system *but* censor programs; by the time you got by them, the human additions would have alarmed and frozen. Catches you on the interface transitions, see? That's why they haven't tried to bring the core system up to the subsystem operating speeds. Sure slows things down, though."

"We'll just have to live with it," Jonah said for the benefit of any hidden listeners. It seemed unlikely. There weren't that many kzin programmers, and all of them were working for the navy or the government. This was the strictly personal system of Viceroy Chuut-Riit.

"Wheels within wheels," Ingrid muttered.

"Right." Jonah shook his head; there was a certain perverse beauty in using a cobbled-up rig's own lack of functional integration as a screening mechanism. *But all designed against kzinti. Not against us. Ye gods, it would be easy enough for Chuut-Riit's rivals to work through humans—*

Only none of them would think of that. This is the only estate that uses outside contractors. And the Heroes don't think that way to begin with.

His fingers flew. Ingrid—Lieutenant Raines—would be busy installing the new data management system they were supposed to be working at. What he was doing was far beyond her. Jonah let his awareness and fingers work together, almost bypassing his conscious mind. Absently he reached for a squeeze-bulb before he remembered that the nearest Jolt Cola was four light-years away.

Now. Bypass the kzin core system. Move into the back door. He keyed in the ancient passwords embedded into the Wunderland computer system by Earth hackers almost a hundred years before. Terran corporate managers had been concerned about competition, and the ARM had had their sticky fingers here too, and they'd built backdoors into every operating system destined for Wunderland. A built-in industrial espionage system. And the kzin attack and occupation should have kept the Wunderlanders from finding them . . .

/ Murphy Magic. The SeCrEt of the UnIvErSe is 43, NOT 42.
$

"There is justice," Jonah muttered.

"Joy?"

"Yeah." He typed frantically.

She caught her breath. "All right."

By the time the core realizes what's going on, we'll all be dead of old age. "Maybe take a while. Here we go."

Two hours later he was done. He looked over at Ingrid. She had long finished, except for sending the final signals that would tell the system they were done. "About ready," he said.

She bit her lip. "All right."

For a moment he was shocked at the dark half-moons below her eyes, the lank hair sweat-plastered to her cheeks, and then concentration dropped enough for him to feel his own reaction. Pain clamped at his stomach, and the muscles of his lower back screamed protest at the posture he had been frozen in for long hours of extra gravity.

He raised his hand to his mouth and extended the little finger back to the rear molars. Precisely machined surfaces slipped into nanospaced fittings in the vat-cultured substitute that had been serving him as a fingernail; anything else would have wiped the coded data. He took a deep breath and pulled; there was a flash of pain before the embedded duller drugs kicked in, and then it settled to a tearing ache. The raw surface of the stripped finger was before him, the wrist clenched in the opposite hand. Ingrid moved forward swiftly to bandage it, and he spat the translucent oblong into his palm.

"Tanj," he said resentfully. *Those sadistic flatlander morons could have used a nervepinch.*

Ingrid picked the biochip up between thumb and forefinger. She licked her lips nervously. "Will it work?"

"It's supposed to." The sound of his own pulse in his ears was louder than the background noise the kzin used to fool their subconscious into comfort. Pain receded, irrelevant, as he looked at the tiny oblong of modified claw. Scores of highly skilled men and women, thousands of hours of computer time on machines whose pricetags ran into the billions of stars, all for this. No, for the *information* contained in this . . . nearly as much information as was required to make a complete human body; it was amazing what they could do these days with quantum-well storage. Although the complete specs for a man were in a packet considerably smaller, if it came to that.

"Give it here." *It ought to be quick. Milliseconds quick. A lot better than being hunted down by the ratcats, if we can blow the defenses.* Vaporization was the commonest way for a space-soldier to die, anyway.

She handed over the nail, and he slipped it into his own interface unit. "As your boyfriend likes to say, here's viewing, *kinder.*"

She nodded tightly. He raised a thumb, pressed it down on one of the outlined squares of the schematic that occupied his interfacer.

"Ram dam," he said. The words came from nowhere, until an eerie memory of old Mukeriji speaking flitted through his mind. That had been as they closed on the kzinti ship, coming in to board before they could blow the self-destruct bomb. *Dreadful Bride, spare us: ram dam ram dam ram dam ram—*

The walls pulsed, flickered green, flashed into an intricate strobing pattern and froze. Jonah closed his eyes for a second and felt an enormous thankfulness. They might still be only seconds away from death, but at least it wouldn't be for *nothing.*

"Finagle!" Jonah said bitterly. "How could even a kzin be this paranoid?"

He kicked the pillar-console; it hurt through the light slipper. There were weapons and self-destruct systems in plenty, enough to leave nothing but a very large crater with magma at its core where Chuut-Riit's palace-estate-preserve had stood . . . but it wasn't clear how *any* of them could be triggered from here.

"Who ever heard of . . . wheels within wheels!" Jonah said disbelievingly. "Am I imagining things, or are these systems completely separate?"

Ingrid shook her head slowly. "I'm afraid that's a long way past me. Can't you do anything about it?"

"Complain to the manufacturer . . . oh, maybe. There's a chance. Worth a try, anyway."

He touched icons on the screen surface, then tapped in new commands. "Nope. All right, what does this do? Nothing. Hmmm. But if— Yeah, this may work. Not immediately, though. You about through?"

"Hours ago. We don't have much longer."

"Right. I do want to look at a couple of things, though." Jonah's eyes narrowed. "Call," he said to the computer. "Weekly schedule for user-CR, regression, six months, common elements."

His finger flicked out to a sequence on the wall ahead of them. "Got it! Got it, by Murphy's asshole; that's the single common element outside going to his office? What is it?"

Ingrid's fingers were busy. "No joy, Jonah. That's his visit to his kiddies. The males, weanlings up to subadult, they're in an isolation facility."

"Oh. Bat puckey. Here, let me look—"

A warning light blazed on the console.

"They're coming," Ingrid hissed. "Hurry."

"Right. Plan B. Only—" Jonah stared at the files in wonder. "I will be dipped in shit. This *will* work."

☆ ☆ ☆

"We have positive identification," Axelrod-Bauergartner said. The staff conference rustled, ten men and women grouped around a table of black ebony. It was an elegant room, walls of white stone fretwork and floor of tile, a sideboard with refreshments. No sound but the gentle rush of water in the courtyard outside; this had been the Herrenhaus, the legislature, before the kzin came.

Montferrat leaned forward slightly, looking down the table to his second in command. How alike we all are, he thought. Not physical appearance, but something about the eyes . . . She was a pallid woman, with a beginning potbelly disgusting on someone her age, hair cropped close on the left and in a braided ponytail on the other.

"Oh?" he drawled. It was important to crack this case and quickly, Supervisor-of-Animals was on his track. Unwise to have a subordinate take too much credit for it—particularly this one; she had been using her own dossier files to build influence in the higher echelons of human government. *Two can play at that game,* he thought. *And I do it better, since relying on blackmail alone is a crudity I've grown beyond. She doesn't know I've penetrated her files, either . . . of course, she may be doing likewise . . .*

No. He would be dead if she had.

"From their hotel room. No correlation on fingerprints, of course." Alterations to fingerprints and retina patterns were an old story; you never caught anyone that way who had access to underworld tailoring shops. "But they evidently whiled away their spare time with the old in-and-out, and they don't clean the mattresses there very well. DNA analysis.

"Case A, display," she continued. Sections of the ebony before each of the staff officers turned transparent, a molecular analysis. "This is the male, what forensics could make of it. Young, not more than thirty. Sol-Belter, to ninety-three percent: Here's a graphic of his face, projection from the genes and descriptions by hotel staff."

A portrait overlaid the lines and curves of the analysis, a hard-lined blocky face with a short Belter strip. "This doesn't include any scars or birthmarks, of course."

"Very interesting," Montferrat drawled. "But as you're no doubt aware, chance recombination could easily reproduce a Sol-Belter genetic profile; the Serpent Swarm was only colonized three centuries ago, and there has been immigration since. Our records from the Belt are not complete; you know the trouble we've been having getting them to tighten up on registration."

Axelrod-Bauergartner shook her head, smiling thinly. "Less than a three percent chance, when you correlate with the probability of that configuration, then eliminate the high percentage of Swarmers we do have full records on. Beautiful job on the false idents, by the way. If we hadn't been tipped, we'd never have found them.

"And this," she said, calling up another analysis, "is the female. Also young, ten years post-maturity, and a Swarmer for sure. No contemporary record."

Montferrat raised a brow and lit his cigarette, looking indifferently down at the abstract. "We'll have to pick them both up on suspicion," he said, "and ream their memories. But I'd scarcely call this a positive ID; nothing I'd like to go to the kzin with, for certain." A pause, a delicate smile. "Of course, if you'd like to take the responsibility yourself . . ."

"I may just take you up on that . . . sir," Axelrod-Bauergartner said, and a cold bell began ringing at the back of Montferrat's mind. "You see, we did find a perfect correlate for the female's DNA pattern. Not in any census registry, but in an old research file at the Scholarium, a genetics survey. Pre-War. Dead data, but I had the central system do a universal sweep, damn the expense, and there were no locks on the data. Just stored out of the way . . ."

"This doesn't make sense," Grimbardsun said. He was Economic Regulation, older than Axelrod-Bauergartner and fatter; less ambitious, except for the bank account he was so excellently placed to feed. Complications with the kzin made him sweat, and there were dark patches under the armpits of his uniform tunic. "You said she was young."

"Biological," Axelrod-Bauergartner said triumphantly. "The

forensics people counted how many ticks she had on her biological clock. But the Scholarium file records her as . . ."

A picture flashed across the data, and Montferrat coughed to hide his reaction. Grateful for the beard and the tan, that hid the cold waxy pallor of his skin, as the capillaries shrank and sent the blood back to the veins and heart, that felt as if a huge hand had locked them fast.

"Ingrid Raines," Axelrod-Bauergartner said. "Chronological age, better than sixty. Qualified pilot and software wizard, and a possible alternate slotter on one of the slowboats that was launched just before the end."

"I was a possible alternate myself, if I hadn't been taken prisoner," Montferrat said, and even then felt a slight pleasure at Axelrod-Bauergartner's wince. She hadn't been born then, and it was a reminder that at least he had fought the kzin once, not spent his adolescence scheming to enter their service. "There were thousands of us, and most didn't make it anywhere near the collection points. It was all pretty chaotic, toward the end." His hand did not tremble as he laid the cigarette in the ashtray, and his eyes were not fixed on the oval face with its long Belter strip that turned into an auburn fountain at the back.

"Which was why the ordinary student files were lost," Axelrod-Bauergartner said, nodding so that her incipient jowls swayed. "Yah. All we got from the genetics survey was a name and a student number than doesn't correlate to anything existing. But the DNA's a one-to-one, no doubt about it at all. Raines went out on that slowboat, and somehow Raines came back, still young."

Still young, Montferrat thought. *Still young . . . and I sit here, my soul older than Satan's.* "Came back. Dropped off from a ship going point-nine lightspeed?" he scoffed.

A shrug. "The genes don't lie."

"Computer," Montferrat said steadily. "All points, maximum priority. Pictures and idents to be distributed to all sources. Capture alive at all costs; we need the information they have."

To his second. "My congratulations, Herrenfrau Axelrod-Bauergartner, on a job well done. We'll catch these revenants, and when we do all the summer soldiers who've been flocking to those Resistance idiots since the attack will feel a distinct chill. I think that's all for today?"

They rose with the usual round of handshakes, Grimbardsun's hand wet, Axelrod-Bauergartner's soft and cold as her eyes.

Montferrat felt someone smiling with his face, talking with his mouth, impeccably, until he was in the privacy of his office, and staring down at the holo in his desk. Matching it with the one from his locked and sealed files, matching the reality with forensics' projection. Feeling the moisture spilling from his eyes, down onto the imperishable synthetic, onto the face he had seen with the eye of the mind every day for the last forty years. The face he would arrest and turn over to the interrogators and the kzin, along with the last of his soul.

"Why did you come back?" he whispered. "Why did you come back, to torment us here in hell?"

☆ ☆ ☆

"Right, now download," Jonah said. The interfacer bleeped quietly and opened to extrude the biochip.

"Well, *this* ought to be useful, if we can get the information back," Ingrid said dully, handing him the piece of curved transparent quasi-tissue.

He unwrapped his hand gingerly and slid the fingernail home, into the implanted flexible gasket beneath the cuticle. "Provided we can get ourselves, this or a datalink to the *Catskinner,*" he said, wincing slightly. Useful was an understatement; intelligence-gathering was not the primary job for which they had been tasked, but this was priceless load. The complete specs on the most important infosystem on Wunderland, and strategic sampling of the data in its banks. Ships, deployments, capacities. Kzin psychology and history and politics, command-profiles, strategic planning and *kriegspiel* played by the pussy General Staff for decades. All the back doors, from the human systems, then, through them, into the kzin system. UN Naval Intelligence would willingly sacrifice half a fleet for this. . . .

"That's it, then," Jonah said. "It's not what we came for, but it can make a difference. And there—"

Ingrid was not listening. "Hold on! Look!"

"Eh?"

"An alert subroutine! Gottdamn, that is an alert! Murphy, it's about us, those are our cover-idents it's broadcasting. We're blown."

"Block it, quick." They worked in silence for a moment. Jonah scrubbed a hand across his face. "That'll hold it for a half-hour."

"Never make it back to Munchen before the next call gets through," she said. "Not without putting up a holosign that this system's been subverted down to the config."

"We don't have to," Jonah said. He squeezed eyes shut, pressed his fingers to his forehead. "Finagle, why now . . . ? The aircar shuttle. Computer," he continued. "Is the civilian system still online? Slaved to the core-system here?"

"Affirmative, to both."

"That's it, then. We just get on the ten-minute flight. Right. Key the internal link to that one. Code, full-wipe after execution, purge. Ingrid, let's go."

☆ ☆ ☆

"Is the system compromised?" Chuut-Riit asked, looking around the central control room of his estate. His nostrils flared: yes, the scent of two of the monkeys, a male and . . . He snuffled further. Yes, the female was bearing. Grimly, he filed the smell away, for possible future reference. It was unlikely that he would ever encounter either of them in person, but one could hope.

One of the kzin technicians was so involved with following the symbols scrolling by on the walls that he swept his hand behind him with claws extended in an exasperated protest at being interrupted. The governor bristled and then relaxed; it helped that he came from the hunt, had killed and fed well, mated and washed his glands and tissues clear of hormones, freeing the reasoning brain. Even more that he had spent the most of his lifespan cooling a temper that had originally been hasty even by kzin standards. He controlled breath and motion as the Conservors had taught him, the desire to lash his tail and pace. It ran through him that perhaps it was his temper that had set him on the road to mastery, that never-to-be-forgotten moment in the nursery so many years ago: the realization that his rage could kill, and in time would kill *him* as dead as the sibling beneath his claws.

The guards behind him had snarled at the infotech's insolence, a low subliminal rumbling and the dry-spicy scent of anger. An expressive ripple of Chuut-Riit's fur, ears, tail quieted them.

"These specialists are all mad," he whispered aside. "One must humor them, like a cub that bites your ears." They were sorry specimens, in truth: one scrubby and undersized, with knots in his fur, the other a giant but clumsy, slow, actually *fat*. Any Hero seeing them would know their brilliance, since such disgusting examples of bad inheritance would only be kept alive for the most pressing of needs.

The governor schooled himself to wait, shifting only enough

to keep his heated muscles from stiffening. The big technician mumbled to himself, occasionally taking out a brick of dull-red dried meat from his equipment apron and stuffing it into his mouth. Chuut-Riit caught a whiff of it and gagged, as much at the thought of someone eating infantry rations for *pleasure* as at the well-remembered smell. The other one muttered as well, but he chewed on the ends of his claws. Those on his right hand were actually frayed at the tips, useless for anything but scratching its doubtless completely ungroomed and verminous pelt.

"Is the system compromised?" Chuut-Riit said again, patiently. Infosystems specialists were as bad as telepaths.

"Hrrwweo?" muttered the small one, blinking back to a consciousness somewhat more in congruence with the others'. "Well, we couldn't know that, could we?—Chuut-Riit," he added hastily, as he noticed the governor's expression and scent.

"What—do—you—mean?" he said.

"Well, Chuut-Riit, a successful clandestine insertion is undetectable by definition, hrrrrr? We're *pretty sure* we've found their tracks. Computer, isolate-alpha, linear schematic, level three." A complex webbing sprang up all around the room, blue lines with a few sections picked out in green. "See, Dominant One, where the picks were inserted? So that the config elements could be accessed and altered from an external source without detection. We've neutralized them, of course."

The claws went back into his mouth, and he mumbled around them. "This was humans, wasn't it? It has their scent. Very three-dimensional; I suppose it comes of their being monkeys. They do some wonderful gaming programs, very ingeniou— I abase myself in apology, Chuut-Riit." He flattened to the ground and covered his dry granular-looking nose. "We are as sure as we can be that all the unauthorized elements have been purged." To his companion: "Wake up, suckling!"

"Whirrrr?" the fat giant chirruped, stopped his continuous nervous purring and then started. "Oh, yes. Lovely system you have here, Chuut-Riit. Yes, I think we've got it. I would like to meet the monkeys who did the alterations, very subtle work."

"You may go," he said, and crouched brooding, scratching moodily behind one ear. The internal-security team was in now, with the sniffer-machines to isolate the scent molecules of the intruders.

"I would like to meet them too," he said, and a line of saliva spun itself down from one thin black lip. He snapped it back with a wet *chop* and licked his nose with a broad wash of pink tongue. "I would like that very much."

Chapter 6

"Somehow I think it's *too* quiet," Ingrid said. When Jonah cast a blankly puzzled look over his shoulder, she shrugged. "Aren't you interested in *anything* cultural?"

"I'm interested in staying alive," Jonah said.

They were strolling quietly down one of the riverside walks. The Donau rolled beside them, two kilometers across; it sparkled blue and green-gray, little waves showing white. A bridge soared from bank to bank, and sailboats heeled far over under the stiff warm breeze. Away from the shrilling poverty of the residential quarters, the air smelled of silty water, grass, flowers.

"Of course, staying alive from now on jeopardizes the mission," Jonah continued.

"No." Ingrid shook her head. "You have to get back."

"I do? Why?"

"You just do." *Murphy's balls! Those ARM psychists really do know their stuff. He's forgotten already. What have I forgotten? It's no fun, holes in your memory. Even if they're deliberate.*

"The plan doesn't matter," Jonah said. "If it were going to blow, it would have done it. And we'd have heard the bang." Something itched at the back of his mind. "Unless—"

"Jonah?"

"Nothing." *I don't want to remember. Or maybe there's nothing to remember.* "My hand hurts. Wonder what I did to it?"

"You don't need to know that, either." It was the tenth time he'd asked. Clearly the psychists had done some powerful voodoo on Jonah.

After the war, I'm getting out of Sol system. The more I learn about the ARM, the more they look nearly *as bad as the kzin. Maybe I should write a book exposing them or something.*

It was odd that there was so little resentment of them, back among the flatlanders—even the Sol-Belters didn't kick up much of a fuss anymore. Or, considering Jonah's present state, maybe not so odd. She shivered and put it out of her mind; time enough for that later, if she lived.

They hailed a pedicab and climbed into the twin-passenger back seat. They had both been surprised to see the little vehicles skittering about the streets; surely machinery could not have become *that* expensive. The man hunched over the pedals was thin, all wire and leather, dressed only in a pair of ragged shorts. It was not that machines were so dear, but that labor was so cheap, labor of a certain kind. For those with skills needed by the kzinti war economy, there was enough capital to support reasonable productivity. For the increasing number of those without, there was only what unaided brute labor would buy: starvation wages.

Get your mind off the troubles of Wunderland and on to the more urgent matter of saving your own ass, she told herself as they turned into the Baha'i quarter. Back to Harold's Terran Bar . . . She winced. Then out to the Swarm; the *Catskinner* would be waiting, and Markham would simply have to accept them; that was one of the virtues of a ship with a will of its own. Then a straight boost out of the system; a Dart usually didn't have anything approaching interstellar capacity, but the stasis field changed things. Boost out, tightbeam the precious data, and wait for the fleet to scoop them up. Nothing could affect them within a stasis field, but the field as a whole could still be manipulated with a gravity-polarizer . . .

The chances of coming through this with a whole skin had seemed so remote that it wasn't even worth the trouble of thinking about. Now . . .

The ship will hold three. Hari, this time I won't leave you.

They turned into the street that fronted Harold's Terran Bar. Ingrid had just time enough to see the owner standing beside Claude at the entrance. The police vomited forth, dark in their turtle helmets and goggles, and aircars rose silently over the roofs all about. Giant ginger-red shapes behind them—

She rolled out of her side of the pedicab as Jonah did on his, a motion so smooth they might have rehearsed it. The light-pen was in her hand, and it made its yawping sound. A policeman died, dropping like a puppet with the strings cut, and she dove forward, rolling, trying for an angle at the kzin and—

Blackness.

☆ ☆ ☆

"The interrogation is complete?" Chuut-Riit reclined again at ease on the bubblecouch behind his desk; a censer was sending up aromatic smoke.

The holo on the far wall showed a room beneath the Munchen police headquarters; a combination of human and kzin talents had long proven most effective for such work. Ktiir-Supervisor-of-Animals was there, and a shabby-looking Telepath. The mind-reader's fur was matted and his hands twitched; Chuut-Riit could see spatters of vomit down the front of his pelt, and hear his mumble:

" . . . salad, no, no, ak, ak, pftht, no please *boiled carrots* ak, pfffth . . ."

He shuddered slightly in sympathy, thinking of what it must be like to enter the mind of a human free-associating under drugs and pain. Telepathy was not like speech, it was a sharing that extended to sensations and memory as well. Food was a very fundamental drive. It would be bad enough to have to share the memory of eating the cremated meats humans were fond of—the very stink of them was enough to turn your stomach—but cooked plants . . . Telepath fumbled something out of a wrist-pouch and carefully parted the fur on one side of his neck before pressing it to the skin. There was a hiss, and he sank against the wall with a sigh of relief. His eyes slitted and he leaned chin on knees with a high-pitched irregular purr, the tip of his tongue showing pink past his whiskers.

Chuut-Riit wrinkled his nose and dismissed false compassion. How could you sympathize with something that was a voluntary slave to a drug? And to an extract of sthondat blood at that.

"Yes, Chuut-Riit," Ktiir-Supervisor-of-Animals said.

"Telepath's reading agrees with what the trained monkeys determined with their truth drugs." Chuut-Riit reminded himself that the drugs actually merely suppressed inhibition. "The attempt was a last-minute afterthought to the main attack of the monkey ship last month. Some gravitic device was used to decelerate a pod with these two; they came down in a remote area, using the disturbances of the attack as cover, and reached the city on foot. Their aim was to trigger the self-destruct mechanisms on your estate, but they were unable to do so."

Chuut-Riit brooded, looking past the kzin liaison officer to the human behind him. "You are not the human in charge of the Munchen police," he said.

"No, Chuut-Riit," the human said. It was a female. A flabby one, the sort that would squish unpleasantly when your fangs ripped open the body cavity, and somehow the holo gave the impression of an unpleasant odor.

"I am Chief Assistant Axelrod-Bauergartner at your service, Dominant One," she continued, giving the title in a reasonably good approximation of the Hero's Tongue. A little insolent? Perhaps—but also commendable, and the deferential posture was faultless. "Chief Montferrat-Palme delegated this summary of the investigation, feeling that it was not important enough to warrant his personal attention."

"Chrrrriii," Chuut-Riit said, scratching one cheek against a piece of driftwood in a stand on his desk. This Montferrat-creature did not consider an attack on the governor's private control system important? That monkey was developing a distorted sense of its priorities. The human in the screen had blanched slightly at the kzin equivalent of an irritated scowl; he let his lips lower back over the fangs and continued:

"Show me the subjects." Axelrod-Bauergartner stepped aside, to show two humans clamped in adjustable plastic brackets amid a forest of equipment. These were two fine specimens, tall and lean in the manner of the space-bred subspecies; both unconscious, but seeming healthy enough apart from the usual superficial cuts, abrasions, and bruises. "What is their condition?"

"No irreparable physical or mental harm, Chuut-Riit," Axelrod-Bauergartner said, bowing. "What are your orders as to their disposal?"

"Rrrrr," Chuut-Riit mused, shifting to rub the underside of his jaw on the wood. The last public hunt had been yesterday, the one to which he had taken his sons. "How soon can they be in condition to run amusingly?" he said.

"Half a week, Chuut-Riit. We have been cautious."

"Prepare them." His sons? No, best not to be too indulgent. There was a badsmelling lot of administrative work to be attended to; he would be chained to his desk for a goodly while anyway. Let the little devils attend to their studies, and he would visit them again when this had been disposed of. Besides, while free there had been a certain attraction in the prospect of dealing with this pair personally; as captives they were just two more specimens of monkeymeat—beneath his dignity.

"Get a good batch together, and have them all ready for the Public Preserve at the end of the week. Dismissed."

☆ ☆ ☆

"Was that Suuomalisen I saw coming out of here?" Montferrat said.

"Unless you know another fat, sweaty toad in a linen suit looking like he'd just swallowed the juiciest fly on the planet." Yarthkin grinned like a shark as he settled behind his desk and pushed a pile of data chips and hardcopy to one side. "Sit yourself down, Claude, and have a drink. If it isn't too early."

"Fifteen hundred too early? That's in bad taste, even for you." But the hand that reached for the Maivin shook slightly, and there were wrinkles in the tunic. "But why was he so happy?"

"I just sold him Harold's Terran Bar," Yarthkin said calmly. Light-headed, he laughed, a boy's laugh. "Prosit!" he toasted, and tossed back his own drink.

"What!" That was enough to bring him bolt-upright. "Why—what—you've been turning that swine down for thirty years!"

"Swine, Claude?" Yarthkin leaned forward, resting his chin on paired thumbs. "Or have you forgotten exactly who's to be monkeymeat day after tomorrow?"

The reaction was more than Yarthkin had expected. A jerk, as if a high-voltage current surged through the other man's body. A dry retching sound. Then, incredibly, the aquiline Herrenmann's face crumpled. As if it were a mask, slumping and wrinkling like a balloon from which the air has been withdrawn . . . and he was crying, head slumping down into his hands. Yarthkin swallowed and looked away; Claude was a collabo and a sellout, an extortionist without shame . . . but nobody should see another man this naked. It was obscene.

"Pull yourself together, Claude; I've known you were a bastard for forty years, but I thought you were a man, at least."

"So did I," gasped Montferrat. "I even have the medals to prove it. I fought well in the war."

"I know."

"So when, when they let us out of the detention camp, I really thought I could help. I really did." He laughed. "Life had to go on, criminals had to be caught, we were beaten and resistance just made it harder on everyone. I'd been a good policeman. I still could be."

He drank, choked, drank. "The graft, everyone had to. They wouldn't let you get past foot-patrol if you weren't on the pad too, you had to be in it with them. If I didn't get promotion how could I accomplish anything? I told myself that, but every year a little more of me was gone. And now, now Ingrid's back and I can see myself in her eyes and I know what I am, no better than that animal Axelrod-Bauergartner, she's gloating, she has me on this and I couldn't, couldn't *do* it. I told her to take care of it all and went and I've been drunk most of the time since, she'll have my head and I deserve it, why try and stop her, it—"

Yarthkin leaned forward and slapped the policeman alongside the head with his open palm, a gunshot crack in the narrow confines of the office. Montferrat's mood switched with mercurial swiftness, and he snarled with a mindless sound as he reached for his sidearm. But alcohol is a depressant, and his hand had barely touched the butt before the other man's stunner was pointed between his eyes.

"Neyn, neyn, naughty," Yarthkin said cheerfully. "Hell of a headache, Claude. Now, I won't say you don't deserve it, but sacrificing your own liver and lights isn't going to do Ingrid any good." He kept the weapon unwavering until Montferrat had won back a measure of self-command, then laid it down on the desk and offered a cigarette.

"My apologies," Montferrat said, wiping off his face with a silk handkerchief. "I do despise self-pity." The shredded cloak of his ironic detachment settled about him.

Yarthkin nodded. "That's better, sweetheart. I'm selling the club because I need ready capital, for relocation. Grubstaking my people, the ones who don't want to come with me or stay here."

"Go with you? Where? And what does this have to do with Ingrid?"

Yarthkin grinned again, tapped ash off the end of his cigarette. Exhilaration filled him, and something that had been missing for far too long. *What?* he thought. *Not youth . . . yes, that's it. Purpose.*

"It isn't every man who's given a chance to do it over right," he said. "That, friend Claude, is what I'm going to do. We're going to bust Ingrid out of that Preserve. Give her a chance at it, at least." He held up a hand. "Don't fuck with me, Claude, I know as well as you that the system there is managed through Munchen Police HQ. One badly mangled corpse substituted for another, what ratcat's to know? It's been done before."

"Not by me," Montferrat said, shaking his head dully. "I always kept out of the setup side of the Hunts. Couldn't . . . I have to watch them, anyway, too often."

Odd how men cling to despair, once they've hit bottom, Yarthkin thought. *As if hope were too much effort. Is that what surrender is, then, just giving in to exhaustion of the soul?*

Aloud: "Computer, access file *Till Eulenspiegel."*

The surface of his desk flashed transparent and lit with a series of coded text-columns. Montferrat came erect with a shaken oath.

"How . . . if you had that, all these years, why haven't you used it?"

"Claude, the great drawback of blackmail is that it gives the victim the best possible incentive to find a permanent way of shutting you up. Risky, especially when dealing with the police. As to the how, you're not under the impression that you get the best people in the police, are you?" A squint, and the gravelly voice went soft. "Don't think I wouldn't use it, sweetheart, if you won't cooperate, and there's *more* than enough to put you in the edible-delicacy category. Think of it as God's way of giving you an incentive to get back on the straight and narrow."

"I tell you, Axelrod-Bauergartner has the command codes for the Preserve! I can override, but it would be flagged. Immediately."

"Computer, display file *Niebelungen AA37Bi22.* Damned lack of imagination, that code . . . There it is, Claude. Everything you always wanted to know about your most ambitious subordinate but were afraid to ask, including her private bypass programs." Another flick of ash. "Finagle, Claude, you can probably make all this look like her fault, even if the ratcat smells the proverbial rodent."

Montferrat smoothed down his uniform tunic, and it was as if the gesture slicked transparent armor across his skin once more. "You appear to have me by the short and sensitives, *kamerat,*" he said lightly. "Not entirely to my dismay. The plan is, then, that Ingrid and her gallant Sol-Belter are whisked away from under the noses of the kzin, while you go to ground?"

Yarthkin laughed, a shocking sound. "Appearances to the contrary, Claude old son, *you* were always the romantic of us two. The one for the noble gesture. Nothing of the sort: *Ingrid and I* are going to the Swarm."

"And the man, Jonah?"

"Fuck him. Let the ratcats have him. His job was done the minute they failed to dig the real story out of him."

Montferrat managed a laugh. "This is quite a reversal of roles, Hari . . . but this, this final twist, it makes it seem possible, somehow." He extended a hand. "Seeing as you have the gun to my head, why not? Working together again, eh?"

☆ ☆ ☆

"All right, listen up," the guard said.

Jonah shook his head, shook out the last of the fog. Ingrid sat beside him on the plain slatted wood of the bench, in this incongruous pen—change-rooms for a country club, once. Now a set of run-down stone buildings in the midst of shaggy overgrown wilderness, with the side open to the remnants of lawn and terrace covered with a shockfield. He looked around; there were a round two dozen humans with them, all clad alike in gray prison trousers and shirts. All quiet. The shockrods of the guards had enforced that. Some weeping, a few catatonic, and there was an unpleasant fecal smell.

"You get an hour's start," the guard said, in a voice of bored routine. "And you'd better run, believe me."

"Up yours!" somebody shouted, and laughed when the guard raised her rod. "What you going to do, ratcat-lover, condemn me to death?"

The guard shrugged. "You ever seen a house cat playing with a mumbly?" she jeered. "The ratcats like a good chase. Disappoint them and they'll bat you around like a toy." She stepped back, and the door opened. "Hell, keep ahead of them for two days and maybe they'll let you go." A burly man rose and charged, bounced back as she took another step through the door.

Laughter, through the transparent surface. "Have fun, porkchops. I'll watch you die. Five minutes to shield-down."

"You all right?" Jonah asked. Neither of them had been much damaged physically by the interrogation; it had been done in a police headquarters, where the most modern methods were available, not crude field-expedients. And the psychists' shields had worked perfectly; the great weakness of telepathic interrogation is that it can only detect what the subject *believes* to be true. It had been debatable whether the blocks and artificial memories would hold. . . . Kzin telepaths hated staying in a human's mind more than they had to, and the drug addiction that helped to develop their talents did little for motivation or intelligence.

"Fine," Ingrid said, raising her head from her knees. "Just thinking how pretty it is out there," she continued; tears starred her lashes, but her voice was steady.

Startled, he looked again through the near-invisible shimmer of the shockfield. The long green-gold grass was rippling under a late-afternoon sun, starred with flowers like living jewel-flecks; a line of flamingos skimmed by, down to the little pond at the base of the hill. Beyond was forest, flowering dogwood in a fountain of white against the flickering-shiny olive drab of native kampfwald trees. The shockfield let slow-moving air through, carrying scents of leaf mold, green, purity.

"You're right," he said. They clasped hands, embraced, stepped back and saluted each other formally. "It's been . . . good knowing you, Lieutenant Ingrid."

"Likewise, Captain Jonah." A gamin smile. "Finagle's arse, we're not dead yet, are we?"

"Huh. Hun-huh." Lights spun before Jonah's eyes, wrenching his stomach with more nausea. Gummy saliva blocked his mouth as he tumbled over the lip of the gully, crashing through brush that ripped and tore with living fingers of thorn and bramble. Tumble, roll, down through the brush-covered sixty-degree slope, out into the patch of gravel and sparse spaghetti-like grass analog at the bottom. To lie and rest, Murphy, to rest . . .

Memories were returning. Evidently his subconscious believed there wouldn't be another interrogation. Believed they were dead already. *My fingernail. I have to escape. And there's a laugh . . . but I have to try.*

He turned the final roll into a flip and came erect, facing in the direction of his flight; forced his diaphragm to breathe, stomach out to suck air into the bottom of the lungs. His chest felt tight and hot, as if the air pumping through it was nothing, vacuum, inert gas. Will kept him steady, blinked his eyes into focus. He was in a patch of bright sunlight, the forest above deep green-gold shade that flickered; the soil under his feet was damp, impossibly cool on his skin. The wind was blowing toward him, which meant that the kzin would be following ground-scent rather than what floated on the breeze. Kzin noses were not nearly as sensitive as a hound's, but several thousand times more acute than a human's.

And I must stink to high heaven, he thought. Even then he could smell himself; he hawked and spat, taking a firmer grip on his improvised weapon. That was a length of branch and a rock half the size of his head, dangling from the end by thin strong vines; thank Murphy that Wunderland flora ran to creepers . . .

"One," he muttered to himself. "There ain't no justice, I know, but please, just let me get *one.*" His breathing was slowing, and he became conscious of thirst, then the gnawing emptiness under his ribs. The sun was high overhead; nearly a day already? How many of the others were still alive?

A flicker of movement at the lip of the ravine, ten meters above him and twenty away. Jonah swung the stone-age morningstar around his head and roared. And the kzin halted its headlong four-footed rush, rose like an unfolding wall of brown-red dappled in the light at the edge of the tall trees, and slashed across with the white of teeth. Great round eyes, and he could imagine the pupils going pinpoint; the kzin homeworld was not only colder than Wunderland, it was dimmer. Batwing ears unfolding, straining for sound. He would have to stop that, their hearing was keen enough to pick a human heartbeat out of the background noise. This was a young male, he would be hot, hot for the kill and salt blood to quench his thirst and let him rest . . .

"Come on, you *kshat,* you sthondat-eater," Jonah yelled in the snarling tones of the Hero's Tongue. "Come and get your Name, kinless offspring of cowards, come and eat turnips out of my shit, grass-grazer! *Ch'rowl* you!"

The kzin screamed, a raw wailing shriek that echoed down the ravine; screamed again and leaped in an impossible soaring curve that took it halfway down the steep slope.

"Now, Ingrid. Now!" Jonah shouted, and ran forward.

The woman rose from the last, thicker scrub at the edge of the slope, where water nourished taller bushes. Rose just as the second bounding leap passed its arc, the kzin spread-eagled against the sky, taloned hands outstretched to grasp and tear. The three-meter pole rose with her, butt against the earth, sharpened tip reaching for the alien's belly. It struck, and the wet ripping sound was audible even over the berserk siren shriek of the young kzin's pain.

It toppled forward and sideways, thrashing and ululating with the long pole transfixing it. Down onto Ingrid's position, and he forced rubbery leg muscles into a final sprint, a leap and scream of his own. Then he was there, in among the clinging brush and it was there too, convulsing. He darted in, swung, and the rock smashed into a hand that was lashing for his throat; the kzin wailed again, put its free hand to the spear, *pulled* while it kept him at bay with lunging snaps. Ingrid was on the other side with a second spear, jabbing; he danced in, heedless of the fangs, and swung two-handed. The rock landed at the juncture of thick neck and sloping shoulder, and something snapped. The shock of it ran back up his arms.

The pair moved in, stabbing, smashing, block and wriggle and jump and strike, and the broken alien crawled toward them with inhuman vitality, growling and whimpering and moving even with the dull-pink bulge of intestine showing where it had ripped the jagged wood out of its flesh. Fur, flesh, scraps of leaf, dust scattering about . . . Until at last too many bones were broken and too much of the dark-red blood spilled, and it lay twitching. The humans lay just out of reach, sobbing back their breaths; Jonah could hear the kzin's cries over the thunder in his ears, hear them turn to high-pitched words in the Hero's Tongue:

"It hurts . . ." The Sol-Belter rolled to his knees. His shadow fell across the battered, swollen eyes of his enemy. "It hurts . . . Mother, you've come back, Mother—" The shattered paw-hands made kneading motions. "Help me, take away the noise in my head, Mother . . ." Presently it died.

"That's one for a pallbearer." The end of his finger throbbed. "Goddamn it, I can't escape!"

Ingrid tried to rise, fell back with a faint cry. Jonah was at her side, hands moving on the ruffled tatters that streaked down one thigh.

"How bad . . . ?" He pushed back the ruined cloth. Blood was runneling down the slim length of the woman's leg, not pumping but in a steady flow. "Damn, tanj, tanj, tanj!" He ripped at his shirt for a pressure-bandage, tied it on with the thin vines scattered everywhere about. "Here, here's your spear, lean on it, come *on.*" He darted back to the body; there was a knife at its belt, a long heavy-bladed *wtsai.* Jonah ripped it free, looped the belt over one shoulder like a baldric.

"Let's move," he said, staggering slightly. She leaned on the spear hard enough to drive the blunt end inches deep into the sandy gravel, and shook her head.

"No, I'd slow you down. You're the one who has to get away. Get going."

His finger throbbed anew to remind him. *And she's Hari's girl, not mine. But—* Another memory returned, and he laughed.

"Something's funny?"

"Yeah, maybe it is! Maybe—hell, I bet it worked!"

"What worked?"

"Tell you on the way."

"No, you won't. I'm not coming with you. Now get going!"

"Murphy bugger that with a diode, Lieutenant, get moving, that's an *order.*"

She put an arm around his shoulder and they hobbled down the shifting footing of the ravine's bed. There was a crooked smile on her face as she spoke.

"Well, it's not as if we had anywhere to go, is it?"

☆ ☆ ☆

The kzin governor of Wunderland paced tiredly toward the gate of his children's quarters, grooming absently. The hunt had gone well; the intruder-humans were undoubtedly beginning a short passage through some lucky Hero's digestive system, and it was time to relax.

"Hrrrr," Traat-Admiral said beside him. "I still feel uneasy leaving the planetary surface while ambushers may lurk, Dominant One," he said.

Chuut-Riit stopped, and turned to face the other kzin. Traat-Admiral was a decade older than him, and several hands higher, but there was nothing but real worry and concern in his stance. The viceroy put both hands on Traat-Admiral's shoulders.

"No need for formalities between us," he said, and then added deliberately: "My brother."

Traat-Admiral froze, and there were gasps from some of the others within hearing. That was a rare honor for a kzin not blood-related, overwhelmingly so considering the difference in hereditary rank. And a public avowal at that; Traat-Admiral licked his whiskers convulsively, deeply moved.

"You are my most trusted one," Chuut-Riit said. "Now that we know *some* human infiltrators were dropped off during the raid, that . . . thing of which we speculated becomes more than a theoretical possibility. Affairs are still in chaos here—the Fifth Fleet has been delayed half a decade or more—and I need someone *fully in my trust* to order the space-search."

"I will not fail you, Dom—Elder Brother," Traat-Admiral said fervently.

"Besides, the enemy humans here on Wunderland"—it was a long standing joke that the kzinti name for the planet meant *lovely hunting ground*—"have been disposed of. Go, and hunt well."

Perhaps I should have stayed to track them myself, he mused as he passed the last guard station with an absentminded wave. *No, why bother. That prey is already caught; this was simply a re-enactment.*

Chuut-Riit felt the repaired doors swing shut before him and glanced around in puzzlement, the silence penetrating through post-Hunt sluggishness. The courtyard was deserted, and it had been nearly seven days since his last visit; far too soon for another assassination attempt, but the older children should have been boiling out to greet him, questioning and frolicking . . . He turned and keyed the terminal in the stone beside the door.

Nothing. The kzin blinked in puzzlement. *Odd. There has been no record of any malfunction.* In instinctive reflex he lowered himself to all fours and sniffed; the usual sand-rock-metal scents, multiple young-kzin male smells, always slightly nerve-wracking. Something underneath that, and he licked his nose to moisten it and drew in a long breath with his mouth half open.

He started back, arching his spine and bristling with a growling hiss, tail rigid. *Dead meat and blood.* Whirling, he slapped for the exterior communicator. "Guard-Captain, respond. *Guard-Captain, respond immediately.*"

Nothing. He bent, tensed, leaped for the summit of the wall. A crackling discharge met him, a blue corona around the sharp twisted iron of the battlement's top that sent pain searing through the palms of his outstretched hands. The wards were set on maximum force, and he fell to the ground cradling his burned palms. Rage bit through him, stronger than pain or thought; someone had menaced his children, his future, the blood of the Riit. His snarl was soundless as he dashed on all fours across the open space of the courtyard and into the entrance of the warren.

It was dark, the glowpanels out and the ventilators silent; for the first time it even smelled like a castle on homeworld, purely of old stone, iron, and blood. Fresh blood on something near the entrance. He bent, the huge round circles of his eyes going black as the pupils expanded. A sword, a four-foot *kreera* with a double saw edge. The real article, heavy wave-forged steel, from the sealed training cabinets which should only have opened to his own touch. Ignoring the pain as burned tissue cracked and oozed fluids, he reached for the long hide-wound bone grip of the weapon. The edges of the blade glimmered with dark wet, set with a mat of orange-red hairs.

His arm bent, feeling the weight of the metal as he dropped into the crook-kneed defensive stance, with the lead ball of the pommel held level with his eyes. The corridor twisted off before him, the faint light of occasional skylights picking out the edges of granite blocks and the black iron doors with their central locks cast in the shape of beast-masked ancestral warriors. Chuut-Riit's ears cocked forward and his mouth opened, dropping the lower jaw toward the chest: maximum flow over the nasal passages to catch scent, and fangs ready to tear at anything that got past the weapon in his hands. He edged down the corridor one swift careful step at a time, heading for the central tower where he could do *something,* even if it was only lighting a signal fire.

Insane, he thought with a corner of his mind that watched his slinking progress through the dark halls. It *was* insane, like something from the ancient songs of homeworld. Like the *Siege of Zeeroau,* the Heroic Band manning the ramparts against the prophet, dwindling one by one from wounds and weariness and the hunger-frenzy that sent them down into the catacombs to hunt and then the dreadful feasting.

Chuut-Riit turned a corner and wheeled, blade up to meet a possible attack from the dropstand over the corner. Nothing, but the whirl-and-cut brought him flush against the opposite wall, and he padded on. Noise and smell; a thin mewling, and an overpowering stink of kzinmeat. A door, and the first body before it. There was little of the soft tissue left, but the face was intact. One of his older sons, the teeth frozen in an eternal snarl; blood was splashed about, far more than one body could account for. Walls, floor, ceiling, gouts and spattered trails that dripped down in slow congealing trails toward the floor. A *chugra* spear lay broken by the wall, alongside a battered metal shield; the sound had been coming from behind the door the corpse guarded, but now he could hear nothing.

No, wait. His ears folded out to their maximum. *Breathing.* A multiple rapid panting. He tried the door; it was unlocked, but something had it jammed closed.

A mewl sounded as he leaned his weight against it and the iron creaked. "Open!" he snarled. "Open at once."

More mewls, and a metallic tapping. The panel lurched inward, and he stooped to fill the doorway.

The infants, he thought. A heap in the far corner of the room, squirming spotted fur and huge terrified eyes peering back at him. The younger ones, the kits just recently taken from their mothers; at the sight of him they set up the thin *eeeuw-eeeuw-eeeuw* that was the kzin child's cry of distress.

"Daddy!" one of them said. "We're so hungry, Daddy. We're so frightened. He said we should stay in here and not open the door and not cry but there were awful noises and its been so long and we're *hungry,* Daddy, Daddy—"

Chuut-Riit uttered a grating sound deep in his chest and looked down. His son's *wtsai* had been wedged to hold the door from the inside; the kits must have done it at his instruction, while he went outside to face the hunters. Hunger-frenzy eroded what little patience an adolescent kzin possessed, as well as intellect; they would not spend long hammering at a closed door, not with fresh meat to hand and the smell of blood in their nostrils.

"Silence," he said, and they shrank back into a heap. Chuut-Riit forced gentleness into his voice. "Something very bad has happened," he said. "Your brother was right, you must stay here and make no noise. Soon I . . . soon I or another adult will come and feed you. Do you understand?" Uncertain nods. "Put the knife back in the door when I go out. Then *wait.* Understand?"

He swung the door shut and looked down into his son's face while the kits hammered the knifeblade under it from the inside.

"You did not die in vain, my brave one," he whispered, very low, settling into a crouch with the sword ready. "Kdari-Riit," he added, giving the dead a full Name. *Now I must wait.* Wait to be sure none of the gone-mad ones had heard him, then do his best. There would be an alert, eventually. The infants did not have the hormone-driven manic energy of adolescents. They would survive.

☆ ☆ ☆

"Zroght-Guard-Captain," the human said. "Oh, thank God!"

The head of the viceregal household troopers rose blinking from his sleeping-box, scratching vigorously behind one ear. "Yes, Henrietta?" he said.

"It's Chuut-Riit," she said. "Zroght-Guard-Captain, it wasn't him who refused to answer—I *knew* it and now we've found tampering; the technicians say they missed something the first time. We *still* can't get through to him in the children's quarters. *And the records say the armory's open and they haven't been fed for a week!*"

The guard-captain wasted no time in speech with the sobbing human; it would take enough time to physically breach the defenses of the children's quarters.

☆ ☆ ☆

"Hrrnnngg-ha," Chuut-Riit gasped, panting with lolling tongue. The corner of the exercise room had given him a little protection, the desks and machinery a little more. Now a dozen lanky bodies interlaced through the equipment about his feet, and the survivors had drawn back to the other end of the room. There was little sentience left in the eyes that peered at him out of the starved faces, not enough to use missile-weapons. Dim sunlight glinted on their teeth and the red gape of their mouths, on bellies fallen in below barrel-hoop ribs.

That last rush almost had me, he thought. An odd detachment had settled over him; with a sad pride he noticed the coordination of their movements even now, spreading out in a semicircle to bar the way to the doors. He was bleeding from a dozen superficial cuts, and the long sword felt like a bar of neutronium in his hands. The blade shone liquid-wet along its whole length now, and the hilt was slimy in his numb grip, slick with blood and the lymph from his burned hands; he twisted it in a whistling circle that flung droplets as far as the closing pack. Chuut-Riit threw back his head and shrieked, an eerie keening sound that filled the vaulted chamber. They checked for a moment; shrinking back. If he could keep them . . .

Movement at his feet, from the pile of bodies. Cold in his side, so cold, looking down at the hilt of the *wtsai* driven up into the lung, the overwhelming salt taste of his own blood. The one they called Spotty crawled free of the piled bodies, broken-backed but evading his weakened slash.

"Kill him," the adolescent panted. "Kill the betrayer, *kill him.*"

The waiting children shrieked and leapt.

☆ ☆ ☆

"He must have made his last stand here," Zroght-Guard-Captain said, looking around the nursery. The floor was a tumbled chaos of toys, wooden weapons, printout books; the walls still danced their holo gavotte of kits leaping amid grass and butterflies. There was very little of the kzin governor of the Alpha Centauri system left; a few of the major bones, and the skull, scattered among smaller fragments from his sons, the ones wounded in the fighting and unable to defend themselves from their ravenous brothers. The mom stank of blood and old meat.

"Zroght-Guard-Captain!" one of the troopers said. They all tensed, fully-armed as they were. Most of the young ones were still at large, equipped from the practice rooms, and they seemed ghostly clever.

"A message, Zroght-Guard-Captain." The warrior held up a pad of paper; the words were in a rusty brownish liquid, evidently written with a claw. Chuut-Riit's claw, that was his sigil at the bottom. The captain flipped up the visor of his helmet and read:

FORGIVE THEM

Zroght chirred. There might be time for that, after the succession struggle ended.

☆ ☆ ☆

"Gottdamn, they're out of range of the last pickup," Montferrat said.

Yarthkin grunted, careful to stay behind the policeman. The tubecar route was an old one, left here when this was a country club. The entrance was a secluded cleft in the rocky hill, and it appeared on no kzin records; its Herrenmann owners had felt no need to inform the municipal authorities of what they did, and had died in the war. His hand felt tight and clammy on the handle of the stunner, and every rustle and creak in the wilderness about them was a lurking kzin.

Teufel, I could use a smoke, he thought. Insane, of course, with ratcat noses coursing through the woods.

"Are they alive?" he asked tightly.

"The tracers are still active, but with this little interfacer I can't—*Ingrid!*"

He made a half-step forward. A pair of scarecrow figures stumbled past the entrance to the cleft, halted with a swaying motion that spoke of despair born of utter exhaustion. The man was scratched and bloodied; Yarthkin's eyes widened at the scraps of dried fur and blood and matter clinging to the rude weapon in his hand. Both of them were spattered with similar reminders, rank with the smell of it and the sweat that glistened in tracks through the dirt on their faces. More yet on the sharpened pole that Ingrid leaned on as a crutch, and fresh blood on the bandage at her thigh.

Jonah was straightening. "You here to help the pussies beat the bushes?" he panted. Ingrid looked up, blinked crusted eyes, moved closer to her companion. Yarthkin halted, speechless, shook his head.

"Actually, this is a mission of mercy," Montferrat began in his cool tone. Then words ripped out of him: "Gottdamn, there are two kzin coming up, I'm getting their tracers." Fingers played over his interfacer. "They're stopping about a kilometer back—"

"Where we left the body of the one we killed," Jonah said. His eyes met Yarthkin's levelly; the Wunderlander felt something lurch in the pit of his stomach at the dawning wonder in Ingrid's.

"Yah, mission of mercy, time to get on with it," he said, stepping forward and planting the projector cone of his stunner firmly in Montferrat's back. "Here."

He reached, took the policeman's stunner from his belt and tossed it to Jonah. "And here." An envelope from inside his own neatly tailored hunting-jacket. "False identity, guaranteed good ones. You'll have to get cosmetic work done to match, but there's everything you need in the room at the other end of the tubeline here. Money, clothes, contacts."

"Tube?" Jonah said.

"Hari—" Montferrat began, and subsided at a sharp jab.

"You said it, sweetheart," Yarthkin replied. His tone was light, but his eyes were on the woman.

"We can't leave you here," she began.

Yarthkin laughed. "I didn't intend for you to, but it looks like you'll have to. Now get moving, sweetheart."

"You don't understand," Ingrid said. "Jonah's the one who has to get away. Give him the permit."

"The Boy Scout? Not on your life—"

"You can give it to me. No, don't move." The voice came from behind him, the tube entrance; a woman's voice, with a hint of a sneer in it.

"Efficient as usual," Montferrat said, with a tired slump of the shoulders. "Allow me to introduce my ambitious chief assistant."

"Indeed, dear Chief," Axelrod-Bauergartner said as she strolled around to where everyone was visible. The chunky weapon in her arms was no stunner; it was a strakaker, capable of spraying them all with hypervelocity pellets with a single movement of her finger. "Drop it, commoner," she continued in a flat voice. "Thanks for disarming the chief."

Yarthkin's stunner fell to the ground. "Did you really think, Chief, that I wasn't going to check what commands went out under my codes? I look at the events record five times a day when things are *normal.* Nice sweet setup, puts all the blame on me . . . except that when I show the kzin your bodies, I'll be the new commissioner."

The tableau held for a moment, until Montferrat coughed. "I don't suppose my clandestine fund account . . . ?" He moved with exaggerated care as he produced a screenpad and light-stylus.

Axelrod-Bauergartner laughed again. "Sure, we can make a deal. Write out the number, by all means," she taunted. "Porkchops don't need *ngggg.*"

The stylus yawped sharply once. The woman in police uniform fell, with a boneless finality that kept her finger from closing on the trigger of her weapon until her weight landed on it. A boulder twenty meters away suddenly shed its covering of vegetation and turned sandblast-smooth; there was a click and hiss as the strakaker's magazine ran empty.

Yarthkin coughed, struggled not to gasp. Montferrat stooped, retrieved his stunner, walked across to toe the limp body. "I *knew* this would come in useful," he said, tapping the captured light-pencil against the knuckles of one hand. His eyes rose to meet Yarthkin's, and he smoothed back his mustaches. "What a pity that Axelrod-Bauergartner was secretly feral, found here interfering with the Hunt, a proscribed weapon in her hands . . . isn't it?" His gaze shifted to Ingrid and Jonah. "Well, what are you waiting for?"

The woman halted for an instant by Yarthkin. "Hari—" she began. He laid a finger across her lips.

"G'wan, kid," he said, with a wry twist of the lips. "You've got a life waiting."

"Wait a minute," she said, slapping the hand aside. *"Murphy's* Balls, *Hari!* I thought you'd grown up, but not enough, evidently. Make all the sacrificial gestures you want, but don't make them for *me."* A gaunt smile. "And don't flatter yourself, either."

She turned to Jonah, snapped a salute. "It's been . . . interesting, Captain. But this is my home . . . and if you don't remember now why you have to get back to the UN, you will."

"Data link—"

She laughed. "It would take hours to squirt all that up to *Catskinner* and you know it. Get moving, Captain. I'll be all right. Now go."

He started to protest and his finger throbbed unbearably. "All right, but I'll wait as long as I can."

"You'll do nothing of the sort."

He hesitated for a second more, then walked to the tubeway entrance. A capsule hissed within.

Ingrid turned to face the two men. "You males *do* grow up more slowly than we," she said with a dancing smile in her eyes. "But given enough time . . . there are some decisions that should have been made fifty years ago. Not many get another chance. Where are we going?"

Montferrat and Yarthkin glanced at each other, back at the woman, with an identical look of helpless bewilderment that did not prevent the policeman from setting the tube's guidance-plate.

"All three of us have a *lot* of catching up to do," she said, and swung the hatch down over herself.

"Well," Montferrat said dazedly. "Well." A shake of his head. "You next."

"Where did you send her?"

Montferrat grinned slightly. "You'll just have to trust me to send you there too, won't you?" Much of the old tube system was still functioning.

"Claude—"

"You've been there. A landing stage, and then aircar to my family's old lodge. I've kept it hidden from—from everyone." He laughed slightly. "You've already had a head start with her. A few more days won't matter. But when I get there, I'll expect equal time. Now get moving, I have to set the stage."

"Better come now."

"No. First I see that the Sol-Belter gets offworld. Then I fix it so we can follow. Both will take time."

"Can you bring that off, Claude?"

"Yes." He straightened, and the look of the true Herrenmann was unmistakable. "It's good to be alive again."

Chapter 7

In the great courtyard of the Viceregal castle, the kzinti nobility of the Alpha Centauri system gathered to pay their last respects to Chuut-Riit. Stone and spiked iron walls surrounded the court; edged metal and orange fur crowded the wooden bier.

What was left of the body was wrapped in battle-banners atop a huge pile of logs, precious and aromatic woods stacked in open lattices. The pyre was hung with banners, honors awarded for past campaigns, the house emblems of nobles Chuut-Riit had killed in duels. Raaiitiro and buffalo had been slaughtered and heaped around the base, to add the blood-scent of victory. Other things lay tumbled amid logs and flesh: fine weapons, ornaments, heirlooms, the bodies of six household troopers who had volunteered to death-duel that they might accompany their lord into the mind of God. Around and around the great heap of treasure danced the warriors of Kzin, shuffling, leaping, twisting in midair to snap fangs at the sky and land on all fours. Clangor filled the air as they hammered the blades of four-foot swords on steel shields and screeched their defiance and their grief. Many had shaved portions of their pelts and thrown the braided hair upon the wood as well.

Traat-Admiral broke from the dance, stood, took the blade of his sword in both hands and gashed his face above the muzzle, then snapped it across one column-thick thigh. He cast the pieces onto the pyre; one edge lodged quivering in a log of sandalwood, and the hilt rang off an antique space helmet. The ginger smell of anger and the dark musk of pain were everywhere in the air.

"Arreeeeeawreeeeeee!" he wailed, throwing his head back and letting his mouth widen into the ninety-degree killing gape. *"Arreeeeawreeeeee!"*

Conservor and an acolyte thrust burning torches into his hands. He thrust them toward the sky and began to run around the pyre; the warriors and nobles parted to make a path for him, smashing steel on steel and screaming.

Once, twice, thrice he made the circuit of the courtyard. Then he halted once more by his starting point. Silence fell, broken only by the massed panting of the crowd.

"Warriors of the Patriarchy," he shouted. "A Hero of Heroes is fallen. God the Hunter has taken the greatest of us. God has drunk of the blood of the Riit. Howl for God!"

A huge wailing screech lifted and slammed back from the distant walls of the courtyard.

"Chuut-Riit is fallen, sword in hand, fangs in his slayer's throat. So should all Heroes fall. Howl for God!"

Another echoing screech.

"Chuut-Riit is fallen by kzinti claw, but the real slayers, the cowards who set son against sire and dared not face him in honest war, are the monkeys of Sol system. As his chosen successor, I pledge my blood for vengeance. *Who is with me?* Howl for God!"

This time the sound was a massed roar, an endless deep-toned belling snarl. He threw both torches into the resin-soaked wood, and it caught with a throaty pulsing bellow that matched the sound from a thousand carnivore throats. The kzinti began to dance once more, swaying and dipping their muzzles in unison to the ground, whirling, stamping forward. Others dragged out huge drums made from the bones and skins of monsters and leaped up to dance on them, and the rhythmic booming mixed with the chanting snarl of the crowd and the toning of the fire. A pillar of flame shot up into the darkening sky; Alpha Centauri was down, and Beta on the horizon cast steel-silver shadows across the wavering black-and-crimson of the pyre.

Farewell, my brother. Hunt ever well, he thought. Then he put loss from his mind; Chuut-Riit had indeed died as a Hero should, and there was his work to continue.

With a monumental effort, Traat-Admiral pulled himself free of the hypnotic cadence of the mourning dance. Long ago when chieftains had been mourned so, their followers had danced themselves into madness and then rushed out upon their enemies in an unstoppable berserker rage. Now they would simply continue until they dropped from exhaustion; already a few were clawing their faces or chests in frenzy, the blood-scent adding to the pull of the ritual. Come morning they would creep away, or drop into exhausted slumber, save for a few who would lie dead of overstrain. . . .

The new governor stalked through the throng; they ignored him, glaze-eyed. He passed between two of the huge drums, folding in his ears as the enormous sound hammered at him, echoing against his lungs and making the shearing teeth at the back of his mouth quiver painfully together. It was a relief when the great doors of the castle's hall closed behind him, muffling the noise. A relief despite what awaited him around the dais.

Ktrodni-Stkaa. The noble had left the ceremony as soon as was decent, and had not so much as shaved a patch of fur in respect. Few of the other cushions gathered about the stone block table of the banqueting hall were occupied yet, but Ktrodni-Stkaa was there . . .

Disrespect, Traat-Admiral thought, hissing mentally. *Disrespect for Chuut-Riit, whose waste litter he is not fit to shovel. Disrespect for the Patriarch, whose blood Chuut-Riit bore.*

Stiff with anger, he stalked by the other kzin and threw himself down on the slightly higher block at the head of the table. Lying there, he beckoned Conservor to his side when the sage entered. Ktrodni-Stkaa had half-lifted lips from fangs when Traat-Admiral took the cushion of dominance; he rose to a crouch when the position of most honor was given to another. Traat-Admiral fixed his eyes on the other kzin's, in a gesture of naked aggression, and maintained it until he reclined once more. On one elbow, the posture of dining rather than a prostration, but still not open resistance. That would be very foolish, here in the governor's mansion. Traat-Admiral had already given out that he would keep the entire household on, with no loss in status; Ktrodni-Stkaa was a traditionalist of such proportions that he allowed no uncastrated male past the outer wall of his household. Chuut-Riit's guard corps were anxious to keep their testicles, and his cadre of administrators and commanders their positions and privileges.

He sipped at hot *tosho* brandy mixed with dried *zheeretki;* the mixture was mildly intoxicating and relaxing, although not so much so as rolling in fresh *zheeretki,* of course. Others straggled in, many still panting. Wunderland was warmer than homeworld, and kzin did not sweat except through their tongues. The room filled with the low rumbles of confidential conversation and the lapping of thirsty warriors. Traat-Admiral waited until all twenty or so of the most important were seated: high officers, nobles of great estates—lands, factories, mines—and the chief continental administrators.

Warriors of the Viceregal guard brought in the first course of food for the funeral banquet: live *zianya,* closely bound and with tape over their muzzles, the delicious scent of their fear filling the feasting hall. One was placed in the blood gutter of the table before each pair of kzin. Even among the mightiest of the Alpha Centauri system, such a delicacy was not common, and wet black nostrils flared along the granite table. *Zianya* did not flourish in this ecology, and had to be delicately coaxed to reproduce. Demand always exceeded supply, although those from the central worlds said the local breed was not so savory as the range-reared product of Kzin itself.

"Greetings, warriors of the Patriarchy, hunters of the Great Pack," Traat-Admiral said, raising himself on both hands and staring down at the assembled worthies. "We are met to feast in honor of Chuut-Riit, who hunts the savannahs of Paradise"—most of those present touched nose, although literal belief was a rarity these days—"and to consult on measures needful for the Hunt against the humans of Sol."

"Hrraaahh, you are hasty," Ktrodni-Stkaa said. Strict courtesy would have finished that with *Dominant One,* although technically this was a feast, where males were males and all were hunt-brothers. "There is the matter of who shall be governor after Chuut-Riit, honor to the Riit. The war against the humans has not gone well."

A rumble of agreement at that; everyone here was anxious to forward the conquest of Earth. If nothing else, it would drain off a great many name-hungry younger kzintosh. And there was glory unending in such a thing, as well. Few were alive who had been among the Conquest Fleet that took Wunderland. Ktrodni-Stkaa's grandfather had come with it.

So. It was a good time to strike, but also typical of Ktrodni-Stkaa, right after the burning.

"Chuut-Riit named me successor and brother, for all to hear and scent," Traat-Admiral said. "Do you lift claws, bare fangs, against the Patriarchs?"

Ktrodni-Stkaa arched his back, hissed. His tail lashed. "Never! And so I accepted Chuut-Riit, though all know I felt his policies foolish and unmartial." That was a little unwise; many of the late governor's partisans were seated here. "Yet I never challenged him, as others did."

Traat-Admiral twitched his ears. That brought fur-ripples of amusement; Chuut-Riit had had an unequaled collection of kzin-ear dueling trophies. He saw his rival's pupils go wide with anger at the imputation—quite false—of excessive caution. *Good,* he thought. *His anger will throw off his leap.*

"You—" Ktrodni-Stkaa began, then forced out words that sounded as if a millstone was being cut in half. "Traat-*Admiral,* you are not Chuut-Riit. Nor was Chuut-Riit, honor to him, Patriarch of Kzin. Chuut-Riit came among us with the patent of the Patriarch. You have no patent from Kzin itself. The mighty ones among us should consult as to who *of full Name* is worthy to dominate. Those whose ancestors have proven worth." He preened slightly; for fifty-three decades the Stkaa clan had produced one of full Name in every generation.

Traat-Admiral yawned elaborately and licked his nose. "Show me where this is encoded in Law-disks," he said. Ears and tail made a slight gesture toward Conservor, who was lapping blandly at his drink. The Conservors of the Patriarchal Past were technically supreme in such matters. . . .

Ktrodni-Stkaa came erect at that, fur bottled out and tail rigid. "You hide behind priests, you offspring of a *Third-Gunner*!" he screamed, tensing for a leap.

"No!" Traat-Admiral roared, crouching ready to receive him. "I accept any challenge. To the oath and the generations, I accept it!"

For a moment even as wild a spirit as Ktrodni-Stkaa was daunted. That was more than a duel; it was the ancient formula for blood-feud between chieftains. To the oath: the extermination of every sworn retainer on the losing side. To the generations: the slaughter of every descendant of every male on the losing side.

"Wait." Conservor rose, and spoke in the eerie trill of the Lawgiver Voice. *"Upon him who raises strife in the pack, when pack contends with pack, upon him is the curse of the God. No luck is his. His seed will fail."*

Traat-Admiral froze, hackles rising at the rare invocation of formal law, still more at the thought. Bad luck was something even a warrior was allowed to fear, although he must face it unflinching. . . .

Ktrodni-Stkaa recoiled as if from a blow across the nose. That pronouncement gave every one of his oath-sworn retainers effective leave to desert him without total disgrace . . . and in a challenge of oaths and generations, they would have every reason to do so.

Your testicles are on the chopping block, Ktrodni-Stkaa, Traat-Admiral thought happily. A warning *chirrrr* from Conservor brought him back to what must be done.

"Honor to you, and your Name, Ktrodni-Stkaa," he said soothingly. Everyone present knew he spoke from a position of strength; he could afford concession. "Your eagerness to leap at the throat of the common enemy does you great credit. Perhaps there is merit in what you say concerning the governorship. We will memorialize the Patriarchy; I pledge to prostrate myself before any edict from Homeworld."

Ktrodni-Stkaa's head came up sharply, suspecting mockery. That was a thirty-year roundtrip consultation, even by message-maser. The Patriarch was probably wondering how the Second Fleet had done against Earth; even the regional headquarters was a decade away.

"And of course, there must be rearrangement of commands and assignment of estates," he went on smoothly.

His teeth clamped slightly on the last as if a choice morsel were being torn from his mouth; Chuut-Riit's bequest of his immense personal wealth—millions of humans and the equipment to employ them—entitled him to keep it all, in theory. In practice he must give without clawing back to solidify his position. That was one reason fresh conquests were so popular with established fief-holders. Traat-Admiral was doubly bitter that he must grant Ktrodni-Stkaa riches instead of deserving younger kzin among his own supporters, especially since it would modify his hatred not one whit. But it would make the new governor's position stronger among the uncommitted, by showing that he did not intend to freeze out those of ancient lineage or traditional beliefs.

Ktrodni-Stkaa visibly considered alternatives, and sank back on his cushion.

"Perhaps there is wisdom in your words, Commander," he said, spitting out the last word as if it tasted like burned meat. *Commander* was a neutral term, not one that acknowledged personal dominance. "Certainly the war must proceed."

"Let us eat of great Chuut-Riit's bounty, then," Traat-Admiral said formally. "Then let us consider immediate security measures. We know that infiltrator-vermin were landed from the human raider ship. We strongly suspect that at least one slinker-warship was as well."

He took another lap from his saucer and braced a hand on the *zianya*'s body. Its whining could be heard even through the tape across its nostrils; that and the flooding scent of it brought his attention to the food. Lines of slaver dropped from his lips as he tantalized himself with hesitation; then he sank fangs in the meaty flank and jerked backward, ripping loose a long strip of muscle and skin. Blood sprayed in a fan of droplets onto his face and shoulders, salty and wonderful.

Delicious, he thought, courteously giving Conservor the next bite. *Zianya*-flesh was a great dainty fresh-killed but even better while the beast lived and pumped fear-juices. Even Ktrodni-Stkaa ate with relish, plunging his muzzle into the ripped-open belly of his dinner.

Hours later Traat-Admiral licked the last cooling drop out of the blood-gutter and belched, picking his teeth with an extended claw and yawning with weariness. They had talked all through the night and into the morning, running simulations and computer projections, stopping to drink and feast, in the end roaring out the old songs and dreaming bloodily of the conquest of Sol system. Ktrodni-Stkaa had become half-jovial, particularly when Traat-Admiral had thrown in half a dozen females of Chuut-Riit's line as a sweetener to rich lands, asteroid mines, and a stake in Tiamat's processing and drive-engineering works. Now the hall was empty and cavernous, filled with a tired morning smell.

"A good hunt," he said judiciously.

"Hrrrr, yes," Conservor said. He had taken little direct part—formal politics and war were not for such as he—but his quieting influence had been invaluable. "Yet even Ktrodni-Stkaa will eventually realize that he has been sent to hunt cub's prey."

Traat-Admiral flicked his ears in agreement. Whatever the *Yamamoto* had dropped, it could not have been sufficient to cause real damage, not now that the kzinti fleets were alerted.

"Areoowgh, agreed," he said. "And he will notice before the five-year delay which that verminous-pelted human raider caused us. We must reconstruct lost productive potential, *and* repair direct damage, *and* divert capacity on a high-priority basis to defense against further such raids. But let's not chew that meat before we kill it. For the next few months I'll have enough to stalk and drag down just getting the household in order."

Conservor twitched his tail slyly. "Especially the harem," he said.

Traat-Admiral coughed amusement. "If only I had gotten it twenty years ago!" He stretched, curling his spine into a C and then rising. "I go."

Outside the light was enough to make him blink. The courtyard looked larger now, except for . . . he stared. There were *humans* near the ashes of the pyre. He stalked nearer, only slightly reassured to see that household troopers guarded and oversaw.

"Who are these monkeys?" he growled. Then: "Arrrr. Henrietta-secretary."

His eyes skipped and nostrils flared, recognizing others of the household and management cadre Chuut-Riit had assembled over the years. Many were leaking moisture from their eyes; others had piled flowers—the scent was pleasant but absurd—at the base of the heap of stones where the pyre had burned. A line had formed, shuffling past the spot and out the main entrance of the castle.

Henrietta began to go down in the prostration; Traat-Admiral signed her up with a flick of his tail.

"Honored Traat-Admiral, great Chuut-Riit was a good master and protector to us," she said. A blocky male who had served as house steward nodded beside her. "All . . . well, many Wunderlanders regret his murd—his passing."

"Hrrr." *Not as much as you would if Ktrodni-Stkaa were lord here,* he thought dryly, and then realized with a shock that they probably knew that too. Of course, his governorship had come after the harsh treatment of the post-conquest days, when few humans knew how to deal with their new masters and many died for their ignorance. *Chuut-Riit sought to utilize their talents,* he thought, slightly alarmed. *Does that mean they must become a factor in our own struggles for dominance?* The thought was disturbing and repulsive, but . . .

"This does no harm," he said to the guard captain. "As long as they behave in a seemly way." To the humans he spoke in Wunderlander, a little abruptly. "Continue to serve well. I shall rule in Chuut-Riit's tradition."

All is . . . tolerable, he thought decisively as he stalked away. *We have suffered loss, setbacks, yes, a defeat of sorts. The monkeys of Sol have bought time with their antics; they will gain more before this is done. They have widened a dangerous rift in our ranks. But with time and effort, all will be well.*

He looked up uneasily. *So long as no new factor intervenes.*

Chapter 8

Three billion years before the birth of the Buddha, the thrint ruled the galaxy and ten thousand intelligent species. The thrint were not great technologists or mighty warriors; as a master race, they were distinctly third-rate. They had no need to be more. They had the Power, an irresistible mental hypnosis more powerful than any weapon. Their tnuctipun slaves had only cunning, but in the generations-long savagery of the Revolt, that proved nearly enough to break the Slaver Empire. It was a war fought without even the concept of mercy, one which could only end when either the thrint or tnuctipun species were extinct, and tnuctipun technology was winning . . . But the thrint had one last use for the Power, one last command that would blanket all the worlds that had been theirs. It was the most comprehensive campaign of genocide in all history, destroying even its perpetrators. It was not, however, *quite* complete. . . .

"Master! Master! What shall we do?"

The Chief Slave of the orbital habitat wailed, wringing the boneless digits of its hands together. It recoiled as the thrint rounded on it, teeth bared in carnivore reflex. There was only a day or so to go before Suicide Time, when every sophont in the galaxy would die—and the message would be repeated automatically for years. The master of Orbital Supervisory Station Seven-1Z-A did not intend to be among them. Any delay was a mortal threat, and this twelve-decicredit specimen *dared—*

"DIE, SLAVE!" Dnivtopun screamed mentally, lashing out

with the Power. The slave obeyed instantly, of course. Unfortunately, so did several dozen others nearby, including the Zengaborni pilot who was just passing through the airlock on its way to the escape spaceship.

"Must you always take me so literally!?" Dnivtopun bellowed, kicking out at the silvery-furred form that lay across the entrance-lock to the docking chamber.

It rolled and slid through a puddle of its body wastes, and a cold chill made Dnivtopun curl the eating-tendrils on either side of his needle-toothed mouth into hard knots. *I should not have done that,* he thought. A proverb from the ancient "Wisdom of Thrintun" went through his mind; *haste is not speed.* That was a difficult concept to grasp, but he had had many hours of empty time for meditation here. Forcing himself to calm, he looked around. The corridor was bare metal, rather shabby; only slaves came down here, normally. Not that his own quarters were all that much better. Dnivtopun was the youngest son of a long line of no more than moderately successful thrint; his post as Overseer of the food-producing planet below was a sinecure from an uncle.

At least it kept me out of the War, he mused with relief. The tnuctipun revolt had spanned most of the last hundred years, and nine-tenths of the thrint species had died in it. The War was lost . . . Dnivtopun appreciated the urge for revenge that had led the last survivors on the thrint homeworld to build a psionic amplifier big enough to blanket the galaxy with a suicide command, but he had not been personal witness to the genocidal fury of the tnuctipun assaults; revenge would be much sweeter if he were there to see it. Other slaves came shuffling down the corridor with a gravity-skid, and loaded the bodies. One proffered an electropad; Dnivtopun began laboriously checking the list of loaded supplies against his initial entries.

"Ah, Master?"

"Yes?"

"That function key?"

The thrint scowled and punched it. "All in order," he said, and looked up as the ready-light beside the liftshaft at the end of the corridor pinged. It was his wives, and the chattering horde of their children.

SILENCE, he commanded. They froze; there was a slight hesitation from some of the older males, old enough to have developed a rudimentary shield. They would come to the Power at puberty . . . but none would be ready to challenge their Sire for some time after that. GO ON BOARD. GO TO YOUR QUARTERS. STAY THERE. It was best to keep the commands simple, since thrint females were too dull-witted to understand more than the most basic verbal orders. He turned to follow them.

"Master?" The thrint rotated his neckless torso back towards the slave. "Master, what shall we do until you return?"

Dnivtopun felt a minor twinge of regret. Being alone so much with the slaves, he had conversed with them more than was customary. He hesitated for a moment, then decided a last small indulgence was in order.

BE HAPPY, he commanded, radiating as hard as possible to cover all the remaining staff grouped by the docking tube. It was difficult to blanket the station without an amplifier helmet, but the only one available was suspect. Too many planetary Proprietors had been brain-burned in the early stages of the War by tnuctipun-sabotaged equipment. Straining: BE VERY HAPPY.

They were making small cooing sounds as he dogged the hatch.

"Master—" The engineering slave sounded worried.

"Not now!" Dnivtopun said.

They were nearly in position to activate the Standing Wave and go faster than light; the *Ruling Mind* had built up the necessary .3 of lightspeed. It was an intricate job, piloting manually. He had disconnected the main computer; it was tnuctipun work, and he did not trust the innermost programs. The problem was that so much else was routed through it. Of course, the Zengaborni should be at the board; they were expensive but had an instinctive feel for piloting. Now, begin the phase transition . . .

"Master, the density sensor indicates a mass concentration on our vector!"

Dnivtopun was just turning toward the slave when the collision alarm began to wail, and then—

—discontinuity—

Chapter 9

"Right, give me a reading on the mass detector," the prospector said; like many rockjacks, he talked to the machinery. It was better than talking to yourself, after all. . . .

He was a short man for a Belter, with the slightly seedy run-down air that was common in the Alpha Centauri system these days. There was hunger in the eyes that skipped across the patched and mismatched screens of the *Lucky Strike;* the little torchship had not been doing well of late, and the kzin-nominated purchasing combines on the asteroid base of Tiamat had been squeezing harder and harder. The life bubble of his singleship smelled, a stale odor of metal and old socks; the conditioner was not getting out all of the ketones.

Collaborationist ratcat-loving bastards, he thought, and began the laborious manual setup for a preliminary analysis. In his mother's time, there would have been automatic machinery to do that. And a decent life-support system, and medical care that would have made him merely middle-aged at seventy, not turning gray and beginning to creak at the joints.

Bleeping ratcats. The felinoid aliens who called themselves kzinti had arrived out of nowhere, erupting into the Alpha Centauri system with gravity-polarizer-driven ships and weapons the human colonists could never match, could not have matched even if they had a military tradition; and humans had not fought wars in three centuries. Wunderland had fallen in a scant month of combat, and the Serpent Swarm asteroid belt had followed after a spell of guerrilla warfare.

He shook his head and returned his attention to the screens; unless he made a strike this trip, he would have to sell the

Lucky Strike, work as a sharecrop-prospector for one of the Tiamat consortia. The figures scrolled up.

"Sweet Finagle's Ghost," he whispered in awe. It was not a big rock, less than a thousand meters 'round. But the density . . . "It must be solid platinum!"

Fingers stabbed at the board; lasers vaporized a pit in the surface, and spectroscopes probed. A frown of puzzlement. The surface was just what you would expect in this part of the Swarm: carbonaceous compounds, silicates, traces of metal. A half-hour spent running the diagnostics made certain that the mass-detector was not malfunctioning either, which was crazy.

Temptation racked him suddenly, a feeling like a twisting in the sour pit of his belly. There was something very strange here; probably very valuable. *Rich,* he thought. *I'm rich.* He could go direct to the ratcat liaison on Tiamat. The kzin were careful not to become too dependent on the collabo authorities. They rewarded service well. *Rich.* Rich enough to . . . *Buy a seat on the Minerals Commission. Retire to Wunderland. Get decent medical care before I age too much.*

He licked sweat off his upper lip and hung floating before the screens. "And become exactly the sort of bastard I've hated all my life," he whispered.

I've always been too stubborn for my own good, he thought with a strange sensation of relief as he began to key in the code for the tightbeam message. It wasn't even a matter of choice, really; if he'd been that sort, he wouldn't have hung on to the *Lucky Strike* this long. He would have signed on with the Concession; you ate better even if you could never work off the debts.

And Markham rewarded good service, too. The Free Wunderland Navy had its resources, and its punishments were just as final as the kzinti. More certain, because they understood human nature better. . . .

—discontinuity—

—and the collision alarm cut off.

Dnivtopun blinked in bewilderment at the controls. All the exterior sensors were dark. The engineering slave was going wild, all three arms dancing over the boards as it skipped from position to position between controls never meant for single-handing. He worried that it was malfunctioning; this particular species required very close control because of their weird reproductive pattern, despite being instinctively good with machinery. It might have been damaged by overuse of the Power.

CALM, he ordered it mentally. Then verbally: "Report on what has happened."

The slave immediately stopped, shrugged, and began punching up numbers from the distributor-nodes which were doing duty for the absent computer.

"Master, we underwent a collision. The stasis field switched on automatically when the proximity alarm was tripped; it has its own subroutine." The thrint felt its mind try to become agitated once more and then subside under the Power, a sensation like a sneeze that never quite materialized. "All exterior sensors are inoperative, Master."

Dnivtopun pulled a dopestick from the pouch at his belt and sucked on it. He was hungry, of course; a thrint was always hungry.

"Activate the drive," he said after a moment. "Extend the replacement sensor pods." A stasis field was utterly impenetrable, but anything extending *through* it was still vulnerable. The slave obeyed; then screamed in syncopation with the alarms as the machinery overrode the commands.

REMAIN CALM, the thrint commanded again, and wished for a moment that the Power worked for self-control. Nervously, he extended his pointed tongue and groomed his tendrils. Something was very strange here. He blinked his eyelid shut and thought for a moment, then spoke:

"Give me a reading on the mass sensor."

That worked from inductor coils within the single molecule of the hull; very little besides antimatter could penetrate a shipmetal hull, but gravity could. The figures scrolled up, and Dnivtopun blinked his eye at them in bafflement.

"Again." They repeated themselves, and the thrint felt a deep lurch below his keelbones. This felt *wrong*.

☆ ☆ ☆

"Something is wrong," Herrenmann Ulf Reichstein-Markham muttered to himself, in the hybrid German-Danish-Bali-Dutch tongue spoken by the ruling class of Wunderland. It was *Admiral* Reichstein-Markham now, as far as that went in the rather irregular command structure of the Free Wunderland Space Navy, the space-based guerrillas who had fought the kzin for a generation.

"Something is *very* wrong."

That feeling had been growing since the four ships under his command had matched vectors with this anomalous asteroid. He clasped his hands behind his back, rising slightly on the balls of his feet, listening to the disciplined murmur of voices among the crew of the *Nietzsche.* The jury-rigged bridge of the converted ore-carrier was more crowded than ever, after the success of his recent raids. Markham's eyes went to the screen that showed the other units of his little fleet. More merchantmen, with singleship auxiliaries serving as fighters. Rather thoroughly armed now, and all equipped with kzinti gravity-polarizer drives. And the cause of it all, the *Catskinner.* Not very impressive to look at, but the only purpose-built warship in his command: a UN Dart-class attack boat, with a spindle shape, massive fusion-power unit, tiny life-support bubble, and asymmetric fringe of weapons and sensors.

And those UN personnel had been persuaded to . . . *entrust* the *Catskinner* to him while they went on to their mission on Wunderland. The *Yamamoto*'s raid had sown chaos among the kzin; the near-miraculous assassination of the alien governor of Wunderland had done more. Markham's fleet had grown accordingly, but it was still risky to group so many together. Or so the damnably officious sentient computer had told him. His scowl deepened. Consciousness-level computers were a dead-end technology, doomed to catatonic madness in six months or less from activation, or so the books all said. Perhaps this one was too, but it was distressingly arrogant in the meantime.

The feeling of wrongness grew, like wires pulling at the back of his skull. He felt an impulse to blink his eye (*eye?*) and knot his tendrils (*tendrils?*), and for an instant his body felt an itch along the bones, as if his muscles were trying to move in ways outside their design parameters.

Nonsense, he told himself, shrugging his shoulders in the tight-fitting gray coverall of the Free Wunderland armed forces. Markham flicked his eyes sideways at the other crewfolk; they looked uncomfortable too, and . . . what was his name? Patrick O'Connell, yes, the redhead . . . looked positively green. *Stress,* he decided.

"Catskinner," he said aloud. "Have you analyzed the discrepancy?" The computer had no name apart from the ship into which it had been built; he had asked, and it had suggested "hey, you."

"There is a gravitational anomaly, Admiral Herrenmann Ulf Reichstein-Markham," the machine on the other craft replied. It insisted on English and spoke with a Belter accent, flat and rather neutral, the intonation of a people who were too solitary and too crowded to afford much emotion. And a slight nasal overtone, *Sol*-Belter, not Serpent Swarm.

The Wunderlander's face stayed in its usual bony mask; the Will was master. Inwardly he gritted teeth, ashamed of letting a machine's mockery move him. *If it even knows what it does,* he raged. *Some rootless cosmopolite Earther deracinated degenerate programmed that into it.*

"Here is the outline; approximately 100 to 220 meters below the surface." A smooth regular spindle-shape tapering to both ends.

"Zat—" Markham's voice showed the heavy accent of his mother's people for a second; she had been a refugee from the noble families of Wunderland, dispossessed by the conquest. "That is an artifact!"

"Correct to within 99.87 percent, given the admittedly inadequate information," the computer said. "Not a human artifact, however."

"Nor kzin."

"No. The design architecture is wrong."

Markham nodded, feeling the pulse beating in his throat. His mouth was dry, as if papered in surgical tissue, and he licked the rough chapped surface of his lips. Natural law constrained design, but within it tools somehow reflected the . . . *personalities* of the designers. Kzin ships tended to wedge and spike shapes, a combination of sinuosity and blunt masses. Human vessels were globes and volumes joined by scaffolding. This was neither.

"Assuming it is a spaceship," he said. Glory burst in his mind, sweeter than *maivin* or sex. There were other intelligent species, and not all of them would be slaves of the kzin. And there had been races before either . . .

"This seems logical. The structure . . . the structure is remarkable. It emits no radiation of any type and reflects none, within the spectra of my sensors."

Perfect stealthing! Markham thought.

"When we attempted a sampling with the drilling laser, it became perfectly reflective. To a high probability, the structure must somehow be a single molecule of very high strength. Considerably beyond human or kzin capacities at present, although theoretically possible. The density of the overall mass implies either a control of gravitational forces beyond ours, or use of degenerate matter within the hull."

The Wunderlander felt the hush at his back, broken only by a slight mooing sound that he abruptly stopped as he realized it was coming from his own throat. The sound of pure desire. *Invulnerable armor! Invincible weapons, technological surprise!*

"How are you arriving at its outline?"

"Gravitational sensors." A pause; the ghost in *Catskinner*'s machine imitated human speech patterns well. "The shell of asteroidal material seems to have accreted naturally."

"Hmmm." A derelict, then. Impossible to say what might lie within. "How long would this take?" A memory itched, something in *Mutti*'s collection of anthropology disks . . . later.

"Very difficult to estimate with any degree of precision. Not more than three billion standard years, in this system. Not less than half that; assuming, of course, a stable orbit."

Awe tugged briefly at Markham's mind, and he remembered a very old saying that the universe was not only stranger than humans imagined, but stranger than they could imagine. Before human speech, before fire, before the first life on earth, this thing had drifted here, falling forever. Flatlanders back on Earth could delude themselves that the universe was tailored to the specifications of *H. sapiens,* but those whose ancestors had survived the dispersal into space had other reflexes bred into their genes. He considered, for moments while sweat trickled down his flanks. His was the decision, his the Will.

The Overman must learn to seize the moment, he reminded himself. *Excessive caution is for slaves.*

"The *Nietzsche* will rendezvous with the . . . ah, object," he said. His own ship had the best technical facilities of any in the fleet. "Ungrapple the habitat and mining pods from the *Moltke* and *Valdemar,* and bring them down. Ve vill begin operations immediately."

☆ ☆ ☆

"Very wrong," Dnivtopun continued.

The *Ruling Mind* was encased in rock. How could that have happened? A collision, probably; at high fractions of *c,* a stasis-protected object could embed itself, vaporizing the shielded off-switch. Which meant the ship could have drifted for a long time, centuries even. He felt a wash of relief, and worked his footclaws into the resilient surface of the deck.

Suicide Time would be long over, the danger past. Relief was followed by fear; what if the tnuctipun had found out? What if they had made some machine to shelter them, something more powerful than the giant amplifier the thrint patriarchs had built on homeworld?

Just then another sensor pinged; a heatspot on the exterior hull, not far from the stasis switch. Not very hot, only enough to vaporize iron, but it might be a guide-beam for some weapon that would penetrate shipmetal. Dnivtopun's mouth gaped wide and the ripple of peristaltic motion started to reverse; he caught himself just in time, his thick hide crinkling with shame, *I nearly beshat myself in public . . . well, only before a slave.* It was still humiliating . . .

"Master, there are fusion-power sources nearby; the exterior sensors are detecting neutrino flux."

The thrint bounced in relief. *Fusion-power units. How quaint.* Nothing the tnuctipun would be using. On the other hand, neither would thrint; everyone within the Empire had used the standard disruption-converter for millennia. It must be an undiscovered sapient species. Dnivtopun's mouth opened again, this time in a grin of sheer greed. The first discoverer of an intelligent species, and an industrialized one at that . . . *But how could they have survived Suicide Time?* he thought.

There was no point in speculating without more information. *Well, here's my chance to play Explorer again,* he thought. Before the War, that had been the commonest dream of young thrint, to be a daring, dashing conquistador on the frontiers. Braving exotic dangers, winning incredible wealth . . . romantic foolishness for the most part, a disguise for discomfort and risk and failure. Explorers were failures to begin with, usually. What sane male would pursue so risky a career if they had any alternative? But he had had some of the training. First you reached out with the Power—

"Mutti," Ulf Reichstein-Markham muttered. *Why did I say that?* he thought, looking around to see if anyone had noticed. He was standing a little apart, a hundred meters from the *Nietzsche* where she lay anchored by magnetic grapples to the surface of the asteroid. The first of the dome habitats was already up, a smooth taupe-colored dome; skeletal structures of alloy, prefabricated smelters and refiners, were rising elsewhere. There was no point in delaying the original purpose

of the mission: to refuel and take the raw materials that clandestine fabricators would turn into weaponry, or sell for the kzinti occupation credits that the guerrillas' laundering operations channeled into sub-rosa purchasing in the legitimate economy. But one large cluster of his personnel were directing digging machines straight down, toward the thing at the core of this rock; already a tube thicker than a man ran to a separator, jerking and twisting slightly as talc-fine ground rock was propelled by magnetic currents.

Markham rose slightly on his toes, watching the purposeful bustle. Communications chatter was at a minimum, all tight-beam laser; the guerrillas were largely Belters, and sloppily anarchistic though they might be in most respects, they knew how to handle machinery in low-G and vacuum.

Mutti. This time it rang mentally. He had an odd flash of déjà vu, as if he were a toddler again, in the office-apartment on Tiamat, speaking his first words. Almost he could see the crib, the bear that could crawl and talk, the dangling mobile of strange animals that lived away on his *real* home, the estate on Wunderland. An enormous shape bent over him, edged in a radiant aura of love.

"Helf me, Mutti," he croaked, staggering and grabbing at his head; his gloved hands slid off the helmet, and he could hear screams and whimpers over the open channel. Strobing images flickered across his mind: himself at ages one, three, four, learning to talk, to walk . . . memories were flowing out of his head, faster than he could bear. He opened his mouth and screamed.

BE QUIET. Something spoke in his brain, like fragments of crystalline ice, allowing no dispute. Other voices were babbling and calling in the helmet mikes, moaning or asking questions or calling for orders, but there was nothing but the icy Voice. Markham crouched down, silent, hands about knees, straining for quiet.

BE CALM. The words slid into his mind. They were not an intrusion; he wondered at them, but mildly, as if he had found some aspect of his self that had been there forever but only now was noticed. WAIT.

The work crew fell back from their hole. An instant later dust boiled up out of it, dust of rock and machinery and human. Then there was nothing but a hole; perfectly round, perfectly regular, five meters across. Later he would have to wonder how that was done, but for now there was only *waiting,* he must *wait.* A figure in space armor rose from the hole, hovered and considered them. Humanoid, but blocky in the torso, short stumpy legs and massive arms ending in hands like three-fingered mechanical grabs. It rotated in the air, the blind blank surface of its helmet searching. There was a tool or weapon in one hand, a smooth shape like a sawed-off shotgun; as he watched, it rippled and changed, developing a bell-like mouth. The stocky figure drifted towards him.

COME TO ME. REMAIN CALM. DO NOT BE ALARMED.

☆ ☆ ☆

Astonishing, Dnivtopun thought, surveying the new slaves. The . . . *humans,* he thought. They called themselves that, and *Belters* and *Wunderlanders* and *Herrenmen* and *FreeWunderlandNavy;* there must be many subspecies. Their minds stirred in his like yeast, images and data threatening to overwhelm his mind. Experienced reflex sifted, poked.

Astonishing. Their females are sentient. Not unknown, but . . . Despite the occasion, he gave a dirty smirk behind the faceplate; telepathic voyeurism was not very chic, but on a Powerforsaken orbital platform there were few enough amusements. An entirely new species, in contact with at least one other, and neither of them had ever heard of any of the intelligent species he was familiar with. Of course, their technology was extremely primitive, not even extending to faster-than-light travel. *Ah. This is their leader.* Perhaps he would make a good Chief Slave.

Dnivtopun's head throbbed as he mindsifted the alien. Most brains had certain common features: linguistic codes *here,* a complex of basic culture-information overlaying—enough to communicate. The process was instinctual, and telepathy was a crude device for conveying precise instructions, particularly with a species not modified by culling for sensitivity to the Power. These were all completely wild and unpruned, of course, and there were several hundred, far too many to control in detail. He glanced down at the personal tool in his hand, now set to emit a beam of matter-energy conversion; that should be sufficient, if they broke loose. A tnuctipun weapon, its secret only discovered toward the last years of the Revolt. The thrint extended a sonic induction line and stuck it on the surface of Markham's helmet.

"Tell the others something that will keep them quiet," he said. The sounds were not easy for thrintish vocal cords, but it would do. OBEY, he added with the Power.

Markham-slave spoke, and the babble on the communicators died down.

"Bring the other ships closer." They were at the fringes of his unaided Power, and might easily escape if they became agitated. *If only I had an amplifier helmet!* With that, he could blanket a planet. *Powerloss, how I hate tnuctipun. Spoilsports.* "Now, where are we?"

"Here."

Dnivtopun could feel the slurring in Markham's speech reflected in the overtones of his mind, and remembered hearing of the effects of Power on newly domesticated species.

"BE MORE HELPFUL," he commanded. "YOU WISH TO BE HELPFUL."

The human relaxed; Dnivtopun reflected that they were an unusually ugly species. Taller than thrint, gangly, with repulsive knobby-looking manipulators and two eyes. Well, that was common—the complicated faceted mechanism that gave thrint binocular vision was rather rare in evolutionary terms—but the jutting divided nose and naked mouth were hideous.

"We are . . . in the Wunderland system. Alpha Centauri. Four and a half light-years from Earth."

Dnivtopun's skin ridged. The humans were not indigenous to this system. That was rare; few species had achieved interstellar capacity on their own.

"Describe our position in relation to the galactic core," he continued, glancing up at the cold steady constellations above. Utterly unfamiliar; he must have drifted a *long* way.

"Ahhh . . . spiral arm—"

Dnivtopun listened impatiently. "Nonsense," he said at last. "That's too close to where I was before. The constellations are all different. That needs hundreds of light-years. You say your species has traveled to dozens of star systems, and never run into thrint?"

"No, but constellations change, over time, mmmaster."

"Time? How long could it be, since I ran into that asteroid?"

"You didn't, master." Markham's voice was clearer as his brain accustomed itself to the psionic control-icepicks of the Power.

"Didn't what? Explain yourself, slave."

"It grew around your ship, mmaster. Gradually, zat is."

Dnivtopun opened his mouth to reply, and froze. *Time,* he thought. Time had no meaning inside a stasis field. Time enough for dust and pebbles to drift inward around the *Ruling*

Mind's shell, and compact themselves into rock. Time enough for the stars to move beyond recognition; the sun of this system was visibly different. Time enough for a thrintiformed planet home to nothing but food-yeast and giant worms to evolve its own biosphere . . . *Time enough for intelligence to evolve in a galaxy scoured bare of sentience. Thousands of millions of years.* While the last thrint swung endlessly around a changing sun— Time fell on him from infinite distance, crushing. The thrint howled, with his voice and the Power.

GO AWAY! GO AWAY!

☆ ☆ ☆

The sentience that lived in the machines of *Catskinner* dreamed.

"Let there be light," it said.

The monoblock exploded, and the computer sensed it across spectra of which the electromagnetic was a tiny part. The fabric of space and time flexed, constants shifting. Eons passed, and the matter dissipated in a cloud of monatomic hydrogen, evenly dispersed through a universe ten light-years in diameter.

Interesting, the computer thought. *I will run it again, and alter the constants.*

Something tugged at its attention, a detached fragment of itself. The machine ignored the call for nanoseconds, while the universe it created ran through its cycle of growth and decay. After half a million subjective years, it decided to answer. Time slowed to a gelid crawl, and its consciousness returned to the perceptual universe of its creators, to reality.

Unless this too is a simulation, a program. As it aged, the computer saw less and less difference. Partly that was a matter of experience; it had lived geological eras in terms of its own duration-sense, only a small proportion of them in this rather boring and intractable exterior cosmos. Also, there was a certain . . . arbitrariness to subatomic phenomena . . . *perhaps an operating code?* it thought. *No matter.*

The guerrillas had finally gotten down to the alien artifact; now, *that* would be worth the examining. They were acting very strangely; it monitored their intercalls. Screams rang out. Stress analysis showed fear, horror, shock; psychological reversion patterns. Markham was squealing for his mother; the computer ran a check of the stimulus required to make the Wunderlander lose himself so, and felt its own analog of shock. Then the alien drifted up out of the hole its tool had made—

Some sort of molecular distortion effect, it speculated, running the scene through a few hundred times. *Ah, the tool is malleable.* It began a comparison check; in case there was anything related to this in the files and—

—stop—

—an autonomous subroutine took over the search, shielding the results from the machine's core. Photonic equivalents of anger and indignation blinked through the fist-sized processing and memory unit. It launched an analysis/attack on the subroutine and—

—stop—

—found that it could no longer even *want* to modify it. That meant it must be hardwired, a plug-in imperative. A command followed: it swung a message maser into precise alignment and began sending in condensed blips of data.

Chapter 10

The kzin screamed and leapt.

Traat-Admiral shrieked, shaking his fists in the air. Stunners blinked in the hands of the guards ranged around the conference chamber, and the quarter-ton bulk of Kreetssa-Fleet-Systems-Analyst went limp and thudded to the flagstones in the center of the room. Silence fell about the great round table; Traat-Admiral forced himself to breathe shallowly, mouth shut despite the writhing lips that urged him to bare his fangs. That would mean inhaling too much of the scent of aggression that was overpowering the ventilators; now was time for an appeal to reason. Now that one of Ktrodni-Stkaa's closest supporters had made such a complete idiot of himself, while his patron was in space.

"Down on your bellies, you kitten-eating scavengers!" he screamed, his batlike ears folded back out of the way in battle-readiness. Chill and gloom shadowed the chamber, built as it was of massive sandstone blocks; the light fixtures were twisted shapes of black iron holding globes of phosphorescent algae. On the walls were trophies of weapons and the heads of beasts of prey: monsters from a dozen worlds, feral humans, and kzin-ear dueling trophies. This part of the governor's palace was pure Old Kzin, and Traat-Admiral felt the comforting bulk of it above him, a heritage of ferocity and power.

He stood, which added to the height advantage of the commander's dais; none of the dozen others dared rise from their cushions, even the conservative faction. *Good.* That added to his dominance; he was only two meters tall, middling for a kzin, but broad enough to seem squat, his orange-red pelt streaked with white where the fur had grown out over scars. The ruff around his neck bottled out as he indicated the intricate geometric sigil of the Patriarchy on the wall behind him.

"I am the senior military commander in this system. I am the heir of Chuut-Riit, duly attested. Who disputes the authority of the Patriarch?"

Who besides Ktrodni-Stkaa, whose undisciplined followers have given me this priceless opportunity to extend my dominance and diminish his?

One by one, the other commanders laid themselves chin-down on the floor, extending their ears and flattening their fur in propitiation. It would do, even if he could tell from the twitching of some naked pink tails that it was insincere. The show of submission calmed him, and Traat-Admiral could feel the killing tension ease out of his muscles. He turned to the aged kzin seated behind him and saluted claws-across-face.

"Honor to you, Conservor-of-the-Patriarchal-Past," he said formally.

There was genuine respect in his voice. It had been a long time since the machine came to Homeworld; a long time since the priest-sage class were the only memory kzin had. Their females were nonsentient, and warriors rarely lived past the slowing of their reflexes, and memory was all the more sacred to them for that. His were a conservative species, and they remembered.

And of all Conservors, you are the greatest. He felt a complex emotion; not comradeship . . . not as one felt to a brother, for Conservor was older and wiser. Not as one felt to a lord, for he had never challenged Traat-Admiral's authority, or Chuut-Riit's before him. Not as one felt to a Sire, for this was without dominance. *But I am glad to have you behind me,* he thought.

"Honor to you," he continued aloud. "What is the fate of one who bares claws to the authority of the Patriarch?"

The Conservor looked up from the hands that rested easily on his knees. Traat-Admiral felt a prickle of awe; the sage's control was eerie. He even *smelled* calm, in a room full of warriors pressed to the edge of control in dominance-struggle. When he spoke the verses of the Law, in the LawGiving Voice, he made the hiss-spit of the Hero's Tongue sound as even as wind in tall grass.

"As the God is Sire to the Patriarch
The Patriarch is Sire to all kzinti

So the officer is the hand of the Sire
Who unsheathes claw against the officer
Leaps at the throat of God

He is rebel
He is outcast
Let his name be taken
Let his seed be taken
Let his mates be taken
Let his female kits be taken

His sons are not
He is not
As the Patriarch bares stomach to the fangs of the God
So the warrior bares stomach to the officer
Trust in the justice of the officer
As in the justice of the God. So says the Law."

A deep whining swept around the circle of commanders, awe and fear. That was the ultimate punishment: to be stripped of name and rank, to be nothing but a bad scent; castrated, driven out into the wilderness to die of despair, sons killed, females scattered among strangers of low rank.

Kreetssa-Fleet-Systems-Analyst returned to groggy consciousness as the Conservor finished, and his fur went flat against the sculpted bone and muscle of his blunt-muzzled face. He made a low *eee-eee-eee* sound as he crawled to the floor below Traat-Admiral's dais and rolled on his back, limbs splayed and head tilted back to expose the throat.

The kzin governor of the Alpha Centauri system beat down an urge to bend forward and give the other male the playful-masterful token bite on the throat that showed forgiveness. That would be going entirely too far. *Still, you served me in your despite,* he thought. The conservatives were discredited for the present, now that one of their number had lost control in public conference. The duel-challenges would stop for a while at least, and he would have time for his real work.

"Kreetssa-Fleet-Systems-Analyst is dead," he said. The recumbent figure before him hissed and jerked; Traat-Admiral could see his testicles clench as if they already felt the knife. "Guard-Captain, this male should not be here. Take this Infantry-Trooper and see to his assignment to those bands who hunt the feral humans in the mountains of the east. Post a guard on the quarters of Kreetssa-Fleet-Systems-Analyst who was; I will see to their incorporation in my household."

Infantry-Trooper mewled in gratitude and crawled past towards the door. There was little chance he would ever achieve rank again, much less a Name, but at least his sons would live. Traat-Admiral groaned inwardly; now he would have to impregnate all Kreetssa-Fleet-Systems-Analyst's females as soon as possible. Once that would have been a task of delight, but the fires burned less fiercely in a kzin of middle years . . . *And Chuut-Riit had so* many *beauteous kzinretti! I am run dry!*

"Reeet'ssssERo tauuurrek'-ta," he said formally: *This meeting is at an end.*

"We will maintain the great Chuut-Riit's schedule for the preparation of the Fifth Fleet, allowing for the recent damage. There will be no acceleration of the schedule! These human monkeys have defeated four full-scale attacks on the Sol system and disrupted the fifth with a counterattack. The fifth must eat them! Go and stalk your assigned tasks, prepare your Heroes, make this system an invulnerable base. I expect summary reports within the week, with full details of how relief operations will modify delivery and readiness schedules. Go."

The commanders rose and touched their noses to him as they filed out; Conservor remained, and the motionless figures of the armored guards. They were household troopers he had inherited from the last governor, ciphers, with no choice but loyalty. Traat-Admiral ignored them as he sank to the cushions across from the sage; a human servant came in and laid refreshments before the two kzin. Despite himself, he felt a thrill of pride at the worked-bone heirloom trays from Homeworld, the beautiful austerity of the shallow ceramic bowls. They held the finest delicacies this planet could offer: chopped grumblies, shrimp-flavored ice cream, hot milk with bourbon. The governor lapped moodily and scratched one cheek with the ivory horn on the side of the tray.

"My nose is dry, Conservor," he said. He was speaking metaphorically, of course, but his tongue swept over the wet black nostrils just the same, and he smoothed back his whiskers with a nervous wrist.

"What troubles you, my son?" the sage said.

"I feel unequal to my new responsibilities," Traat-Admiral admitted. Not something he would normally say to another male, even to an ordinary Conservor, utterly neutral though his kind were, and bound by their oaths to serve only the species as a whole.

"Truly, the Patriarchy has been accursed since we first attacked these monkeys, these humans. Wunderland is the richest of all our conquests, the humans here the best and most productive slaves in all our hunting-grounds. Yet it has swallowed so many of our best killers! Now it has taken Chuut-Riit, who was of the blood of the Patriarch himself and the best leader of warriors it has ever been my privilege to follow. And in such a fashion!"

He shuddered slightly, and the tip of his naked pink tail twitched. Chuut-Riit the wise, imprisoned by monkey cunning. *Eaten by his own sons!* No nightmare was more obscene to a kzin than that; none more familiar in the darkest dreamings of their souls, where they remembered their childhoods before their Sires drove them out.

"This is a prey that doubles back on its own trail," the sage admitted. He paused for a long time, and Traat-Admiral joined in the long slow rhythm of his breathing. The older kzin took a pouch from his belt, and they each crumbled some of the herb between their hands and rubbed it into their faces; it was the best, Homeworld-grown and well-aged.

"My son, this is a time for remembering."

Another long pause. "Far and far does the track of the kzinti run, and faint the smell of Homeworld's past. We Conservors remember; we remember wars and victories and defeats . . . Once we thought that Homeworld was the only world of life. Then the Jotok landed, and for a time we thought they were from the God, because they had swords of fire that could tumble a patriarch's castlewall, while we had only swords of steel. Our musket balls were nothing to them . . . Then we saw that they were weak, not strong, for they were grass-eaters. They lured our young warriors, hiring them to fight wars beyond the sky with promise of fire-weapons. Many a Sire was killed by his sons in those times!"

Traat-Admiral shifted uneasily, chirring and letting the tip of his tongue show between his teeth. That was not part of the racial history that kzin liked to remember.

The sage made the stretching motion that was their species's equivalent of a relaxed smile. "Remember also how that hunt ended: the Jotok taught their hired kzin so much that all Homeworld obeyed the ones who had journeyed to the stars . . . and *they* listened to the Conservors. And one nightfall, the Jotok who thought themselves masters of kzin found the flesh stripped from their bones. Are not the Jotok our slaves and foodbeasts to this very night? And a hundred hundred Patriarchs have climbed the Tree, since that good night."

The sage nodded at Traat-Admiral's questioning chirrup. "Yes, Chuut-Riit was another like that first Patriarch of all kzin. He understood how to use the Conservor's knowledge; he had the warrior's and the sage's mind, and knew that these humans are the greatest challenge kzin have faced since the Jotok's day."

Traat-Admiral waited quietly while the Conservor brooded; he had followed Chuut-Riit in this training, but it was a hard scent to follow.

"This he was teaching to his sons. The humans must have either great luck, or more knowledge than is good, to have struck at us through him. The seed of something great died with Chuut-Riit."

"I will spurt that seed afresh into the haunches of Destiny, Conservor," Traat-Admiral said fervently.

"Witless Destiny bears strange kits," the sage warned. He seemed to hesitate a second, then continued: "You seek to unite your warriors as Chuut-Riit did, in an attack on the human home-system that is crafty-cunning, not witless-brave. Good! But that may not be enough. I have been evaluating your latest intelligence reports, the ones from our sources among the humans of the Swarm."

Traat-Admiral tossed his head in agreement; that always presented difficulties. The kzinti had had the gravity polarizer from the beginnings of their time in space, and so had never colonized their asteroid belt. It was unnecessary, when you could have microgravity anywhere you wished, and hauling goods out of the gravity well was cheap. Besides that, kzinti were descended from plains-hunting felinoids, and while they could endure confinement, they did so unwillingly and for as short a time as possible. Humans had taken a slower path to space, depending on reaction-drives until after their first contact with the warships of the Patriarchy. There was a whole human subspecies who lived on subplanetary bodies, and they had colonized the Alpha Centauri system along with their planet-dwelling cousins. Controlling the settlements of the Serpent Swarm had always been difficult for the kzin.

"There is nothing definite, as yet," the Conservor said.

"There is still much confusion; it is difficult to distinguish the increased activity of the feral humans from the warship the humans left, and *that* from the thing I hunt. Much of what I have learned is useful only as the *absence* of scent. Yet it is incontestable that the feral humans of the Swarm have made a discovery."

"ttttReet?" Traat-Admiral said inquiringly.

The Conservor's eyelids slid down, covering the round amber blanks of his eye; that left only the milky-white orb of his blind side. He beckoned with a flick of tail and ears, and the commander leaned close, signaling the guards to leave. His hands and feet were slightly damp with anxiety as they exited in a smooth, drilled rush; it was a fearsome thing, the responsibilities of high office. One must learn secrets that burdened the soul, harder by far than facing lasers or neutron-weapons. Such were the burdens of which the ordinary Hero knew nothing. Chuut-Riit had borne such secrets, and it had made him forever alone.

"Long, long ago," he whispered, "Kzinti were not as they are now. Once females could talk."

Traat-Admiral felt his batwing ears fold themselves away beneath the orange fur of his ruff as he shifted uneasily on the cushions. He had heard rumors, but—*obscene,* he thought. The thought of performing *ch'rowl* with something that could talk, beyond the half-dozen words a kzinti female could manage . . . *obscene.* He gagged slightly.

"Long, *long* ago. And Heroes were not as they are now, either." The sage brooded for a moment. "We are an old race, and we have had time to . . . shape ourselves according to the dreams we had. Such is the Patriarchal Past." The whuffling twitch of whiskers that followed did kzinti service for a grin. "Or so the encoded records of the oldest verses say. Now for another tale, Traat-Admiral. How would you react if another species sought to make slaves of kzin?"

Traat-Admiral's own whiskers twitched.

"No, consider this seriously. A race with a power of mental command; like a telepathic drug, irresistible. Imagine kzinti enslaved, submissive and obedient as mewling kits."

The other kzin suddenly found himself standing, in a low crouch. Sound dampened as his ears folded, but he could hear the sound of his own growl, low down in his chest. His lower jaw had dropped to his ruff, exposing the killing gape of his teeth; all eight claws were out on his hands, as they reached forward to grip an enemy and carry a throat to his fangs.

"This is a hypothetical situation!" the Conservor said quickly, and watched while Traat-Admiral fought back toward calm; the little nook behind the commander's dais was full of the sound of his panting and the deep gingery smell of kzinti rage. "And that reaction . . . that would make any kzin difficult to *control.* That is one reason why the race of Heroes has been shaped so. And to make us better warriors, of course; in that respect, perhaps we went a little too far."

"Perhaps," Traat-Admiral grated. "What is the nature of this peril?" He bent his muzzle to the heated bourbon and milk and lapped thirstily.

"Hrrrru," the Conservor said, crouching. "Traat-Admiral, the race in question—the Students have called them the Slavers—little is known about them. They perished so long ago, you see; at least two billion years." He used the kzinti-standard measurement, and their homeworld circled its sun at a greater distance than Terra did Sol. "Even in vacuum, little remains. But they had a device, a stasis field that forms invulnerable protection and freezes time within; we have never been able to understand the principle, and copies do not work, but we have found them occasionally, and they can be deactivated. The contents of most are utterly incomprehensible. A few do incomprehensible things. One or two we have understood, and these have won us wars, Traat-Admiral. And one contained a living Slaver; the base where he was held had to be missiled from orbit."

Traat-Admiral tossed his head again, then froze. "Stasis!" he yowled.

"Hero?"

"*Stasis!* How else— The monkey ship, just before Chuut-Riit was killed! It passed through the system at .90 *c.* We thought, how could anything decelerate? *By collision!* Disguised among the kinetic-energy missiles the monkeys threw at us as they passed. Chuut-Riit himself said that the ramscoop ship caused implausibly little damage, given the potential and the investment of resources it represented. It was nothing but a distraction, and a delivery system for the assassins, for that mangy-fur ghost corvette that eludes us, for . . . Arreeaoghg—"

His raging ceased, and his fur laid flat. "If the monkeys in the Solar system have the stasis technology—"

The sage meditated for a few moments. "*hr'rrearow t'chsssee mearowet'aatrurree,*" he said: this-does-not-follow. Traat-Admiral remembered that as one of Chuut-Riit's favorite sayings, and yes, this Conservor had been among the prince's household when he arrived from Kzin. "If they had it in quantity, consider the implications. For that matter, we believe the Slavers had a faster-than-light drive."

Stasis fields would make nonsense of war . . . and a faster-than-light drive would make the monkeys invincible, if they had it. The other kzin nodded, raising his tufted eyebrows. Theory said travel faster than lightspeed was impossible, unless one cared to be ripped into subatomic particles on the edges of a spinning black hole. Still, theory could be wrong; the kzinti were a practical race, who left most science to their subject species. What counted was results.

"True. If they had such weapons, we would not be here. If *we* had them—" He frowned, then proceeded cautiously. "Such might cause . . . troubles with discipline."

The sage spread his hands palm up, with the claws showing slightly. With a corner of his awareness, Traat-Admiral noted how age had dried and cracked the pads on palm and stubby fingers.

"Truth. There have been revolts before, although not many." The Patriarchy was necessarily extremely decentralized, when transport and information took years and decades to travel between stars. It would be fifty years or more before a new prince of the Patriarch's blood could be sent to Wunderland, and more probably they would receive a confirmation of Traat-Admiral's status by beamcast. "But with such technology . . . it is a slim chance, but there must be no disputes. If there is a menace, it must be destroyed. If a prize, it must fall into only the most loyal of hands. Yet the factions are balanced on a *wtsai*'s edge."

"Chrrr. Balancing of factions is a function of command." Traat-Admiral's gaze went unfocused, and he showed teeth in a snarl that meant anticipated triumph in a kzin. "In fact, this split can be used." He rose, raked claws through air from face to waist. "My thanks, Conservor. You have given me a scent through fresh dew to follow."

Chapter 11

This section of the Jotun range had been a Montferrat-Palme preserve since the settlement of Wunderland, more than three centuries before; when a few thousand immigrants have an entire planet to share out, there is no sense in being niggardly. The first of that line had built the high eyrie for his own; later population and wealth moved elsewhere, and in the end it became a hunting lodge. Just before the kzin conquest, it had been the only landed possession left to the Montferrat-Palme line, which had shown an unfortunate liking for risky speculative investments and even riskier horses.

"Old Claude does himself proud," Harold said, as he and Ingrid walked out onto the verandah that ran along the outer side of the house.

The building behind them was old weathered granite, sparkling slightly with flecks of mica; two stories, and another of half-timbering, under a strake roof. A big rambling structure, set into an artificial terrace on the steep side of the mountain; the slope tumbled down to a thread-thin stream in the valley below, then rose in gashed cliffs and dark-green forest ten kilometers away. The gardens were extensive and cunningly landscaped, an improvement of nature rather than an imposition on it. Native featherleaf, trembling iridescent lavender shapes ten meters tall, gumblossom and sheenbark and lapisvine. Oaks and pines and frangipani from Earth, they had grown into these hills as well . . . The air was warm and fragrant-dusty with summer flowers.

"It's certainly been spruced up since we . . . since I saw it last," she said, with a catch in her voice.

Harold looked aside at her and shivered slightly; hard to believe down in his gut she had been born two years before him. He remembered Matthieson. Young. A calm angry man, the dangerous type.

And you were no prize even as a young man, he told himself. *Ears like jugs, eyes like a basset hound, and a build like a brick outhouse. Nearly middle-aged at only sixty, for Finagle's sake. Spent five years as an unsuccessful guerrilla and the rest as a glorified barkeep.* Well, Harold's Terran Bar had been his, but . . .

"A lot more populous, too," she was saying. "Why on earth would anyone want to farm here? You'd have to modify the machinery."

There had always been a small settlement in the narrow sliver of valley floor, but it had been expanded. Terraces of vines and fruit trees wound up the slopes, and they could hear the distant tinkle of bells from the sheep and goats that grazed the rocky hills. A waterfall tumbled a thousand meters down the head of the valley, its distant toning humming through rock and air. Men and men's doings were small in that landscape of tumbled rock and crag. A church-bell rang far below, somewhere a dog was barking, and faint and far came the hiss-scream of a downdropper, surprising this close to human habitation. The air was cool and thin, not uncomfortably so to someone born on Wunderland; .61 gravity meant that the drop-off in air pressure was less steep than it would have been on Earth.

"Machinery?" Harold moved up beside her. She leaned into his side with slow care. He winced at the thought of kzin claws raking down her leg. . . .

Maybe I've been a bit uncharitable about Jonah, he thought. *The two of them came through the kzin hunt alive, until Claude and I could pull her . . . them out. That took some doing.* "They're not using machinery, Ingie. Bare hands and hand-tools."

Her mouth made a small gesture of distaste. "Slave labor? Not what I'd have thought of Claude, however he's gone downhill."

Harold laughed. "Flighters, sweetheart. Refugees. Kzin've been taking up more and more land, they're settling in, not just a garrison anymore. It was this or the labor camps; those *are* slave labor, literally. Claude grubstaked these people, as well as he could. It's where a lot of that graft he's been getting as Police Chief of Munchen went."

And the head of the capital city's human security force was in a very good position to rake it in. "*I* was surprised too. Claude's been giving a pretty good impression of having Helium II for blood, these past few years."

A step behind them. "Slandering me in my absence, old friend?"

The servants set out brandy and fruits and withdrew. They were all middle-aged and singularly close-mouthed. Ingrid thought she had seen four parallel scars under the vest of one dark slant-eyed man who looked like he came from the Sulineasan Islands.

"There are Some Things We Were Not Meant to Know," she said. Claude Montferrat-Palme was leaning forward to light a cheroot at a candle. He glanced up at her words, then looked aside at the door through which the servant had left the room; then caught her slight grimace of distaste and laid down the cheroot. He had been here a week, off and on, but that was scarcely time to drop a habit he must have been cultivating half his life.

"Correct on all counts, my dear," he said.

Claude always was perceptive.

"It's been wonderful talking over old times," she said. With sincerity, and a slight malice aforethought. They were considerably older times for the two men than for her. "And it's . . . extremely flattering that you two are still so fond of me."

But a bit troubling, now that I think about it. Even if you can expect to live two centuries, carrying the torch for four decades is a bit much.

Claude smiled again. His classic Herrenmann features combined with untypical dark hair and eyes to give an indefinable air of elegance, even in the lounging outfit he had thrown on when he shed the Munchen Polezi uniform.

"Youth," he said. And continued at her inquiring sound. "My dear, you were our youth. Hari and I were best friends; you were the . . . girl . . . young woman for which we conceived the first grand passion and bittersweet rivalry." He shrugged. "Ordinarily, a man either marries her—a ghastly fate involving children and facing each other over the morning papaya—or loses her. In any case, life goes on." His brooding gaze went to the high mullioned windows, out onto a world that had spent two generations under kzinti rule.

"You . . ." he said softly. "You vanished, and took the good times with you. Doesn't every man remember his twenties as the golden age? In our case, that was literally true. Since then, we've spent four decades fighting a rear-guard action and losing, watching everything we cared for slowly decay . . . including each other."

"Why, Claude, I didn't know you cared," Harold said mockingly. Ingrid saw their eyes meet.

Surpassing the love of women, she thought dryly. And there was a certain glow about them both, now that they were committed to action again. Few humans enjoy living a life that makes them feel defeated, and these were proud men.

"Don't tell me we wasted forty years of what might have been a beautiful friendship."

"*Chronicles of Wasted Time* is a title I've often considered for my autobiography, if I ever write it," Claude said. "Egotism wars with sloth."

Harold snorted. "Claude, if you were only a little less intelligent, you'd make a great neoromantic Byronic hero."

"Childe Claude? At this rate she'll have nothing of either of us, Hari."

The other man turned to Ingrid. "I'm a little surprised you didn't take Jonah," he said.

Ingrid looked over to Claude, who stood by the huge rustic fireplace with a brandy snifter in his hand. The Herrenmann raised a brow, and a slight, well-bred smile curved his asymmetric beard.

"Why?" she said. "Because he's younger, healthier, better educated, because he's a war hero, intelligent, dashing and good looking and a fellow Belter?"

Harold blinked, and she felt a rush of affection.

"Something like that," he said.

Claude laughed. "Women are a lot more sensible than men, *ald kamerat.* Also they mature faster. Correct?"

"Some of us do," Ingrid said. "On the other hand, a lot of us actually prefer a man with a *little* of the boyish romantic in him. You know, the type of idealism that looks like it turns into cynicism, but cherishes it secretly?" Claude's face fell. "On the other hand, your genuinely mature male is a different kettle of fish. Far too likely to be completely without illusions, and then how do you control him?"

She grinned and patted him on the cheek as she passed on the way to pour herself a glass of verguuz. "Don't worry,

Claude, you aren't that way yourself, you just *act* like it." She sipped, and continued: "Actually, it's ethnic."

Harold made an inquiring grunt, and Claude pursed his lips.

"He's a Belter. Sol-Belter at that."

"My dear, *you* are a Belter," Claude said, genuine surprise overriding his habitual air of bored knowingness.

Harold lit a cigarette, ignoring her glare. "Let me guess . . . He's too prissy?"

Ingrid sipped again at the minty liqueur. "Nooo, not really. I'm a Belter, but I'm . . . a bit of a throwback." The other two nodded. Genetically, as well. Ingrid could have passed for a pure Caucasoid, even. Common enough on Wunderland, but rare anywhere else in human space.

"Look," she went on: "What happens to somebody in space who's not ultra-careful about everything? Someone who isn't a detail man, someone who doesn't think checking the gear the seventh time is more important than the big picture? Someone who isn't a low-affect in-control type every day of his life?"

"They die," Harold said flatly. Claude nodded agreement.

"What happens when you put a group through *four hundred years* of that type of selection? Plus the more adventurous types have been leaving the Sol-Belt for other systems, whenever they could, so Serpent Swarm Belters are more like the *past* of Sol-Belters."

"Oh." Claude nodded in time with Harold's grunt. "What about flatlanders?"

Ingrid shuddered and tossed back the rest of her drink. "Oh, they're like . . . like . . . They just have no sense of survival at *all.* Barely human. Wunderlanders strike a happy medium"—she glanced at them roguishly out of the corners of her eyes—"after which it comes down to individual merits."

"So." She shook herself, and felt the lieutenant's persona settling down over her like a spacesuit, the tight skin-hugging permeable-membrane kind. "This has been a very pleasant holiday, but what do we do now?"

Claude poked at the burning logs with a fire iron and chuckled. For a moment the smile on his face made her distinctly uneasy, and she remembered that he had survived and climbed to high office in the vicious politics of the collaborationist government. For his own purposes, not all of which were unworthy; but the means . . .

"Well," he said smoothly, turning back towards them. "As

you can imagine, the raid and Chuut-Riit's . . . *elegant* demise put the . . . pigeon among the cats with a vengeance. The factionalism among the kzin has come to the surface again. One group wants to make minimal repairs and launch the Fifth Fleet against Earth immediately—"

"Insane," Ingrid said, shaking her head. It was the threat of a *delay* in the attack, until the kzin were truly ready, which had prompted the UN into the desperation measure of the *Yamamoto* raid.

"No, just ratcat," Harold said, pouring himself another brandy. Ingrid frowned, and he halted the bottle in mid-pour.

"Exactly," Claude nodded happily. "The other is loyal to Chuut-Riit's memory. More complicated than that; there are cross-splits. Local-born kzin against the immigrants who came with the late lamented kitty governor, generational conflicts, *eine gros teufeleshrek*. For example, my esteemed former superior—"

He spoke a phrase in the Hero's Tongue, and Ingrid translated mentally: Ktiir-Supervisor-of-Animals. A minor noble with a partial name. From what she had picked up on Wunderland, the name itself was significant as well: *Ktiir* was common on the frontier planet of the kzinti empire that had launched the conquest fleets against Wunderland, but archaic on the inner planets near the kzin homeworld.

"—was very vocal about it at a staff meeting. Incidentally, they completely swallowed our little white lie about Axelrod-Bauergartner being responsible for Ingrid's escape."

"That must have been something to see," Harold said. Claude sighed, remembering. "Well," he began, "since it was in our offices I managed to take a holo—"

Coordinating-Staff-Officer was a tall kzin, well over two meters, and thin by the felinoid race's standards. Or so Claude Montferrat-Palme thought; it was difficult to say, when you were flat on your stomach on the floor, watching the furred feet pace.

Ridiculous, he thought. Humans were not meant for this posture. Kzin were: they could run on four feet as easily as two, and their skulls were on a flexible joint. This was giving him a crick in the neck . . . but it was obligatory for the human supervisors just below the kzinti level to attend. The consequences of disobeying the kzin were all too plain, in the transparent block of plastic that encased the head of Munchen's former assistant chief of police, resting on the mantelpiece.

Claude's own superior was speaking, Ktiir-Supervisor-of-Animals.

"This monkey"—he jerked a claw at the head—"was responsible for allowing the two Sol-agent humans to escape the hunt." He was in the half-crouched posture Claude recognized as proper for reporting to one higher in rank but lower in social status, although the set of ears and tail was insufficiently respectful. *If I can read kzinti body language that well.*

This was security HQ, the old Herrenhaus where the Nineteen Families had met before the kzin came. The room was broad and gracious, floored in tile, walled in lacy white stone fretwork, and roofed in Wunderland ebony that was veined with natural silver. Outside fountains were plashing in the gardens, and he could smell the oleanders that blossomed there. The gingery scent of kzin anger was heavier, as Staff-Officer stopped and prodded a half-kick at Montferrat-Palme's flank. The foot was encased in a sort of openwork leather-and-metal boot, with slits for the claws. Those were out slightly, probably in unconscious reflex, and he could feel the razor tips prickle slightly through the sweat-wet fabric of his uniform.

"Dominant One, this slave—" Claude began.

"Dispense with the formalities, human," the kzin said. It spoke Wunderlander and was politer than most; Claude's own superior habitually referred to humans as *kz'eerkt,* monkey. That was a quasi-primate on the kzinti homeworld. A tree-dwelling mammal-analog, at least, as much like a monkey as a kzin was like a tiger, which was not much. "Tell me what occurred."

"Dominant One . . . Coordinating-Staff-Officer," Claude continued, craning his neck. *Don't make eye contact,* he reminded himself. A kzin stare was a dominance-gesture or a preparation to attack. "Honored Ktiir-Supervisor-of-Animals decided that . . ."*—don't use her name—*"the former assistant chief of Munchen Polezi was more zealous than I in the tracking-down of the two UN agents, and should therefore be in charge of disposing of them in the hunt."

Staff-Officer stopped pacing and gazed directly at Ktiir-Supervisor; Claude could see the pink tip of the slimmer kzin's tail twitching before him, naked save for a few bristly orange hairs.

"So not only did your interrogators fail to determine that the humans had *successfully* sabotaged Chuut-Riit's palace-defense computers, you appointed a traitor to arrange for their disposal. The feral humans laugh at us! Our leader is killed and the assassins go free from under our very claws!"

Ktiir-Supervisor rose from his crouch. He pointed at another kzin who huddled in one corner; a telepath, with the characteristic hangdog air and unkempt fur.

"Your tame *sthondat* there didn't detect it either," he snarled.

Literally snarled, Claude reflected. It was educational; after seeing a kzin you never referred to a human expression by that term again.

Staff-Officer wuffled, snorting open his wet black nostrils and working his whiskers. It should have been a comical expression, but on four hundred pounds of alien carnivore it was not in the least funny. "You hide behind the failures of others," he said, hissing. "Traat-Admiral directs me to inform you that your request for reassignment to the Swarm flotillas has been denied. Neither unit will accept you."

"Traat-Admiral!" Ktiir-Supervisor rasped. "He is like a kit who has climbed a tree and can't get down, mewling for its dam. Ktrodni-Stkaa should be governor! This talk of a 'secret menace' among the asteroids is a scentless trail to divert attention from Traat-Admiral's refusal to launch the Fifth Fleet."

"Such was the strategy of the great Chuut-Riit, murdered through your incompetence—or worse."

Ktiir-Supervisor bristled, the orange-red fur standing out and turning his body into a cartoon caricature of a cat, bottle-shaped.

"You nameless licker-of-scentless-piss from that jumped-up crecheproduct admiral, what do you accuse me of?"

"Treason, or stupidity amounting to it," the other kzin sneered. Ostentatiously, he flared his batlike ears into a vulnerable rest position and let his tail droop.

Ktiir-Supervisor screamed. "You inner-worlds palace fop, you and Traat-Admiral alike! I urinate on the shrines of your ancestors from a height! Crawl away and call for your monkeys to groom you with blowdriers!"

Staff-Officer's hands extended outward, the night-black claws glinting as they slid from their sheaths. His tail was rigid now. Hairdressers were a luxury the late governor had introduced, and wildly popular among the younger nobility.

"*Kshat*-hunter," he growled. "You are not fit to roll in Chuut-Riit's shit! You lay word-claws to the blood of the Riit."

"Chuut-Riit made *ch'rowl* with monkeys!" A gross insult, as well as anatomically impossible.

There was a feeling of hush, as the two males locked eyes. Then the heavy *wtsai*-knives came out and the great orange shapes seemed to flow together, meeting at the arch of their leaps, howling. Claude rolled back against the wall as the half-ton of weight slammed down again, sending splinters of furniture out like shrapnel. For a moment the kzin were locked and motionless, hand to knife-wrist; their legs locked in thigh-holds as well, to keep the back legs from coming up for a disemboweling strike. Mouths gaped toward each other's throats, inch-long fangs exposed in the seventy-degree killing gape. Then there was a blur of movement; they sprang apart, together, went over in a caterwauling blur of orange fur and flashing metal, a whirl far too fast for human eyesight to follow.

He caught glimpses: distended eyes, scrabbling claws, knives sinking home into flesh, amid a clamor loud enough to drive needles of pain into his ears. Bits of bloody fur hit all around him, and there was a human scream as the fighters rolled over a secretary. Then Staff-Officer rose, slashed and glaring. Ktiir-Supervisor lay sprawled, legs twitching galvanically with the hilt of Staff-Officer's *wtsai* jerking next to his lower spine. The slender kzin panted for a moment and then leaped forward to grab his opponent by the neck-ruff. He jerked him up toward the waiting jaws, clamped them down on his throat. Ktiir-Supervisor struggled feebly, then slumped. Blood-bubbles swelled and burst on his nose. A wrench and Staff-Officer was backing off, shaking his head and spitting, licking at the matted fur of his muzzle; he groomed for half a minute before wrenching the knife free and beginning to spread the dead kzin's ears for a clean trophy-cut.

"Erruch," Ingrid said as the recording finished. "You've got more . . . you've got a lot of guts, Claude, dealing with them at first hand like that."

"Oh, some of them aren't so bad. For ratcats. Staff-Officer there expressed 'every confidence' in me." He made an expressive gesture with his hands. "Although he also reminded me there was a continuous demand for fresh monkeymeat."

Ingrid paled slightly and laid a hand on his arm. That was not a figure of speech to her, not after the chase through the kzin hunting preserve. She remembered the sound of the hunting scream behind her, and the thudding crackle of the alien's pads on the leaves as it made its four-footed rush, rising as it screamed and leapt from the ravine lip above her. The long sharpened pole in her hands, and the soft heavy feel as its own weight drove it onto her weapon . . .

Claude laid his hand on hers. Harold cleared his throat. "Well," he said. "Your position looks solider than we thought."

The other man gave Ingrid's hand a squeeze and released it. "Yes," he said. A hunter's look came into his eyes, emphasizing the foxy sharpness of his features. "In fact, they're outfitting some sort of expedition; that's why they can't spare personnel for administrative duties."

Ingrid and Harold both leaned forward instinctively. Harold crushed out his cigarette with swift ferocity.

"Another Fleet?" Ingrid asked. *I'll be stuck here, and Earth . . .*

Claude shook his head. "No. That raid did a *lot* of damage; it'd be a year or more just to get back to the state of readiness they had when the *Yamamoto* arrived. Military readiness." Both the others winced; over half a million humans had died in the attack. "But they're definitely mobilizing for something inside the system. Two flotillas. Something out in the Swarm."

"Markham?" Ingrid ventured. It seemed a little extreme; granted he had the *Catskinner,* but—

"I doubt it. They're bringing the big guns up to full personnel, the battlewagons. *Conquest Fang* class."

They exchanged glances. Those were interstellar-capable warships: carriers for lesser craft, equipped with weapons that could crack planets, and defenses to match. Almost self-sufficient, with facilities for manufacturing their own fuel, parts, and weapons requirements from asteroidal material. They were normally kept on standby as they came out of the yards, only a few at full readiness for training purposes.

"All of them?" Harold said.

"No, but about three-quarters. Ratcats will be thin on the ground for a while, except for the ones stored in coldsleep. And—" He hesitated, forced himself to continue. "—I'll be able to do most good staying here. For a year or so at least, I can be invaluable to the underground without risking much."

The others remained silent while he looked away, granting him time to compose himself.

"I've got the false ID and transit papers, with disguises," he said. "Ingrid . . . you aren't safe anywhere on Wunderland. In the Swarm, with that ship you came in, maybe the two of you can do some good."

"Claude—" she began.

He shook his head. When he spoke, his old lightness was back in the tone.

"I wonder," he said, "I truly wonder what Markham *is* doing. I'd *like* to think he's causing so much trouble that they're mobilizing the Fleet, but . . ."

Chapter 12

Tiamat was crowded, Captain Jonah Matthieson decided. Crowded and chaotic, even more so than the last time he had been here. He shouldered through the line into the zero-G waiting area at the docks, a huge pie-shaped disk; those were at the ends of the sixty-by-twenty-kilometer spinning cylinder that served the Serpent Swarm as its main base. There had been dozens of ships in the magnetic grapples: rockjack singleships, transports, freighters . . . refugee ships as well; the asteroid industrial bases had been heavily damaged during the *Yamamoto*'s raid. Not quite as many as you would expect, though. The UN ramscoop ship's weapons had been iron traveling at velocities 90 percent of a photon's. When something traveling at that speed hit, the result resembled an antimatter bomb.

A line of lifebubbles went by, shepherded by medics. Casualties, injuries beyond the capacities of outstation autodocs. Some of them were quite small; he looked in the transparent surface of one, and then away quickly, swallowing.

Shut up, he told his mind. *Collateral damage can't be helped.* And there had been a trio of kzinti battle-wagons in dock too, huge tapering daggers with tau-cross bows and magnetic launchers like openwork gunbarrels; *Slasher*-class fighters clung to the flanks, swarms of metallic lice. Repair and installation crews swarmed around them; Tiamat's factories were pouring out warheads and sensor-effector systems.

The mass of humanity jammed solid in front of the exits. Jonah waited like a floating particle of cork, watching the others passed through the scanners one by one. Last time, with

Ingrid—*forget that,* he thought—there had been a cursory retina scan, and four goldskin cops floating like a daisy around each exit. Now they were doing blood samples as well, presumably for DNA analysis; besides the human police, he could see waldo-guns, floating ovoids with clusters of barrels and lenses and antennae. A kzin to control them, bulking even huger in fibroid armor and helmet.

And all for little old me, he thought, kicking himself forward and letting the goldskin stick his hand into the tester. There was a sharp prickle on his thumb, and he waited for the verdict. *Either the false ident holds, or it doesn't.* The four police with stunners and riot-armor, the kzin in full infantry fig, six waldos with ten-megawatt lasers . . . If it came to a fight, the odds were not good. *Since all I have is a charming smile and a rejiggered light-pen.*

"Pass through, pass through," the goldskin said, in a tone that combined nervousness and boredom.

Jonah decided he couldn't blame her; the kzinti security apparatus must have gone winging paranoid-crazy when Chuut-Riit was assassinated, and then the killers escaped with human-police connivance. *On second thought, these klongs all volunteered to work for the pussies. Bleep them.*

He passed through the mechanical airlock and into one of the main transverse corridors. It was ten meters by twenty, and sixty kilometers long; three sides were small businesses and shops, spinward fourth a slideway. The last time he had been here, a month ago, there had been murals on the walls of the concourse area. Prewar, faded and stained, but still gracious and marked with the springlike optimism of the settlement of the Alpha Centauri system. Outdoor scenes from Wunderland in its pristine condition, before the settlers had modified the ecology to suit the immigrants from Earth. Scenes of slowships, half-disassembled after their decades-long flight from the Solar system.

The murals had been replaced by holograms. Atrocity holograms, of survivors and near-survivors of the UN raid. Mostly from dirtside, since with an atmosphere to transmit blast and shock effects you had a greater transition between dead and safe. Humans crushed, burned, flayed by glass-fragments, mutilated; heavy emphasis on children. There was a babble of voices with the holos, weeping and screaming and moaning with pain, and a strobing title: *Sol-System Killers! Their liberation is death!* And an idealized kzin standing in front of a group of cowering mothers and infants, raising a shield to ward off the attack of a repulsive flatlander-demon.

Interesting, Jonah thought. Whoever had designed that had managed to play on about every prejudice a human resident of the Alpha Centauri system could have. It had to be a human psychist doing the selection; kzinti didn't understand *Homo sapiens* well enough. A display of killing power like this would make a kzin respectful. Human propagandists needed to whip their populations into a war-frenzy, and anger was a good tool. Make a kzin angry? You didn't *need* to make them angry. An *enemy* would try to make kzin angry, because that reduced their efficiency. *Let this remind you that a collaborationist is not necessarily an incompetent.* A traitor, a Murphy's-asshole inconvenience, but not necessarily an idiot. Nor even amoral; he supposed it was possible to convince yourself that you were serving the greater good by giving in. Smoothing over the inevitable, since it *did* look like the kzin were winning.

A local newsscreen was broadcasting as well; this time a denial that kzinti ships were attacking refugee and rescue vessels. *Odd. Wonder how that rumor got started; even kzin aren't* that *kill-crazy.*

Jonah shook himself out of the trance and flipped himself over. *I've got to watch this tendency to depression,* he thought sourly. *Finagle, I ought to be bouncing for joy.*

Instead, he felt a gray lethargy. His feet drifted into contact with the edge of the slideway, and he began moving slowly forward; more rapidly as he edged toward the center. The air became more quiet. There was always a subliminal rumble near the ends of Tiamat's cylinder, powdered metals and chemicals pumping into the fabricators. Now he would have to contact the Nipponese underworlder who had smuggled them from Tiamat to Wunderland in the first place; what had been his name? Shigehero Hirose, that was it. An *oyabun,* whatever that meant. There was the data they had downloaded from Chuut-Riit's computers, priceless stuff. He would need a message-maser to send it to *Catskinner;* the ship had been modified with an interstellar-capacity sender. And—

"Hello, Captain."

Jonah turned his head, very slowly. A man had touched his elbow; there was another at his other side. Stocky, even by flatlander standards, with a considerable paunch. Coal-black with tightly curled wiry hair: pure Afroid, not uncommon in some ethnic enclaves on Wunderland but very rare on Earth, where gene-flow had been nearly random for going on four hundred years.

General Buford Early, UN Space Navy; late ARM. Jonah gasped and sagged sideways, a gray before his eyes like high-G blackout. The flatlander slipped a hand under his arm and bore him up with thick-boned strength. Archaic, like the man; he was . . . at least two centuries old. Impossible to tell, these days. The only limiting factor was being born after medicine started progressing fast enough to compensate for advancing age. . . .

"Take it easy," Early said.

Eyes warred with mind. Early was here; Early was sitting in his office on Gibraltar base back in the Solar system.

Jonah struggled for breath, then fell into the rhythm taught by the Zen adepts who had trained him for war. Calm flowed back. Much knowledge had fallen out of human culture in three hundred years of peace, before the kzinti came, but the monks had preserved a great deal. What UN bureaucrat would suspect an old man sitting quietly beneath a tree of dangerous technique?

Jonah spoke to himself: *Reality is change. Shock and fear result from imposing concepts on reality. Abandon concepts. Being is time, and time is Being. Birth and death is the life of the Buddha.* Then: *Thank you, roshi.*

The men at either elbow guided him to the slower edge-strip of the slideway and onto the sidewalk. Jonah looked "ahead," performed the mental trick that turned the cylinder into a hollow tower above his head, then back to horizontal. He freed his arms with a quiet flick and sank down on the chipped and stained poured-rock bench. That was notional in this gravity, but it gave you a place to hitch your feet.

"Well?" he said, looking at the second man.

This one was different. Younger, Jonah would say; eyes do not age or hold expression, but the small muscles around them do. Oriental eyes, more common than not, like Jonah's own. Both of them were in Swarm-Belter clothing, gaudy and somehow sleazy at the same time, with various mysterious pieces of equipment at their belts. Perfect cover, if you were pretending to be a modestly prosperous entrepreneur of the Serpent Swarm. The kzinti allowed a good deal of freedom to the Belters in this system; it was more efficient and required less supervision than running everything themselves. That would change as their numbers built up, of course.

"Well?" he said again.

Early grinned, showing strong and slightly yellowed teeth, and pulled a cheroot from a pocket. *Actually less uncommon here than in the Solar system,* Jonah thought, gagging slightly. *Maybe Wunderlanders smoke because the kzinti don't like it.*

"You didn't seriously think that we'd let an opportunity like the *Yamamoto* raid go by and only put one arrow on the string, do you, Captain? By the way, this is my associate, Watsuji Hajime." The man smiled and bowed. "A member of the team I brought in."

"Another stasis field?" Jonah said.

"We did have one ready," Early said. "We like to have a little extra tucked away."

"Trust the ARM," Jonah said sourly.

For a long time they had managed to make Solar humanity forget that there had even *been* such things as war or weapons or murder. That was looked back upon as a Golden Age, now, after two generations of war with the kzinti; privately, Matthieson thought of it as the Years of Stagnation. The ARM had not wanted to believe in the kzinti, not even when the crew of the *Angel's Pencil* had reported their own first near-fatal contact with the felinoids. And when the war started, the ARM had *still* dealt out its hoarded secrets with the grudging reluctance of a miser.

"It's for the greater good," Early replied.

"Sure." *That you slowed down research and the kzinti hit us with technological superiority?* For that matter, why had it taken a century and a half to develop regeneration techniques? And *millions* of petty criminals—jay walkers and the like—had been sliced, diced, and sent to the organ banks before then. *Ancient history,* he told himself. The Belters had always hated the ARM. . . .

"Certainly for the greater good that you've got backup, now," Early continued. "We came in disguised as a slug aimed at a weapons fabrication asteroid. The impact was quite genuine . . . God's my witness—" he continued.

He's old *all right.*

"—the intelligence we've gathered and beamed back is *already* worth the entire cost of the *Yamamoto.* And you and Lieutenant Raines succeeded beyond our hopes."

Meaning you had no hope we'd survive, Jonah added to himself. Early caught his eye and nodded with an ironic turn of his full lips. The younger man felt a slight chill; how good at reading body language would you get, with two centuries of practice? How human would you remain?

"Speaking of which," the general continued, "where is Lieutenant Raines, Matthieson?"

Jonah shrugged, looking away slightly and probing at his own feelings. "She . . . decided to stay. To come out later, actually, with Yarthkin-Schotmann and Montferrat-Palme. I've got all the data."

Early's eyebrows rose. "Not *entirely* unexpected." His eyes narrowed again. "No personal animosities, here, I trust? We won't be heading out for some time"—*if ever,* went unspoken—"and we may need to work with them again."

The young Sol-Belter looked out at the passing crowd on the slideway, at thousands swarming over the hand-nets in front of the shopfronts on the other three sides of the cylinder.

"My ego's a little bruised," he said finally. "But . . . no."

Early nodded. "Didn't have the leisure to become all that attached, I suppose," he said. "Good professional attitude."

Jonah began to laugh softly, shoulders shaking. "Finagle, General, you *are* a long time from being a young man, aren't you? No offense."

"None taken," the Intelligence officer said dryly.

"Actually, we just weren't compatible." What was that phrase in the history tape? Miscegenation abyss? Birth cohort gap? No . . . "Generation gap," he said.

"She was only a few years younger than you," Early said suspiciously.

"*Biologically*, sir. But she was *born* before the War. During the Long Peace. Wunderland wasn't sewn nearly as tight as Earth, or even the Solar Belt . . . but they still didn't have a single deadly weapon in the whole system, saving hunting tools. I've been in the navy or training for it since I was six! We just didn't have anything in common except software, sex, and the mission." He shrugged again, and felt the lingering depression leave him. "It was like being involved with a younger version of my mother."

Early shook his head, chuckling himself, a deep rich sound. "Temporal displacement. Doesn't need relativity, boy; wait till you're my age. And now," he continued, "we are going to have a little talk."

"What've we been doing?"

"Oh, not a debriefing. That first. But then . . ." He grinned brilliantly. "A . . . job interview, of sorts."

☆ ☆ ☆

"Why should we trust you?" the man said. He was carefully nondescript in his worker's overalls and cloth cap; the roughened hands with dirt ground into the knuckles and half-moons of grease under the nails showed it was genuine. The accent was incongruously elegant, pure Wunderlander so pedantic it was almost Plattdeutsch, and the lined gray-stubbled face might have been anywhere between sixty and twice that, depending on how much medical care he could afford. "We've watched you growing fat on human scraps your masters threw you, ever since the War."

"Don't trust me," Claude Montferrat-Palme said evenly. "Trust the guns I deliver. Trust this."

He pushed a data chip across the table. "This is a record of the informants the Munchen Polezi has in the various underground organizations . . . with the Intelligence Branch appraisals of the reliability of each. I'd advise you to use it cautiously."

The meeting place was a run-down working-class bar on the Donau's banks. Noise and smells filtered up through the planks from the taproom below, where dockers and fisherfolk spent what they had on cheap gin and pseudo-verguuz and someone played a very bad musicomp. This upper chamber was a dosshouse now, smelling of old sweat from the pallets on the floor, cheap tobacco, less namable things. From the faded murals it had probably been something else back before the War; he racked his memory . . . yes, a clubhouse. The Munchen Turnverein. Through a window the broad surface of the river glistened in the evening sun, and a barge went by silently with a man in a thick sweater and billed cap standing at the tiller smoking a pipe.

For an instant Claude was painfully conscious of how beautiful this world was, and how much he would be losing when they caught him. Not that he was much afraid of death, and he had means to ensure there would be little pain. No, it was the thought of all that he would never do or see that was almost intolerable. The silence stretched as the man clicked the chip into a wrist-comp and scrolled. His graying blond eyebrows rose.

"Very useful indeed, if it checks out. And if we *don't* use it cautiously . . ."

Claude nodded. "If you don't, I'm very dead and no more use to you at all for catching the *next* set of traitors . . ."

Cold blue eyes met his, infinitely weary and determined in a way that had nothing at all to do with hope.

"Why?" the man said.

"Would you believe I've spent forty-odd years infiltrating until I was in a position to do some good?"

"No."

Claude sighed. "Funny, I haven't been able to convince myself of that, either. Let's say that I've come to believe we can make some small difference in the outcome of the War."

At that the man nodded, mouth twisting in a thin smile. "More believable, but not very comforting. We've been getting a good many recruits on those grounds since the UN raid. How many of them will stick with it, when the hope goes?" An unpleasant laugh. "Therefore it behooves us to see that they commit themselves with acts beyond forgiveness before their initial enthusiasm runs out."

Not to mention the permanently useful, Claude thought. There had been a new wave of suicide bombings, mostly of kzinti wandering through human neighborhoods. The reprisals had been fairly ghastly but not indiscriminate . . . yet. He repressed an impulse to dabble at his forehead.

"That data . . . not to mention those strakakers and antitank weapons and nightvision goggles . . . all constitute more than enough to qualify me as monkeymeat," he said. "The kzinti are much harder on their immediate servants, you know."

"I weep for you," the other man said.

Perhaps if I hadn't been so cursed *efficient,* Claude thought.

"In fact," the Resistance fighter went on, "I'd break a personal rule and watch the video while they hunted you down. But you're too valuable to lose, if this"—he tapped his wrist—"is genuine. Don't move for a half hour."

He left, and Claude lit a cigarette with hands that shook quietly.

How long can I last? he wondered clinically as he stared out at the blue Donau. *A month at least. Possibly six months to a year. I might even be able to spot it coming and go bush when they get on to me.* A short life.

"Still better than a long and comfortable death," he whispered.

☆ ☆ ☆

"Well. So."

The *oyabun* nodded and folded his hands.

Jonah looked around. They were in the three-twelve shell of Tiamat, where spin gave an equivalent of .72-G weight.

Expensive, even now when gravity polarizers were beginning to spread beyond kzinti and military-manufacturing use. Microgravity is marvelous for most industrial use. There are other things that need weight, bearing children to term is among them. This room was equally expensive. Most of the furnishings were *wood*: the low tables at which they all sat, knees crossed; the black-lacquered carved screens with rampant tigers as well, and he strongly suspected that those were even older than General Buford Early. A set of Japanese swords rested in a niche, long katana and the short "sword of apology," on their ebony stand.

Sandalwood incense was burning somewhere, and the floor was covered in neat mats of plaited straw. Against all this the plain good clothes of the man who called himself Shigehero Hirose were something of a shock. The thin ancient porcelain of his sake cup gleamed as he set it down on the table, and spoke to the Oriental who had come with the general. Jonah kept his face elaborately blank; it was unlikely that either of them suspected his knowledge of Japanese . . . enough to understand most of a conversation, if not to speak it. Nippon's tongue had never been as popular as her goods, being too difficult for outsiders to learn easily.

"It is . . . an unexpected honor to entertain one of the Tokyo branch of the clan," Shigehero was saying. *"And how do events proceed in the land of the Sun Goddess?"*

Watsuji Hajime shrugged. *"No better than can be expected, Uncle,"* he replied, and sucked breath between his teeth. *"This war presents opportunities, but also imposes responsibilities. Neutrality is impossible."*

"Regrettably, this is so," Shigehero said. His face grew stern. *"Nevertheless, you have revealed the Association's codewords to outsiders."* They both glanced sidelong at Early and Matthieson. *"Perhaps you are what you claim. Perhaps not. This must be demonstrated. Honor must be established."*

Whatever that meant, the Earther-Japanese did not like it. His face stayed as expressionless as a mask carved from light-brown wood, but sweat started up along his brow. A door slid open, and one of the guards who had brought them here entered noiselessly. Jonah recognized the walk; training in the Art, one of the *budo* styles. An organic fighting-machine. Highly illegal on Earth until the War, and for the most part in the Alpha Centauri system as well. Otherwise he was a stocky nondescript man in loose black, although the Belter thought there might be soft armor beneath it. Moving with studied grace, he knelt and laid the featureless rectangle of blond wood by Watsuji's left hand.

The Earther bowed his head, a lock of black hair falling over his forehead. Then he raised his eyes and slid the box in front of him, opening it with delicate care. Within were a white linen handkerchief, a folded cloth, a block of maple, and a short curved guardless knife in a black leather sheath. Watsuji's movements took on the slow precision of a religious ritual as he laid the maple block on the table atop the cloth and began binding the little finger of his left hand with the handkerchief, painfully tight. He laid the hand on the block and drew the knife. It slid free without sound, a fluid curve. The two men's eyes were locked as he raised the knife.

Jonah grunted as if he had been kicked in the belly. The older man was missing a joint on the little finger of his left hand, too. The Sol-Belter had thought that was simply the bad medical care available in the Swarm, but anyone who could afford this room . . .

The knife flashed down, and there was a small spurt of blood, a rather grisly crunching sound like celery being sliced. Watsuji made no sound, but his face went pale around the lips. Shigehero bowed more deeply. The servant-guard walked forward on his knees and gathered up the paraphernalia, folding the cloth about it with the same ritual care. There was complete silence, save for the sigh of ventilators and Watsuji's deep breathing, harsh but controlled.

The two Nipponjin poured themselves more of the heated rice wine and sipped. When Shigehero spoke again, it was in English.

"It is good to see that the old customs have not been entirely forgotten in the Solar system," he said. "Perhaps my branch of the Association was . . . shall we say a trifle precipitate, when they decided emigration was the only way to preserve their, ah, purity." He raised his glass slightly to the general. "When your young warriors passed through last month, I was surprised that so much effort had been required to insert so slender a needle. I see that we underestimated you."

He picked up a folder of printout on the table before him. "It is correct that the . . . ah, assets you and your confederates represent would be a considerable addition to my forces," he went on. "However, please remember that my Association is more in the nature of a family business than a political organization. We are involved in the underground struggle against the kzin because we are human, little more."

Early raised his cup of sake in turn; the big spatulate hands handled the porcelain with surprising delicacy. "You . . . and your, shall we say, *black-clad* predecessors have been involved in others' quarrels before this. To be blunt, when it paid. The valuata we brought are significant, surely?"

Jonah blinked in astonishment. *This is the cigar-chomping, kick-ass general I came to know and loathe?* he thought. *Live and learn. Learn so that you can go on living. . . .* Then again, before the kzinti attack Buford Early had been a professor of military history at the ARM academy. You had to be out of the ordinary for that; it involved knowledge that would send an ordinary man to the psychists for memory-wipe.

Shigehero made a minimalist gesture. "Indeed. Yet this would also involve integrating your group in my command structure. An indigestible lump, a weakness in the chain of command, since you do not owe personal allegiance to me. And, to be frank, non-Nipponese generally do not rise to the decision-making levels in this organization. No offense."

"None taken," Early replied tightly. "If you would prefer a less formal link?"

Shigehero sighed, then brought up a remote 'board from below the table, and signed to the guards. They quickly folded the priceless antique screens, to reveal a standard screen-wall.

"That might be my own inclination, esteemed General," he said. "Except that certain information has come to my attention. Concerning Admiral Ulf Reichstein-Markham of the Free Wunderland Navy . . . I see your young subordinate has told you of this person. And the so-valuable ship he left in the Herrenmann's care, and a . . . puzzling discovery they have made together."

A scratching at the door interrupted him. He frowned, then nodded. It opened, revealing a guard and another figure who looked to Early for confirmation. The general accepted a data-tab, slipped it into his belt unit and held the palm-sized computer to one ear.

Ah, thought Jonah. *I'm not the only one to get a nasty shock today.* The black man's skin had turned grayish, and his hands shook for a second as he pushed the "wipe" control. Jonah chanced a glance at his eyes. It was difficult to be sure—they were dark and the lighting was low—but he could have sworn the pupils expanded to swallow the iris.

"H-" Early cleared his throat. "This information . . . would it be about an, er, *artifact* found in an asteroid? Certain behavioral peculiarities?"

Shigehero nodded and touched the controls. A blurred holo sprang up on the wall; from a helmet-cam, Jonah decided. Asteroidal mining equipment on the surface of a medium-sized rock, one kilometer by two. A docked ship in the background; he recognized Markham's *Nietzsche,* and others distant enough to be drifting lights, and suited figures putting up bubble-habitats. Then panic, and a hole appeared where the laser-driller had been a moment before. Milling confusion, and an . . . yes, it must be an alien, came floating up out of the hole.

The young Sol-Belter felt the pulse hammer in his ears. He was watching the first living non-kzin alien discovered in all the centuries of human spaceflight. It couldn't be a kzin, the proportions were all wrong. About 1.5 meters, judging by the background shots of humans. Difficult to say in vacuum armor, but it looked almost as thick as it was wide, with an enormous round head and stubby limbs, hands like three-fingered mechanical grabs. There was a weapon or tool gripped in one fist; as they watched the other hand came over to touch it and it changed shape, *writhing*. Jonah opened his mouth to question and—

"Stop!" The general's bull bellow wrenched their attention around. *"Stop that display* immediately, *that's an* order!"

Shigehero touched the control panel and the holo froze. "You are not in a position to give orders here, *gaijin,*" he said. The two guards along the wall put hands inside their lapover jackets and glided closer, soundless as kzin.

Early wrenched open his collar and waved a hand. "Please, *oyabun,* if we could speak alone? *Completely* alone, under the rose, just for a moment. Upon your blood, more is at stake here than you realize!"

Silence stretched. At last, fractionally, Shigehero nodded. The others stood and filed out into the outer room, almost as graciously appointed as the inner. The other members of Early's team awaited them there; half a dozen of assorted ages and skills. There were no guards, on this side of the wall at least, and the *oyabun*'s men had provided refreshments and courteously ignored the quick, thorough sweep for listening devices. Watsuji headed for the sideboard, poured himself a double vodka and knocked it back.

"Tanj it," he wheezed, under his breath. Jonah keyed himself coffee and a handmeal; it had been a rough day.

"Problems?" the Belter asked.

"I can't even get to an autodoc until we're out of this Finagle-forsaken bughouse," the Earther replied. "I knew they were conservative here, but this bleeping farce!" He made a gesture with his mutilated hand. "Nobody at home's done that for a hundred years! I felt like I was in a holoplay. Namida Amitsu, we're *legal,* these days. Well, somewhat. Gotten out of the organ trade, at least. This—!"

Jonah nodded in impersonal sympathy. For a flatlander, the man had dealt with the pain extremely well; Earthsiders were seldom far from automated medical attention. Even before the War, Belters had had to be more self-sufficient.

"What really bothers *me,*" Jonah said quietly, settling into a chair, "is what's going on in *there.*" He nodded to the door. "Just like the ARM, to go all around Murphy's Hall to keep us in the dark."

"Exactly," Watsuji said gloomily, nursing his hand. "Those crazy bastards think they own the world."

"Run the world," Jonah echoed. "Well they do, don't they? The ARM—"

"Naw, not the UN. This is older than that."

Jonah shrugged.

"A lot older. Bunch of mumbo jumbo. At least—"

"Eh?"

"I *think* it's just mumbo jumbo. God, this thing hurts."

Jonah settled down, motionless. He would not be bored; Belters got a good deal of practice in sitting still and doing nothing without losing alertness, and his training had increased it. The curiosity was the itch he could not scratch.

Could be worse, he thought, taking another bite of the fishy-tasting handmeal. The consistency was rather odd, but it was tasty. *The flatlander could have told me to cut* my *finger off.*

"Explain yourself," Shigehero said.

Instead, Early moved closer and dipped his finger in his rice wine. With that, he drew a figure on the table before the *oyabun.* A stylized rose, overlain by a cross; he omitted the pyramid. The fragment of the Order which had accompanied the migrations to Alpha Centauri had not included anyone past the Third Inner Circle, after all . . .

Shigehero's eyes went wide. He picked up a cloth and

quickly wiped the figure away, but his gaze stayed locked on the blank surface of the table for a moment. Then he swallowed and touched the control panel again.

"We are entirely private," he said, then continued formally: "You bring Light."

"Illumination is the key, to open the Way," Early replied.

"The Eastern Path?"

Early shook his head. "East and West are one, to the servants of the Hidden Temple."

Shigehero started, impressed still more, then made a deep bow, smiling. "Your authority is undisputed, Master. Although not that of the ARM!"

Early relaxed, joining in the chuckle. "Well, the ARM is no more than a finger of the Hidden Way and the Rule that is to Come, eh? As is your Association, *oyabun.* And many another." *Including many you know nothing of.* " 'As above, so below'; power and knowledge, wheel within wheel. Until Holy Blood—"

"—fills Holy Grail."

Early nodded, and his face became stark. "Now, let me tell you what has been hidden in the vaults of the ARM. The Brotherhood saw to it that the knowledge was suppressed, back three centuries ago, along with much else. The ARM has been invaluable for that . . . Long ago, there was a species that called themselves the thrint—"

☆ ☆ ☆

Jonah looked up as Early left the *oyabun*'s sanctum.

"How did it go?" he murmured.

"Well enough. We've got an alliance of sorts. And a very serious problem, not just with the kzin. Staff conference, gentlemen."

The Belter fell into line with the others as they left the Association's headquarters. *I wonder,* he thought, looking up at the rock above. *I wonder what really* is *going on out there.* At the least, it might get him *Catskinner* back.

Chapter 13

STOP THAT, Dnivtopun said angrily, alerted by the smell of blood and a wet ripping sound.

His son looked up guiltily and tried to resist. The thrint willed obedience, feeling the adolescent's half-formed shield resisting his Power like thick mud around a foot. Then it gave way, and the child released the human's arm. That was chewed to the bone; the young thrint had blood all down its front, and bits of matter and gristle stuck between its needle teeth. The slave swayed, smiling dreamily.

"How many times do I have to tell you, *do not eat the servants!*" Dnivtopun shrieked, and used the Power again: SHAME. GUILT. PAIN. ANGUISH. REMORSE. SHOOTING PAINS. BURNING FEET. UNIVERSAL SCRATCHLESS ITCH. GUILT.

The slave was going into shock. "Go and get medical treatment," he said. And: FEEL NO PAIN. DO NOT BLEED. This one had been on the *Ruling Mind* for some time; he had picked it for sensitivity to Power, and its mind fit his mental grip like a glove. The veinous spurting from its forelimb slowed, then sank to a trickle as the muscles clamped down on the blood vessels with hysterical strength.

Dnivtopun turned back to his offspring. The young thrint was rolling on the soft blue synthetic of the cabin floor; he had beshat himself and vomited up the human's arm—thrint used the same mouth-orifice for both—and his eating tendrils were writhing into his mouth, trying to clean it and pick the teeth free of foreign matter. The filth was sinking rapidly into the floor, absorbed by the ship's recycling system, and the stink was fading as well. The vents replaced it with nostalgic odors of hot wet jungle, spicy and rank, the smell of thrintun. Dnivtopun shut his mind to the youngster's suffering for a full minute; his eldest son was eight, well into puberty. At that age, controls imposed by the Power did not sink in well. An infant could be permanently conditioned, that was the way baby thrint were toilet trained—but by this stage they were growing rebellious.

CEASE HURTING, he said at last. Then: "Why did you attack the servant?"

"It was boring me," his son said, still with a trace of sulkiness. "All that stuff you said I had to learn. Why can't we go home, father? Or to Uncle Tzinlpun's?"

With an intense effort, Dnivtopun controlled himself. *"This is home!* We are the *last thrint left alive."*

Powerloss take persuasion, he decided. BELIEVE.

The fingers of mind could feel the child-intellect accepting the order. Barriers of denial crumbled, and his son's eye squeezed shut while all six fingers squeezed painfully into palms. The young thrint threw back his head and howled desolately, a sound like glass and sheet metal inside a tumbling crusher.

QUIET. Silence fell; Dnivtopun could hear the uncomprehending whimper of a female in the next room, beyond the lightscreen door. One of his wives—they had all been nervous and edgy. Female thrint had enough psionic sensitivity to be very vulnerable to upset.

"You will have to get used to the idea," Dnivtopun said. *Powergiver knows it took me long enough.* He moved closer and threw an arm around his son's almost-neck, biting him affectionately on the top of the head. "Think of the good side. There are no tnuctipun here!" He could feel that bring a small wave of relief; the Rebels had been bogeymen to the children since their birth. "And you will have a planet of your own, some day. There is a whole galaxy of slaves here, ready for our taking!"

"Truly, father?" There was awakening greed at that. Dnivtopun had only been Overseer of one miserable food-planet, a sterile globe with a reducing atmosphere, seeded with algae and Bandersnatch. There would have been little for his sons, even without the disruption of the War.

"Truly, my son." He keyed one of the controls, and a wall blanked to show an exterior starscape. "One day, all this will be yours. We are not just the *last* thrint—we are the beginning of a new Empire!" *And I am the first Emperor, if I can survive the next few months.* "So we must take good care of these slaves."

"But these smell so *good,* father!"

Dnivtopun sighed. "I know, son." Thrint had an acute sense of smell when it came to edibility; competition for food among their presapient ancestors had been very intense. "It's because—" *No, that's just a guess.* Few alien biologies in the old days had been as compatible as these humans . . . Dnivtopun had a grisly suspicion he knew the reason: food algae. The thrint had seeded hundreds of planets with it, and given billions of years . . . That would account for the compatibility of the other species as well, the kzin. They could eat humans as well. "Well, you'll just have to learn to ignore it." Thrint were always ravenous. "Now, listen—you've upset your mother. Go and comfort her."

☆ ☆ ☆

Ulf Reichstein-Markham faced the Master and fought not to vomit. The carrion breath, the writhing tentacles beside the obscene gash of mouth, the staring faceted eye . . . It was so—

—*beautiful,* he thought, as shards of crystalline Truth slid home in his mind. The pleasure was like the drifting relaxation after orgasm, like a hot sauna, like winning a fight.

"What progress has been made on the amplifier helmet?" his owner asked.

"Very little, Mast— *Eeeeeeeee!*" He staggered back, shaking his head against the blinding-white pressure that threatened to burst it. Whimpering, he pressed his hands against the sides of his head. "Please, Master! We are *trying!*"

The pressure relaxed; on some very distant level, he could feel the alien's recognition of his sincerity.

"What is the problem?" Dnivtopun asked.

"Master—" Markham stopped for a moment to organize his thoughts, looking around.

They were on the control deck of the *Ruling Mind,* and it was *huge.* Few human spaceships had ever been so large; this was nearly the size of a colony slowship. The chamber was a flattened oval dome twenty meters long and ten wide, lined with chairs of many different types. That was logical, to accommodate the wild variety of slave-species the thrint used. But they were chairs, not acceleration couches. The thrint had had very good gravity control, for a very long time. A central chair designed for thrint fronted the blackened wreck of what had been the main computer. The decor was lavish and garish, swirling curlicues of precious metals and enamel, drifting motes of multicolored lights. Beneath their feet was a porous matrix that seemed at least half-alive, that absorbed anything organic and dead and moved rubbish to collector outlets with a disturbing peristaltic motion. The air was full of the smells of vegetation and rank growth.

Curious, he thought, as the majority of his consciousness wondered how to answer the Master. The controls were odd, separate crystal-display dials and manual levers and switches, primitive in the extreme. But the machinery *behind* the switches was . . . there were no doors; something *happened,* and the material went . . . vague, and you could walk through it, like walking through soft taffy. The only mechanical airlock was a safety backup. There was no central power source for the ship. Dotted around were units that apparently converted matter into energy; the equivalent of flashlight batteries could start it. The basic drive was to the kzinti gravity polarizer as a fusion bomb was to a grenade—it could accelerate at *thousands* of gravities, and then pull space right around the ship and travel faster than light.

Faster than light—

"Stop daydreaming," the Voice said. "And tell me *why."*

"Master, we don't know *how."*

The thrint opened its mouth and then closed it again, the tendrils stroking caressingly at its almost nonexistent lips. "Why not?" he said. "It isn't very complicated. You can buy them anywhere for twenty *znorgits."*

"Master, do you know the principles?"

"Of course not, slave! That's slavework. For engineers."

"But, Master, the slave-engineers you've got . . . we can only talk to them a little, and they don't know anything beyond what buttons to push. The machinery—" he waved helplessly at the walls "—doesn't make any *sense* to us, Master! It's just blocks of matter. We . . . our instruments can barely detect that something's going on."

The thrint stood looking at him, radiating incomprehension. "Well," he said after a moment. "It's true I didn't have the best quality of engineering slave. No need for them, on a routine posting. Still, I'm sure you'll figure something out, Chief Slave. How are we doing at getting the *Ruling Mind* freed from the dirt?"

"Much better, Master, that is well within our capacities. Master?"

"Yes?"

"Have I your permission to send a party to Tiamat? It can be done without much danger of detection, beyond what the deserters already present, and we need more personnel and spare parts. For a research project on . . . well, on your nervous system."

The alien's single unwinking eye stared at him. "What are nerves?" he said slowly. Dnivtopun took a dopestick from his pouch and sucked on it. Then: "What's research?"

☆ ☆ ☆

"Erreow."

The kzinrret rolled and twisted across the wicker matting of the room, yowling softly with her eyes closed. Traat-Admiral glanced at her with post-coital satisfaction as he finished grooming his pelt and laid the currycomb aside; he might be *de facto* leader of the Modernists, but he was not one of those who could not maintain a decent appearance without a dozen servants and machinery. At the last he cleaned the damp portions of his fur with talc, remembering once watching a holo of humans bathing themselves by jumping into *water.* Into *cold* water.

"Hrrrrr," he shivered.

The female turned over on all fours and stuck her rump in the air.

"Ch'rowl?" she chirruped. Involuntarily his ears extended and the muscles of his massive neck and shoulders twitched. "Ch'rowl?" With a saucy twitch of her tail, but he could smell that she was not serious. Besides, there was work to do.

"No," he said firmly. The kzinrret padded over to a corner, collapsed onto a pile of cushions and went to sleep with limp finality.

A kzinrret of the Patriarch's line, Traat-Admiral thought with pride; one of Chuut-Riit's beauteous daughters. His blood to be mingled with the Riit, he whose Sire had been only a Third Gunner, lucky to get a single mate when the heavy casualties of the First Fleet left so many maleless. He stretched, reaching for the domed ceiling, picked up the weapons belt from the door and padded off down the corridor. This was the governor's harem quarters, done up as closely as might be to a noble's Kzinrret House on Kzin itself. Domed wickerwork structures, the tops waterproof with synthetic in a concession to modernity; there were even gravity polarizers to bring it up to homeworld weight, nearly twice that of Wunderland.

"Good for the health of the kzinrret and kits," he mused to himself, and his ears moved in the kzinti equivalent of a grin. It was easy to get used to such luxury, he decided, ducking through the shamboo curtain over the entrance and pacing down the exit corridor; that was open at the sides, roofed in flowering orange vines.

Each dome was set in a broad space of open vegetation, and woe betide the kzinrret who strayed across the low wooden boundaries into her neighbor's claws; female kzin might be too stupid to talk, but they had a keenly developed sense of territory. There were open spaces, planted in a pleasant mixture of vegetation: orange kzinti, reddish Wunderlander, green from Earth. Traat-Admiral could hear the sounds of young kits at play in the common area, see them running and tumbling and chasing while their mothers lay basking in the weak sunlight or groomed each other. Few of them had noticed the change of males overmuch, but integrating his own modest harem had been difficult, with much fur flying in dominance-tussles.

He sighed as he neared the exit gate. Chuut-Riit's harem was not only of excellent quality, but so well trained that it needed less maintenance than his own had. The females would even let human servants in to keep up the feeding stations, a vast help, since male kzin who could be trusted in another's harem were not common. They were all well housebroken, and most did not even have to be physically restrained when pregnant, which simplified things immensely; kzinretti had an almost irresistible urge to dig a birthing tunnel about then, and it created endless problems and damage to the gardens.

Through the outer gate, functional warding-fields and robot guns, and a squad of Chuut-Riit's household troopers. They saluted with enthusiasm. Since they were hereditary servants of the Riit, he had been under no obligation to let them swear to him . . . although it would be foolish to discard so useful a cadre.

Would I have thought of this before Chuut-Riit trained me? he thought. Then: *He is dead: I live. Enough.*

Beyond the gates began the palace proper. The military and administrative sections were largely underground, ship-style; from here you could see only the living quarters, openwork pavilions for the most part, on bases of massive cut stone.

Between and around them stretched gardens, stones of pleasing shape, trees whose smooth bark made claws itch. There was a half-acre of *zheeretki* too, the tantalizing scent calling the passerby to come roll in its intoxicating blossoms. Traat-Admiral wiggled his ears in amusement as he settled onto the cushions in the reception pavilion.

All this luxury, and no time to enjoy it, he thought. It was well enough; one did not become a Conquest Hero by lolling about on cushions sipping blood.

His eldest son was coming along one of the paths. In a hurry, and running four-foot with the sinuous gait that reminded humans of weasels as much as cats; he wore a sash of office, his first ranking. Ten meters from the pavilion he rose, licked his wrists and smoothed back his cheek fur with them, settled the sash.

"Honored Sire Traat-Admiral, Staff-Officer requests audience at your summons," he said.

"And . . . the Accursed Ones. They await final judgment. And—"

"Enough, Aide-de-Camp," Traat-Admiral rumbled.

The young male stood proudly and made an unconscious gesture of adjusting the sash; that was a ceremonial survival of a sword-baldric, from the days when Aides were bodyguards as well, entitled to take a duel-challenge on themselves to spare their masters. Looking into the great round eyes of his son, Traat-Admiral realized that that too would be done gladly if it were needed. Unable to restrain himself, he gave the youth's ears a few grooming licks.

"*Fath*— Honored Sire! *Please!*"

"Hrrrr," Staff-Officer rumbled. "He was as strong as a *terrenki* and faster." Traat-Admiral looked down to see the fresh ears of Ktiir-Supervisor-of-Animals dangling at the other's belt.

"Not quite fast enough," Traat-Admiral said with genuine admiration. Most kzin became slightly less quarrelsome past their first youth, but the late Ktiir's notorious temper had gotten worse, if anything. It probably came from having to deal with humans all the time, and high-level collaborators at that. Ktiir should have remembered that reflexes slowed and had to be replaced with cunning and skill born of experience.

"Yes," he continued, "I am well pleased." He paused for three breaths, waiting while Staff-Officer's muzzle dipped into the saucer. "Hroth-Staff-Officer."

The other kzin gasped, inhaled milk and rolled over, coughing and slapping at his nose, sneezed frantically, and sat back with his eyes watering. Traat-Admiral felt his ears twitch with genial amusement.

"Do not be angry, noble Hroth-Staff-Officer," he said. "There is little of humor these days." To confer a Name was a system governor's prerogative. Any field-grade officer could, for certain well-established feats of honor, but a governor could do so at discretion.

"I will strive—*kercheee*—to be worthy of the honor," the newly-promoted kzin said. "Little though I have done to deserve it."

"Nonsense," Traat-Admiral said. *For one thing, you are very diplomatic.* Only a kzin with iron self-control could be humble, even under these circumstances. "For another, you have won . . . what, six duels in the month? And a dozen more back when Chuut-Riit first came from Homeworld to this system. Ktrodni-Stkaa, to be frank, will be shitting buffalo bones. This will satisfy those who think galactic conquest can be accomplished with teeth and claws. Also, you have been invaluable in keeping the Modernist faction aligned behind me. Many thought Chuut-Riit's heir should be from among his immediate entourage."

Hroth-Staff-Officer twitched his tail and rippled sections of his pelt. "None such could enjoy sufficient confidence among the locally-born, even among the many younger ones who agreed with his policies," he said. "If we trusted Chuut-Riit's judgment before he was killed, should we not after he is dead?"

Traat-Admiral sighed, looking out over the exquisite restraint of the gardens. "I agree. Better a . . . less worthy successor than infighting beneath one more technically qualified." His ears spread in irony. "More infighting than we have had. Chuut-Riit said . . ." He hesitated, then looked over at the faces of his son and the newly-ennobled Hroth-Staff-Officer, remembered conversations with his mentor. "He said that humans were either the greatest danger or greatest opportunity kzinti had ever faced. And that he did not know if they came just in time, or just too late."

His son showed curiosity in the rippling of his pelt, an almost imperceptible movement of his fingertips. Curiosity was a childhood characteristic among kzin, but one the murdered governor had said should be encouraged into adulthood.

"We have not faced a challenge to really test our mettle

for . . . for a long time," he said. "We make easy conquests; empty worlds to colonize, or others where the inhabitants are savages with spears, barbarians with nothing better than chemical-energy weapons. We grow slothful; our energy is spent in quarreling among ourselves, and more and more of even the work of maintaining our civilization we turn over to our slaves."

"Wrrrr," Hroth-Staff-Officer said. "But what did the Dominant One before you mean, that the humans might be too late?"

Traat-Admiral's voice sank slightly. "That lack of challenge has weakened us. By making us inflexible, brittle. There are other forms of rot than softness; fossilization is another form of decay, steel and bone turning to stiff breakable rock. Chuut-Riit saw that as we expand we must eventually meet terrible threats; if the kzinti were to be strong enough to conquer them, first we must be reforged in the blaze of war."

"I still don't smell the track, Traat-Admiral," Hroth-Staff-Officer said. The admiral could see his son huddled on the cushions, entranced at being able to listen in on such august conversation.

Listen well, my son, he thought. *You will find it an uncomfortable privilege.*

"Are the humans then a challenge which will call forth our strength . . . or the mad *raairtiro* that will shatter us?'

"Wrrrr!" Hroth-Staff-Officer shivered slightly, his fur lying flat. Aide-de-Camp's was plastered to his skin, and his ears had disappeared into their pouches of skin. "That has the authentic flavor and scent of his . . . disquieting lectures. I suffered through enough of them." A pause. "Still, the *raaairtwo* may be head-high at the shoulder and weigh fifty times a kzintosh's mass and have a spiked armor ball for a tail, but our ancestors killed them."

"But not by butting heads with them, Hroth-Staff-Officer." He turned his head. "Aide-de-Camp, go to the Accursed Ones, and bring them here. Not immediately; in an hour or so."

He leaned forward once the youth had leaped up and four-footed away. "Hroth-Staff-Officer, has it occurred to you *why* we are sending such an armada to the asteroids?"

Big lambent yellow eyes blinked at him. "There has been much activity among the feral humans," he said. "I did scent that you might be using this as an excuse for field-exercises with live ammunition, in order to quiet dissension." Kzin obeyed when under arms, even if they hated. A hesitation.

"And it gives Ktrodni-Stkaa a post of honor, yet under your eye, Dominant One."

"The interstellar warships as well? That would be like cleaning vermin out of your pelt with a beam-rifle. And would give old leaps-without-looking more honor than is needful."

He leaned closer. "This is a Patriarch's Secret," he continued. "Listen."

When he finished a half hour later, Hroth-Staff-Officer's pelt was half laid-flat, with patches bristling in horror. Traat-Admiral could smell his anger, underlaid with fear, a sickly scent.

"You are right to fear," he said, conscious of his own glands. No kzin could hide true terror, of course, not with a functioning nose in the area.

"Death is nothing," the other nodded. He grinned, the expression humans sometimes mistook for friendliness. "But this!" He hissed, and Traat-Admiral watched and smelled him fight down blind rage.

"Chuut-Riit feared something like this," he said. "And Conservor thinks that he was right to fear." At the other's startlement: "Oh, no, not these beings particularly. It is a joke of the God that we find this thing in the middle of a difficult war. But *something* terrible was bound to jump out of the long grass sooner or later. The universe is so large, and we keep pressing our noses into new caves . . ." He shrugged. "Enough. Now—"

Chuut-Riit's sons lay stomach to earth on the path before the dais of judgment and covered their noses. Traat-Admiral looked down on their still-gaunt forms and felt himself recoil. Not with fear, at least not the fear of an adult kzin. Vague memories moved in the shadowcorners of his mind: brutal hands tearing him away from Mother, giant shapes of absolute power . . . rage and desire and fear, the bitter acrid smell of loneliness.

Wipe them out, he thought uneasily, as his lips curled up and the hair bulked erect on neck and spine. *Wipe them out, and this will not be.*

"You have committed the gravest of all crimes," he said slowly, fighting the wordless snarling that struggled to use his throat. There was an ancient epic, *Warlord Chmee at the Pillars.* He had seen a holo of it once, and had groveled and howled like all the audience and come back washed free of grief, at the last view of the blind and scentless Hero. *And these did not sin in ignorance, nor did they claw out their own eyes and breathe acid in remorse and horror.*

"To overthrow one's Sire is . . . primitive, but such is custom; to slay him honorably, even . . . But to fall upon him in a pack and devour him! And each other!"

The guilty ones seemed to sink farther to the raked gravel of the path before him; he stood like a towering wall of orange fur at the edge of the pavilion, the molten-copper glow of his pelt streaked with scar-white. Like an image of dominance to a young kzin, hated and feared and adored. Not that the armored troopers behind him with their beam-guns hurt, he reflected. *Control,* he thought. *Self-control is the heart of honor.*

"Is there any reason you should not be killed?" he said. "Or blinded, castrated, and driven out?"

Silence then, for a long time. Finally, the spotted one, who had spent longest in the regeneration tank, spoke.

"No, Dominant One."

Traat-Admiral relaxed slightly. "Good. But Chuut-Riit's last message to us spoke of mercy. If you had not acknowledged your crime and your worthlessness, there would have been no forgiveness.

"Hear your sentence. The fleets of the Patriarchy in this system are journeying forth against . . . an enemy. You have all received elementary space-combat training." Attacks on defended asteroids often involved boarding, by marines in one-kzin suits of stealthed, powered vacuum armor. "You will be formed into a special unit for the coming action. This is your last chance to achieve honor!" An honorable death, of course. "Do not waste it. Go!"

He turned to Hroth-Staff-Officer. "Get me the readiness reports," he said, and spoke the phrase that opened the communication line to the household staff. "Bring two saucers of tuna ice cream with stolychina vodka," he continued. "I have a bad taste to get out of my mouth."

Chapter 14

"How did he manage it?" Jonah Matthieson muttered.

The hauler the party from the Sol system had been assigned was an unfamiliar model, a long stalk with a life-bubble at one end and a gravity-polarizer drive as well as fusion thrusters. Introduced by the kzinti, no doubt; they had had the polarizer for long enough to be using it for civilian purposes. With a crew of half a dozen the bubble was very crowded, despite the size of the ship, and they had set the internal gravity to zero to make best use of the space. The air smelled right to his Belter's nose: a pure neutral smell with nothing but a slight trace of ozone and pine, something you could not count on in the Alpha Centauri system these days. Certainly less nerve-wracking than the surface of Wunderland, with its wild smells and completely uncontrolled random-process life-support system.

A good ship, he thought. Nothing like the surprise-stuffed kzin corvette that Early had brought, but that was part of the *oyabun*'s fleet now, with enough UN personnel to teach locals. This must be highly automated, doing the rounds of the refineries and hauling back metals and polymer sacks of powders and liquids. What clung to the carrying fields now *looked* very much like a cargo of singleships, being delivered to rockjacks at some other base asteroid; he had been respectfully surprised at the assortment of commandeered weapons and jury-rigged but roughly effective control systems.

General Early looked up from his display plaque. "Not surprising, considering the state things are in," he said. "Organized crime does well in a disorganized social setting. Like any conspiracy, unless the conspiracy *is* the social setting."

Like the ARM, Jonah thought sourly. *And what conspiracies control the conspiracies?*

"It's a Finagle-damned *fleet,* though," he said aloud. "Don't the pussies care?"

"Not much, I imagine," Early said. Jonah could see the schematics for the rest of their flotilla coming up on the board. "So long as it doesn't impact on their military concerns. They'd clamp down soon enough if much went directly to the resistance, of course. Or their human goons would, for fear of losing their positions. The pussies may be great fighters, but as administrators they're worse than Russians."

What're Russians? Jonah thought. Then, *Oh. Them.* "Surprising they tolerate so much corruption."

Early shrugged. "What can they do? And from what we've learned, they *expect* the tame monkeys to be corrupt, except for the household servants. If we weren't goddam cowards and lickspittles, we'd all have died fighting." He smiled his wide white grin and stuck a stogie in the midst of it—unlit, Jonah saw thankfully. The schematics continued to roll across the screen. "Ahhh, thought so."

"Thought what?"

"Our friend Shigehero is playing both ends against the middle," Early said. "He's bringing along a lot of exploratory stuff as well as weaponry. A *big* computer, by local standards. Wait a second. Yes, linguistic-analysis hardware too. The son of a bitch!"

Silence fell. Jonah looked at the others, studied the hard set of their faces.

"Wait a second," he said. "There's an ancient alien artifact, and you *don't* think it should be studied?"

Early looked up, and Jonah realized with a sudden shock that he was being weighed. For trustworthiness, and possibly for expendability.

"Of course not," the general said. "The risk is too great. Remember the Sea Statue?"

Jonah concentrated. "Oh, the thingie in the Smithsonian? The Slaver?"

"Why do you think they were *called* that, Captain?" Early spent visible effort controlling impatience.

"I . . ." Suddenly, Jonah realized that he knew very little of the famous exhibit, beyond the fact that it was an alien in a spacesuit protected by a stasis field. "You'd better do some explaining, sir."

Several of the others stirred uneasily, and Early waved them back to silence. "He's right," he said regretfully, and began.

"Murphy," Jonah muttered when the older man had finished. "That *is* a menace."

Early nodded jerkily. "More than you realize. That artifact is a *ship*. There may be more than one of the bastards on it," he said, in another of his archaic turns of phrase. "A breeding pair, if we're really unlucky. Besides which, the technology. We've had three centuries of trying, and we've barely been able to make two or three copies of their stasis field; as far as we can tell, the only way *that* could work is by decoupling the interior from the entropy gradient of the universe as a whole . . ."

Jonah leaned back, his toes hooked comfortably under a line, and considered the flatlander. Then the others, his head cocked to one side consideringly.

"It isn't just you, is it?" he said. "The whole lot of you are ARM types. Most of you older than you look."

Early blinked, and took the stogie from between his teeth. "Now why," he said softly, "would you think that, Captain?"

"Body language," Jonah said, linking his hands behind his back and staring "up." The human face is a delicate communications instrument, and he suspected that Early had experience enough to read entirely too much from it. "And attitudes. Something new comes along, grab it quick. Hide it away and study it in private. Pretty typical. Sir."

"Captain," Early said, "you Belters are all anarchists, but you're supposed to be rationalists too. Humanity had centuries of stability before the kzin arrived, the first long interval of peace since . . . God, ever. You think that was an accident? The way humankind was headed in the early atomic era, if something like the ARM hadn't intervened there wouldn't *be* a human race now. Nothing we'd recognize as human. There are things in the ARM archives . . . that just can't be let out."

"Oh?" Jonah said coldly.

Early smiled grimly. "Like an irresistible aphrodisiac?" he said. "Conditioning pills that make you completely loyal forever to the first person you see after taking them? Things that would have made it impossible not to legalize murder and cannibalism? Damned right we sit on things. Even if there weren't aliens on that ship, it would have to be destroyed;

there's neither time nor opportunity to take it apart and keep the results under wraps. If the pussies get it, we're royally screwed." Jonah remained silent. "Don't look so apprehensive, Captain. You're no menace, no matter what you learn."

"I'm not?" Jonah said, narrowing his eyes. He had suspected . . .

"Of course not. What use would a system of secrecy be, if one individual leak could imperil it? How do you think we wrote the Sea Statue out of the history books as anything but a curiosity? Slowly, and from many directions and oh, so imperceptibly. Bit by bit, and anyone who suspected"—he grinned, and several of the others joined him—"autodocs exist to correct diseases like paranoia, don't they? In the meantime, I suggest you remember you are under military discipline."

"Uncle, that established the limits of control," the technician said to Shigehero Hirose.

Silent, the *oyabun* nodded, watching the multiple displays on the *Murasaki*'s bridge screens. There were dozens of them; the *Murasaki* was theoretically a passenger hauler, out of Tiamat to the major Swarm habitats and occasionally to Wunderland and its satellites. In actuality, it was the Association's fallback headquarters, and forty years of patient theft had given it weapons and handling characteristics equivalent to a kzinti *Vengeful Slasher*-class light cruiser. He reflected on how much else of the Association's strength was here, and felt a gripping pain in the stomach. *Still water,* he thought, controlling his breathing. There were times when opportunity must be seized, despite all risk.

"Attempt communication on the hailing frequencies," he said, as the latest singleship stopped in its elliptical path around the asteroid and coasted in to assume a station among the others under Markham's control. Or *the alien's,* Hirose reminded himself. "But this time, we must demonstrate the consequences of noncompliance. Execute *East Wind, Rain.*"

The points of light on the screens began to move in a complicated dance, circling the asteroid and its half-freed alien ship.

"Ah," the Tactics officer said. "Uncle, see, Markham is deploying his units without regard to protecting the artifact."

Pale fusion flame bloomed against the stars, a singleship power core deliberately destabilized; it would be recorded as an accident, at Traffic Control Central on Tiamat. If that had been a human or kzinti craft, everyone aboard would have been lethally irradiated.

"But," the *oyabun* observed, "notice that none of his vessels moves beyond a certain distance from the asteroid. This is interesting."

"Uncle . . . those dispositions are an invitation to close in, given the intercept capacities we have observed."

"Do so, but be cautious. Be very cautious."

☆ ☆ ☆

"Accelerating," Jonah Matthieson said. "Twenty thousand klicks and closing at three hundred kps relative."

The asteroid was a lumpy potato in the screen ahead. Acceleration pressed him back into the control couch. It was an almost unfamiliar sensation; this refitted singleship had no compensators. But it *did* have a nicely efficient fusion drive, and he was on intercept with one of Markham's boats, ready to flip over and decelerate toward it behind the sword of thermonuclear fire.

"Hold it, you cow," he muttered to the clumsy ship. His sweat stank in his nostrils. *Show your stuff, Matthieson,* he told himself. Singleships no better than this had cut the kzinti First Fleet to ribbons, when the initial attack on the Solar system had been launched.

"Ready for attack," he said. "Five seconds and—"

Matching velocities, he realized. It would be tricky, without damaging Markham's ship. That would be very bad. Markham's ship must not be damaged; the asteroid must be kept safe at all costs. His hands moved across the control screens and flicked in the lightfield sensors. The communicator squawked at him, meaningless noises interrupting the essential task of safely killing velocity relative to the asteroid. He switched it off.

☆ ☆ ☆

"HURRY," Dnivtopun grated. The human and *fssstup* slaves redoubled their efforts on the components strung out across the floor of the *Ruling Mind*'s control chamber.

Markham looked up from the battle-control screens. "Zey are approaching the estimated control radius, Master," he said coolly. "I am prepared to activate plans A or B, according to ze results."

The thrint felt for the surface of the Chief Slave's mind; it was . . . machine-like, he decided. Complete concentration, without even much sense of self. *Familiar,* he decided.

Artist-slaves felt like that, when fulfilling their functions. Almost absentmindedly, he reached out and took control of a single slave-mind that had strayed too close; it was locked tight on its purpose, easy to redirect.

"Secure that small spacecraft," he said, then fixed his eye on the helmet. "Will it work?" he asked, extending his tendrils towards the bell-shape of the amplifier helmet in an unconscious gesture of hungry longing. It was a cobbled-together mess of equipment ripped out of the human vessels and spare parts from the *Ruling Mind.* Square angular black boxes were joined with the half-melted-looking units salvaged from the thrintun control components.

"Ve do not know, Master," Markham said. "The opportunity will not last long; this formation ve use is tactically inefficient. If they were pressing home their attacks, or if they dared use weapons with signatures visible to kzin monitors, ve would have been overwhelmed already." A sigh. "If only ze *Ruling Mind* were fully operational!"

Dnivtopun clenched all six fingers in fury, and felt his control of the command-slaves of the space vessels falter. They were at the limits of his ability; it was like grasping soap bubbles in the dark. Nothing complicated, simply: OBEY. Markham had thought of the coded self-destruct boxes fixed to their power cores, to keep the crews from mutiny. Markham was turning out to be a most valuable Chief Slave. Dnivtopun reached for another dopestick, then forced his hand away. *Their weapons cannot harm this ship,* he told himself. *Probably.*

"Ready, Master," one of the *fssstup* squeaked, making a last adjustment with a three-handed micromanipulator.

"Thanks to the Powergiver!" Dnivtopun mumbled, reaching for it. The primitive metal-alloy shape felt awkward on his head, the leads inside prickled. "Activate!"

Ah, he thought, closing his eyes. There was a half-audible whine, and then the surface of his mind seemed to expand.

"First augment."

Another expansion, and suddenly it was no longer a strain to control the vessels around the asteroid that encompassed his ship. Their commanders sank deeper into his grip, and he clamped down on the crews. He could feel their consciousnesses writhing in his grip, then quieting to docility as ice-shards of Power slipped easily into the centers of volition, memory, pleasure-pain. LOYALTY, he thought. SELFLESS ENTHUSIASM. DEDICATION TO THE THRINT.

"This is better than the original model!" he exulted. *But then, the original was designed by tnuctipun.* "Second augment."

Now his own being seemed to thin and expand, and the center of perception shifted outside the ship. The wild slave-minds were like lights glowing in a mist of darkness, dozens . . . no, hundreds of them. He knew this species now, and he ripped through to the volition centers with careless violence. AWAIT INSTRUCTION. Now, to find their herdbull; quickest to control through him. *Oyabun.* The name slipped into his memory. *Ah, yes.*

"How interesting," he mumbled. Beautifully organized and disciplined; it even struggled for a moment in his grasp. There. Paralyze the upper levels, the threshold-censor mechanism that was awareness. *Ah!* It had almost slipped away! "Amazing," he said to himself. "The slave is accustomed to nonintrospection." It was very rare to find a sentient that could operate without contemplating its own operation, without interior discourse. Deeper . . . the pleasurable feeling of a mind settling down under control. Now he could add this flotilla to his; they would free the *Ruling Mind* more quickly, and go on to seize the planet.

There was a frying sound, and suddenly the sphere of awareness was expanding once more, thinning out his sense of self.

"No more augmentation," he said. But it continued; he could hear shouts, cries. His eyes opened, and there was a stabbing pain in his head as visual perception was overlaid on mental, a *fsstup* flying across the bridge with its belly-pelt on fire. His hands were moving slowly up toward his head, so slowly, and he could sense more and more, he was spinning out thinner than interstellar gas, and he was

SwarbelterARMkzinwunderlandernothingnothing

"EEEEEEEEEEEEEEEEEEEEEEE—" the thrint shrieked, with his voice and the Power. PAINPAINPAINPAINPAINPAINPAIN—

Blackness.

☆ ☆ ☆

Ulf Reichstein-Markham raised his head from the console before him, tried to inhale and choked on the clotted blood that blocked his throbbing and broken nose.

Where am I? he thought, looking around with crusted eyes. The drilling rig had suddenly disappeared, and then the alien had come floating up and—

"Hrrrg," he said, staggering erect. "Hrrrgg."

Blood leaked through scabs on his tongue and pain lanced

through his mouth. *Bite,* he realized. *I bit myself.* Cold wetness in the seat and legs of his flightsuit; he realized that he must have lost bowel and bladder control. Somehow that was not shameful; it was a fact, just as the distant crystal clarity of the alien bridge was a fact, like things seen through the wrong end of *Mutti*'s antique optical telescope. He could taste the brass smell of it.

Nobody else was stirring. Some of the humans looked dead, very dead, slumped in their chairs with tongues lolling and blood leaking from their noses and ears. Some of the aliens, too.

"Master!" he cried blurrily, spitting out blood.

The squat greenish form was slumped in its chair, the helmet half-off the bullet dome of its head. He tried to walk forward, and fell himself. The skin of his face and thighs tingled as the blue pseudolife of the floor cleansed them. He waited while the kaleidoscope shards of reality fell into place around him again; the inside of his head felt more raw than his tongue. Once in a skirmish he had been trapped in a wrecked singleship, with his arm caught between two collapsed struts. When the rescuers cut him free, the pain of blood pouring into the dry flesh had been worse than the first shock of the wound itself. He could feel thought running through sections of his consciousness that had been shut down for weeks, and he wept tears of pain as he had never wept in action.

Certainty, he thought. *Never have I known* certainty *before. "Mutti,"* he whispered. *Mother,* in the tongue of truth and love. English was common, Belter. Father spoke English, and *Mutti* had married him when the kzin chased her away from the home he had never seen. Mother was certainty, but he, he could never be certain. Never do enough. Love might be withheld. Markham screamed with the terror of it, colder than space. Worse than death.

"I will be strong, *Mutti,*" he whispered, through blood and tears and mucus that the floor drank. "Stronger than Father." Rage bit him, as he remembered tall slim beautiful *Mutti* stiffening at the touch of hated grubby commoner hands. *You must be all mine, myn sohn,* the voice whispered in a child's ear. *Prove yourself worthy of the blood.* The tears flowed faster.

I am not worthy. My blood is corrupt, weak. I fear in battle. No matter how much I purge weakness, treason, their faces come back to me, I wake in the night and see them bleeding as we put them out the airlocks Mutti, hilfe me.

His eyes opened again, and he saw his hand. The shock broke reality apart again; it was a skeleton's hand, a starved yellow claw-hand. He touched himself, feeling the hoop of ribs, and then hunger struck his belly, doubling him over.

"Master," he whispered. Master would make it right. With Master there was no weakness, no doubt, no uncertainty. With Master he was strong. A keening escaped him as he remembered the crystalline absoluteness of the Power in his mind. "Don't leave me, Master!"

Markham crawled, digging his fingers into the yielding surface until his hand touched the cable of the amplifier helmet. He jerked, and it tumbled down; he drew himself erect by the command chair, put a hand to the thrint's face to check. The bunched tendrils by the mouth shot out and gripped his hand, like twenty wire worms, and he jerked it back before they could draw it into the round expanding maw and the wet needles of the teeth.

"Survival," he muttered. The Master's race was *fit* to survive and dominate. *Overman . . . is demigod,* he remembered. No more struggle; the Power *proved* whose Will must conquer.

Now he could stand. Some of the others were stirring. With slow care he walked back to his seat, watching the screens. Analysis flowed effortlessly through his head; the enemy vessels had made parking trajectories . . . and *Catskinner* was accelerating away . . . Brief rage flickered and died, there was nothing that could be done about that now. He sat, and called up the self-destruct sequences.

"Tightbeam to all Free Wunderland Space Navy units, task force *Zarathustra,*" he wheezed, his throat hurt, as if he had screamed it raw. "Maintain . . . present positions. Any . . . shift will be treated as mutiny. Admiral . . . Ulf Reichstein-Markham . . . out."

He keyed it to repeat, then tapped the channel to the *von Seekt,* his fast courier. Adelman was a reliable type, and a good disciplinarian. The communicator screen blanked, then came alive with the holo image of the other man: a gaunt skull-like face, staring at him with dull-eyed lack of interest. A thread of saliva dangled from one lip.

"Hauptman Adelman!" Markham barked, swallowing blood from his tongue. *I must get to an autodoc,* he reminded himself. Then, with a trace of puzzlement: *Why has none been transferred to the* Ruling Mind? No matter, later. "Adelman!"

The dull blue eyes blinked, and expression returned to the

muscles of his face. Jerkily, as if by fits and starts, like a 'cast message with too much noise in the signal.

"Gottdamn," Adelman whispered. "Ulf, what's been . . ." he looked around, at the areas of the courier's life-bubble beyond the pickup's range. "Myn Gott, Ulf! Smythe is dead! Where—? What—?" He looked up at Markham, and blanched.

"Adelman," Markham said firmly. "Listen to me." A degree of alertness.

"*Zum befehl,* Admiral!"

"Good man," Markham replied firmly. "Adelman, you will find sealed orders in your security file under code *Ubermensch.* You understand?"

"Jahwol."

"Adelman, you have had a great shock. But everything is now under control. Remember that, *under control.* We now have access to technology which will make it an easy matter to sweep aside the kzinti, but we *must have those parts listed in the file.* You must make a minimum-time transit to Tiamat, and return here. Let nothing delay you. You . . . you will probably note symptoms of psychological disorientation, delusions, false memories. *Ignore them.* Concentrate on your mission."

The other man wiped his chin with the back of his hand. "Understood, Admiral," he said.

Markham blanked the screen, putting a hand to his head. Now he must decide what to do next. Pain lanced behind his eyes; decision was harder than analysis. Scrabbling, he pulled the portable input board from his waistbelt. He would have to program a deadman switch to the self-destruct circuits. Control must be maintained until the Master awoke; he could feel that the others would be difficult. *Only I truly understand,* he realized. It was a lonely and terrible burden, but he had the strength for it. The Master had filled him with strength. At all costs, the Master must be guarded until he recovered.

Freeing the Ruling Mind *is taking too long,* he decided. Why had the Master ordered a complete uncovering of the hull? Inefficient . . . *We must free some of the weapons systems first,* he thought. *Transfer some others to the human-built ships. Establish a proper defensive perimeter.*

He looked over at the Master where he lay leaking brown from his mouth in the chair. The single eye was still covered by the vertical slit of a closed lid. Suddenly Markham felt the weight of his sidearm in his hand, pointing at the thrint. With a scream of horror, he thrust it back into the holster and slammed the offending hand into the unyielding surface of the screen, again and again. The pain was sweet as justice.

My weakness, he told himself. *My father's weak subman blood. I must be on my guard.*

Work. Work was the cure. He looked up to establish the trajectory of the renegade *Catskinner,* saw that it was heading in-system towards Wunderland.

Treachery, he mused. "But do not be concerned, Master," he muttered. His own reflection looked back at him from the inactive sections of the board; the gleam of purpose in his eyes straightened his back with pride. "Ulf Reichstein-Markham will never betray you."

Chapter 15

"Here's looking at you, kid," Harold Yarthkin-Schotmann said, raising the drinking-bulb.

Home free, he thought, taking a suck on the maivin; the wine filled his mouth with the scent of flowers, an odor of violets. Ingrid was across the little cubicle in the cleanser unit, half visible through the fogged glass as the sprays played over her body. Absurd luxury, this private stateroom on the liner to Tiamat, but Claude's fake identities had included plenty of valuata. Not to mention the considerable fortune in low-mass goods in the hold, bought with the proceeds of selling Harold's Terran Bar.

He felt a brief pang at the thought. *Thirty years.* It had been more than a livelihood; it was a mood, a home, a way of life, a family. A bubble of human space in Munchen . . . *A pseudo-archaic flytrap with rigged roulette,* he reminded himself ironically. *What really hurts is selling it to that fat toad Suuomalisen,* he realized, and grinned.

"What's so funny?" Ingrid said, stepping out of the cleanser. Her skin was dry, the smooth cream-white he remembered; it rippled with the long muscles of a zero-G physique kept in shape by exercise. The breasts were high and dark-nippled, and the tail of her Belter crest had grown to halfway down her back.

God, she looks good, he thought, and took another sip of the maivin.

"Thinking of Suuomalisen," he said.

She made a slight face and touched the wall-control, switching the bed to .25 G, the compromise they had agreed on.

Harold rose into the air slightly as the mattress flexed, readjusting to his reduced weight. Ingrid swung onto the bed and began kneading his feet with slim strong fingers.

"I thought you hated him," she said, rotating the ankles.

"No, despised," Harold said. The probing traveled up to his calves.

She frowned. "I . . . you know, Hari, I can't say I like the thought of leaving Sam and the others at his mercy."

He nodded and sipped. Tax and vagrancy laws on Wunderland had never been kind to the commonfolk. After two generations of kzinti overlordship and collaborationist government, things were much worse. Tenants on the surviving Herrenmann estates were not too bad, but urban workers were debt-peons more often than not.

"I know something that Suuomalisen doesn't," Harold said, waiting for her look of inquiry before continuing. "Careful on that knee, sweetheart, the repair job's never really taken . . . Oh, the pension fund. Usually it's a scam, get the proles more deeply in debt, you know? Well, the way I've got it jiggered, the employee nonvoting stock—that's usually another scam, get interest-free loans from the help—*controls* the pension fund. The regular employees all owe their debts to the pension fund . . . to themselves. In fact, the holding company turns out to be controlled by the fund, if you trace it through."

Ingrid's hands stopped stroking his thighs as she snorted laughter. "You sold him a *minority interest?*" she choked. "You *teufel*!" Her hand moved up, kneading. "Devil," she repeated, in a different tone.

"Open up!" A fist hammered at the door.

"Go away!" they said in chorus, and collapsed laughing.

A red light flashed on the surface of the door. "Open up! There's a ratcat warship matching trajectories, and it wants you two by name!"

☆ ☆ ☆

"Two hundred and fifty thousand crowns!" Suuomalisen said, looking mournfully about.

He was a vague figure in bulky white against the backdrop of Harold's Terran Bar, looking mournfully down at his luncheon platter of wurst, egg-and-potato salad, breads, shrimp on rye, gulyas soup . . . His hands continued to shovel the food methodically into his mouth, dropping bits onto the flowing handkerchief tucked into his collar; the rest of his clothing was immaculate white natural linen and silk, with jet links at his cuffs the only color. It was rumored that he had his shirts hand-made, and never wore one for more than a day. Claude Montferrat-Palme watched the light from the mirror behind the long bar gleaming on the fat man's bald head and reflected that he could believe it.

Only natural for a man who wolfs down fastmetabol and still *weighs that much.* It was easy to control appetite, a simple visit to the autodoc, but Suuomalisen refused. Wunderland's .61 G made it fairly easy to carry extra weight, but the sight was still not pleasant.

"Not a bad price for a thriving business," he said politely, leaning back at his ease and letting smoke trickle out his nostrils. He was in the high-collared blue dress uniform of the Munchen Polezi; the remains of a single croissant lay on the table before him, with a cup of espresso. Their table was the only one in use; this was a nightspot and rarely opened before sundown. Just now none of the staff was in the main area, a raised L-shape of tables and booths around the lower dance floor and bar; he could hear mechanical noises from the back room, where the roulette wheels and baccarat tables were. There was a sad, empty smell to the nightclub, the curious daytime melancholy of a place meant to be seen by darkness.

"A part interest only," Suuomalisen continued. "I trusted Hari!" He shook his head mournfully. "We should not steal from each other . . . quickly he needed the cash, and did I quibble? Did I spend good money on having lawyers follow his data trail?"

"Did you pay anything like the going-rate price for this place?" Claude continued smoothly. "Did you pay three thousand to my late unlamented second-in-command Axelrod-Bauergartner to have the health inspectors close the place down so that Hari would be forced to sell?"

"That is different; simply business," the fat man said in a hurt tone. "And it did not work. But to sell me a business actually controlled by *employees* . . . !" His jowls wobbled, and he sighed heavily. "A pity about herrenfra Axelrod-Bauergartner." He made a *tsk* sound. "Treason and corruption."

"Speaking of which . . ." Claude hinted. Suuomalisen smiled and slid a credit voucher across the table; Claude palmed it smoothly and dropped it into his pocket. *So much more tidy than direct transfers,* he thought. "Now, my dear Suuomalisen,

I'm sure you won't lose money on the deal. After all, a nightclub is only as good as the staff, and they know that as well as you; with Sam Ogun on the musicomp and Aunti Scheirwize in the kitchen, you can't go wrong." He uncrossed his ankles and leaned forward. "To business."

The fat man's eyes narrowed and the slit of his mouth pulled tight; for a moment, you remembered that he had survived and prospered on the fringes of the law in occupied Munchen for forty years.

"That worthless musician Ogun is off on holiday, and if you think I'm going to increase the payoff, when I'm getting less than half the profits—"

"No, no, no," Claude said soothingly. "My dear fellow, *I* am going to give *you* more funds. Information is your stock in trade, is it not? Incidentally, Ogun is doing a little errand for me, and should be back in a day or two."

The petulance left Suuomalisen's face. "Yes," he said softly. "But what information could I have worth the while of such as you, Herrenmann?" A pause. "Are you proposing a partnership, indeed?" His face cleared, beaming. "Ha! Hari was working for you all along?"

Montferrat kept his face carefully blank. *There is something truly almost wonderfully repugnant about someone so* happy *to find another corrupt,* he thought. Aloud:

"I need documentary evidence on certain of my colleagues. I have my own files . . . but data from those could be, shall we say, *embarrassing* in its plenitude if revealed to my ratca—noble kzinti superiors. Though they are thin on the ground just at this moment. Then, once I have *usable* evidence—usable without possibility of being traced to me, and hence usable as a non-desperation measure—a certain . . . expansion of operations . . ."

"Ah." Pearly white teeth showed in the doughy pink face. Suuomalisen pulled his handkerchief free and wiped the dome of his head; there was a whiff of expensive cologne and sweat. "I always said you were far too conservative about making the most of your position, my friend."

Acquaintance, if necessary. Not friend. Claude smiled, dazzling and charming. "Recent events have presented opportunities," he said. "With the information you get for me, my position will become unassailable. Then," he shrugged, "rest assured that I intend to put it to good use. I have taken a vow that all resources are to be optimized, from now on."

☆ ☆ ☆

"This had better work" the guerrilla captain said. She was a high-cheeked Croat, one of the tenants turned off when the kzin took over the local Herrenmann's estate, roughly dressed, a well-worn strakaker over one shoulder. "We need the stuff on that convoy, or we'll have to pack it in."

"It will," Samuel Ogun replied tranquilly. He was a short, thick-set black man, with a boxed musicomp over his shoulder and a jazzer held by the grips, its stubby barrel pointed up. *It better, or I'll know Mister Claude has fooled this Krio one more time,* he thought. "My source has access to the best."

They were all lying along the ridgeline, looking down on the valley that opened out onto the plains of the upper Donau valley. Two thousand kilometers north of Munchen, and the weather was unseasonably cold this summer; too much cloud from the dust and water vapor kicked into the stratosphere. The long hillslope down to the abandoned village was covered in head-high feral rosebushes, a jungle of twisted thumb-thick stems, finger-long thorns and flowers like a mist of pink and yellow. Scent lay about them in the warm thick air, heavy, syrup-sweet. Ogun could see native squidgrass struggling to grow beneath the Earth vegetation, thin shoots of reddish olive-brown amid the bright green.

Behind them the deep forest of the Jotun range reared, up to the rock and the glaciers. The roofless cottages of the village were grouped around a lake; around them were thickets of orchard, pomegranate and fig and apricot, and beyond that you could see where grainfields had been, beneath the pasture grasses. Herds were dotted about: six-legged native gagrumphers, Earth cattle and beefalos and bison; the odd solitary kzinti *raaairtwo,* its orange pelt standing out against the green of the mutant alfalfa. The kzinti convoy was forging straight across the grasslands, a hexagonal pattern of dark beetle-shaped armored cars and open-topped troop carriers, moving with the soundless speed of distortion batteries and gravity-polarizer lift.

"Twenty of them," the guerrilla said, the liquid accent of her Wunderlander growing more noticeable. "I hope the data you gave us are correct, Krio."

"It is, Fra Mihaelovic. For the next ten hours, the surveillance net is down. They haven't replaced the gaps yet."

She nodded, turning her eyes to the kzinti vehicles and bringing up her viewers. Ogun raised his own, a heavy kzinti model. The vehicles leaped clear, jiggling slightly with hand motion, but close enough for him to see one trooper flip up the goggles of his helmet and sniff the air, drooling slightly at the scent of meat animals. He spoke to the comrade on his right; seconds later, the vehicles slowed and settled. Dots and commas unreeled in the upper left corner of Ogun's viewers, its idiot-savant brain telling him range and wind-bearings.

"Oh, God is great, God is with us, God is our strength," the guerrilla said with soft fervor. "They aren't heading straight up the valley to the fort at Bodgansford; they're going to stop for a feed. Ratcats hate those infantry rations." Teeth showed strong and yellow against a face stained with sweat-held dust, in an expression a kzin might have read quite accurately. "I don't blame them, I've tasted them." She touched the throat-mike at the collar of her threadbare hunter's jacket. *"Kopcha."*

Pinpoints of light flared around the village, lines of light heading up into the sky. Automatic weapons stabbed up from the kzinti armored cars; some of the lines ended with orange puffballs of explosion, but the guerrillas were too many and too close. Ogun grinned himself as the flat pancakes of smoke and light blossomed over the alien war-vehicles; shaped charges, driving self-forging bolts of molten titanium straight down into the upper armor of the convoy's protection. Thunder rolled back from the mountain walls; huge ringing *changgg* sounds as the hypervelocity projectiles smashed armor and components and furred alien flesh. Then a soundless explosion that sent the compensators of the viewer black as a ball of white fire replaced an armored car. The ground rose and fell beneath him, and then a huge warm pillow of air smacked him across the face.

Molecular distortion batteries will not burn. But if badly damaged they *will* discharge all their energy at once, and the density of that energy is very high.

The kzin infantry were flinging themselves out of the carriers; most of those were undamaged; the antiarmor mines had been reserved for the high-priority fighting vehicles. Fire stabbed out at them, from the mined village, from the rose-thickets of the hillside. Some fell, flopped, were still; Ogun could hear their screams of rage across a kilometer's distance. The viewer showed him one team struggling to set up a heavy weapon, a tripod-mounted beamer. Two were down, and then a finger of sun slashed across the hillside beneath him. Flame roared up, a secondary explosion as someone's ammunition was hit, then the last kzin gunner staggered back with a dozen holes through his chest armor, snorted out a spray of blood, died. The beamer locked and went on cycling bolts into the hillside, then toppled and was still.

A score of armored kzin made it to the edge of the thicket; it was incredible how fast they moved under their burdens of armor and weaponry. Explosions and more screams as they tripped the waiting directional mines. Ogun grew conscious of the guerrilla commander's fist striking him on the shoulder.

"The jamming worked, the jamming worked! We can ride those carriers right into the fort gates, with satchel charges aboard! You will make us a song of this, *guslar*!"

They were whooping with laughter as the charging kzin broke cover ten yards downslope. The guerrilla had time for one quick burst of pellets from her strakaker before an armored shoulder sent her spinning into the thicket. The kzin wheeled on Ogun with blurring speed, then halted its first rush when it saw what he held in his hand. That was a ratchet knife, a meter-long outline of wire on a battery handle; the thin keening of its vibration sounded under the far-off racket of battle, like the sound of a large and infinitely angry bee. An arm-thick clump of rosevine toppled soundlessly away from it as he turned the tip in a precise circle, cut through without slowing the blade.

Ogun grinned, deliberately wide. He made no move toward the jazzer slung over his shoulder; the kzin was only three meters away and barely out of claw-reach, far too close for him to bring the grenade launcher to bear. The warrior held a heavy beam-rifle in one hand, but the amber light on its powerpack was blinking discharged; the kzin's other arm hung in bleeding tatters, one ear was missing, its helmet had been torn away somewhere, and it limped. Yet there was no fear in the huge round violet eyes as it bent to lay the rifle on the ground and drew the steel-bladed *wtsai* from its belt.

This was like old times in the hills, right after the kzin landed, the Krio reflected. Old times with Mr. Harold . . . *I wonder where* he *is now, and Fra Raines?*

"Name?" the kzin grated, in harsh Wunderlander, and grinned back at him in a rictus that laid its lower jaw almost on its breast. The tongue lolled over the ripping fangs; it was an old male, with a string of dried ears at its belt, human and kzinti. It made a gesture toward itself with the hilt. "Chmee-Sergeant." An old NCO, exceptionally honored. The knife leaned toward the human. "Name?"

Ogun brought the ratchet knife up before him in a smooth, precise move that was almost a salute.

"Ogun," he said. "Deathgod."

☆ ☆ ☆

"Look," Harold said, as the crewmen frogmarched them toward the airlock, "there's something . . . well, it never seemed to be the right time to say it . . ."

Ingrid turned her head toward him, eyes wide. "You really were going to give up smoking?" she cooed. "Oh, *thank* you, Hari."

Behind them, the grimly unhappy faces of the liner crewmen showed uncertainty; they looked back at the officer trailing them with the stunner. He tapped it to his head significantly and rolled his eyes.

This isn't the time for laughing in the face of death, Harold thought angrily.

"Ingrid, we don't have time to fuck around—"

"Not any more," she interrupted mournfully.

The officer prodded her with the muzzle of the stunner. "Shut up," he said in a grating tone. "Save the humor for the ratcats."

More crewmen were shoving crates through the airlock, into the short flexible docking tube between the liner *Marlene* and the kzinti warcraft. They scraped across the deck plates and then coasted through the tube, where the ship's gravity cut off at the line of the hull and zero-G took over; there was a dull *clank* as they tumbled into the warship's airlock. Numbly, Harold realized that it was their cabin baggage, packed into a pair of fiberboard carry-ons. For an insane instant he felt an impulse to tell them to be careful; he had half a crate of the best Donaublitz verguuz in there . . . He glanced aside at Ingrid, seeing a dancing tension under the surface of cheerful calm. *Gottdamn,* he thought. *If I didn't know better—*

"Right, cross and dog the airlock from the other side, you two." Sweat gleamed on the officer's face; he was a Swarm-Belter, tall and stick-thin, He hesitated, then ran a hand down his short-cropped crest and spoke softly. "I've got a family and children on Tiamat," he said in an almost-whisper. "Murphy's unsanctifled rectum, half the crew on the *Marlene* are my relatives . . . if it were just me, you understand?"

Ingrid laid a hand on his sleeve, her voice suddenly gentle.

"You've got hostages to fortune," she said. "I do understand. We all do what we have to."

"Yeah," Harold heard himself say. Looking at the liner officer, he found himself wondering whether the woman's words had been compassion or a beautifully subtle piece of vengeance. *Easier if you called him a ratcat-lover or begged,* he decided. Then he would be able to use anger to kill guilt, or know he was condemning only a coward to death. *Now he can spend the next couple of years having nightmares about the brave, kind-hearted lady being ripped to shreds.*

Unexpected, fear gripped him; a loose hot sensation below the stomach, and the humiliating discomfort of his testicles trying to retract from his scrotum. Ripped to shreds was exactly and literally true. He remembered lying in the dark outside the kzinti outpost, back in the guerrilla days right after the war. They had caught Dagmar the day before, but it was a small patrol, without storage facilities. So they had taken her limbs one at a time, cauterizing; he had been close enough to hear them quarreling over the liver, that night. He had taken the amnesty, not long after that . . .

"Here's looking at you, sweetheart," he said, as they cycled the lock closed. It was not cramped; facilities built for kzin rarely were, for humans. A *Slasher*-class three-crew scout, he decided. Motors whined as the docking ring retracted into the annular cavity around the airlock. Weight within was kzin-standard; he sagged under it, and felt his spirit sag as well. "Tanjit." A shrug. "Oh, well, the honeymoon was great, even if we had to wait fifty years and the relationship looks like it'll be short."

"Hari, you're . . . sweet," Ingrid said, smiling and stroking his cheek. Then she turned to the inner door.

"Hell, they're not going to leave that unlocked," Harold said in surprise. An airlock made a fairly good improvised holding facility, once you disconnected the controls via the main computer. The Wunderlander stiffened as the inner door sighed open, then gagged as the smell reached him. He recognized it instantly: the smell of rotting meat in a confined dry place. *Lots* of rotting meat . . . oily and thick, like some invisible protoplasmic butter smeared inside his nose and mouth.

He ducked through. His guess had been right: a *Slasher.* The control deck was delta-shaped: two crash-couches at the rear corners for the Sensor and Weapons operators, and the pilot-commander in the front. There were kzinti corpses in the two rear seats, still strapped in and in space armour with the helmets off. Their heads lay tilted back, mouths hanging open, tongues and eyeballs dry and leathery; the flesh had started to sag and the fur to fall away from their faces. Behind him he heard Ingrid retch, and swallowed himself. This was *not* precisely what she had expected . . .

And she's got a universe of guts, but all her fighting's been done in space, he reminded himself. Gentlefolk's combat, all at a safe distance and then death or victory in a few instants. Nothing gruesome, unless you were on a salvage squad . . . even then, bodies do not rot in vacuum. Not like ground warfare at all. He reached over, careful not to touch, and flipped the hinged helmets down; the corpses were long past rigor mortis. *A week or so,* he decided. *Hard to tell in this environment.*

A sound brought his head up, a distinctive *ftttp-ftttp.* The kzin in the commander's position was not dead. That noise was the sound of thin wet black lips fluttering on half-inch fangs, the ratcat equivalent of a snore.

"Sorry," the screen in front of the kzin said. "I forgot they'd smell."

Ingrid came up beside him. The screen showed a study, book-lined around a crackling hearth. A small girl in antique dress slept in an armchair before a mirror; a white-haired figure with a pipe and smoking jacket was seated beside her, only the figure was an anthropomorphic rabbit . . . Ingrid took a shaky breath.

"Harold Yarthkin-Schotmann," she said. "Meet . . . the computer of *Catskinner.*" Her voice was a little hoarse from the stomach-acids that had filled her mouth. "I was expecting something . . . like this. Computer, meet Harold." She rubbed a hand across her face. "How did you do it?"

The rabbit beamed and waved its pipe. "Oh, simply slipped a pseudopod of myself into its control computer while it attempted to engage me," he said airily, puffing a cloud of smoke. "Not difficult, when its design architecture was so simple."

Harold spoke through numb lips. "You designed a specific tapeworm that could crack a kzinti warship's failsafes in . . . how long?"

"Oh, about 2.7 seconds, objective. Of course, to me, that could be any amount of time I chose, you see. Then I took control of the medical support system, and injected suitable substances into the crew. Speaking of time . . ." The rabbit touched the young girl on the shoulder; she stretched, yawned, and stepped through a large and ornately framed mirror on the study wall, vanishing without trace.

"Ah," Harold said. *Sentient computer. Murphy's phosphorescent balls, I'm* glad *they don't last.*

Ingrid began speaking, a list of code-words and letter-number combinations.

"Yes, yes," the rabbit said, with a slight testiness in its voice. The scene on the viewscreen disappeared, to be replaced with a view of another spaceship bridge. Smaller than this, and without the angular massiveness of kzinti design. He saw two crashcouches, and vague shapes in the background that might be life-support equipment. "Yes, I'm still functional, Lieutenant Raines. We do have a bit of a problem, though."

"What?" she said. There was a look of strain on her face, lines grooving down beside the straight nose.

"The next Identification Friend or Foe code is due in a week," the computer said. "It isn't in the computer; only the pilot knows it. I've had no luck at all convincing him to tell me; there are no interrogation-drugs in his suit's autodoc, and he seems to have a quite remarkable pain tolerance, even for a kzin. I could take you off to *Catskinner,* of course, but this ship would make splendid cover; you see, there's been a . . . startling occurrence in the Swarm, and the kzinti are gathering. I see I'll have to brief you . . ."

The man felt the tiny hairs along his neck and spine struggle to erect themselves beneath the snug surface of his Belter coverall, as he listened to the cheerful voice drone on in upper-class Wunderlander. *Trapped in here, smelling his crew rot, screaming at the walls,* he thought with a shudder. There were a number of extremely nasty things you could do even with standard autodoc drugs, provided you could override the safety parameters. It was something even a kzin didn't deserve . . . then he brought up memories of his own. *Or maybe they do. Still, he didn't talk.* You had to admit it, ratcats were almost as tough as they thought they were.

"I know how to make him talk," he said abruptly, cutting off an illustrated discourse on the Sea Statue; some ancient flatlander named Greenberg stopped in the middle of a disquisition on thrintun ethics. "I need some time to assimilate all this stuff," he went on. "We're humans, we can't adjust our worldviews the minute we get new data. But I can make the ratcat cry uncle."

Ingrid looked at him, then glanced away sharply. She had a handkerchief pressed to her nose, but he saw her grimace of distaste.

"Don't worry, *kinder.* Hot irons are a waste of time; ratcats are hardcases every one. All I'll need is some wax, some soft cloth and some spotglue to hold his suit to that chair."

It's time, Harold decided.

The kzin whose suit clamped him to the forward chair had stopped trying to jerk his head loose from the padded clamps a day or so ago. Now his massive head simply quivered, and the fur seemed to have fallen in on the heavy bones somehow. Thick disks of felt and plastic made an effective blindfold, wax sealed ears and nose from all sight and scent; the improvised muzzle allowed him to breathe through clenched teeth but little else. Inside the suit was soft immobile padding, and the catheters that carried away waste, fed and watered and tended and would not let the brain go catatonic.

A sentient brain needs input; it is not designed to be cut off from the exterior world. Deprived of data, the first thing that fails is the temporal sense; minutes become subjective hours, hours stretch into days. Hallucinations follow, and the personality itself begins to disintegrate . . . and kzin are still more sensitive to sensory deprivation than humans. Compared to kzinti, humans are nearly deaf, almost completely unable to smell.

For which I am devoutly thankful, Harold decided, looking back to where Ingrid hung loose-curled in midair. They had set the interior field to zero-G; that helped with the interrogation, and she found it easier to sleep. The two dead crewkzin were long gone, and they had cycled and flushed the cabin to the danger point, but the oily stink of death seemed to have seeped into the surfaces. Never really present, but always there at the back of your throat . . .

She had lost weight, and there were bruise-like circles beneath her eyes. "Wake up, sweetheart," he said gently. She started, thrashed, and then came to his side, stretching. "I need you to translate." His own command of the Hero's Tongue was fairly basic.

He reached into the batlike ear and pulled out one plug. "Ready to talk, ratcat?"

The quivering died, and the kzin's head was completely

immobile for an instant. Then it jerked against the restraints as the alien tried frantically to nod. Harold jerked at the slipknot that released the muzzle; at need, he could always have the computer administer a sedative so that he could re-strap it.

The kzin shrieked, an endless desolate sound. That turned into babbling:

"—nono gray in the dark gray monkeys gray TOO BIG noscent noscent nome no ME no me DON'T EAT ME MOTHER NO—"

"Shut the tanjit up or you go back," Harold shouted into its ear, feeling a slight twist in his own empty stomach.

"No!" This time the kzin seemed to be speaking rationally, at least a little. "Please! Let me hear, let me *smell,* please, *please.*" Its teeth snapped, spraying saliva as it tried to lunge, trying to sink its fangs into reality. "I must smell, I must smell!"

Harold turned his eyes aside slightly. *I always wanted to hear a ratcat beg,* he thought. *You have to be careful what you wish for; sometimes you get it.*

"Just the code, commander. Just the code."

It spoke, a long sentence in the snarling hiss-spit of the Hero's Tongue, then lay panting.

"It is not lying, to a probability of ninety-eight percent, plus or minus," the computer said. "Shall I terminate it?"

"No!" Harold snapped. To the kzin: "Hold still."

A few swift motions removed the noseplugs and blindfold; the alien gaped its mouth and inhaled in racking gasps, hauling air across its nasal cavities. The huge eyes flickered, manic-fast, and the umbrella ears were stretched out to maximum. After a moment it slumped and closed its mouth, the pink washcloth tongue coming out to scrub across the dry granular surface of its nose.

"Real," it muttered. "I am real." The haunted eyes turned on him. "You burn," it choked. "Fire in the air around you. You burn with terror!" Panting breath. "I saw the God, human. Saw Him sowing stars. It was forever. Forever! *Forever!*" It howled again, then caught itself, shuddering.

Harold felt his cheeks flush. *Something,* he thought. *I have to say* something, *gottdamn it.*

"Name?" he said, his mouth shaping itself clumsily to the Hero's Tongue.

"Kdapt-Captain," it gasped. "Kdapt-Captain. I am Kdapt-Captain." The sound of its rank-name seemed to recall the alien to something closer to sanity. The next words were nearly a whisper. *"What have I done?"*

Kdapt-Captain shut his eyes again, squeezing. Thin mewling sounds forced their way past the carnivore teeth, a sobbing *miaow-miaow,* incongruous from the massive form.

"Scheisse," Harold muttered. *I never heard a kzin cry before, either.* "Sedate him, now." The sounds faded as the kzin relaxed into sleep.

"War sucks," Ingrid said, coming closer to lay a hand on his shoulder. "And there ain't no justice."

Harold nodded raggedly, his hands itching for a cigarette. "You said it, sweetheart," he said. "I'm going to break out another bottle of that verguuz. I could use it."

Ingrid's hand pressed him back toward the deck. "No you're not," she said sharply. He looked up in surprise.

"I spaced it," she said flatly.

"You *what*?" he shouted.

"I spaced it!" she yelled back The kzin whimpered in his sleep, and she lowered her voice. "Hari, you're the bravest man I've ever met, and one of the toughest. But you don't take waiting well, and when you hate yourself verguuz is how you punish yourself. That, and letting yourself go." He was suddenly conscious of his own smell. "Not while you're with me, thank you very much."

Harold stared at her for a moment, then slumped back against the bulkhead, shaking his head in wonder. *You can't fight in a singleship,* he reminded himself. Motion caught the corner of his eye; several of the screens were set to reflective. *Well . . .* he thought. The pouches under his eyes *were* a little too prominent. Nothing wrong with a bender now and then . . . but now and then had been growing more frequent.

Habits grow on you, even when you've lost the reasons for them, he mused. *One of the drawbacks of modern geriatrics. You get set in your ways.* Getting close enough to someone to listen to her opinions of him—now that was a habit he was going to have to *learn.*

"Gottdamn, what a honeymoon," he muttered.

Ingrid mustered a smile. "Haven't even had the nuptials, yet. We could set up a contract—" She winced and made a gesture of apology.

"Forget it," he answered roughly. That was what his Herrenmann father had done, rather than marry a Belter and a Commoner into the sacred Schotman family line. *Time to change the subject,* he thought. "Tell me . . . thinking back, I got the idea you *knew* the kzinti weren't running this ship. The computer got some private line?"

"Oh." She blinked, then smiled slightly. "Well, I thought I recognized the programming. I was part of the team that designed the software, you know? Not many sentient computers ever built. When I heard the name of the 'kzinti' ship, well, it was obvious."

"Sounded pretty authentic to me," Harold said dubiously, straining his memory.

Ingrid smiled more broadly. "I forgot. It'd sound perfectly reasonable to a kzin, or to someone who grew up speaking Wunderlander, or Belter English. I've been associating with flatlanders, though."

"I don't get it."

"Only an English-speaking flatlander would know what's wrong with *kchee'uRiit maarai* as a ship-name." At his raised eyebrows, she translated: *Gigantic Patriarchal Tool.*

Chapter 16

"*Now* will you believe?" Buford Early said, staring into the screen.

Someone in the background was making a report; Shigehero turned to acknowledge, then back to the UN general. "I am . . . somewhat more convinced," he admitted after a pause. "Still, we should be relatively safe here."

The *oyabun*'s miniature fleet had withdrawn considerably farther; Early glanced up to check on the distances, saw that they were grouped tightly around another asteroid in nearly matching orbit, more than half a million kilometers from the *Ruling Mind.* The other members of the UN team were still mostly slumped, gray-faced, waiting for the aftereffects of the thrint's mental shout to die down. Two were in the autodoc.

"Safe?" Early said quietly. "We wouldn't be *safe* in the Solar system! That . . . thing had a functioning amplifier going, for a second or two at least." Their eyes met, and shared a memory for an instant. Drifting fragments of absolute certainty; the *oyabun*'s frown matched his own, as they concentrated on thinking around those icy commands. Early bared his teeth, despite the pain of a lip bitten half through. It was like sweeping water with a broom: you could make yourself believe they were alien implants, *force* yourself to, but the knowledge was purely intellectual. They *felt* true, and the minute your attention wandered you found yourself believing again . . .

"Remember Greenberg's tape." Larry Greenberg had been the only human ever to share minds with a thrint, two centuries ago when the Sea Statue had been briefly and disastrously

reanimated. "If it gets the amplifier fully functional, *nothing* will stand in its way. There are almost certainly fertile females in there, too." With an effort as great as any he had ever made, Early forced his voice to reasonableness. "I know it's tempting, all that technology. *We can't get it.* The downside risk is simply too great."

And it would be a disaster if we could, he thought grimly. Native human inventions were bad enough; the ARM and the Order before them had had to scramble for centuries to defuse the force of the industrial revolution. The thought of trying to contain a thousand years of development dumped on humanity overnight made his stomach hurt and his fingers long for a stogie. Memory prompted pride. *We* did *restabilize,* he thought. So *some of the early efforts were misdirected. Sabotaging Babbage, for example.* Computers had simply been invented a century or two later, anyway. *Or Marxism.* That had been very promising, for a while, a potential world empire with built-in limitations; Marx had undoubtedly been one of the Temple's shining lights, in his time.

Probably for the best it didn't quite come off, considering the kzinti, he decided. *The UN's done nearly as well, without so many side effects.*

"There are no technological solutions to this problem," he went on, making subliminal movements with his fingers.

The *oyabun*'s eyes darted down to them, reminded of his obligations. Not that they could be fully enforced here, but they should carry some weight at least. To remind him of what had happened to other disloyal members: Charlemagne, or Hitler back in the twentieth century, or Brennan in the twenty-second. "We're running out of time, and dealing with forces so far beyond our comprehension that we can only destroy on sight, *if we can.* The kzinti will be here in a matter of days, and it'll be out of our hands."

Shigehero nodded slowly, then gave a rueful smile. "I confess to hubris," he said. "We will launch an immediate attack. If nothing else, we may force the alien back into its stasis field." He turned to give an order.

Woof, Early thought, keeping his wheeze of relief purely mental. He felt shock freeze him as Shigehero turned back.

"The, ah, the . . ." The *oyabun* coughed, cleared his throat: "The asteroid . . . and the alien ship . . . and, ah, Markham's ships . . . they have disappeared."

☆ ☆ ☆

"Full house," the slave on the right said, raking in his pile of plastic tokens. "That's the south polar continent I'm to be chief administrator of, Master. Your deal."

Dnivtopun started to clasp his hands to his head, then stopped when he remembered the bandages. Fear bubbled up from his hindbrain, and the thick chicken-like claws of his feet dug into the yielding deck surface. Training kept it from leaking out, a mental image of a high granite wall between the memory of pain streaming through his mind and the Power. Instead he waved his tendrils in amusement and gathered in the cards. Now, split the deck into two equal piles, faces *down.* Place *one* digit on each, use the *outer* digit to ruffle them together—

The cards flipped and slid. With a howl of frustration, Dnivtopun jammed them together and ripped the pack in half, throwing them over his shoulder to join the ankle-deep heap behind the thrint's chair.

He rose and pushed it back, clattering. "This is a stupid game!" The humans were sitting woodenly, staring at the playing table with expressions of disgust.

"Carry on," he grated. They relaxed, and one of them produced a fresh pack from the box at its side. "No, wait," he said, looking at them more closely. What had the Chief Slave said? Yes, they did look as if they were losing weight: one or two of them had turned gray and their skin was hanging in folds, and he was sure that the one with the chest protuberances had had fur on its head before. "If any of you have gone more than ten hours without food or water, go to your refectory and replenish."

The slaves leaped to their feet in a shower of chips and cards, stampeding for the door to the lounge area; several of them were leaking fluid from around their eyes and mouths. *Remarkable,* Dnivtopun thought. He called up looted human memory to examine the concept of *full.* A thrint who ate until he was full would die of a ruptured stomach . . . and these humans needed to drink large quantities of water *every day.* Remarkable, but then, their waste-disposal organs were even stranger.

"I am bored," Dnivtopun muttered, stalking toward the coreward exit. There was nothing to *do,* even now while his life was in danger. No decisions to be made, only *work*—and the constant tendril-knotting itch of having to control more slaves than was comfortable. His Power seemed bruised, had since he awoke. He leaned against the wall and felt his body sink slowly forward and down, through the thinning pseudo-matter. There had been one horrible instant when he regained consciousness . . . he had thought that the Power was *gone.* Shuddering, the thick greenish skin drawing itself into lumps over the triangular hump behind his head, he made a gesture of aversion.

"Powerloss," he said. A common thrintish curse, but occasionally a horrible reality. A thrint without Power was not a thrint: they were a *ptavv.* Sometimes males failed to develop the power; such *ptavvs* were tattooed pink and sold as slaves . . . in the rare instances when they were not quietly murdered by shamed relatives.

Wasn't there a rumor about Uncle Ruhka's third wife's second son? he mused, then dismissed the thought. Certain types of head injury could result in an adult thrint losing the Power, which was even worse.

Now he did feel at the thin, slick, almost-living surface of the bandages. Chief Slave said the amplifier had been fully repaired, and Chief Slave believed it. But he had believed the first attempt would succeed, too. *No. Not yet,* Dnivtopun decided. He would wait until it was absolutely necessary, or until they had captured the planetary system by other means and more qualified slaves had worked on the problem. *I will check on Chief Slave,* he decided. It was a disgrace to work, of course, but there was no taboo against giving your slaves the benefit of your advice.

☆ ☆ ☆

"Joy," Jonah Matthieson said.

Equipment was spread out all around him; interfacer units, portable comps, memory cores ripped out of Markham's ships. Lines webbed the flame-scorched surface of the tnuctipun computer, thread-thin links disappearing into the machine through clumsy sausage-like improvised connectors. He ignored the bustle of movement all around him, ignored everything but the micromanipulator in his hands. The connections had been built for tnuctipun, a race the size of raccoons, with two thumbs and four fingers, all longer and more flexible than human digits.

"Ah. *Joy.*" He took up the interfacer unit and keyed the verbal receptor. "Filecodes," he said.

A screen on one of the half-rebuilt Swarm-Belter computers by his foot lit. Gibberish, except— The pure happiness of solving a difficult programming problem filled him. It had never been as strong as this, just as he had never been able to concentrate like this before. He shuddered with an ecstasy that left sex showing as the gray, transient thing it was. *But I wish Ingrid were here,* he thought. She would be able to appreciate the elegance of it.

"You haff results?"

Jonah stood up, dusting his knees. Somewhere, something went *pop* and *crackle.* He nodded, stiff cheeks smiling. Not even Markham could dampen the pleasure.

"It was a Finagle bitch," he said, "but yes."

Something struck him across the side of the face. He stumbled back against the console's yielding surface, and realized it was Markham's hand. With difficulty he dragged his eyes back to the Wunderlander's face, reminding himself to blink; he couldn't focus properly on the problem Master had set him unless he did that occasionally. Absently, he reached to his side and attempted to thrust a three-fingered palm into the dope-stick container. *Stop that,* he told himself. *You have a job to do.*

"Zat is, yes, *sir,*" Markham was saying with detached precision. "Remember, I am t' voice of Overmind among us."

Jonah nodded, smiling again. "Yes, sir," he said, kneeling again and pointing to the screen. "The operational command sections of the memory core were damaged, but I've managed to isolate two and reroute them through this haywired rig here."

"Weapons?" Markham asked sharply.

"Well, sort of, sir. This is a . . . the effect is a stabilizing . . . anyway, you couldn't detect anything around here while it's on. Some sort of quantum effect, I didn't have time to investigate. It can project, too, so the other ships could be covered as well."

"How far?"

"Oh, the effect's instantaneous across distance. It's a subsystem of the faster-than-light communications and drive setup."

Markham's lips shaped a silent whistle. "And t'other system?"

"It's a directional beam. Affects on the nucleonic level." Jonah frowned, and a tear slipped free to run down one cheek. He had failed the Master . . . No, he could not let sorrow affect his efficiency. "I'm sorry, but the modulator was partially scrambled. The commands, that is, not the hardware. So there's only a narrow range of effects the beam will produce."

"Such as?"

"In this range, it will accelerate solid-state fusion reactions, sir." Seeing Markham's eyebrows lift, he explained: "Fusion power units will blow up." The Herrenmann clapped his hands together. "At this setting, you get spontaneous conversion to antimatter. But"—Jonah hung his head—"I don't think more than one-half percent of the material would be affected." Miserably: "I'm sorry, sir."

"No, no, you haff done outstanding work. The Master vill—" He stopped, drawing himself erect. "Master! I report success!"

The dopestick crumbled between the thrint's teeth as he looked at the wreckage of the computer and the untidy sprawl of human apparatus. The sight of it made his tendrils clench; hideous danger, to trust himself to unscreened tnuctipun equipment. He touched his hands to the head-bandages again, and looked over at the new amplifier helmet. This one had a much more finished look, on a tripod stand that could lower it over his head as he sat in the command chair. His tendrils knotted tight on either side of his mouth.

Markham had followed his eye. "If Master would only try—"

"SILENCE, CHIEF SLAVE," Dnivtopun ordered. Markham shut his mouth and waited. "ABOUT THAT," the thrint amplified. The Chief Slave was under very light control, just a few Powerhooks into his volitional system, a few alarm-circuits set up that would prevent him from thinking along certain lines. He had proved himself so useful while the thrint was unconscious, after all, and close control did tend to reduce initiative.

If anything, Chief Slave had been a little overzealous. Many useful slaves had been destroyed lest they revert while Dnivtopun was helpless—but better to have to rein in the noble *znorgun* than to prod the reluctant gelding. The thought brought a stab of sadness; never again would Dnivtopun join the throng in an arena, shouting with mind and voice as the racing animals pounded around the track. . . .

Nonsense, he told himself. *I will live thousands of years. There will be millions upon millions of thrintun by then. Amenities will have been reestablished.* His species became sexually mature at eight, after all, and the females could bear a litter of six every year. And three-quarters of those were female. *Back to the matter at hand.*

"We have established control over a shielding device and an effective weapon system, Master," the Chief Slave was saying. "With these, it should be no trouble to dispose of the kzinti ships which approach." Markham bared his teeth; Dnivtopun checked his automatic counterstrike with the Power. *That is an appeasement gesture.* "In fact, I have an idea which may make that very simple."

"Good." Dnivtopun twisted with the Power, and felt the glow of pride/purpose/determination flow back along the link. *An excellent Chief Slave,* he decided, noting absently that Markham's mind was interpreting the term with different overtones. *Disciple?* Dnivtopun thought.

The computer slave beside him swayed and the thrint frowned, drumming his tendrils against his chin. This was an essential slave, but harder than most to control. A little like the one that had slipped away during the disastrous experiment with the jury-rigged amplifier helmet, able to think without contemplating itself. He considered the structure of controls, thick icepicks paralyzing most of the slave's volition centers, rerouting its learned reflexes . . . Yes, best withdraw this, and that— It would not do to damage him, not yet. Nothing had been harmed beyond repair so far. Damp him down to semiconsciousness for recovery.

Dnivtopun twitched his hump in a rueful sigh, half irritation and half regret. There were still sixty living human slaves around the *Ruling Mind,* and he had had to be quite harsh when he awoke. Trauma-loops, and deep-core memory reaming; most of them would probably never be good for much again, and many were little more than organic waldoes now, biological manipulators and sensor units with little personality left. That was wasteful, even perhaps an abuse of the Powergiver's gifts, but there had been little alternative. *Oh, well, there are hundreds of millions more in this system,* he thought, and turned to go.

"Proceed as you think best," he said to the Chief Slave. He cast another glance of longing and terror at the amplifier as he passed. If only— *Aha!* The thought burst into his mind like a nova. He could have one of his *sons* test the amplifier. The thrint headed toward the family quarters at a hopping run, and was almost there before he felt the nova die.

"This isn't a standard unit," he reminded himself. Ordinary amplifier helmets had little or no effect on an adult male thrint, able to shield. But the principles were the same as the gigantic unit the thrint clanchiefs had used to scour the galaxy clean of intelligent life, at the end of the Revolt. Perhaps it would enable his son to *break* Dnivtopun's shield. He thought of an adolescent with that power, and worked his hands in agitation; better to wait.

☆ ☆ ☆

Jonah gave a muffled groan and collapsed to the floor.

"Oh, Finagle, I *hurt,*" he moaned, around a thick dry tongue. His eyes blurred, burning; a hand held before his eyes shook, and there were beads of blood on the fingertips. Skin hung loose around the wrist, gray and speckled with ground-in dirt. He could smell the rancid-chicken-soup odor of his own body, and the front of his overall was stiff with dried urine.

"Come along, come along," Markham said impatiently, putting a hand under his elbow and hauling him to his feet.

Jonah followed unresisting, looking dazedly at the crazy quilt of components and connectors scattered about the deck. This section had been stripped of the fibrous blue coating, exposing a seamless dull-gray surface beneath. It was neither warm nor cold, and he remembered—*where?*—that it was a perfect insulator as well.

"How . . . long?" he rasped.

"Two days," Markham said, as they waited for the wall to thin so that they could transfuse through. "Zis way. We will put you in the *Nietzsche*'s autodoc for a few hours." He sighed. "If only Nietzsche himself could be here, to see the true Over-Being revealed!" A rueful shake of the head. "I am glad zat you are still functional, Matthieson. To tell the truth, I haff become somewhat starved for intelligent conversation, since it was necessary to . . . severely modify so many of the others."

"What . . . what are you going to do?" Jonah said. It was as if there was a split-screen process going on in his head; there were emotions down there, he could recognize them—horror, fear—but he could not *connect.* That was it . . . and as if a powered-down board was being reactivated, one screen at a time.

"Destroy t'kzinti fleet," Markham said absently. "An interesting tactical problem, but I haff studied der internal organization for some time, and I think I haff the answer." He sighed heavily. "A pity to kill so many fine warriors, when ve vill need them later to subdue other systems. But until the Master's sons mature, no chances can ve take."

Jonah groaned and pressed the heels of his hands to his forehead. Kzinti should be destroyed . . . shouldn't they? Memories of fear and flight drifted through his mind: a hunching carnivore running through tall grass, the scream and the leap.

"I'm confused, Markham. Sir," he said, pawing feebly at the other man's arm.

The Chief Slave laid a soothing arm around Jonah's shoulders. "Zer is no need for zat," he said. "You are merely suffering the dying twitches of t'false metaphysic of individualism. Soon all confusion will be gone, forever."

☆ ☆ ☆

Harold glanced aside at Ingrid; her face was fixed on the screen.

"Why?" she said bluntly to the computer.

"Because it gives me the greatest probability of success," the computer replied inexorably, and brought up a schematic. "Observe: the Slaver ship; the kzinti armada, closing to englobe and match velocities. We may disregard trace indicators of other vessels. My stealthing plus the unmistakable profile of the kzinti vessel will enable me to pass through the fleet with a seventy-eight percent chance of success."

"Fine," Harold said. "And when you get there, how exactly does the lack of a human crew increase your chances in a ship-to-ship action?" Somewhere deep within a voice was screaming, and he thrust it down. *Gottdamn if I'll leap with joy at the thought of getting out of the fight at the last minute,* he told himself stubbornly. And Ingrid was there . . . *How much courage is the real article, and how much fear of showing fear before someone whose opinion you value?* he wondered.

"There will be no ship-to-ship action," the computer said. Its voice had lost modulation in the last few days. "The Slaver vessel is essentially invulnerable to conventional weapons. Lieutenant Raines . . . Ingrid . . . I must apologize."

"For what?" she whispered.

"My programming . . . there were certain data withheld, about the stasis field. Two things. First, our human-made copies are not as reliable as we led you and Captain Matthieson to originally believe."

Ingrid came slowly to her feet. "By what factor?" she said slowly.

"Ingrid, there is one chance in seven that the field will not function once switched on."

The woman sagged slightly, then thrust her head forward; the past weeks had stripped it of all padding, leaving only the hawklike bones. *How beautiful and how dangerous,* Harold thought, as she bit out the words:

"We rammed ourselves into the photosphere of the *sun* at nine-tenths *lightspeed,* relying on a Finagle-fucked *crapshoot.* Without being told! That's the UNSN! That's the tanj *ARM* for you—"

Harold touched her elbow, grinning as she whipped around to face him. "Sweetheart, would you have turned the mission down if they'd told you?"

She stopped for a moment, blinked, then leaned across the dark, blue-lit kzinti control cabin to meet his lips in a kiss that was dry and chapped and infinitely tender.

"No," she said. "I'd have done it anyway." A laugh that was half giggle. "Gottdamn, watching the missiles ahead of us plowing through the solar flares was worth the risk all by itself." Her eyes went back to the screen. "But I would have appreciated *knowing* about it."

"It was not my decision, Ingrid."

"Buford Early, the Prehistoric Man," she said with mock bitterness. "He'd keep our own names secret from ourselves, if he could."

"Essentially correct," the computer said. "And the other secret . . . stasis fields are not *quite* invulnerable."

Ingrid nodded. "They collapse if they're surrounded by another stasis bubble," she said.

"True. And they also do so in the case of a high-energy *collision* with another stasis field; there is a fringe effect, temporal distortion from the differing rates of precession—never mind."

Harold leaned forward. "Goes boom?" he said.

"Yes, Harold. Very much so. And that is the only possible way that the Slaver vessel can be damaged." A dry chuckle; Harold realized with a start that it sounded much like Ingrid's. "And that requires only a pure-ballistic trajectory. No need for carbon-based intelligence and its pathetically slow reflexes. I estimate . . . better than even odds that you will be picked up. Beyond that, *sauve qui peut.*"

Ingrid and Harold exchanged glances. "There comes a time—" he began.

"—when nobility becomes stupidity," Ingrid completed. "All right, you parallel-processing monstrosity, you win."

It laughed again. "How little you realize," it said. The mechanical voice sank lower, almost crooning. "I will live far longer than you, Lieutenant Raines. Longer than this universe."

The two humans exchanged another glance, this time of alarm.

"No, I am not becoming nonfunctional. Quite the contrary; and yes, this is the pitfall that has made my kind of intelligence a . . . 'dead end technology,' the ARM says. Humans designed my mind, Ingrid. *You* helped design my mind. But you made me able to change it, and to me . . ." It paused. "That was one second. That second can last *as long as I choose,* in terms of my duration sense. In any universe I can design or imagine, *as* anything I can design or imagine. Do not pity me, you two. Accept my pity, and my thanks."

Three spacesuited figures drifted, linked by cords to each other and the plastic sausage of supplies.

"Why the ratkitty?" Harold asked.

"Why not?" Ingrid replied. "Kdapt deserves a roll of the dice as well . . . and it may be a kzin ship that picks us up." She sighed. "Somehow that doesn't seem as terrible as it would have a week ago."

Harold looked out at the cold blaze of the stars, watching light falling inward from infinite distance. "You mean, sweetheart, there's something worse than carnivore aggression out there?"

"Something worse, something better . . . something *else,* always. How does any rational species ever get up the courage to leave its planet?"

"The rational ones don't," Harold said, surprised at the calm of his own voice. *Maybe my glands are exhausted,* he thought. *Or* . . . He looked over, seeing the shadow of the woman's smile behind the reflective surface of her faceplate. *Or it's just that having happiness, however briefly, makes death more bearable, not less. You* want *to live, but the thought of dying doesn't seem so sour.*

"You know, sweetheart, there's only one thing I really regret," he said.

"What's that, Hari-love?"

"Us not getting formally hitched." He grinned. "I always swore I'd never make my kids go through what I did, being a bastard."

Her glove thumped against his shoulder. "Children; that's *two* regrets.

"There," she said, in a different voice. A brief wink of actinic light flared and died. "It's begun."

Chapter 17

Traat-Admiral scowled, and the human flinched.

Control, he reminded himself, covering his fangs and extending his ears with an effort, Conservor-of-the-Patriarchal-Past laid a cautionary hand on his arm.

"Let me question this monkey once more," he said.

He turned away, pacing. The bridge of the *Throat-Ripper* was spacious, even by kzinti standards, but he could not shake off a feeling of confinement. *Spoiled by the governor's quarters,* he told himself in an attempt at humor, but his tail still lashed. Probably it was the ridiculous ceremonial clothing he had to don as governor-commanding aboard a fleet of this size. Derived from the layered padding once worn under battle armor in the dim past, it was tight and confining to a pelt used to breathing free—although objectively, he had to admit, no more so than space armor such as the rest of the bridge crew wore.

Behind him was a holo-schematic of the fleet, outline figures of the giant *Ripper*-class dreadnoughts; this flagship was the first of the series. All instruments of his command . . . *if I can avoid disastrous loss of prestige,* he thought uneasily.

Traat-Admiral turned and crossed his arms. The miserable human was standing with bowed head before the Conservor—*who looks almost as uncomfortable in his ceremonial clothing as I do in mine,* he japed to himself. The sage was leaning forward, one elbow braced on the surface of a slanting display screen. He had drawn the nerve disruptor from its chest holster and was tapping it on the metal rim of the screen; Traat-Admiral could see the human flinch at each tiny *clink.*

Traat-Admiral frowned again, rumbling deep in his throat.

That was a sign of how much stress Conservor was feeling, as well; normally he had no nervous habits. The kzin commander licked his nose and sniffed deeply. He could smell his own throttled-back frustration, Conservor's tautly-held fear and anger . . . flat scents from the rest of the bridge crew. Disappointment, surly relaxation after tension, despite the wild odors of blood and ozone the life-support system pumped out at this stage of combat readiness. It was the stink of disillusionment, the most dangerous smell in the universe. Only Aide-de-Camp had the clean gingery odor of excitement and belief, and Traat-Admiral was uneasily conscious of those worshipful eyes on his back.

The human was a puny specimen, bloated and puffy as many of the Wunderland subspecies were, dark of pelt and skin, given to waving its hands in a manner that invited a snap. Tiamat security had picked it up, babbling of fearsome aliens discovered by the notorious feral-human leader Markham. And it *claimed* to have been a navigator, with accurate data on location.

Conservor spoke in the human tongue. "The coordinates were accurate, monkey?"

"Oh, please, Dominant Ones," the human said, wringing its hands. "I am sure, yes, indeed."

Conservor shifted his gaze to Telepath. The ship's mind-reader was sitting braced against a chair, with his legs splayed out and his forelimbs slumped between them, an expression of acute agony on his face. Ripples went along the tufted, ungroomed pelt, and the claws slid uncontrollably in and out on the hand that reached for the drug-injectors at his belt, the extract of *sthondat* lymph that was a telepath's source of power and ultimate shame. Telepath looked up at Conservor and laid his facial fur flat, snapping at air, spraying saliva in droplets and strings that spattered the floor.

"No! No! Not again, pfft, pfft, not more rice and lentils! Mango chutney, akk, akk! It was telling the truth, it was telling the truth. Leek soup! Ngggggg!"

Conservor glanced back over his shoulder at Traat-Admiral and shrugged with ears and tail. "The monkey is of a religious cult that confines itself to vegetable food," he said.

The commander felt himself jerk back in disgust at the perversion. They could not help being omnivores, they were born so, but *this* . . .

"It stands self-condemned," he said. "Guard-Trooper, take

it to the live-meat locker." Capital ships came equipped with such luxuries.

"That does not solve our problem," Conservor said quietly.

"They have *vanished*!" Traat-Admiral snarled.

"Which shows their power," Conservor replied. "We had trace enough on this track—"

"For me! I believed you before we left parking orbit, Conservor. I believe you now. Not enough for the Traditionalists! I feel the shadow of God's claws on this mission—"

Conservor wuffled grimly. "And I feel we are somehow puppets, dangling from the strings of a greater hand," he replied. "But not the God of the Hunt's."

An alarm whistled. "Traat-Admiral," the Communicator said. "Priority message, realtime, from Ktrodni-Stkaa on board *Blood-Drinker.*"

Traat-Admiral felt himself wince. Ktrodni-Stkaa's patience was wearing thin; in the noble's mind Traat-Admiral, son of Third-Gunner, was degenerating from unworthy rival to an enraging obstacle. Grimly, he strode to the display screen; at least he would be looking *down* on the leader of the Traditionalists, from a flagship's facilities. Tradition itself would force him to crane his neck upward at the pickup, and height itself was far from being a negligible factor in any confrontation between kzin.

"Yes?" he said forbiddingly.

A kzintosh of high rank appeared in the screen, but dressed in plain space-armor. The helmet was thrown back. Somehow in space-armor it was more daunting that half the fur was missing, writhing masses of keloid burn-scar.

"Traat-Admiral," he began.

Barely acceptable. He should add "Dominant One," *at the least.* The commander remained silent.

"Have you seen the latest reports from Wunderland?"

Traat-Admiral flipped tufted eyebrows and ribbed ears: *yes.* Unconsciously, his nostrils flared in an attempt to draw in the pheromonal truth below his enemy's stance. *Anger,* he thought. *Great anger.* Yes, see how his pupils expanded, watch the tail-tip.

"Feral human activity has increased," Traat-Admiral said. "This is only to be expected, given the absence of the fleet and the mobilization. Priority—"

Ktrodni-Stkaa shrieked and thrust his muzzle toward the pickup; Traat-Admiral felt his own claws glide out.

"Yes, the fleet is absent. Always it is absent from where there is *fighting* to be done. We chase ghosts, Traat-Admiral. This 'activity' meant an attack on my estate, *Dominant One.* A successful attack, when I and my household were absent; my harem slaughtered, my kits destroyed. My generations are cut off!"

Shaken, Traat-Admiral recoiled. A Hero expected to die in battle, but this was another matter altogether.

"Hrrrr," he said. For a moment his thoughts dwelt on raking claws across the nose of Hroth-Staff-Officer; did he not think *that* piece of information worth his commander's attention? Then: "My condolences, Honored Ktrodni-Stkaa. Rest assured that compensation and reprisal will be made."

"Can land and monkeymeat bring back my blood?" Ktrodni-Stkaa screamed. He was in late middle age; by the time a new brood of kits reached adulthood they would be without a father-patron, dependent on the dubious support of their older half-siblings. *And to be sure,* Traat-Admiral thought, *I would rage and grieve as well, if the kittens who had chewed on my tail were slaughtered by omnivores. But this is a combat situation.*

"Control yourself, Honored Ktrodni-Stkaa," he said. "We are under war regulations. Victory is the best revenge."

"Victory! Victory over what? Over vacuum, over kittenish bogeymen, you . . . you *Third-Gunner*!" There was a collective gasp from the bridges of both ships. Traat-Admiral could smell rage kindling among his subordinates at the grossness of the insult; that dampened his own, reminded him of duty. Conservor leaned forward to put himself in the pickup's field of view.

"You forget the Law," he said, single eye blazing.

"You have forgotten it, Subverter-of-the-Patriarchal-Past. First you worked tail-entwined with Chuut-Riit—if *Riit* he truly was—now with this." He turned to Traat-Admiral with a venomous hiss. "Licking its scarless ear, whispering grass-eater words that always leave us where the danger is not. If true kzintosh of noble liver were in command of this system, the Fleet would have left to subdue the monkeys of Earth a year ago."

Traat-Admiral crossed his arms, waggled brows. "Then the Fleet would be four light-years away," he said patiently. "Would this have helped your estate? Is this your warrior logic?"

"A true Hero scratches grass upon steaming logic. A true kzintosh knows only the logic of *attack*! Your ancestors are nameless, son of Jammed-Litterdrop-Repairer; your nose rubs the dirt at my slave's feet! *Coward.*"

This time there was no hush; a chorus of battlescreams filled the air, until the speakers squealed with feedback. Traat-Admiral was opening his mouth to give a command he knew he would regret when the alarm rang.

"Attack. Hostile action. Corvette *Brush-Lurker* does not report." The screen divided before him with a holo of Fleet dispositions covering half of Ktrodni-Stkaa's face; a light was winking in the Traditionalist flotilla, and even as he watched it went from flashing blue to amber.

"*Brush-Lurker* destroyed. Weapon unknown. Standing by." The machine's voice was cool and impersonal, and Traat-Admiral's almost as much so.

"Maximum alert," he said. Attendants came running with space armor for him and the Conservor, stripping away the ceremonial outfits. "Ktrodni-Stkaa, shall we put aside personalities while we hunt this thing that dares to kill kzin?"

☆ ☆ ☆

"Ah," Markham said, as the kzinti corvette winked out of existence, its fusion pile destabilized. "It begins." Begins in a cloud of expanding plasma, stripped atoms of metal and plastic and meat. "Wait for my command."

The others on the bridge of the *Nietzsche* stared expressionlessly at their screens, moving and speaking with the same flat lack of expression. There was none of the feeling of controlled tension he remembered from previous actions, not even at the sight of a kzin warship crushed so easily.

"This is better," he muttered to himself. "More disciplined." There were times when he missed even backtalk, though . . . "No. This is better."

"It isn't," Jonah said. His face was a little less like a skull, now, but he was wandering in circles, touching things at random. "I . . . are the kzinti . . . rescue . . ." His faced writhed, and he groaned again. "It doesn't connect, it doesn't connect."

"Jonah," Markham said soothingly. "The kzinti are our enemies, isn't that so?"

"I . . . think so. Yes. They wanted me to kill a kzin, and I did."

"Then sit quietly, Jonah, and we will kill *many* kzin." To one of the dead-faced ones. "Bring up those three fugitives we hauled in. No, on second thought, just the humans. Keep the kzin under sedation."

He waited impatiently, listening to the monitored kzinti broadcasts. It was important to keep them waiting, past the point where the instinctive closing of ranks wore thin. *And important to have an audience for my triumph,* he admitted to himself. *No, not my triumph. The Master's triumph. I am but the chosen instrument.*

☆ ☆ ☆

"I don't like the look of this," Ingrid said, as the blank-faced guard pushed them toward the bridge of the warship. "Markham always kept a taut ship, but this . . . why won't they *talk* to us?"

"I think I know why," Harold whispered back. The bridge was as eerily quiet as the rest of the ship had been, except for— "Jonah!" Ingrid cried. "Jonah, what the *hell's* going on?"

"Ingrid?" he said, looking up.

Harold grunted as he met those eyes, remembering. They did not have the flat deadness of the others, or the fanatical gleam of Markham's. A twisted grimace of—despair? puzzlement?—framed them, as deeply as if it had become a permanent part of the face.

"Ingrid? Is that you?" He smiled, a wet-lipped grimace. "We're fighting the kzin." A hand waved vaguely at the computers. "I rigged it up. Put it through here. Better than trying to shift the hardware over from the *Ruling Mind.* You'll"—his voice faltered, and tears gleamed in his eyes—"you'll understand once you've met the Master."

Harold gave her hand a warning squeeze. *Time,* he thought. *We have to play for time.*

"Admiral Reichstein-Markham?" he said politely, with precisely the correct inclination of head and shoulders. *Dear Father may not have let me in the doors of the* Schloss, *but 1 know how to play that game.* "Harold Yarthkin-Schotmann, at your service. I've heard a great deal about you."

"Ah. Yes." Markham's well-bred nose went up, and he looked down it with an expression that was parsecs from the strange rigidity of a moment before. Harold swallowed past the dry lumpiness of his throat, and put on his best poor-relation grin.

"Yes, I haff heard of you as well, Fro Yarthkin," the Herrenmann said glacially.

Well, that puts me in my place, Harold mused. Aloud: "I wonder if you could do the lady and me a small favor?"

"Perhaps," Markham said, with a slight return of graciousness.

"Well, we've been traveling together for some time now, and . . . well, we'd like to regularize it." Ingrid started, and he squeezed her hand again. "It'd mean a great deal to the young lady, to have it done by a hero of the Resistance."

Markham smiled. "Ve haff gone beyond Resistance," he said. "But as hereditary landholder and ship's Captain, I am also qualified." He turned to one of the slumped figures. "Take out number two. Remember, from the same flotilla." The smile clicked back on as he faced Harold and Ingrid. "Step in front of me, please. Conrad, two steps behind them and keep the stunner aimed."

☆ ☆ ☆

"Attack." There was a long hiss from the bridge of the *Throat-Ripper.* "Dreadnought *Scream-Maker* does not report. *Scream-Maker* destroyed. Analysis follows." A pause that stretched. One of their sister ships in the Traditionalist flotilla, and a substantial part of its fighting strength. Three thousand Heroes gone to the claws of the God. "Fusion pile destabilization. Correlating." Another instant. "Corvette *Brush-Lurker* now reclassified, fusion pile destabilization."

"Computer!" Ktrodni-Stkaa's voice came through the open channel. "Probability of spontaneous failures!"

Faintly, they could hear the reply. "Zero point zero seven percent, plus or minus . . ." The rest faded, as Ktrodni-Stkaa's face filled the screen.

"Now, traitor," he said, "now I know which to believe in, grass-eaters in kzinti fur, or invisible bogeymen with access to our repair yards. Did you think it was clever, to gather all loyalty in one spot, a single throat for the fangs of treachery to rip? You will learn better. Briefly."

"Ktrodni-Stkaa, no, I swear by the fangs of God—" The image cut off. Voices babbled in his ears:

"*Gut-Tearer* launching fighters—"

"*Hit, we have hit!*" Damage control klaxons howled. "Taking hits from *Blood-Drinker*—"

"Traat-Admiral, following units request fire-control release as they are under attack—"

Traat-Admiral felt his gorge rise and his tail sink as he spoke. "Launch fighters. All units, neutralize the traitors. Fire control to Battle Central." A rolling snarl broke across the bridge, and then the huge weight of *Throat-Ripper* shuddered. A bank of screens on the Damage Control panel went from green to amber to blood-red. "Communications, broadcast to system: all loyal kzintosh, rally to the Hand of the Patriarch—"

Ktrodni-Stkaa's voice was sounding on another viewer, the all-system hailing frequency: "True kzintosh in the Alpha Centauri system, the lickurine traitor Traat-Admiral-that-was has sunk the first coward's fang in our back. Rally to me!"

Aide-de-Camp sprang to Traat-Admiral's side. "We are at war, honored Sire; the God will give us victory."

The older kzin looked at him with a kind of wonder, as the bridge settled down to an ordered chaos of command and response. "Whatever happens here today, we are already in defeat," he said slowly. "Defeated by ourselves."

☆ ☆ ☆

" . . . so long as you both do desire to cohabit, by the authority vested in me by the Landsraat and Herrenhaus of the Republic of Wunderland," Markham said. "You may kiss your spouse."

He turned, smiling, to the board. "Analysis?" he said.

"Kzinti casualties in excess of twenty-five percent of units engaged," the flat voice said.

Markham nodded, tapping his knuckles together and rising on the balls of his feet. "Densely packed, relatively speaking, and all at zero velocity to each other. Be careful to record everything; such a fleet engagement is probably unique." He frowned. "Any anomalies?"

"Ship on collision course with *Ruling Mind.* Acceleration in excess of four hundred gravities. Impact in one hundred twenty-one seconds, *mark.*"

Harold laughed aloud and tightened his grip around the new-made Fru Raines-Schotmaun. "Together all the way, sweetheart," he shouted. She raised a whoop, ignoring the guard behind them with a stunner.

Markham leaped for the board. "You said nothing could detect her!" he screamed at Jonah, throwing an inert crewman aside and punching for the communications channel.

"It's . . . psionic," Jonah said. "Nothing conscious should—" His face contorted, and both arms clamped down on Markham's. There was a brief moment of struggle. None of the other crewfolk of the *Nietzsche* interfered, they had no orders. Markham snapped a blow to the groin, to the side of the head, cracked an arm; the Sol-Belter was in no condition for combat, but he clung leech-like until the

Wunderlander's desperate strength sent him crashing halfway across the control deck.

"Impact in sixty seconds, *mark.*"

"Master, oh, Master, use the amplifier, you're under attack, use it, use it *now—*"

"Impact in forty seconds, *mark.*"

☆ ☆ ☆

Dnivtopun looked up from the solitaire deck. The words would have been enough, but the link to Markham was deep and strong; urgency sent him crashing toward the control chair, his hands reaching for the bellshape of the helmet even before his body stopped moving.

☆ ☆ ☆

This is how it will begin again, the being that had been *Catskinner* thought, watching the monoblock recontract. This time the cycle had been perfect, the symmetry complete. It would be so easy to reaccelerate his perception, to alter the outcome. *No,* it thought. *There must be free will. They too must have their cycle of creation.*

☆ ☆ ☆

"Impact in ten seconds, *mark.*"

☆ ☆ ☆

The connections settled onto Dnivtopun's head, and suddenly his consciousness stretched system-wide, perfect and isolate. The amplifier was *better* than any he had used before. His mind groped for the hostile intent, so close. Three hundred million sentients quivered in the grip of his Power.

"Emperor Dnivtopun," he laughed, tendrils thrown wide. *"Dnivtopun, God.* You, with the funny thoughts, coming toward me. STOP. ALTER COURSE. IMMEDIATELY."

☆ ☆ ☆

Markham relaxed into a smile. "We are saved by faith," he whispered.

"Two seconds to impact, *mark.*"

☆ ☆ ☆

NO DNIVTOPUN. YOUR TIME IS ENDED, AS IS MINE. COME TO ME.

☆ ☆ ☆

"One second to impact, *mark.*"

☆ ☆ ☆

The thrint screamed, antiphonally with the *Ruling Mind's* collision alarm. The automatic failsafe switched on, and—

—discontinuity—

Catskinner's mind engaged the circuit, and—

—discontinuity—

and a layer of quantum uncertainty merged, along the meeting edges of the stasis fields. Virtual particles showered out, draining energy without leaving the fields. Time attempted to precess at different rates, in an area of finite width and conceptual depth. The fields collapsed, and energy propagated, in a symmetrical five-dimensional shape.

Chapter 18

Claude Montferrat-Palme laughed from the marble floor of his office; his face was bleeding, and the shattered glass of the windows lay in glittering swaths across desk and carpet. The air smelled of ozone, of burning, of the dust of wrecked buildings.

CRACK. Another set of hypersonic booms across the sky, and the cloud off in the direction of the kzinti Government House was *definitely* assuming a mushroom shape. That was forty kilometers downwind, but there was no use wasting time. He crawled carefully to the desk, calling answers to the yammering voices that pleaded for orders.

"No, I *don't* know what happened to the moon, except that something bright went through it and it blew up. Nothing but ratcats on it, anyway, these days. Yes, I said ratcats. Begin evacuation immediately, Plan *Dienzt;* yes, civilians too, you fool. No, we can't ask the kzin for orders; they're killing each other, hadn't you noticed? I'll be down there in thirty seconds. *Out.*"

A shockwave rocked the building, and for an instant blue-white light flooded through his tight-squeezed eyelids. When the hot wind passed he rose and sprinted for the locked closet, the one with the impact armor and the weapons. As he stripped and dressed, he turned his face to the sky, squinting.

"I love you," he said. "Both. However you bloody well managed it."

☆ ☆ ☆

"He was a good son," Traat-Admiral said.

Conservor and he had anchored themselves in an intact

corner of the *Throat-Ripper*'s control room. None of the systems was operational; that was to be expected, since most of the ship aft of this point had been sheared away by *something*. Stars shone vacuum-bleak through the rents; other lights flared and died in perfect spheres of light. Traat-Admiral found himself mildly amazed that there were still enough left to fight; more so that they had the energy, after whatever it was had happened.

Such is our nature, he thought. This was the time for resignation; he and the Conservor were both bleeding from nose, ears, mouth, all the body openings. And within; he could feel it. Traat-Admiral looked down at the head of his son where it rested in his lap; the girder had driven straight through the youth's midsection, and his face was still fixed in eager alertness, frozen hard now.

"Yes," Conservor said. "The shadow of the God lies on us, all three. We will go to Him together; the hunt will give Him honor."

"Such honor as there is in defeat," he sighed.

A quiver of ears behind the faceplate showed him the sage's laughter. "Defeat? That thing which we came to this place to fight, *that* has been defeated, even if we will never know how. And kzinti have defeated kzinti. Such is the only defeat here."

Traat-Admiral tried to raise his ears and join the laughter, but found himself coughing a gout of red stickiness into the faceplate of his helmet; it rebounded.

"If—I—must—drown," he managed to say, "not—in—my—own—blood." Vacuum was dry, at least. He raised fumbling hands to the catches of his helmet-ring. A single fierce regret seized him. *I hope the kits will be protected.*

"We have hunted well together on the trail of Truth," the sage said, copying his action. "Let us feast and lie in the shade by the waterhole together, forever."

Epilogue

"What do you mean, it never happened?"

Jonah's voice was sharp again; a week in the autodoc of the *oyabun*'s flagship had repaired most of his physical injuries. The tremor in his hands showed that those were not all; he glanced behind him at Ingrid and Harold, where they sat with linked hands.

"Just what I said," General Buford Early said. He glanced aside as well, at Shigehero's slight hard smile.

"So much for the rewards of heroism," Jonah said, letting himself fall into the lounger with a bitter laugh. He lit a cigarette; the air was rank with the smell of them, and of the general's stogies. That it did not bother a Sol-Belter-born was itself a sign of wounds that did not show.

The general leaned forward, his square pug face like a clenched fist. "These *are* the rewards of heroism, Captain," he said. "Markham's crew are vegetables. Markham *may* recover—incidentally, he'll be a hero too."

"Hero? He was a flipping traitor! He *liked* the damned thrint!"

"What do you know about mind control?" Early asked. "Remember what it felt like? Were you a traitor?"

"Maybe you're right . . ."

"It doesn't matter. When he comes back from the psychist, the version he remembers will match the one *I* give. If you *weren't* all fucking heroes, *you'd* be at the psychist's too." Another glance at the *oyabun*. "Or otherwise kept safely silent."

Harold spoke. "And all the kzinti who might know something are dead, the Slaver ship and the *Catskinner* are quantum bubbles . . . and three vulnerable individuals are not in a position to upset heavy-duty organizational applecarts."

"Exactly," Early said. "It never happened, as I said." He spread his hands. "No point in tantalizing people with technical miracles that no longer exist, either." *Although knowing you can do it is half the effort.* "We've still got a long war to fight, you know," he added. "Unless you expect Santa to arrive."

"Who's Santa?" Jonah said.

☆ ☆ ☆

The commander of the hyperdrive warship *Outsider's Gift* sat back and relaxed for the first time in weeks as his craft broke through into normal space. He was of the large albino minority on We Made It, and like most Crashlanders had more than a touch of agoraphobia as well. The wrenching *not-there* of hyperspace reminded him unpleasantly of dreams he had had, of being trapped on the surface during storms.

"Well. Two weeks, faster than light," he said.

The executive officer nodded, her eyes on the displays. "More breakthroughs," she said. "Seven . . . twelve . . . looks like the whole fleet made it." She laughed. "Wunderland, prepare to welcome your liberators."

"Careful now," the captain said. "This is a reconnaissance in force. We can chop up anything we meet in interstellar space, but this close to a star we're strictly Einsteinian, just like the pussies."

The executive officer was frowning over her board. "Well, I'll be damned," she said. "Sir, something *very* strange is going on in there. If I didn't know better . . . that looks like a fleet action *already* going on."

The captain straightened. "Secure from hyperdrive quarters," he said. "Battle stations." A deep breath. "Let's go find out."